THE
THINGS
WE
PROMISE

J.C. BURKE

ALLEN&UNWIN
SYDNEY · MELBOURNE · AUCKLAND · LONDON

First published by Allen & Unwin in 2017

Copyright © J.C. Burke 2017

The moral right of J.C. Burke to be identified as the author of this work has been asserted by her in accordance with the United Kingdom's *Copyright, Designs and Patents Act 1988*.

Allen & Unwin – Australia
83 Alexander Street, Crows Nest NSW 2065, Australia
Phone: (61 2) 8425 0100
Email: info@allenandunwin.com
Web: www.allenandunwin.com

Allen & Unwin – UK
Ormond House, 26–27 Boswell Street,
London WC1N 3JZ, UK
Phone: +44 (0) 20 8785 5995
Email: info@murdochbooks.co.uk
Web: www.murdochbooks.co.uk

A Cataloguing-in-Publication entry is available from the National Library of Australia: www.trove.nla.gov.au.

A catalogue record for this book is available from the British Library.

ISBN (AUS) 978 1 76029 040 5
ISBN (UK) 978 1 74336 953 1

Cover and text design by Astred Hicks, Design Cherry
Cover photo by Alexey Kuzma/Stocksy
Set in 11 pt Adobe Caslon Pro by Midland Typesetters, Australia
Printed by McPherson's Printing Group, Australia

10 9 8 7 6 5 4 3 2 1

For Ned,
REACH FOR THE STARS

THERE ARE TWO THINGS YOU NEED TO KNOW about me. The first is that I remember life by what I was wearing. The second is that I think too much.

I know that night, the night when it all began, I went to bed wearing Billy's black-and-white INXS T-shirt. It was my total favourite to sleep in. The cotton was soft and it was big and baggy. When I was cold I stretched it over my knees and watched Michael Hutchence's face elongate as though he were staring into a trick mirror at an amusement park.

I was trying to balance a cup of tea and a *Cleo* magazine on my lap when I spilt my tea everywhere. It kind of served me right because I didn't even like herbal tea. I'd only convinced Mum to buy some because, according to Andrea, everyone was drinking chamomile tea at bedtime. It turned out that the tea was a greeny yellow colour – if I'd known that beforehand then I probably wouldn't have tried to be a herbal trendoid – but at least it didn't leave a stain on Billy's T-shirt. Still, it was wet so I'd changed into the first one my hand grabbed off the shelf.

Saul had bought this T-shirt for my brother but it was my least favourite. Obviously Billy didn't like it either or he would've taken it back to New York, not left it on my bed for me to add to my sleepwear collection.

Silence = Death. The big black letters stood out against the white fabric. How impressed would my English teacher be? I was wearing irony. Or rather it was wearing me.

But that's the thing about irony – you don't always know it at the time.

It was almost 10 p.m. and I desperately needed to call Andrea because after nearly three weeks of searching, I'd found the perfect hairdo for her. But the problem was that Mum had been on the phone for hours and Andrea would be going to bed any minute now because Elizabeth Taylor recommended eight hours of beauty sleep – and what Elizabeth Taylor said, Andrea did.

Andrea had nominated me to find her a hairstyle that Billy could do for our formal, which wasn't till the middle of October, but was pretty much all we could think about. It wasn't just about the dress and the hair, we're not total empty heads. It was also because my brother, Billy, Aussie from unknown suburb Down Under, had become one of New York's 'up-and-coming' hair and make-up artists, and last Christmas he had made me a promise. A promise that no matter what, he would come home especially for my formal, because, in Billy's words, he was going to 'create magic' on me.

As soon as he'd made the promise, I'd asked Billy if he could do Andrea's too.

'As if I didn't think I would be,' he answered. 'I mean, you two are virtually joined at the hip.'

Andrea had been my best buddy since Grade 3. Or the 'wind beneath her wings' as she'd started calling me last holidays after we saw the movie *Beaches*. Bette Midler sang it about her best friend who dies at the end. Andrea blubbered so loudly that the usher shone a torch in her face asking her if she was okay.

'How about you, Andrea . . .' Billy suggested, then said, 'and one other friend?'

The second friend hadn't been decided on. Justin said not to waste a position on him. He didn't need Billy, because he could create his own magic with a jar of hair gel. Andrea wasn't convinced we needed a third person. She reckoned the formal should be our moment to shine. Our turn to shove a couple of the up-their-bum prissy girls out of the way. Watch their jaws drop and their skin go green as for once everybody turned to look at us.

But word somehow got around Year 11. According to Andrea, that was the reason why we suddenly found ourselves with a new 'friend'. Louise Lovejoy.

Louise Lovejoy had been one of those prissy girls until last year when she got off with Bronnie Perry's boyfriend Simon Finkler, aka 'the Fink'. Bad move.

The following Monday, Louise Lovejoy turned up to school with a black eye and a nose that sat a bit flatter on her face. Within twenty-four hours she'd lost her looks and her popularity. Everyone still called her Louise Lovejoy to her face, but there were other names that I'd heard muttered along the school corridors.

'Louise Lovejoy is definitely hanging around like a bad smell,' Andrea had said a couple of weeks ago. 'But you know what' – when Andrea began to speak out the side of her mouth you knew she was about to deliver a whammy – 'I don't even know if Billy can save that face.'

No one could hit the truth like Andrea and that's why I loved her. I had seven minutes left to call her about the hairstyle I'd found. But Mum was still gasbagging on the phone – plus her bedroom door was closed. That meant she was talking to Billy and they could chat for hours. Lately he seemed to call every night.

When I couldn't wait any longer I knocked on the door. Mum didn't say the usual, 'Oh Billy, I hear the ears on legs.' There'd always be a few seconds of silence as Billy replied. Then Mum'd answer, 'Yes, it's little sister Gemma. Shall we let her in?' That was my cue to walk in and say a quick 'hi' to Billy. I was only ever allowed about thirty seconds because Mum would stand there mouthing, 'This is costing a lot of money,' even though Billy was the one who paid our phone bill. But this night, the night I wore the *Silence = Death* T-shirt, there was nothing when I knocked. Not a sound. So I knocked again, louder.

'Piss off, Gemma!' Mum shrieked, which had me scampering back to bed.

I sat on top of the covers, trying to pull the T-shirt over my knees. That wasn't Billy on the phone. That must've been my father.

※

Andrea's verdict was that the hairdo wasn't right. Too Madonna and she's more Cindy Crawford, which I interpreted as meaning it wasn't 'big' enough. Billy had told me 'big hair' was over in New York but that he didn't expect home to catch on anytime soon.

I had a free period before lunch so it was back to hairstyle research. *Hamlet*, photosynthesis and World War I could wait at the back of the queue where they belonged.

I sank into one of the library's beanbags and started on a stack of magazines. They were mostly from last year, but

Andrea wasn't up with the latest fashion – even though she thought she was.

Just as I'd got myself perfectly moulded into the beanbag, with just the right amount of beans on either side, Vanessa Harding walked in.

The best thing about Vanessa was her twin brother Ralph. He was a major spunk on two legs. I'd only said about two hundred words to him and that was mostly in Literature Circle, which had ended last year, so it was unlikely I'd make it past two hundred and fifty by the time we'd finished high school.

Vanessa was a model but she wasn't one of the prissy girls. She didn't really hang out with anyone, probably because she was away for half the school year and now she was repeating Year 10, which would seriously suck.

For some reason, Vanessa seemed to be making a beeline for me. I tried not to look at her but it was hard not to have a quick peek. She didn't walk like a model, her big glasses took up most of her face and the gap between her front teeth was wide enough to hold a cigarette (I'd seen this firsthand). But she had amazing thick dark hair and was very, very tall.

'She's not a natural beauty.' That was Andrea's opinion. 'Vanessa's look will date and she'll be washed-up and out of business before school's over.'

'Hi, Gemma.' Vanessa was standing right in front of me. It was a strain on my neck to look all the way up at her. 'How are you?'

'Oh, hi, Vanessa.' I acted surprised. I didn't want her to think I'd been watching her.

'How are you?' she asked again.

'Good. You?'

'Yeah, good.' She was still vertical and I was wondering how long my neck could support this position. 'Although *Pride and Prejudice* is so hard to read. It's killing me.' Vanessa groaned. She flopped into the beanbag next to mine, her legs spreading out in front of her. I looked at them thinking that apart from being ridiculously long, her legs looked just like mine. Not like a model's. She had bruises, mozzie bites and knobbly knees that were dry on top.

Vanessa pointed at one of my folders that was lying on the floor. 'I love that picture of Madonna!'

'It's from *Interview*—'

'Yeah, *Interview* magazine! That's my total favourite.'

'My brother sends them to me from New York.'

Vanessa was nodding like she already knew. 'Did Billy tell you we were hanging out last month? In New York, at a fashion shoot. It went for days and days,' she said. 'It was so boring except for Billy being there.'

'You saw Billy?'

'Just a few weeks ago,' she said. 'Cool, hey! You didn't know?'

I was shaking my head.

'I love your brother. He's become my family away from home.'

My brother had told me when he'd met Vanessa for the first time last year. But I hadn't really taken much notice because every time someone mentioned Vanessa all I did was think about Ralph.

'As soon as he heard my accent he came up to me and said, "I bet you're Vanessa."'

Straight away my brain went into overdrive, flicking through all the things I'd probably said to Billy about

Vanessa. *She doesn't have any friends. She has a hunky twin brother called Ralph.* And I was sure I'd borrowed Andrea's lines: *She's not a natural beauty. She won't last.* The list was incriminating but the only thing I desperately hoped Billy hadn't let slip was the line about Ralph. The rest I could live with.

'Billy was telling me how he's flying in later this year for the formal. That's so nice.'

'I know,' I agreed. 'He promised.'

'Does he ring home much?'

'These days it's pretty much every night.'

'He's probably lonely.'

'No, it wouldn't be that. Billy has a boyfriend, Saul. He's a lawyer, or an "attorney" as they say in America. You know they've been together five years? They're like a married couple.' I didn't know why I was telling Vanessa this. All I knew was that I couldn't stop. 'Saul comes home with Billy every Christmas. Except last Christmas. Last Christmas he couldn't.'

'I know,' Vanessa answered, collecting her long limbs out of the beanbag and disappearing into the nonfiction shelves.

I watched her, wondering why Vanessa Harding suddenly thought she was some expert on our family.

After we'd eaten lunch, Andrea, Justin, Louise Lovejoy and I lay on the roof of the gymnasium, soaking up the last rays of summer and arguing over what length a formal dress should be.

Andrea was convinced on long. I was fighting for short, and Justin's all-important 'guy opinion' was that short was great but only if you had good legs. Louise Lovejoy didn't seem to have anything to add, which was predictably boring of her.

'Which one of you stinks of garlic?' Andrea whined.

'Guilty, your honour,' I said. 'Mrs C's lasagne.'

'That woman makes a totally wicked lasagne,' added Justin. 'I've only eaten it once and I still dream about it.'

Of course Louise Lovejoy asked, 'Who's Mrs C?' because she was still too new to the group to have heard any of my Mr and Mrs Carpinetta stories. Like when I was thirteen and I moved upstairs to their flat for two weeks while Mum and Aunty Penny went overseas to visit Billy. Mrs C made Mr C take all the soccer posters off their son's old bedroom wall and replace them with Boy George posters because she knew I was obsessed.

Even after Mum returned, I spent most of that year upstairs in their flat stuffing my face with lasagne or cannoli and watching *Dallas* while Mrs C plaited my hair, threading through ribbons of every colour. Just like Boy George.

Mr C wasn't sure about my idol. 'I no understand this Bob George.' He could never get his name right. 'Man or woman, Gemma? He no decide. One day in dress, next day in trouser.'

Some days when Mr C was on a rave about what the world was coming to, or as he'd say, 'what the world gone to', I'd catch Mrs C shaking her head at him. I knew what that meant. It was Mrs C's warning to her husband not to let the 'P' word slip.

Poofter. It wasn't such a bad word. I never cared when Mr C said it. I'd heard worse from my father's mouth. Phrases that had me imagining things I hadn't known I could imagine. Poofter was fine with me. In fact, I rather liked the soft sound my lips made when I said it.

'Hey, newsflash,' I said, suddenly sitting up and giving Andrea's leg a whack. 'Vanessa told me she was hanging out with Billy at a fashion shoot in New York. Can you believe it?'

Andrea sat up too and started speaking in the posh voice she adopted whenever Vanessa was the subject. 'Ooooh, on the catwalk? How soooper. And what did Vanessa have to say about *our* Billy?'

'Not much,' I replied. 'He told Vanessa he's coming back for the formal.'

The posh voice spontaneously combusted and Andrea was squawking. 'Vanessa better not be expecting Billy to do her make-up and hair! That'd be so, so unfair because, because . . .'

'. . . because she's so pretty she doesn't need any make-up,' Justin managed to slot in. I shot him a *you're an idiot* look and he grinned back.

'You are mental in the head,' Andrea began. A snorting giggle escaped from Louise Lovejoy, who hadn't quite acclimatised to Andrea's acts of tough love. 'Do you really think someone like Vanessa . . .' Andrea's lips had narrowed and she had started to speak from the side of her mouth. I wanted to block my ears, or rather block Justin's, because I feared what was to come. '. . . would actually notice a five-foot-two, fuzzy-haired boy who still plays Dungeons & Dragons?'

Justin started laughing because he loved getting a rise out of Andrea.

'Let's go,' I said, climbing off the roof. I didn't want

this to turn into one of Andrea's hissy fits. Andrea could be a bad sport and I could feel a storm brewing around her.

I have always been able to sense 'bad' coming. Not just with Andrea, with life too. Mum reckoned I was born a pessimist. 'Polly Pessimistic' she called me. She joked that the first expression I ever pulled was a frown. But it's true, I can feel it. Sometimes I sense it early. Sometimes it's not till it's almost on top of me.

At the moment a little bit of 'bad' was lurking at home. Why had Mum been talking to my father last night? My birthday was ages away and that was usually the only time Mum called him. 'It's just a gentle reminder, Garth,' I'd hear her say. 'No need to jump down my throat.'

But Dad was a professional 'jumper down the throat'. Whatever we did, it was never good enough. 'How many times have I told you not to do it like that!' was his all-time favourite line.

When I was ten and Billy was eighteen, Billy'd take shelter in my room. He'd lie on my bed, flicking through the pages of his bankbook, calculating how long it'd be before he had enough money for an airfare to America.

'Then I'll be out of his hair forever,' he'd say about Dad.

But just before my eleventh birthday, Dad removed himself from our hair. He quit his job at the hardware shop and took a job up north, on an oil rig. I hadn't seen it coming, not one little bit. At the start, I was mad. Then I began to miss him.

The first year he came home for Easter and Christmas. Easter was bad but Christmas was really, really bad. That was when Dad had called my brother those horrible words that had me doing acrobatics in my mind. *Limp-wristed, pillow-biting, doughnut-punching bum bandit.* There were more, but I tried my hardest not to remember them. I didn't miss him again after that.

Up ahead, Andrea, Justin and Louise Lovejoy were walking back to class. Andrea's arms were flapping around, which meant she was probably still stuck on the topic of Vanessa.

Usually, I'd call out to them to wait. But today I didn't. There was something bugging me about Vanessa's last words. I just couldn't put my finger on what it was.

2

MUM HAD A MOUTHFUL OF PINS AND WAS circumnavigating the kitchen table she made her clients stand on while she measured and pinned their gowns. Once I told her I didn't think it was a particularly hygienic practice. She bit my head off, saying, 'What do you suggest when my workroom is the size of a mouse's house?'

'. . . ma sis is trtina.' Mum introduced me to Catrina, her latest bride-to-be, who didn't look a lot older than me.

'Catrina,' she told me with a little wave. 'Hi.'

'Hi,' I answered. 'Believe it or not, I can understand Mum through a mouthful of pins. Years of training.'

The hem was pinned and Mum was smiling. 'I like this new length. Now hubby will be able to admire your nice slim ankles.'

Catrina blushed. I grabbed an apple from the lopsided papier-mâché fruit bowl I'd made for Mum in Grade 4 and went off to my room, ignoring the call of, 'How was school, darl?' because I was too busy wondering why Catrina was turning red over her future husband seeing her ankles. Surely the guy she was about to marry had seen more than that?

I wasn't a 'sexpert', as Andrea liked to call herself

because she had done it with three boys and I'd still only had the one. Fergus Eames, a year ago in the back of his mother's Holden Camira.

I had been wearing a blue-and-white dress that laced up at the back. I felt it go in all right but the problem was that it was over so quickly that I wondered if we'd really done it properly. I didn't want to walk around unsure if I was still a virgin or not but it wasn't the sort of thing you could ask. Fergus Eames just mumbled something like, 'Thanks, that was nice,' buttoned up his jeans and then told me we'd better get back to the party.

The first time I'd ever contemplated slapping Andrea across the face was five minutes later. Fergus was still in earshot but Andrea had rushed up to me and said, a bit too loudly, 'Why don't you ask Fergus to our Year 11 formal next year?'

'Why would I do that?' I'd answered. 'That's over a year and a half away.'

She'd shrugged. There were so many things that shrug could have been saying and none of them were good.

'Andrea,' I started, hemming her into a corner just to make my point a bit firmer, 'stop trying to organise my life! I just wanted to get my first screw out of the way. That's all. Fergus was there and he doesn't have six heads so I decided he'd do. That's where Fergus and I start and finish. Got it?'

'Take a chill pill,' she'd muttered back.

That was the God's honest truth. It was something I'd wanted to get out of the way. Like a box I needed to tick on my mental list of things to achieve before I finished high school. I knew that sex could be and should be more than that. But in time it'd happen. There was no point flying into a panic about it now.

Last Christmas, Billy told me that when he'd met Saul and fallen so deeply in love he realised that the good sex he thought he'd been having was like thinking oranges were tasty until you discovered mangoes.

That night, I was wearing my new Christmas pyjamas. Red spotty shorts and a singlet with one giant red cherry in the very centre. Maybe that's what gave Billy the idea of the fruit analogy but I was extremely relieved he'd left it at that. Hearing any more details would've totally grossed me out.

I didn't tell him about Fergus and me. In fact, that night we hadn't been talking about sex. We hadn't been talking at all. It was hot and we were lying on my bed with the fan blowing cool air into our faces. He'd said it, just out of the blue, like it was a thought that had turned into words.

Billy was missing Saul, I could tell. He was quieter, didn't go out as much and slept a lot. But mostly he talked about how much he loved Saul.

It was the first Christmas in four years that Billy had come home on his own.

I was disappointed. I missed Saul and his funny whistling snore that sounded like a plane landing. I knew that Christmas wouldn't be nearly as much fun without him. After we were stuffed full of turkey and Christmas pudding, Saul would start the games, like my favourite, when someone sticks a movie star's name on your forehead and you have to ask questions to guess who you are. The year before last, at the end of the night, Saul had dressed up as Mrs Claus and performed a hysterical cabaret act that ended with him and Aunty Penny doing a tap dance to Rudolph the Red-Nosed Reindeer.

Most importantly of all, Saul was a big present-giver. One Christmas he gave Aunty Penny a CD player, Mum a new state-of-the-art sewing machine and me a pair of sapphire studs. I got the special present because I was his 'number one gal'.

Saul had to stay in New York last year because he had family issues to deal with. It was hard to get a straight answer from Billy when I asked what these 'family issues' were.

'Just the usual.'

'What?' I questioned. 'That his parents can't handle he's a poof?'

'All that stuff.'

'Do they hate you?'

'They're . . .' he started. 'They're just not too happy about it.'

'That sucks.'

'Gems, they're no different to Dad. We all have a parent sob story. You should come to some of our dinner parties.'

'So yours isn't the best?'

'It's up there. But Dad still rings home. Like when it's your birthday. Even if he does need a prod from Mum.'

'Wow, give the man an award!'

'It's something.'

'Yeah, right!' I spat. 'It's pathetic. He's pathetic. Have you ever written to him?'

Billy sighed.

'Exactly! And I haven't written to him either. Ever. I'd shoot myself before I did that.'

'Gem. Come on.'

I didn't know why he wasn't cooperating. Usually Billy would join me or sometimes even lead the stampede in the verbal assassination of our father and all the things we could do to him. But that night, he didn't.

I'd finished my Biology homework and scanned through the crib notes of *Hamlet*, yet Mum and Catrina were still in the kitchen discussing her wedding dress. I wandered out there, opened and closed the fridge a few times and generally started making noises about dinner and how hungry I was.

But Mum and Catrina stayed locked in their deep and meaningful.

'Maryanne, how do you know if you're doing the right thing?' Catrina was asking Mum. 'How do you know if he's the one?'

'Do you love him?' When my mother answered a question with another question it either meant that she didn't know the answer or she didn't want to say it.

'Yes. I think so.'

'Can you imagine your life without him?'

'Gee, Maryanne, I . . .' Catrina started.

But Mum was up for a soliloquy. 'That's the question you need to ask yourself, Catrina. Can you imagine your life without him? If he were gone, would it feel like half your limbs had disappeared or that you were suddenly just a shadow and not a whole person? That's how you know if it's love. If you can't bear to think of your life without him.' Mum was burying herself thigh-high in the mud of life. I wondered where these lines were coming from because I was fairly sure it wasn't the way Mum had ever described her relationship with my father.

Anyway, Mum's speech did the trick or perhaps Catrina

was wishing she'd never asked because she simply said, 'Thanks, Maryanne. See you in two weeks,' and left.

'About time!' I groaned. 'Gee, Mum, you could replace Donahue or Oprah. When you get started there's no . . .'

But Mum was heading for the bathroom. Almost jogging there.

No doubt Andrea was jumping around somewhere playing netball, and Justin smashing cardboard in his karate lesson. Not me. Saturday mornings were spent watching *Video Hits* on the couch with a bowl of cereal so huge the milk spilt over the edge and into my lap.

It was almost 11 a.m. and Mum was still in bed, which wasn't that unusual for a weekend. I stood at the doorway of her room watching her fingers trying to adjust the blinkers she wore at night.

'A bit to the left,' I offered.

She mumbled, 'Is that you, Gem?'

'No, it's Coco Chanel.'

'She's dead,' Mum said, pushing her eye mask up onto her forehead. 'But oh, all the things I'd ask her.'

I crawled under the covers and hooked my arm around Mum but instead of a handful of flesh I found a handful of tissues.

'You know you're lying on a mound of tissues,' I told her, throwing them onto the bedside table so I could cuddle her properly. 'Are you getting a cold?'

'Maybe.'

But she said it so softly that I asked again, louder. 'Are you?'

She yawned back.

'Mum, do you think Saul will come out with Billy in October?' I asked. 'Maybe they could both stay until Christmas?'

Mum's answer was half snap, half sigh. 'That's months and months away.'

'Mum?'

'What?'

'Is there something you're not telling me?'

'Gemma, please don't invite Polly Pessimistic into bed with us.'

'They're not breaking up, are they?'

'Sweetheart, Billy and Saul love each other,' she told me. 'More than any other couple I've ever known.'

'Did you and Dad love each other?'

'At the time I thought we did,' she said.

'You were talking to Dad the other night, weren't you?' I asked. 'When you shouted at me to piss off.'

'Ah.' Mum sighed. 'Right. I thought you'd forgotten about that.'

'I'm not mad at you. That's not why I asked.'

'I'm sorry,' she answered, tightening her arm around me. 'I shouldn't swear at you.'

'Piss off isn't really swearing, Mum. Not in my books.'

'Well, it is in mine.'

'Does Dad ever ask how Billy is?'

'Darling, I really don't feel like talking about your father.'

'You're going to say "it's complicated", aren't you?'

'Because it is.' For a while Mum didn't speak. But by the way she was breathing I knew she wasn't finished. It was that kind of thinking breathing. So I waited. 'Of course your father loves Billy. He loves you both. I'm just not sure he knew how to be a good dad,' Mum said. 'His father died when he was so young and his mother was one cold fish.'

'Did she really never kiss you?'

'She probably did on our wedding day. I can't remember.'

'But she liked Billy?'

'Everyone loved Billy. He was such a gorgeous kid. He could even make Uncle Roddy smile and that was a beautiful sight. Your father's little brother was always so kind to me. I liked him very much.'

'Is that why you have the photo of Billy and him on your chest of drawers?' I asked.

'I just like that photo. That's all,' she answered. 'They look so happy. Especially Billy.'

'Mum, do you honestly not know where Uncle Roddy is?'

'He could be dead for all I know.'

'But you've never seen his name in the death notices and it's not like you don't read them.'

'Gemma, a family member or a friend has to put your death notice in the newspaper. It doesn't just automatically happen because you die.'

'Well, I'm going to start checking for his name in the death notices. At least we'll know then if he's dead or alive.'

Aunty Penny, my mum's little sister, was the only aunty I had and it didn't look like she was going to get married and give me cousins. She was a nurse and looked after men's 'waterworks'. I had no idea what that meant, but she said that she saw a lot of willies, so she was turned off men for life. Really, Mum had told me, Penny didn't trust men because a guy called Dean had broken her heart.

Lying in bed, snuggled under Mum's arm, her soft fingertips running across my skin while she answered my thousand and one questions, was my most favourite thing in the world. Then, I wasn't the sixteen-year-old girl who had a mental list of things she wanted to do before high school was finished; who had a friend like Andrea who was a full-time job to keep up with; and who had a formal at the end of the year that ended in the ultimate, but never-going-to-happen, fantasy of getting off with Vanessa's twin brother Ralph.

Right now, there was no 'bad' to sense. Instead I felt completely safe, as though Mum and I lived together in a bubble, away from all the horrible things that could ruin our lives.

I was nine years old the first time that I really understood what fear was. A girl called Meg Docker, the same age as me and who didn't live that far away, had disappeared. Her parents were always on the news, their words garbled as they pleaded for anyone who had information to come forward. 'Please, please help us,' they'd beg.

I've never ever told anyone, but I took it upon myself to help. At every drain I'd pass on the footpath or road, I'd stand there, even crouch if Mum or Dad or Billy weren't looking, straining my ears in case I could hear her cries.

When they found her body, I went to my room and sobbed. Mum told me it was a tragedy but that I was safe and nothing bad would ever happen to me.

'But how do you know? How do you know?' I choked out the words through my tears.

And for the first time in my life, Mum couldn't give me an answer.

I WAS BENT OVER THE BATH, SCRUBBING IT till it sparkled. Mum's instructions. No sparkle, no pocket money.

Mum was standing in the doorway, watching me clean. 'Billy's friend Claude has found some great material for your formal dress,' she said. 'He's sending us a few swatches in the post.'

'What are swatches again?' I asked.

'Little samples of fabric, Gemma!' Mum groaned. 'You've been living with a dressmaker all your life. How could you still not know what a swatch is?'

'Mum, sewing and I aren't friends,' I said. 'Just like how you and housework will never be friends.'

'Yes, but I don't get a choice.'

'Mum, no offence, but I'm not sure you'd clean the house if Bob Hawke was coming over.'

'Oh dear, I've grown a new wrinkle. It definitely wasn't there last week.' Mum was studying herself in the bathroom mirror. I watched as she leaned in closer, her fingers pulling at the skin on her forehead. 'Are you still thinking about your formal dress being as short as the one in the picture on the fridge?'

'Why? Are you still wanting to make that train thing for the back of it?' I grumbled. 'Err, gross, Mum. You forget that I'm sixteen, not thirty-six!'

'It was good enough for Jodie Foster to wear to the Oscars last year.'

'I think you mean Demi Moore?'

'Sorry if I'm not up on all their names! I know some glamorous movie star wore a train.'

'Mum, I hate to break it to you, but I'm not going to the Oscars,' I answered.

'I think a long dress is more appropriate for a school formal. Andrea's wearing long.'

'All the more reason not to. Plus she's wearing hot pink. Spew!' I said. 'How many bits of these swatch things has Billy sent? Did he say what they're like? Did he get them from that fabric shop he saw Madonna in?'

'I'm not sure if he's seen them.'

'But Billy's meant to be picking the fabric at that shop he told us about,' I complained. 'I don't even know this Claude guy. His taste might suck. He might've got them from somewhere else?'

'I'm sure your brother wouldn't ask someone whose taste sucked!'

'I don't know why Billy can't do it himself,' I grunted. 'That was the deal.'

Mum spun around. She caught me off balance and I hit my knee against the edge of the bath. 'Ouch!' I yelped.

It was like Mum hadn't noticed or if she had she didn't care. 'Your brother is obviously caught up . . . with . . . more important things.' It seemed each word was measured and weighed before it spat from her lips.

'Take a chill pill,' I muttered.

But Mum had left and her bedroom door was slamming.

Someone's a bit oversensitive today, I thought. I perched on the edge of the bath, studying my knee. A monstrous bruise would appear by tomorrow and Monday was sports day, which meant shorts plus my bruise on display for everyone to look at and go, *Yuck! Disgusting! What happened?* and I'd feel like a child-abuse victim.

I was about to go back to cleaning the bathroom when I suddenly changed my mind. This was my formal and my formal dress. I didn't want some long, daggy train trailing behind me because my mother thought it was more appropriate, and I didn't want some nobody called Claude picking my fabric either. The formal was meant to be my night to shine, and at the moment it wasn't feeling like that.

I ripped off the rubber gloves, chucked them into the basin and marched down the hall.

'Mum?' I announced, throwing open her bedroom door. 'I need to call Billy about the swatches.'

'Sorry, Gemma, it's the middle of the night in New York.'

'It's eleven-fifteen,' I told her. I'd been smart enough to calculate the time difference before I made my demands, because I knew that would be the quickest and easiest way for her to shut me down. 'Billy and Saul won't be asleep yet, and if they're out, I'll leave a message.'

Mum was rummaging around in her chest of drawers. She didn't stop. She didn't turn around to look at me. She simply answered, 'No.'

'I'll give you the money for the call?'

'I said no. End of conversation.'

'You don't get to tell me whether or not I can call my brother.'

'Yes, I do, Gemma. I pay the phone bill.'

'Billy pays the phone bill.'

'Excuse me?'

'You heard what I said.'

'Yes. And I didn't like it.'

Now Mum was facing me. Her cheeks were flushed and red. When she tucked some hair behind her ear, her hand was shaking. I realised a freak attack was coming my way.

I always got a couple of seconds' warning before Mum unleashed the freak. The first sign was a snarl that came right from the back of her throat. There was never much volume. But trust me, the explosion was only seconds away.

'I am telling you. You can*not* ring your brother,' she began. 'Did you not *hear* what I said before, Gemma? That's final.'

'But that's not fair!' I snapped back, ready for battle. 'Billy promised he'd pick the fabric samples himself. It's my formal, my dress and I don't want some—'

'You spoilt little brat! Is that all you can think about? Hmm? Hmm?' Then the explosion erupted in full force. Shouting, arms waving, spit flying, the psycho eyes. This was going to be the annual technicolour humdinger and murder was not out of the question. My mother's pointed finger moved closer and closer to my chest. *'You selfish, selfish, ungrateful girl!'* Mum yelled as the tip of her finger jabbed me with each word. *'Your brother has been so good to you. So, sooo good to you. Generous. Kind. But at the moment he doesn't have time to run around New York for your silly formal dress! You brat! You don't deserve . . .'*

Sometimes you have to accept when you've lost. Except that I hadn't actually lost. I'd just come up with a new plan.

I backed out of the room, grabbed my wallet and made a run for it.

I had my own money. I could ring my brother, or anyone for that matter, whenever I wanted to. This was between Billy and me, and my mother could go and jab her finger in someone else's chest.

Besides, it wasn't as though I was going to call Billy to abuse him. I just wanted to ask why he was sending someone I'd never heard of to pick the fabric. And did this Claude know that I despised every variation of the colour pink?

All that was in my wallet was one precious ten-dollar note. I'd been hanging on to it so I could finish the lay-by I had on a pair of earrings, but I needed change for the phone. The corner shop was closed because it was Sunday. So I had to hike all the way up to the junction and buy a packet of chewing gum to break the note.

By the time I trudged back, none of my questions felt so urgent. Still, I went into the phone box, closed the door and carefully laid the coins along the ledge.

Seeing the silver stacked up in little piles and thinking about how many times I'd have to scrub the bath to earn the money back had me wondering if I'd overreacted.

Plus now it was almost midnight in New York. Once when I'd called in the middle of the night, Saul had been cranky that I'd woken him up. I'd definitely lose it if Saul had a freak attack at me too.

So I stood in the phone box, wondering, worrying and wasting more time. Billy used to call the phone box his 'office'. He'd come down here every night so he could call his boyfriend, Matt Leong. That was back when Dad was still at home and Billy had to sneak around while Mum and I covered for him.

I owned part of this phone box too. One weekend, Andrea and I had left a trail of messages here after we'd had a fight in Year 7.

The words had faded but I could still read them clearly.

Dear Andrea, You really hurt my feelings when you said you hated me. G xo

I was cut because you said I was a big know-all.
A xoxo

That's because you kept saying I like Justin and I don't! G xoxoxo

You always sit next to him in Science. Not me.
A xoxoxoxo

That's because he's good at science and I'm hopeless at it. But I promise I will sit next to you now.
G xoxoxoxoxo

I'm sorry. A xoxoxoxoxoxo

Me 2. G xoxoxoxoxoxoxoxoxoxoxoxoxoxoxoxoxoxoxoxoxoxox
oxoxoxoxoxoxoxoxoxoxoxoxoxoxoxoxoxoxoxoxoxoxoxoxoxoxo

Me 3 A.xoxoxoxoxoxoxoxoxoxoxoxoxoxoxoxoxoxoxoxoxoxo
xoxoxoxoxoxoxoxoxox

When I got home, the door to Mum's bedroom was shut. I stood outside and whispered, 'I didn't call Billy.' Of course, there was no answer and there definitely weren't going to be any apologies either.

So I crept out of the flat and upstairs to see Mr and Mrs C. They'd probably heard Mum and me shouting earlier and they were always good for some sympathy. Their door was never closed. As I came up the stairs I could see the silhouette of Mr C on the couch watching TV.

'Hello?' I called. 'It's me.'

'*Mia cara*, Gemma,' Mrs C sang back. 'I'm in the *cucina*.'

Mrs C was the most insane cook ever. There wasn't a better sight than walking into the Carpinettas' kitchen and finding Mrs C in her black apron, her big arms rolling out enough pastry to feed Southern Italy.

'You can fill cannoli for me, Gemma, when they come out of oven,' she said. 'And taste the first one.'

I groaned in reply. 'They're soooooo fattening. But I love them.'

'Gemma, you never fat! And one cannoli not hurt you.'

'I can't stop at one.'

Mrs C kissed me on the head.

'Did you hear Mum and me fighting?' I asked her.

She kissed me on the head again.

'Did you?'

'It's okay, darling. Grown-ups get cross. They have a lot on their mind.'

'I didn't do anything wrong.'

'Come here, *mia cara*.' Mrs C began to hug me. She was tall, giant tall, and when she hugged me it always felt like I was going to suffocate in her massive boobs that squashed up against my face. 'You be good to Mamma. She need you, Gemma.'

I untangled myself and wandered into the living room.

'Hi, Mr C,' I said, plonking myself on the couch next to him.

Mr C was engrossed in his favourite Sunday night TV show, *Degrassi High*. Mrs C said grown men who watched that show were '*coglioni*', which kind of meant 'idiot' even though the actual translation was 'testicles', but I thought it was cute that he watched it.

'Fat Dwayne got a girlfriend,' Mr C began to tell me as though Fat Dwayne was one of his close personal friends. 'And Joey is gonna walk through school with no clothes because he want to buy a car.'

'Got it,' I replied, even though I didn't. Mr C had a habit of talking me through every episode, but to be honest I'm not sure he really understood it himself.

'They have condong machine in every bathroom,' he told me.

'Huh?'

'Condong machine in the school bathroom.'

'Condong?

'Yeah. For the . . .'

'Oh – condom?' I spluttered.

'*Si!*' Then he whispered, 'For the disease.'

'What?'

'Fat Dwayne, he think he—'

'*Spegnerlo*, Giuseppe!' Mrs C shouted. Suddenly she was storming into the living room, standing in front of the TV. '*Spegni il televisore, stupido idiota!*'

Mr C was usually up for a good shouting match with his wife but he just sat there like a little boy.

'Come, Gemma.' Mrs C was taking my hand, pulling me off the couch. 'We need to fill cannoli now. *Pronto!*'

'Oh? Oh?' I think I said it a hundred times because I was answering the hundred questions spinning through my head, each one popping up before I had a chance to answer the one before that. And the person asking them all was Polly Pessimistic.

Louise Lovejoy had watched *Degrassi High*. 'It was an amazing episode,' she told us the next day during our study period in the library. 'Dwayne found out he's got AIDS. It was really sad. He went mental and bashed up the condom machine in the bathroom. He actually ripped it off the wall.'

'What? Dwayne's got AIDS?' Andrea asked. 'But doesn't he – you know – like girls?'

'Isn't a poof, you mean?'

'Well, yes, Gemma,' Andrea replied. 'But you know I don't like saying that word.' It was actually Andrea's mother who had the hang-up about the word and my brother being one. Mum reckoned every time Deidre asked her about Billy she'd put on this sad voice as though there was something wrong with him.

'My brother's a poof,' I explained to Louise Lovejoy.

'I don't care,' she answered.

'But he has a boyfriend. They've been together five years. They are like an old married couple. Aren't they, Andrea?'

'You want my theory about Mrs C?' Andrea offered, although I was fairly sure it was non-negotiable. 'She probably didn't want you to watch it because of the condom machine. I mean, they're old, plus they're Catholic! Derr Gemma, birth control is against their religion.'

Justin, who'd been busy finishing his Biology assignment, looked up at us and said, 'Does Dwayne have AIDS or is he HIV-positive? They're not the same thing.'

'Mr Technical,' Andrea chimed back. 'What difference does it make? He's still going to die!'

'Yeah, but—'

'Maybe not,' Louise Lovejoy interrupted and we all turned to look at her. 'They had a sex-ed class on *Degrassi High* and there were these guys who had AIDS giving a talk. They said it wasn't a death sentence.'

'Oh, great,' Andrea said. 'So they're going to go around infecting everyone now?'

'Andrea!' Justin groaned. 'Get your facts straight. That's why they use condoms. Don't you know anything?'

'Oh, go back to Dungeons & Dragons, Justin!' Then Andrea's voice dropped an octave. 'Anyway,' she started, 'I don't think we should be talking about this in front of Gemma.'

'Why not?' I snapped back.

'I know Billy and Saul are different, but – but,' she stammered, 'I just don't think we should.'

The bell rang and for four different reasons the four of us jumped out of our seats at the same time. Andrea, because she never liked being wrong. Justin, because he realised Andrea was probably a minute away from going psycho at him. Louise Lovejoy, because she was well aware she'd started the whole thing and she couldn't afford to make any more enemies. Me? I'm not sure. I just felt weird.

At home, there was a note under the fruit bowl.

Out with Penny. Back by 6 p.m. Can you peel spuds in sink? M x

I wandered into Billy's room. I knew that I was going to do this when I got home from school today. Even though it wasn't on my mental list of things to do, like copy Justin's

Biology homework, shave my legs and see what my hair looked like parted on the other side.

Neat is the word I'd use to describe my brother's room. Unlike Mum and me, Billy had always been a bit of a neat freak. He'd tidy his room before he went back to New York and it would stay in this pristine state until he came home again.

While he was away his room felt like a giant vacuum of nothing. When he first left for America, I used to come in here and take deep breaths until the hairs in my nose tingled. Hoping I'd find a hint of him, like the rich coconut smell of his hair gel. But I never did. That'd have me sinking onto his bed thinking, *This is what it'd be like if Billy was dead.*

It started to weird me out so Mum told me not to go in there anymore. She'd said, 'I never do, there's no need.' So I told her I'd stop. But I didn't. Five years later I was still sneaking in to see if I could find a bit of him. There were times I liked to lie on his bed and chat as though he was actually there, lying next to me.

Today, something looked different on the shelves. The photo of Billy at his Year 12 school formal was on the second shelf, in front of his magazines, not on the third shelf, where it usually sat next to his NSW State Championships swimming trophy.

Sprung, Maryanne! I thought as I walked over and picked up the picture frame. Mum obviously did make the occasional visit.

The photo was one big bad fashion moment from 1982. Billy wore a pale blue tuxedo. His date, Pauline, looked even worse in a purple taffeta dress with sleeves like balloons. But what really made me chuckle were their hairdos. It was like they'd got each other's mixed up. Pauline had short back and sides and Billy's hair was so long it almost reached his waist.

That was the night Billy had met Matt Leong. Matt was trying to elbow his way to the front of the dance floor because his favourite band Snake Head was playing. But Matt was short and skinny and it was almost impossible for him to push his way through the crowd. Plus, as Billy said, 'He was the lone Asian and no one was going to let him get past.'

Billy scooped Matt up and sat him on his shoulders. Everyone shouted at Matt to get down but Billy said that together they were like one of those dancing Chinese dragons. They were unstoppable.

Matt became Billy's first proper boyfriend. When I asked Billy, 'How did you know that Matt was the same as you?' he said, 'You just know, Gem.'

Billy could barely eat, let alone study, he was so in love. All day, he'd be on the phone to Matt, and when Dad got home from work Billy would disappear down the street to his 'office', the public phone box. Some nights, if Matt and he had fought, Billy would still be there after midnight and Mum would be spinning Dad some lie about the library being open late.

Billy reckoned Matt Leong was the final straw for Dad. 'Finding out your son's a poofter and then a week later walking in on him in bed with a gook. That was it for the old man. He was out the door.'

I put the photo back on the shelf and took a magazine from the top of the pile. It was the January edition of *City Star*. It was a kind of half newspaper, half magazine that Billy picked up from The Carousel, the dance club he partied at when he was home.

The first page was an ad for the Gay and Lesbian Mardi Gras. I flipped over to the next page where there was another big ad. No pictures in this one. Just words covering the whole page. It took several seconds before I registered what I was actually reading.

Q. Does having just one partner guarantee protection from AIDS?
R. NO.

Sometimes your body takes matters into its own hands: the brain switches off and the legs start moving. Right now, that was happening to me. I was closing the door of Billy's room. Then the front door. I was going down the stairs, out the gate and into the crisp afternoon air.

My Walkman and my jumper were at the bottom of my schoolbag but I knew my legs weren't going to take me back upstairs to get them.

I could sense 'bad'. I was sure of it. Mum could tell me I was a pessimist all she liked but she wouldn't be able to sense 'bad' if it rang the doorbell and introduced itself to her.

Mum, in her own words, was a pragmatist. I was the pessimist and Billy was somewhere in the middle. Mum never said I'd inherited the pessimist gene from Dad, but I knew that's what she thought.

Well, I had the pessimisms right now. Polly Pessimistic was holding my funeral and no one was going to turn up. That's how bad I had it.

I fished through my pocket, checking I had the right coin, because I knew I was headed to the phone box.

I didn't make the call straight away. I had to fine-tune

my story first. For a moment I wondered if I should call Andrea but I couldn't talk to her about that.

My fingers dropped in the coin and started dialling.

'Hello? Louise speaking.'

The only reason I knew Louise Lovejoy's number was because the last four numbers were the date of my birthday, then Billy's – 2127. 'Hi, Louise . . .' I had to catch myself not to add 'Lovejoy'. 'It's Gemma here.'

'Oh? Hi, Gemma.'

'I forgot to bring my *Hamlet* questions home. Have you got yours?'

'Hang on two secs, I'll get them.'

I rehearsed my line. It sounded okay but I had to find a way to slip it in.

Louise Lovejoy was puffing when I heard her voice again. 'You know, I think a short formal dress is way cooler, Gemma.'

'You do?'

'Totally. My mum gets the English *Vogue* and—'

'So does mine. She's a dressmaker so she gets all the mags.'

'That's why your folders look so amazing. I've been eyeballing them in English. That picture you have of Madonna is the best ever!'

'It's from *Interview*. One of the magazines my brother brings home from New York.'

'Gemma?' Louise Lovejoy's tone suddenly changed. 'I felt really bad after our study period. You know when I was talking about *Degrassi High* and . . .'

Louise Lovejoy had just thrown open the door and invited me in. If it was possible to have squeezed through the phone and hugged her, I would've. For a second I actually thought I was going to cry.

'That's okay,' I answered. 'It's not your fault.'

'Do you worry about your brother? Sorry, is that too personal a question?'

'No. No. It's not,' I said. Yet from anyone else, at any other time, that question that I'd never been asked before would've turned me into a three-headed monster. But right now, for the first time ever, I wanted to talk about it. 'I try not to think about it,' I started. 'But sometimes it feels like it's everywhere. Posters or ads on TV. I was in the supermarket the other day and there was a caller on the radio saying, "They all deserve AIDS and God made it on purpose." Stuff like that.'

'That sucks.'

'My mum says I don't need to worry about my brother because he's been with his boyfriend for so long.'

'Five years?'

'Yeah. How did you know?'

'You told me today.'

'Louise?' I took a deep breath. 'Can I ask you something? Did . . . did they say anything else about AIDS on *Degrassi High*?'

'Not really.'

'Nothing?'

'Not that I can think of. Sorry, Gemma,' she offered. 'I know there are special numbers you can call, like the AIDS hotline.'

'No, it's okay. But thanks.'

'I won't say anything,' Louise Lovejoy said. It was as though she could read my mind.

4

MONDAY WAS THE DAY AFTER APRIL FOOLS'
Day, but that didn't stop anyone. When you have a friend
like Andrea, even the second of April is a day of high alert.

Lunch was predictable. A student had got on the loudspeaker announcing that the principal said we could all
go home, someone planted a trail of fake dog poo in the
locker room, and the joke that sucked everyone in and
even had a few girls crying was that Princess Diana was
dead.

As far as I was concerned, April Fools' Day was over for
another year. But Andrea executed her prank in the afternoon, when my complacency had set in.

The last period was in the drama room and was a total
bludge. We were seated on the grey felt carpet that always
gave me an itchy bum, watching a theatre group perform an
act from *Hamlet*. I was sitting next to Louise Lovejoy and
Andrea was behind us.

Andrea started to touch my back. Sometimes when
we couldn't talk, she spelled messages to me that way.
I thought that's what she was doing, because a second before
the play started she'd launched into some complicated story
about Martin Searles. How she'd found out what party he

was going to on Saturday night and she was pretty sure we could gatecrash with no dramas.

So I was concentrating on the supposed message she was writing on my back, trying to work out what words she was spelling. Not realising that in between strokes, she was gathering up the back of my uniform (which I stupidly wasn't sitting on, even though I usually did because of the itch factor!) and pinning the hem up. Way, way up. So that at the end of *Hamlet* when I stood up, my hungry bum, swallowing my red-striped undies, was on full show for everyone to see. Including Ralph.

Louise Lovejoy was in the same predicament. She seemed to catch on quicker and pasted herself against the wall squealing that she'd been 'got real good'!

We had been got real good. The only reason I didn't kill Andrea was because Louise Lovejoy laughed about it. Really hard and really loud. So I had to as well or I would've looked like a total spoilsport in front of everyone.

But when I walked in the front door from school, the prank still sat sour on my lips.

Mum was busy fitting some girl's ugly pink bridesmaid dress to the plastic mannequin we called 'Neuta', because there was nothing downstairs. Apart from the boobs, you couldn't tell if it was a male or female.

'Neuta and I have been so excited for you to get home,' Mum said. She picked up a tiny yellow package and began to wave it in my face. 'Guess what's inside, Gemma?'

'What?' I grumped back.

'The swatches for your formal dress!'

'I'm not going to the formal anymore.' I hadn't actually thought of that possibility before I said it. But at that moment it seemed like a good idea even though I one hundred per cent didn't mean it. It's just that Ralph witnessing my bum had been beyond mortifying, even though he hadn't laughed and pointed like the prissy girls had. 'I'm not going back to school tomorrow, Mum. Or ever again for that matter. I'm going to become a hairdresser.'

But Mum was ignoring me. She'd already opened the package and was stroking a small square of jade green velvet like it was a kitten. 'Isn't it beautiful?' she purred.

'Yuck,' I said, even though it wasn't too bad.

'Yuck.' Mum imitated me, screwing up her nose like I had. She kept it that way while she said in a nasal voice, 'You know if the wind changes you'll be stuck with a nose like this forever.'

I groaned because I wasn't in the mood for any more jokes.

Mum's fingers pulled another swatch from the envelope. Black velvet.

'Do you like this one?'

'It's a bit better.'

'Now keep an open mind with this one.' Out of the package she pulled a piece of salmon pink satin. 'Stunning, isn't it?'

'That's pink!' The tiny piece of material detonated my explode button. 'I hate pink! Pale pink, candy pink, hot pink, every pink ever invented, and if Billy had picked the fabric himself instead of some guy who doesn't know the foggiest about me, then, then . . .' I didn't know what I was trying to say. We'd barely mentioned the swatches since our last fight. I stormed into my room and slammed the door behind me, tears choking me as I threw myself on the bed, face-first into the pillow.

The next day I couldn't even give Andrea the cold shoulder. People were still congratulating her on what an unreal April Fools' Day prank she'd pulled and Louise Lovejoy and I on what good sports we'd been. Even Sonia Darue, one of the prissy girls, came up to me and said, 'If that was me I would've totally burst into tears. But you were so cool about it, Genna.'

'It's Gemma,' I muttered back, thinking, *I almost liked you then*.

Andrea lapped up every compliment until she was peaking so much she found herself at Martin Searles' locker, asking him to be her date at the formal.

'That's months away,' Martin mumbled.

'I like to be in control of things,' Andrea told him, her fingers running up and down the locker handle.

I snuck off to the bubbler because this was clearly not a conversation for three. When I looked up Andrea was beaming and Martin Searles was walking away.

'So?' I nudged Andrea.

'So, looks like I have a date for the formal.'

'He said yes?'

Andrea was nodding.

'Oh my God! He said yes?'

'Well, as good as,' she replied. 'Anyway, I told Marty we're planning on crashing Simon Finkler's party on Saturday night.'

'Marty?' I choked.

Andrea was glowing. 'I can't wait.'

'We are going to crash the Fink's party?' I gulped. Simon Finkler was in the year above. He was big, tough, mean and not one to appreciate girls like Andrea and me crashing his party. 'The Fink? Tell me you're kidding. Please?'

'I'm deadly serious.' Andrea pulled a face. It was the annoying one where she sucked in her cheeks and pouted her lips until they resembled a bumhole. The problem was that Andrea thought it looked sexy, so I'd probably be seeing a lot more of it now that 'Marty' was suddenly on the scene. 'Marty will get us an invitation,' she was saying. 'If that's what you're worried about.'

'That's not my main concern,' I answered. 'I'm more worried about Bronnie Perry. You know, the girl who rearranged Louise Lovejoy's face? Derr.'

'It's different. I'm not after the Fink. Louise Lovejoy was an idiot. She asked for it.'

'Andrea! That's a horrible thing to say.'

'Are you best friends with Louise Lovejoy now?'

'What?'

'It's a joke, Gemma,' she told me. 'But I've been thinking. I'm not sure Louise Lovejoy should be the other person who Billy makes up. I think we should keep that spot open for a while.'

'Too late.' I had just made my decision and I'd never been so sure of anything. 'I've already asked her,' I lied. I walked off, leaving Andrea glued to the ground.

The rest of the week was about one thing and one thing only. Simon Finkler's party. Actually that's not true. Simon Finkler's party was merely the venue. Everything was about Andrea and Martin 'Marty' Searles.

What was Andrea going to wear? Should she trim her

fringe so that she could tease it better? Were the black kitten heels too dressed up? Where could she buy the new Revlon Bronze Lame lipstick?

Her questions and obsessions went on and on, while all I wanted to ask was, *Does Martin Searles actually know that you're going to the party?*

If I subscribed to lessons of tough love like Andrea did, then I'd substitute 'know' with 'care' because that was more like the truth. Three times this week I'd had the agony of watching Andrea sidle up to his locker only for him to turn on his heel and walk away as though he hadn't seen her. The problem was that he had. But Andrea was thick-skinned, and more than that she could convince herself of anything.

'Marty's just playing hard to get,' she told me. 'He's actually flirting with me, Gemma. We're like animals. It's a mating game we're playing.'

It didn't matter how much I rolled my eyeballs. We were going to the party and that was that.

'I'm a bloody good friend,' I reminded her at every opportunity.

'I'd do the same for you, Gemma,' Andrea replied each time.

But some days I wondered if she would.

On Saturday night Andrea knocked on the door. She'd cut her fringe and teased the life out of it. She was wearing the black kitten heels and after travelling six train stops had finally found the Revlon Bronze Lame lipstick that was painted thick on her lips, so when she pulled the annoying pout her mouth resembled a bumhole that sparkled.

'You look very' – Mum paused – 'dressed up tonight, Andrea.'

'Too dressed up?'

'No,' I butted in, because I could sense a fashion crisis ahead. 'Mum just means you look dressed up next to me.'

I was in my uniform: Levi's 501s, my faithful Doc Martens, a tight black long-sleeve midriff and the chunky gold hoops that Saul had given me for my fifteenth birthday.

When I'd opened Saul's present I couldn't hide my disappointment, because I'd hoped they were going to be the amazing Christian Lacroix earrings that I'd shown Saul in a magazine. I wasn't trying to drop a hint. It was just that I gasped so loudly, Saul had come over to see what the fuss was about.

'Look! Look!' I'd said, pointing to the picture. They were big, chunky gold crosses. 'I would die to have these.'

I really liked the gold hoops. I wore them all the time. Sometimes I worried whether Saul could tell I was disappointed that day.

Andrea pointed to the picture of my dream formal dress on the fridge. 'Is this strapless number still the one?' she asked me.

'Something like that. Maybe in black velvet instead.'

'I still think it's a bit boring. No offence.'

'And I still think Gemma's dress should be long,' Mum piped up. 'It is a formal. Not a party.'

'I agree, Maryanne.'

'Louise Lovejoy's wearing short,' I bravely announced.

'How do you know?'

I stalled on purpose, because I could almost hear Andrea panting.

'How?' Andrea snapped and Mum did her little cough that meant *Andrea's pushing you around again.*

'She told me,' I answered casually, dragging out her agony a bit longer. 'Louise's in love with the dress that the lead singer of Roxette wore on the cover of the single "Dressed for Success".' I paused. 'It's tight, red and short.'

'Hmm,' Andrea said, and I knew that meant she didn't like what she was hearing. She was pretending to study the picture, and I wondered what drama had just started in that head of hers.

'We should hit the road, Gemma,' she suddenly said.

'Do you girls want a lift to the party?'

'No.' Andrea beat my answer of 'yes'. Then she gave me the big saucer-eyes that said *shut up, we don't want a lift*. 'No, thank you, Maryanne,' she finished in a sucking-up, sweet voice. 'We don't want to put you out. It's only a ten-minute walk.'

'Have a good time then.' Mum tucked my hair behind my ears. 'Shows off your earrings better,' she whispered.

'Yes, Mother.'

'Midnight, Gemma, and not a minute later. Or I will hunt you down and publicly humiliate you at the party.'

'Bye, Maryanne.'

We weren't even out of the apartment block before I was blasting Andrea. 'Ten-minute walk!' I spat. 'More like twenty-five. Correction, forty with you in those heels.'

'I have to get supplies. A just-in-case item,' Andrea answered as she linked her arm through mine.

'Sorry, you've lost me.'

'Condoms.'

'Condoms?'

'Exactly. We are headed to that late-night chemist up the junction.'

'But that's the opposite way,' I moaned.

'I don't know why you're complaining, Gemma. I'm the one in the heels!'

'So when did you decide you were going to have sex?' I asked.

'It's not like I've decided, but if Marty asks, I want to be prepared.'

'Always thinking of others, Andrea.'

'Gemma, do you think your mother really would hunt you down and publicly humiliate you?'

'No, Andrea. It was a joke.'

We clip-clopped along the street, or rather Andrea clip-clopped with the occasional stumble because she really hadn't nailed the art of walking in kitten heels. I'm not saying I had, but Billy had shown me how the models are taught to walk on the catwalk. Hips forward, feet forward in the shoes, look forward and pretend you're walking on a tightrope.

Twenty-five minutes later we arrived at the late-night chemist.

Open 364 days the neon sign flashed. All that sign ever did was present me with a huge conundrum: what one day of the year were they closed? Was it Christmas? Boxing Day? Good Friday? The owner's birthday? Because for some reason they didn't bother to specify.

Andrea scanned the shelves while I stood there trying not to look awkward. The chemist, a man who was about a hundred years old, was watching us like we were either shoplifters or sex maniacs.

Andrea kept picking up box after box of condoms, reading the information, then putting them back down again. I couldn't bear it any longer so when she'd got to about the fourth packet I whispered in her ear, 'Why are you taking so long to choose?'

'The first two are ultra thin and this box' – she was now holding another one – 'says thin.'

'So?'

'So I don't want thin or ultra thin.' Andrea was talking normally. Actually almost a bit louder than normal. We may as well have been discussing the difference between Rice Bubbles and Coco Pops. The chemist was now peering over at us from the opposite shelf. 'Although ultra thin would be worse. Much worse.'

'Why?'

'Derr, Gemma,' she said. 'Less protection! And I can't risk that. Not anymore. Look at Fat Dwayne. We all have to be extra careful now.'

'You mean . . .?'

'AIDS, Gemma.' Finally she was whispering. 'Look, you know I don't like talking about it in front of you. And I know Saul and Billy are different to – to all the others.' She suddenly stopped mid-sentence, marched up to the counter, bought the condoms and we left the shop.

It was only then, when we were outside, that she started talking again. On and on and on she went. '. . . the Grim Reaper ad was right, Gemma! Mothers and fathers and children all dropping dead because of them . . .'

I watched her. Her arms waving around, her eyes wide and her gold lips stretched over every word. And I knew that night for sure, the night of the Fink's party, when I wore my Levi's 501s, a tight black long-sleeve midriff, chunky gold hoops and Doc Martens, that I would never, ever be able to share my fears with Andrea.

*

At the party, Andrea handed me a big plastic cup of wine and uttered from the side of her mouth, 'You're looking like Nigel no friends.'

Believe me, that was not a good thing. I took a big gulp. I didn't like wine and it made me burp, but I was going to be stuck at the Fink's party for a while and I was sick of standing against the wall with my arms crossed. From my position, I had two views: couples rolling around on the carpet or couples groping each other on the dance floor.

I had another gulp of wine and then another, and a few cups later I was on the dance floor too.

I wasn't a big one for dancing. I left that up to the prissy girls. But when Salt-N-Pepa came on, Andrea had dragged me up. 'Come on, Gem,' she yelled over the music. 'You have to dance with me!'

At the end of Year 8, I'd ditched Boy George and had a brief and intense love affair with Salt-N-Pepa. Andrea and I had spent the whole Christmas holidays making up dances to go with their songs. We then subjected Billy and Saul to countless dance performances. If they were out, Mum or Aunty Penny would be our victims.

'You remember the moves?' Andrea was squealing. I did and suddenly I wasn't shy.

Bum to hip rotation. Spin. Bum out. Bum in. Spin. Tap hand on the ground. We still had it. *Arms up. Arms down. Spin. Bum to hip rotation.* All the steps were coming back. *Quick down on the floor. Three push-ups.*

A crowd had gathered, but that didn't stop us. *Bum to hip rotation. Arms up. Arms down. Spin. Bum out. Bum in.* Andrea even remembered the bit where she had to slide between my legs. I was only just ready for her too, but we pulled it off.

The circle around us were clapping in time. Now it was Sonia Darue and a few of the other prissy girls from our year, standing against the wall with their arms crossed. I spotted Ralph in the crowd, clapping and laughing. I waved at him and he actually waved back.

Our moves were getting bigger and bolder. Andrea and I were singing at the top of our lungs. We were having a moment and it was fantastic.

Afterwards, we joked that it was our dress rehearsal for the formal. A little warm-up to warn the prissy girls we were coming.

But it would be a very different occasion when I next danced to that song.

5

ON SUNDAY MORNING I OPENED SATURDAY'S
papers but I had a bit of a white wine headache so I was
only pretending to read.

Mum was busy with Catrina, who'd just arrived for an
emergency bridal fitting. Catrina had called that morning
in tears because she'd just found out she was pregnant and
the wedding wasn't for another four months.

'I'm already fourteen weeks,' she was blubbering to my
mother. 'I missed a couple of periods but I do when I'm
stressed. I didn't think anything of it.'

'It'll be okay. You're not the first pregnant bride I've had
to dress.'

'But I wanted to look beautiful, Maryanne.'

'You will. I promise.'

Oh, Mum, I thought, *that's a promise you're not going to be
able to keep. In three months' time, Catrina's going to look like
a giant marshmallow walking down the aisle and she's going to
blame you when she does.*

'If we let out the seam here,' Mum was explaining, 'and
I make a tiny tuck here and loosen . . .'

I went back to the newspaper and started reading it
properly. It was the third week in my quest to search for

Uncle Roddy's name in the death notices. It had been going well too. By well, I mean I hadn't found the name 'Roderick John Longrigg'.

Mum said Saturday was the best day to look because some families waited for the Saturday newspaper even if their loved one died on a Wednesday. It didn't make sense to me, but Mum knew more about this business than I did. Although I had noticed she'd stopped reading the death notices.

The prospect of having to read through the entire list of dead old fogies was way too boring. Perhaps I was cutting corners, but I felt like I only needed to look through the surnames beginning with 'L'. I had a system that was quick, efficient and foolproof. I'd find the start of the 'L's and my index finger would scan down the list of names, slowing considerably when it hit 'LO'. The annoying thing about this paper was that the 'L's started at the bottom of one column then resumed at the top of the next. Slowly my index finger slid down to the bottom of the page.

There it froze at the very last name.

Matthew Thomas Leong.

I kept reading. *Aged twenty-five. Died after a short illness. Loved by his family and friends.* That was it.

'Mum?' I called.

'Mmm?' she answered through a mouthful of pins.

'Remember Matt Leong?'

'Mmm.'

'Do you know what his middle name was?'

'. . . ohmas? I ink.'

I waited until Catrina had gone and then I showed Mum the death notice. She took it really badly. I held her as tight as I could and when she folded her body onto the floor I folded with her. We sat, huddled together on the cold kitchen tiles, while Mum cried and cried.

Maybe Mum didn't realise, but I guessed how Matt had died.

In January when it was just Billy and me at home, Billy had started thumping his fist on the kitchen table. He'd been reading the *City Star*. 'No! No! No! No!' he uttered with each thump. 'Bloody hell!'

'What's up?' I asked.

'Another guy I know has died.'

'Who?'

'Adam Haydele. I met him through Aunty Mame. He was a country boy. Sweet guy.'

'That's sad.'

Then Billy said, 'I hate the way they write *Died after a short illness*. It's such a pathetic, empty line.'

'What does it mean?' I asked.

'It means he died of AIDS.'

There were two things that stayed with me that day. Occasionally I still push them around my head and wonder. The first was that Billy seemed almost casual about his friend's death. I don't mean he didn't care, it just didn't seem to be a shock to him. But I'd be really shocked if I heard about someone I knew who died. Even if I didn't know them that well. Like when the man who lived in the flat downstairs died.

The second thing was that it was one of the few times I'd heard Billy say the 'A' word. I'd assumed he didn't talk about it because it'd upset him. But Billy seemed fine. Not at all freaked out.

That morning, I clearly remember saying to myself, *Ask him about it now. Ask him all the things you want to know.*

It was the perfect opportunity because Mum was out and it was such a no-go topic with her.

Yet it wasn't the right time. Billy wasn't hysterical like I would've been, but he was still sad. So I didn't ask. I just said what I knew Mum would say. 'I'll put the kettle on.'

Matt Leong was the first person I really knew who had died. That night, I slept in bed with Mum. I told her I didn't want her to be alone, but to be truthful, it was me who didn't want to be alone.

Mum fell asleep quickly, probably because of all the crying she'd done. I lay there, staring at the ceiling, trying to recall Matt Leong's face. I couldn't get the picture right but I could hear his voice and remember the way he used to say Billy's name, 'Beelee.'

A few weeks after Dad left Billy went pyscho. Afterwards, he refused to come out of his room for two days. Mum asked Matt to come over and try to coax him out of his self-imposed confinement. Matt stood outside the door of my brother's room. 'Beelee? Beelee?' he pleaded over and over again. 'It not your fault. Beelee?'

Matt was nice. His parents owned the corner shop and he used to bring me musk sticks and cobbers.

After Dad went, Billy and Matt could stop pretending they were just mates. But at the Leongs', they still had to play the game. Billy reckoned Mrs Leong was one of the scariest women he'd ever met. She never spoke to Billy; she just stared at him.

Mrs Leong definitely looked scary. I could picture her standing behind the shop counter. Her hair pulled back in a super tight bun and her eyebrows drawn in with black pencil like two little upside-down 'C's. It was true too that she barely spoke. When you asked her where something was, she'd just grunt and point to a shelf. Matt's family moved away about the same time Billy left for New York.

I must've finally fallen asleep wondering where they'd moved to, but when I woke up and rolled over in the bed, I could feel that Mum wasn't there.

It was pitch black. The bedroom door was closed. My hands fumbled for the lamp. It was 3.24 a.m and the phone that usually sat next to the clock was gone. That meant one thing: Mum was making the call to Billy.

She'd said she'd have to tell him about Matt. She'd said she didn't want to, that maybe she'd wait a few days. Obviously she'd changed her mind.

I crept out. Mum was in the living room, huddled in the corner of the couch with a blanket around her shoulders. She was crying, soft, tiny hiccups. The ones you make when you've been crying for a long time. 'Please, Billy,' she was saying. 'Please, Billy. Please.' Then Mum was nodding and wiping her nose with the blanket. 'Okay, darling,' she said. 'Okay. You too.'

When Mum looked up and saw me, she gasped, really sucking in the air like I'd given her a fright. 'How long have you been standing there, Gem?' she asked.

To me, right then at that moment, it seemed like a strange thing to say.

The week didn't get any better. On Tuesday when I got home from school, Mum was crying. On Wednesday, she hadn't changed out of her pyjamas. By Thursday, she was in bed and barely able to speak. Matt Leong's death seemed to have sucked the life out of her.

But when Friday arrived, it was my turn to have the nervous breakdown.

Apparently that morning, Martin Searles had fingered Andrea on the bus. Gross. But she was acting like he'd given her a diamond ring and proposed.

We were walking to a sex-education forum everyone in Year 11 had to attend, but for Louise Lovejoy and me it'd been going all day.

'Andrea! No more details,' I barked. 'That's enough.'

Louise Lovejoy was pressing her lips together but I was way beyond thinking it was funny anymore.

'Do you think maybe we're going round now?' Andrea asked. It was about the twentieth time she'd presented us with this delusionary idea of hers. 'It has to mean something.'

'Martin Searles is a bit of a user.' At least Louise Lovejoy was brave enough to hint at the truth.

Of course Andrea shut her down in two seconds. 'How would you know, Louise?' And in true Andrea style she went that bit too far. 'He's not the same as Simon Finkler,' she uttered from the corner of her mouth.

Louise Lovejoy just shrugged it off, but it must've hurt. I squeezed her elbow and she whispered, 'I'm fine. Don't worry.'

A teacher was yelling at us to form a line so we could walk into the auditorium in single file. 'You'll be given a handout at the door. So please remember to pick it up before you go in and sit down.'

Andrea had the huffs now. She pushed into the front of the line and didn't look back at us once.

'I said the wrong thing, didn't I?' Louise Lovejoy whispered to me.

'Andrea can be a schizo.'

'She's really sensitive.'

'Only if we're talking about her!' I answered. Louise Lovejoy and I took our handouts. I tucked mine under my arm and kept talking. 'I'm sorry about what she said to you. That was harsh.'

'It's true though,' Louise Lovejoy said. 'Simon Finkler isn't like Martin Searles. Simon Finkler's much worse.'

'How do you mean?' I asked.

'He's just not a very nice person,' she answered, then started reading the handout. The silence that suddenly sat between us clearly told me that the topic of Simon Finkler was closed.

So I started to flick through my *How to keep safe* handout too. I wasn't really reading it, just opening the pages so I had something to do because it was obvious Louise Lovejoy had shut up shop for the day.

Typically, this was the page I opened. *Most cases of HIV are men who have sex with other men . . . Blah, blah, blah,* I said to myself. But I kept reading. *. . . estimated that over 300,000 cases of AIDS have been reported to the World . . . in the USA . . .* I was just about to turn the page when I spotted the line *. . . New York City has the highest incidence of AIDS in . . .* Suddenly my eyes were flicking across phrases and sentences, just grabbing snatches here and there. *Young men . . . AIDS . . . short illness . . . rapid death . . .*

I'd frozen at the entrance to the auditorium. 'Come on. Move it.' Students were shoving but even with the weight of the queue pushing against me, I couldn't lift my foot to take a step.

'Gemma?' It was Louise Lovejoy's voice and I could feel a hand taking my arm. 'Gemma, are you okay?'

'I . . . I have to go.'

'I'll come with you.' I could see that she was still holding my arm but I couldn't feel her grip anymore. 'Gemma? I'm coming with you.'

'No. No, it's fine,' I stammered. 'I'd like to be alone.'

I think that's when I started running.

I didn't stop. I didn't even collect my bag. I just had to get away.

When I got home, Mum was lying on the couch. She didn't look up and see my red face drenched in sweat and she didn't hear my panting breath either. She didn't even speak.

I didn't bother telling her what'd happened. Besides, what would I say? That I freaked out over a paragraph in a sex-education booklet? She'd just tell me the usual, that I didn't need to worry.

So I went to bed. I stayed there until it was a new day and it felt safe to get up.

6

APRIL 30TH, I WROTE AT THE TOP OF MY
Hamlet exam. *What a long month,* I thought. Mum had got
over Matt Leong's death but now she'd turned totally psycho.

One day she was on the couch, still in her pyjamas, the
next she was out of them and on a crazy bridal frenzy. Now
Neuta really didn't know if it was Arthur or Martha; it had
on a new outfit every day. Mum seemed to be up all hours
of the night cutting white satin and sewing beads onto
bodices that didn't need to be finished until September.
The only dress she couldn't attack was Catrina's, because
Catrina was growing fatter by the minute with twins.

Even worse, Mum was on a cleaning frenzy too. Yet,
she agreed she wouldn't clean the house even if the prime
minister was visiting. But this week she'd scrubbed the
kitchen cupboards, thrown out every old jar of gherkins
from the fridge, cleaned the oven, washed the curtains.
I even caught her standing on the table, vacuuming the
ceiling. That's when I announced I was going upstairs to
Mr and Mrs C's, where there was peace and quiet and
grown-ups who fed and fussed over me.

The *Hamlet* exam was a doozy. When I got home,
all I wanted to do was lie in a hot bath, close my eyes

and pretend I was Ophelia floating down the river, dead.

Not that anyone would notice. Especially Ralph. For as I had just discovered, I was invisible.

On the way home from school, Vanessa and Ralph had almost run me down at the zebra crossing in their unmissable lime-green car. Maybe since Literature Circle had ended, Ralph had forgotten I even existed? He had waved at me on the dance floor the night of the Fink's party. At least, I thought he had. Maybe he had been waving to someone behind me?

There was no time for self-pity or hyperventilation, which was what I was on the verge of, because my mother wasn't home to complain to and had instead left me an irritating note about Claude and the swatches.

Hi Gemma.

Hope Hamlet exam okay. I'm out with Penny. We'll be home about six-thirty with pizzas. I promise yours will not contain anchovies. Time is running out and we need to start on your formal dress. Can you go through ALL the swatches (bad salmon pink has been chucked!) and decide which fabric you like best so Claude can buy from the NYC shop. (Yes, the one Madonna's been seen in!) Also did you want gold braid edging like in the photo? Or just plain? Need to know so Claude can order as well. Getting exciting!!!

Penny's reserved the video A Fish Called Wanda. Meant to be really funny and I think we all need a laugh and a big bowl of chocolate chip ice-cream.

MA xxx

PS Swatches in yellow envelope on kitchen bench.

The swatches weren't on the kitchen bench. There was no yellow envelope to be found. I went through the pile of mail and newspapers twice, searched the drawers, even checked inside the fridge because Mum sometimes hid bills in there when she couldn't deal with them.

The only other place they could be was Mum's room. But they weren't on her bedside table or her chest of drawers or her basket of things to file. I checked the top drawer, which was my go-to place when I needed spare change. No yellow envelope, just the usual tangle of earrings and chains that hadn't been worn for years.

The next drawer was underwear, so not a likely spot. But I opened it anyway and began to rummage through Mum's bras and undies that were seriously old and gross. Straight away my fingers found the edge of an envelope, wedged in a far corner under the winter socks.

I pulled it out and lay on Mum's bed. I was fairly sure I was going with black velvet but I wanted to look at the others in case I had a sudden brainwave.

I turned on the lamp, got comfy and opened the envelope. But instead of swatches, I found photos. Only two, but I'd never seen them before.

It took me a while to figure out that it was Saul I was staring at. He was at a fancy dress ball. The room was crammed with people and red balloons covered the entire ceiling.

Typical Saul had taken the 'dress up' theme seriously. He was wearing a black-and-white all-in-one suit and his face was painted in black and white stripes like a zebra. He even had pointed fabric ears stuck over his own.

I held the photo under the lamp so I could study it better in the light. Billy had gone beyond 'working his magic' on Saul. He'd created a work of art.

The stripes on Saul's face were painted exactly the same as on a zebra's hide. Each one was different in width and length yet all came to a pointed end. But what finished it off was the black circle my brother had painted from the tip of Saul's nose to the bottom of his chin. Billy was a genius.

The other photo in the envelope was of Billy and Saul. Billy was dressed up as a circus ringmaster with a curly black moustache and a top hat. Alone he would have looked pretty good, but next to Saul he was dead boring. Written on the back of the photo in Saul's handwriting was, *Thanks to my love, you'd never know.*

I put the pictures back in the envelope and left them on Mum's bedside table. Then I went and ran a bath. Mum hated me using the phone in the bath. She said it was dangerous and I'd get electrocuted if I dropped it in. But Mum was out. After I'd eased myself into a steaming bubble bath, I telephoned Louise Lovejoy.

'Hi. It's Gemma.'

'How hard was that *Hamlet* exam?' she exploded. 'Who gives a fluff about Rosencrantz and Guildenstern! They're hardly the main characters.'

'Not according to Justin.'

'What's happened to Justin? He's always in the library, these days.'

'Justin's turned into a nerd That's what's happened. Anyway, don't worry,' I told her, 'I flunked for sure.'

'That makes two of us then,' Louise Lovejoy said. 'My father will kill me.'

'Over flunking a *Hamlet* essay?'

'Yep. He's a freak.'

'Don't worry, so's my mother. She's already hassling me about my formal dress. Acting like it's tomorrow, not six months away. This is what happens when your mother makes your dress. Sometimes I wish I could just go to a shop and buy it like a normal person.'

'Are you still going short?'

'That's exactly what I was ringing you about! Are you?'

'Totally. My dress is going to be exactly like the Roxette girl's.'

'Good. If you're going short then I will too,' I said. 'I just didn't want to be the only one.'

'So should I find a hairdo too?' Louise Lovejoy hesitated. 'For your brother to do? That's if he has time. I mean, it's fine if he doesn't. I'm just stoked about the make-up.'

'Start going through the mags,' I told her.

'I'm beyond excited! Thank you so, so much, Gemma.'

'Don't be stupid. You don't need to thank me. Andrea does though. I've spent ages going through magazines for her and now she's decided she wants a French roll. She thinks it'll be very Liz Taylor. Vomit!'

'What's with her obsession with Elizabeth Taylor?'

'Her mum and grandma worship her so she joined the fan club,' I answered. 'To be fair, Elizabeth Taylor was really beautiful when she was young but I reckon she looks like a transvestite now!'

Louise Lovejoy was laughing. 'I wouldn't know,' she said. 'I've never seen one!'

'Come to my place when Billy and Saul are home,' I answered. 'They have this good friend Aunty Mame. She does shows where she calls herself Madame Tutti Frutti, and she wears these amazing headdresses with bananas and oranges.'

'So you say "she" even though . . .'

'Yeah. I know it's confusing.'

'And she's not your actual aunty?'

'No!' I laughed. 'She's called "Aunty" because she helps guys come out. She shows them around town and introduces them to other guys,' I explained. 'If you've come from the country to get away from your family because they don't know you're queer, or rather they don't want to know you because you are queer, then you arrive in the big city and it's really scary. That's where the aunties help.'

'That's way cool.'

It was easy talking to Louise Lovejoy. She didn't hog the conversation. She was a good listener and her mind didn't just shut down when she heard something a bit different. Once I'd tried to explain the 'Aunty' thing to Andrea's mother. I was almost halfway through the explanation when I noticed Deidre's nose was starting to screw up like someone had let off a fart. I cut the story short because I suddenly felt embarrassed.

I was still dying to ask Louise about Simon Finkler. A few days ago, I'd almost had the chance because I saw Bronnie Perry walk up to Louise Lovejoy and say something. I was sure it had to be bad but when I asked Louise if she was okay she'd simply said, 'Fine. Bronnie was just asking if the buses are still on strike this afternoon.'

The Fink and Bronnie Perry had broken up, but it still didn't make sense. Why would the girl who'd rearranged your face ask you a mundane question about the bus? Actually, why would she speak to you at all? And why would you speak back? There was something suss and it was going to be a delicate extraction to get the real story out of Louise. But now wasn't the time.

'I'd better go,' I told Louise. 'My mum and Aunty Penny will be home in a minute and I'll be majorly busted if they find out I'm using the phone in the bath.'

I went into Mum's room and used her hair dryer because mine was about to die and had been taking an hour to dry three hairs. Mum's rule was that I had to wait until it cooled down before I put it back in her cupboard or it might set the flat on fire.

While I waited, I stood in front of the mirror pretending I was asking Ralph to be my partner at the formal because, let's face it, he wasn't going to ask me.

I began by smiling at my reflection. 'Hi, Ralph.'

Hi, Gemma. How're you going?

'I'm good.' I nodded in a coy kind of way because I didn't want to seem like a full-on stalker. 'How are you?'

Good. I keep thinking about that dance you did at the Fink's party. It was cool.

'Really?' I shrugged and gave a giggle. A husky one. Not a girly one.

Yeah. You're a good dancer, Gemma.

Suddenly real voices echoed down the hall. 'Pizzas are here. One minus anchovies.'

I took the yellow envelope off Mum's bedside table and wandered into the kitchen.

'Hey, I found these in your drawer, Mum. They are way cool. Saul looks incredible.'

Mum dropped the pizzas on the table, but one of the boxes fell onto the floor.

'I'll fix that,' Aunty Penny said, dropping to her knees.

'I hope that's one with anchovies.' I laughed. 'Because I'm starving.' Mum was staring at me. 'What?' I said.

Her keys were in one hand and the other kept hitting the table. Not hard, more like a slow, rhythmical thud. *Thud . . . thud . . . thud . . .* And then I understood: she was trying to think of something to say.

'Why were you going through my drawers, Gemma?'

'I was looking for the swatches,' I told her. 'I couldn't find them anywhere.'

Aunty Penny was furiously digging through Mum's bag. She pulled out a package. 'We accidently took them with us. I like the black velvet the best too.'

'Do you?' I mumbled, because I was busy watching Mum walk out of the kitchen – or rather the way she was walking out of the kitchen

'Is Mum drunk?' I asked Penny.

'No!'

'Well, what's her problem? She's walking funny. And she's acting funny too!'

Penny was fussing around. Opening and closing cupboards, getting out plates and glasses. 'She mentioned she was feeling a bit sick.'

'Well, that's a lot of pizza for just you and me to eat. Or rather you, Penny, because the margherita is mine.'

I opened the envelope and showed the photo of Saul to Penny. 'Have you seen this? How amazing does Saul look?' Penny was nodding and I couldn't work out why she wasn't saying how incredible my brother's work was. 'Saul's written this cryptic message on the back. *Thanks to my love, you'd never know*,' I read. 'Never know what? That's he's actually a human and not a real zebra?'

Aunty Penny didn't laugh at my joke. Instead she left the room, muttering something about the toilet. But I saw her go into Mum's bedroom and close the door.

'Schizo sisters!' I muttered to myself.

I ate the margherita pizza. I flicked through the *Woman's Day* that had been sticking out of Penny's bag, along with a pamphlet for a Bachelor and Spinster Ball. But mostly

I listened to the muffled cheers of the soccer game Mr C was watching upstairs. Really, what I was waiting for was my mother's laughter as Aunty Penny snapped her out of whatever mood she was in.

But there was nothing.

I stood up and left the table, feeling merely curious. But once I was there, standing outside my mother's closed bedroom door, my sense of 'bad' loomed up out of nowhere and wrapped its hands around my neck.

There are moments when silence feels like the loudest noise you can actually hear. Right now, in the hall, it was beyond deafening.

Something had happened. I could feel it. The 'bad' was bubbling up through the carpet, seeping through the walls.

I didn't knock. Instead I barged into Mum's room. 'What's going on?' I demanded.

Mum and Aunty Penny were sitting on the bed, holding hands. But when they saw me, they let go. If they weren't sisters, I would've been suspicious they were having an affair because they both had guilt pasted all over their faces.

'I know you're hiding something. Both of you.'

'What on earth would we be hiding?' Penny said.

'You tell me!'

'Gemma, what are you suggesting?' Penny continued.

'Well, if I knew I wouldn't have to ask, would I?'

'Why are you raising your voice at your aunt?' Mum said.

'Because!' I suddenly yelled really, really loudly because I wasn't going to be *shooshed* this time. I wasn't going to be answered with another question or told 'it's complicated'. The 'bad' was strangling me now. Its hands were so tight around my throat I could barely catch a breath. 'Because neither of you are talking to me!'

'Put your voice down. We live in a block of flats.'

So I snarled at my mother instead. 'You've gone all weird. And I want to know why!'

'What have I done that's weird?'

'Yes. How's your mother being weird?' Penny added.

'I know what you're both doing!' I snapped. 'You're answering my questions with other questions. Don't worry, I do know your tactics by now.'

No answer from them. They knew they'd been caught red-handed.

'Since we found out Matt Leong died, you haven't been yourself, Mum,' I started. 'You barely got out of bed for ten days and now you've gone on this cleaning, sewing frenzy. I can handle the sewing but not the cleaning. The cleaning is seriously weirding me out. And . . . and it's not me being Polly Pessimistic. I know when things aren't right, and don't say it's complicated! Tell me. Now!'

Aunty Penny stood up and left the room, closing the door behind her. Suddenly I was terrified.

'Mum?'

Mum was peering up at me. 'Sit next to me, Gem,' she said softly.

So I did. Mum took my hands, curling her fingers over mine, swaddling them in her palms until both her hands were wrapped over them.

'Mum, you're scaring me,' I whispered.

Mum took a deep breath in. The air heaved through her nose like she was trying to suck up courage. She held it in for a moment, then the awful words escaped with a single breath. 'Saul has been sick. Very sick.'

'What are you saying?'

'I'm saying that he's been very sick.'

'And he's . . .'

'He's not going to get better, Gemma.'

I didn't scream and cry the way I'd imagined I would if I heard bad news about someone I loved. It was more like I suddenly couldn't move and inside, my body had gone very, very quiet and still.

'Is it . . .'

Mum nodded.

'No!' A sob escaped. 'What about Billy? Is he . . .'

She shook her head.

I started crying. I buried my head in Mum's lap and cried so hard it scared me. I was crying because I loved Saul and I didn't want him to die. But mixed in there were sobs of relief because my brother was okay.

I could've stayed cradled in my mother's lap all night. But I actually started to feel like I was drowning in my tears. I'd always thought that was just a saying. Yet at that moment, I couldn't breathe. My nose was blocked, my face was wet and there was liquid gurgling in my throat.

When I sat up Aunty Penny was back, sitting on the bed too, and we were all drowning in our tears. Saul was dying of AIDS. It'd started with a cancer called Kaposi's sarcoma. Aunty Penny wrote the two words on paper. *Ka-po-si's sar-coma.*

It began with a single purple spot on his chest. Not much bigger than a fleck of dust. Now the lesions were all over his face. That was the reason Billy had turned Saul into a zebra. So no one would see. *Thanks to my love, you'd never know.* That's what the words had meant.

7

MAY

THE NEXT MORNING, I WOKE AT 11.51 A.M.
with almost half the school day over. Every muscle ached.
My eyes looked like two slits in my face and my head
throbbed more than it ever had after white wine. And, to
be honest, there was a part of me that woke up mad.

Why hadn't I known Saul was sick? Why did no one tell
me? I'd sensed something wasn't right but all I'd got back
was 'You're being Polly Pessimistic'.

In the kitchen I could hear the whir of the sewing
machine and a whining voice on the radio complaining that
the trains were never on time.

'Who cares,' I snapped at the anonymous voice. 'Don't
you realise there are bigger things happening in the
world?'

I rolled onto my back and closed my eyes. I needed to
block out how cranky and ripped off and left out I felt.
I needed to lie here quietly and think, because there was
only one thing on my mental list of things to do today and
it was enormous and terrifying. Not like yesterday. Yesterday
morning when I'd woken up the first thing I'd thought
was: *Do I have time to shave my legs before school?*

Today it was making a phone call to Billy and Saul.

What would I say to them? That's what terrified me. *I'm sorry? How are you, Saul? Are you okay, Billy?*

Then I thought of all the things I'd like to ask Billy in private. *Is Saul really going to die? When? Are you scared? Is he scared?*

I made a cup of tea. I tried to eat some toast but I wasn't sure I could swallow food.

'It's nearly midnight in New York,' I called to Mum.

'Too late to ring, Gem.'

'I know.'

I heaped another spoonful of sugar into my tea. I usually had two, but today I couldn't taste the sweetness on my tongue.

'That's why Billy couldn't pick my formal dress fabric, isn't it? And that's why Saul didn't come home for Christmas?'

The whirring of the sewing machine stopped and Mum appeared in the kitchen.

'Why didn't you tell me, Mum?'

'I had no choice. I promised Billy,' she said. 'He wanted to tell you everything himself.'

Mum was leaning against the fridge with her arms crossed and the tip of her right elbow just covering the picture of my formal dress. Suddenly the answers I wanted didn't matter. Instead, I wanted to vomit. Imagine if I had called Billy the afternoon I was mad about the swatches? I had changed my mind at the very last second. A mixture of not wanting to spend my money, feeling foolish over making a scene and being scared that Saul might blast me for calling so late. But if I had called, maybe Saul would've answered? Maybe he wouldn't have been mad? Maybe he would've been happy to hear my voice because he knew he wouldn't be hearing it too many more times?

Now I had a new question for Mum. 'Have you spoken to Saul?'

'Yes.'

'How did he sound?'

'Weak. Tired.'

'Did he ask about me? Did he say, "How's Gemma?"'

'He said, "Tell Gem she's still my number one gal."'

'Did he say it in that funny voice?'

'Yes, he did.'

'I'd like to talk to him.'

Mum swallowed. I heard it clearly and I thought I knew what it meant.

'I'll be okay,' I told her. 'I mean, I'll probably cry, and I'm scared because I know he might not sound like Saul, but I should talk to him, shouldn't I?'

'Saul knew you loved him. That's what was important.'

'Stop talking about him like he's already dead!' It was hearing my words, not Mum's, that made me realise. 'Mum? Mum?' I could barely breathe. 'Saul's already dead, isn't he?'

✳

Saul was dead and buried. He'd died almost a week after I'd found Matt Leong's death notice in the newspaper. At the end, he hadn't even known who Billy was.

Saul's funeral has just been his family plus Billy. Billy had told Mum that he'd felt like the outsider. That it was as though Saul's family were farewelling a man Billy hadn't known.

It was Saul the Attorney, Saul the Valedictorian, Saul the 100-metre University Sprinter, Saul the Good Son and Eldest Brother. Billy, Saul's partner of five years, wasn't even mentioned. But Billy had told Mum that he felt lucky to have been invited at all.

Now he was away with friends at a place called Martha's Vineyard. He said to Mum that this would be his time to remember his true love.

But my mother had been furious. A red-faced, roaring, homicidal, spit-flying, crazy madwoman. She had been holding on to this rage and now that I knew everything, she was letting it out and letting it rip. What she'd say and what she'd do if she ran into Saul's mother, which just as well for both of them was never going to happen or my mother would be spending the rest of her life behind bars.

On Wednesday afternoon we went to the supermarket. Neither of us felt like eating but we always did the shop on a Wednesday after school.

Mum hurled cans and jars into the shopping trolley. Then she bit the check-out chick's head off because she was too slow. But it was on the drive home that she had the psycho moment of the century.

We were remembering the Christmas when Saul had carried a drunk Mrs C up to her flat and how we had heard the echo of his groans as he climbed each stair. We were laughing really hard. That kind of laughter that at any second could turn into hysterical, blubbering tears.

We pulled up at the traffic lights next to the church where Andrea and her family went. Now we were bathing in that warm, fuzzy silence that comes after a memory that both devastates and delights. That silence where you're both still there, lost somewhere in the story. I was on the verge of letting out a big, long sigh when Mum suddenly yanked on the handbrake and jumped out of the car.

In a split second she was charging up the stairs to the church and ripping a poster off the noticeboard. Then she leapt back into the car and we were driving away, sticky tape caught on the cuffs of her jumper.

If I hadn't been feeling so lousy I would've burst out laughing because it was the craziest thing I'd ever seen my mother do.

'Why'd you do that?'

'I hate bigots.' Mum's fingers were strangling the steering wheel and her nose was almost pressed up against the windscreen.

'Okay. But . . . what did the poster say?'

'The usual.'

'Like?'

'Like crap about love between a man and a woman.' The brakes screeched as Mum took the corner too fast.

'Okay,' I said again, pulling on the strap of my seatbelt to check if it was fastened properly. 'Can you elaborate?'

'Isn't love just love? Why does it matter who it's between? It's like saying one love is better than another.'

By the time we arrived home and were lugging the shopping up the stairs my mother had flipped so badly she was quoting lines from the Bible. 'Love comes from God. Everyone who loves has been born of God. That's John. Or is it Paul? I can't remember now. They're just a bunch of bigots.'

'Mum, how about I put the kettle on?' I said as she unlocked the door.

The answering machine was beeping. Mum dashed in and just about pounced on the message. 'Hey, Gemma . . .' the voice started.

'Oh, it's Andrea,' Mum moaned.

Andrea's voice was a jerk back into reality. A reminder that the world outside was still turning. 'Bludging again, hey? Are you coming to school tomorrow? Call me. It's urgent. Marty update.'

'You still haven't told Andrea about Saul, have you?' Mum asked.

'I haven't felt like talking to anyone,' I answered. Yet I'd thought about calling Justin. I'd even thought about ringing Louise Lovejoy. But Andrea? I wasn't ready to tell Andrea, and that had never happened before.

Andrea was my first stop for everything. The Saturday morning in Year 8 when I woke up with my period. She was the first to know, even before Mum. My first pash at summer camp with the lip-gnawing Timmy O'Brien. We'd barely parted and I was dashing down to the tennis courts to find Andrea. The day after Boxing Day when Dad had slammed the door and we understood he wasn't ever coming back. It was Andrea who met me at the phone box and whose arms I collapsed into. My virginity, my exam results, my fights with Mum, my broken hearts. My Year 9 identity crisis when for a night and a day I thought I might be a lesbian. It was Andrea who I'd whispered my fears to.

We were best friends. I was the wind beneath her wings.

But the idea of telling her about Saul terrified me because I honestly didn't know what she'd say. Scarier than that, I didn't know how I'd react.

Mum didn't know about the time I'd slapped Andrea across the face. I didn't tell her because I didn't want her to hate Andrea. It was the day before Billy and Saul arrived for Christmas last year, except at that time I didn't know it was only going to be Billy because, yet again, no one had found the need to tell me.

We were sunbaking by the pool at Andrea's place and sharing a mango. I was going through my black-and-white phase and was wearing a white bandeau bikini top and black boy-short bottoms. Andrea was attempting to copy my look but typically had it all wrong; she was wearing white bottoms and a black top with ugly yellow flowers.

I tried to explain to her that the colours didn't balance that way and you were meant to wear it the other way around. She'd rolled her eyeballs at me and said, 'Gemma, you are such a walking fashion think-you-know-everything.'

But that's not why I slapped her.

About five minutes after that Andrea had finished licking the last of the mango juice off her fingers and was busy slathering coconut oil all over her legs. 'You excited to see Billy and Saul tomorrow?'

'Yeah,' I'd answered.

'I wonder what Saul's bought you for Christmas? Do you reckon he's ever going to buy you those Christian Lacross earrings you wanted?'

'It's Christian Lacroix,' I corrected her in my best French accent, dragging the spit up from my throat. 'One day he will. He promised.'

'But all that posh French stuff is so expensive. Just say Saul bought you a pair of earrings from some cheap place and told you they were Lacock or whatever his name is. I bet you wouldn't know the difference.'

'I bet I would!'

'You'll never get them,' Andrea said. 'They're too expensive. You shouldn't have pulled that big, sad puppy dog face when you saw the gold hoops. Poor Saul.'

'Thanks for the lecture.'

'So Saul and Billy are staying at your place?'

'Derr. Where else would they stay?'

'I don't know.' She shrugged. 'Maybe they want some privacy? Like your room is right next door. Hello? You must hear noises.'

'Why do you always ask that? You've got some weird fascination with Billy and Saul.'

'I'm just curious.'

'Well, for the billionth time, I've never heard a thing,' I answered. 'Chuck me the oil.'

'Maybe they gag each other?'

'Andrea!' I'd almost missed catching the oil. 'You're off!'

'My parents wouldn't let my sisters or me sleep in the same bed as our boyfriend unless we were married.'

'Your parents still think you're a virgin.'

'Well, my dad would kill me if he knew I wasn't.'

'Or maybe he'd just leave, like my dad.'

'But if Billy wasn't a, wasn't a . . .'

'Poofter? You can say it, Andrea.'

'Yeah, one of them,' she said. 'If he wasn't, then your dad wouldn't have left and your parents would still be together.'

'No they wouldn't!'

'My mum reckons they would. Because you must admit your mum had to choose between her son and her husband.'

'No she didn't!'

'Mum says she did.'

'How would your mother know?'

Andrea shrugged.

'How?'

Her next words were muttered through the side of her mouth and that had me sitting up. 'It's pretty obvious.'

'Excuse me?'

'What?'

'What did you just say, Andrea?'

'When?'

'A second ago,' I said. Inside, I could feel my chest starting to burn. 'I heard you, Andrea. You said, "It's pretty obvious."'

Now Andrea was sitting up too because I was on my feet and leaning over her. 'Hello?' I barked into her face. 'Can't you speak now?'

'Well, it is,' she replied.

'Is what?'

'Is obvious.'

'What's obvious? Hey?'

Andrea dealt me another pathetic shrug then looked the other way.

'What's obvious?' I was shouting and I was so close to her I could smell the mango on her breath. 'Hey? Tell me.'

'It's obvious . . . your dad couldn't handle his only son being a bum bandit.'

Whack! It happened so fast. I still remember watching my hand reach out of nowhere, as though it had a mind of its own, and slap her across the face, one cheek to the next.

I know I hit her hard. It wasn't just because I heard her yelp and my palm was red and stung like crazy, it was because I had hit her for her crime – plus my father's too.

I didn't go back to school for the rest of the week and I didn't call Andrea, Justin or Louise Lovejoy. I mooched around the house, watched television and made the odd visit to see the Carpinettas.

The first time I went upstairs, Mrs C stood up from the kitchen table and walked towards me with outstretched arms. '*Cara, cara, cara, cara,*' is all she kept saying.

We had a little cry together. It was nice. Not over the top. Just enough.

'You know this is your home, Gemma,' Mrs C told me. 'Whenever it get too much you come up here to Mr C and me.'

I wanted to ask her what 'too much' meant. Too much crying? Too much of Mum being sad? Too much of what exactly? But it was too hard to dissect the real meaning of words from someone whose first language wasn't English. So I left it at that.

Mum finally had to deal with Andrea after she called for the eighth time because I still wasn't up to telling her about Saul. Mum spun some story about me having suspected glandular fever that was possibly infectious so it was best not to visit. I told Mum that she'd missed her calling and she should've been an actress, or a professional liar if there was such a job.

Mum didn't laugh at my joke. She stopped ironing the hem of the flower girl's dress she was working on. 'I don't like what I'm doing, Gemma,' she said. 'One day when you're a parent you'll understand that you'd do anything to protect your children. If you can give them one less day of pain, then you do it. Even if it's wrong. But you won't understand that until you're a mother. Maybe then you'll forgive me.'

'Chill. I wasn't saying it was a bad thing,' I told her.

Mum came over and wrapped her arms around me. She didn't say anything, she just held me. I loved being cuddled by Mum, but this felt different.

I wasn't exactly sure why, but I was sure of one thing. There was more 'bad' coming our way.

8

**23 weeks
to formal**

ON MONDAY MORNING MUM WAS UP EARLY, sorting through the bathroom. The cleaning freak had returned, bigger and scarier than ever. Mum was swiping jars and half-empty tubes off the shelves and into a garbage bag.

'What are you doing?'

'Cleaning the clutter and junk out of the bathroom.' Mum was puffing. She'd worked up a sweat too. 'There were six half-used bottles of shampoo and conditioner in this cupboard and none of them had lids.'

'Hey, that's my hair wax!' I said, watching it fly into the bag along with a comb, a frilly shower cap and two faded cakes of soap. 'It's still half full!'

'It doesn't have a lid either.'

'But it's still fine to use.'

'I'll buy you another one,' she told me, then went over to the shower and started unclipping our map of the world shower curtain. 'This is so disgusting. Disgusting!' she was muttering. 'I've bought a nice blue-and-white striped one.'

'I love that shower curtain,' I whined. 'It's how I learnt where all the countries are and—'

'I don't know how,' Mum said. 'The Northern Hemisphere is covered with mould!'

'That's one of the first things Billy brought back from New York.'

'Exactly! So it's had a good run but now it's time for the garbage.' Mum yanked the shower curtain off the last hook.

'That's sad.'

'You'll like the new one.'

'Bet I won't.'

'From now on, Gemma, I want you to do your hair and all that stuff in your room,' she said, tying up the rubbish bag. 'I don't want this mess in the bathroom anymore. You can keep your toiletries in a bag and just bring them in when you're using them. We need to have a system.'

'Yes, sir.'

'I'm serious!' Mum snapped, but straight away she apologised.

'It's okay,' I said. 'It's been a tough week.'

Mum didn't answer. She threw the garbage bag over her shoulder and I followed her into the kitchen. 'When's Billy back from Martha's Garden or whatever it's called? Because I still haven't spoken to him.'

'I promise you will talk to Billy tonight,' Mum said and just like that she started crying.

'Maybe I shouldn't go to school today?'

'No, Gemma. The world can't stop just because . . .'

'Just because Saul died?'

'Just because,' Mum answered.

School was a better option. At least it was predictable, which wasn't what home felt like at the moment. Number one prediction was that Andrea would be waiting by my locker and, of course, she was.

'At last!' she announced, throwing her arms around me. 'I was starting to think you'd died.'

Lucky for me, my face was pressed into her shoulder because I needed a second to pull my expression together. Maybe it was the word 'died' or maybe I just wasn't as ready as I thought I was.

'Thanks for returning my calls – not,' she said, cutting off the embrace and getting straight down to business. 'I have a Marty situation on my hands and I've needed you!'

'I've been sick.'

'I know. The Infection Gestapo told me.'

'The who?'

'Your mother,' Andrea answered. 'She told me not to come over! Did you know? I couldn't believe it. What a cow!'

'She—' I began.

'I'm not lying, Gemma. Your mother said I wasn't allowed to visit. I felt like saying, "Derr, Maryanne, Gemma would want me there."'

I opened my mouth to say something in my mother's defence, because if anyone could be accused of being in the Infection Gestapo it was Andrea's mother.

But the effort of trying to think of a comeback was too hard.

Yesterday I'd almost felt like I was ready to tell Andrea about Saul. But today the door had slammed on the idea. I couldn't tell Andrea now. I didn't know when I would be able to but it wasn't today and it probably wouldn't be tomorrow either. It's hard to describe but it felt a bit like my armour didn't fit properly and I had to wait until it did.

So I held on to it like it was my dirty little secret.

We walked to English. Andrea couldn't get the words out quick enough. They were toppling over one another in a cascade of what Marty did next. '. . . he was hanging around Miss Prissy Sonia Darue and she was lapping it up and I couldn't stand it any longer so when I saw Marty in the hall after assembly I said, "Why haven't you spoken to me?" and Simon Finkler started laughing, like pissing his pants laughing, and then he said to me, the Fink, not Marty, "Piss off, you slag," and I was standing there and they just walked off and I know Sonia Darue heard the whole thing.'

'That sounds horrible,' I said to Andrea.

'It was.' Andrea's bottom lip had turned south. 'It was really horrible . . .' she spluttered. 'I needed you, Gemma, and you weren't here. I know you've been sick but you, you still could've called me. I don't think that's too much to ask of your best friend.'

I did feel sorry for her. I wasn't thinking, *Boo hoo, Andrea, worse things have happened*. It was strange yet comforting that our stupid little world with Andrea at the very epicentre was still here and still exactly the same. I knew this world. I knew how to deal with it.

So much had changed in the last week and now I wasn't sure how the big world worked anymore. Saul had died. Mum had ripped posters off church billboards and become a cleaning freak. Our map of the world shower curtain had gone, the fridge was spotless and all the old jars of gherkins had disappeared.

But what was shaking my world the most, what had the ground shifting under my feet, was how could Billy possibly be okay?

In the last week I had spent so much time thinking about it. How was Billy not HIV-positive? Was he sure he was negative? Had he had another test? In Billy's fag mag there were stories about guys being told their results were negative when it was wrong. I wanted to ask Aunty Penny how he could be negative when his boyfriend of five years had just died of AIDS.

But I couldn't reduce Saul to some medical mystery.

Saul was a wound in all our hearts. He had carved his way in not just because he was Billy's boyfriend but because he was kind and real and generous. From day one, Saul had fitted into our somewhat strange little family. He had found a gap that none of us had filled and he'd simply slipped in and made it his own. My world would never be the same without Saul, and if I felt like this then I couldn't imagine how my brother must feel.

There was no way Andrea was going to let me go straight home after school, because Andrea was, in her words, 'going mental' and 'men in little white coats were about to cart her off to hospital'. Marty was ignoring her; Sonia Darue was having an 'S party' on the weekend, which Andrea wasn't invited to but Marty was, and she knew Sonia would try and conquer him that night; and worst of all was that Andrea didn't know if he was still her date for the formal.

But Andrea had a plan and she wanted to discuss it over coffee at Cafe Francais.

The red-and-white checked tablecloths that I thought were a total cliché, Andrea thought were exotic. She had zero money, which was typical. But the idea that we couldn't afford Cafe Francais never occurred to her, which was even more typical.

I was counting all my coins, which came to five dollars and sixty-five cents, while she was whining, 'Are you sure that's all you have, Gemma?'

We calculated that we could afford to share a cappuccino and an almond croissant, even though at the milk bar around the corner we could both have had a vanilla thickshake with enough money left for a giant bag of mixed lollies each.

'What the hell am I going to do?' Andrea collapsed into a chair. 'I'm so humiliated. Sonia's stupid party is not the problem. When I asked Marty if he was still coming to the formal with me he said he didn't know what I was talking about Now can you understand why I think I'm going mental?'

The waitress brought over our food. 'Merci, Madame,' Andrea said, helping herself to the croissant and taking an enormous bite. 'I mean, you're my witness, Gemma. You were there when Marty said yes to me. You remember, don't you?' she asked through lips covered in flakes of pastry. 'Don't you?'

'Hmm,' I answered, grateful to be mid-sip of cappuccino, because I wasn't sure Martin Searles had agreed to anything.

'So there's only one thing to do, and this is our plan,' Andrea announced, taking the cup from my hand and putting it back on the saucer. 'Billy has to work *all* his magic on me! Forget Louise Lovejoy – she's beyond help. Forget you too, Gemma, because you'll look good anyway. Billy needs to concentrate on me so I look totally, totally amaaaaaazing,' she neighed. 'When I walk into the school hall I want Marty to regret that Miss Prissy Darue is his date instead of me.' She sat back in the chair, smiling and nodding. 'Mum and I have discussed this over and over and I have decided to definitely do the Elizabeth Taylor look. I had my doubts for a bit because you and Louise Lovejoy are going short. But Mum said elegant and classic always wins, because boys want their dates to look classy. And don't say it shouldn't matter what the boys think, because I do. Mum also said – no offence, Gemma – short dresses are a little bit slutty for a formal. I'm not surprised Louise is going short.'

'There's lots to organise,' she continued. 'I'd like to have a big chat with Billy at least two days before. I'll show him the photos in my Elizabeth Taylor book that Grandma gave me. He can do buns and French rolls, can't he?' she quizzed. 'Billy is my magic bullet. That's what Mum said. Now, when's Billy actually getting here?' I wouldn't have been surprised if Andrea got out her diary and started marking the dates. 'Hopefully not the day of the formal?'

'Um, no. I'd say probably a few days before,' I answered, realising it was another question that I didn't know the answer to anymore.

Andrea was standing up. 'I have to go. Mum's waiting for me so we can try out her new Jane Fonda exercise video, *Abs, Buns & Thighs.*'

I followed her, pretending to listen, because really I was thinking, *You, Justin and Louise Lovejoy have no idea what's happening in my life.*

Andrea and I always said goodbye at a pole that randomly stood smack bang in the middle of a sunless, grassless nature strip. We called this halfway mark 'Nigel', because the name was engraved on the pole.

Andrea and I had had many discussions about who Nigel was. Had he carved his name there himself or was it someone else who'd had a crush on him?

'Bye,' I said.

'Your brother is my magic bullet. Thank you for being related to him.'

She disappeared down her fork of the road, singing 'Wind Beneath My Wings' at the top of her lungs.

I watched her go. I watched her till she was so tiny she could've been anyone and not Andrea. Andrea, who had the knack of sucking the life out of you. The problem was, today I didn't have as much life in me to give as I usually did.

I stood there for a while and just breathed. It felt like I needed to refuel before I got home because who knew what would be happening in there. Would Mum be cleaning? Would she be back in bed with the crying disease? Maybe she'd driven past another church and seen a sign she didn't like?

I wasn't ready to go home, so I sat on the kerb and breathed while the cars rushed past and an icy wind streaked across my legs.

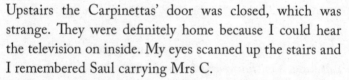

Upstairs the Carpinettas' door was closed, which was strange. They were definitely home because I could hear the television on inside. My eyes scanned up the stairs and I remembered Saul carrying Mrs C.

There were seventeen stairs in total and I wondered if that meant Saul had groaned seventeen times. Once for each step.

When he'd come back down he said he'd done a hammy and slipped a disc. None of us cared. We all just burst out laughing. Maybe it wasn't a joke? Maybe Saul was already sick. Maybe it really had been too much for him.

Tonight, Billy would be calling – and I was terrified. Terrified of how Billy would sound. Terrified that I'd say the wrong thing because I didn't even know how to start the conversation.

I unlocked the front door to our flat, wondering if it would be too chicken of me to get Mum to talk to Billy first. Just in case he wasn't up to speaking to me yet. As I closed the door behind me I decided that it wasn't too chicken. That way would be easier for both of us.

But there was no need to ask because on the couch, sitting there in the dark like a shadow, was my brother.

The next couple of minutes were a blur. One second I was at the door and the next Billy and I were on the couch, a tangled, sobbing ball.

It was a while before I realised that I had stopped crying. I went to break away but Billy pulled me back tighter into his hug, like he couldn't let go. His sobs sounded like some strange animal, low and braying, and it was freaking me out.

'Billy,' I was whispering in his ear. 'Billy. Oh, Billy.'

I was racking my brains to try to think of what Mum would do. Straight away, I thought about the day that Matt Leong and Billy had broken up. Billy had fallen into Mum's arms, just like he'd done with me, and cried and cried. She didn't try to stop him. All she did was rub his back and utter his name. Just like I was doing now.

Mum appeared at the doorway holding two mugs, steam spiralling from the top of them. I knew one was for Billy because it was his *I Love New York* mug. Saul had given it to him. Billy brought it back here the first Christmas he came home from New York. Apart from last Christmas, that was the only time Saul hadn't come home too.

Later, Billy had confessed that he didn't know what Saul would think of our daggy flat and fifteen-year-old car that didn't even have FM radio.

Mum put the two cups of tea on the coffee table and turned on the light.

Now, I could look at Billy. Scan him up and down for any hints of what his body might be cooking, because it wasn't the sort of thing I could just come straight out and ask.

His face was thin like the stuffing had been sucked out of his cheeks. It made his nose look even longer than usual and I knew that when he was feeling a bit better I could tease him about that and it might make him laugh. Apart from that, he didn't look too bad. Just tired. Maybe he was okay?

Mum sat on the arm of the couch, her hand hanging over Billy's shoulder so easy, like he'd never been away. Suddenly I noticed that Mum's face was thinner too.

'How are you, Gem?' Billy said, squeezing my knee. 'I've missed you. I could've done with having you around these last few weeks.'

'That's the mug Saul gave you,' I said.

'Sure is,' Billy answered. 'He gave it to me as a reminder that I loved New York. When I got back after that Christmas I said to him, "It's you I love." That was the real beginning of us.' Billy hung his head and started to cry again.

'I'm sorry,' I whispered. I wanted to kick myself for being such an idiot.

'Gem, it's not your fault,' he answered. 'I'm just very, very sad. Everything makes me cry at the moment.'

'Is that my tea?' I asked Mum and straight away wanted to kick myself again for following up with such a pathetic question when all I wanted was to say something deep and meaningful.

'Tea with three sugars,' Mum said.

'Three sugars?' Billy raised his head and looked at me. 'Since when?'

'Since, since . . .' But I stopped myself from saying it.

'Sugar's bad for you,' Billy said. 'At least have honey instead.'

'Honey? Yuck!'

'Honey? Yuck!' Billy imitated me, crinkling up his nose the way I did.

That only made me burst into tears. Suddenly, in one long sob, I was blurting out all the things I wanted to say. 'I'm so sorry. I'm so sorry. I didn't know Saul was sick. No one told me. If I did I would've called him. I would've called you to see how you were. But I didn't know. How are we going to have Christmas without him? It won't be the same. Poor Saul. Poor Saul. I can't believe I'm never going to see him again. Oh, Billy, you must be so sad.'

The next morning, I didn't bother getting up for school. Mum didn't come into my room clapping her hands in my face like she usually would if I'd slept in.

The TV was on upstairs at the Carpinettas' but our house was quiet. I crept past Billy's room on the way to the bathroom. The door was ajar and I could hear him snoring. A short piggy snort, but not with every breath. That was Billy's tune. Sometimes they could be minutes apart and suddenly you'd hear one and jump.

But what was missing today was the other half of the melody: Saul's whistling hiss. Constant and with every breath he took. Saul's whistle sounded like he was imitating a landing plane. It started at the top and down, down the sound descended until there was silence.

But I would never hear that sound again. The song of Billy and Saul was never to return. It hurt. I felt it right in that little triangle, the point below the chest, with the funny name. The point I'd learnt about when doing my Bronze Medallion. The place you have to feel for, then measure two finger spaces before you lay your hands on the patient's chest to perform CPR. The tip of my finger touched it now and I tried not to think about whether they did CPR on Saul.

Billy hadn't told me much about Saul dying. All I knew was that he died in hospital at 6.22 a.m. Billy was the only one there. He said Saul was off with the pixies when he died, that he didn't know what was happening.

Billy said that he was sorry that they hadn't told me Saul was sick, but Saul hadn't wanted me to worry. How could I argue with that? You can't argue with someone who's dead and buried.

I walked back to my room and peered through my curtains. I wasn't ready to fully open them and let the punishing light in. It was easier to be here in the dark because it was almost like it was a blanket on my sadness. Somehow the darkness soothed it. Kept it bedded down. Kept it quiet.

Tomorrow would be the eighth of May. The tree across the road that Billy used to tell me fairies lived in was almost bare. It struck me how ugly and stern it suddenly looked without its covering of green.

It made me feel horrible so I crawled back into bed. I wrapped my arms around the pillow and lay there in the dark wondering how long this sadness was going to hang around.

9

SAUL HAD BEEN IN HOSPITAL FOR THREE
weeks before he died. Again I kept my lips zipped but I
was shocked I hadn't known that either.

At least one thing made sense: all those days that Mum
had cried. Now I understood that only some of her tears
had been for Matt Leong. Most of them had been for Saul.

Saul and Billy had made a video. Now Mum, Billy and
I were sitting up on the couch, waiting for it to start like
it was a new release we'd hired for the night. But it wasn't
like that. I was so tense I couldn't even sit back into the
cushions.

The screen went fuzzy like it always did the second
before a video was about to start. The first shot was of
someone's feet. There was the sound of Billy and Saul
laughing and suddenly my breath was escaping in a long,
singing sigh.

'Gem, are you okay?' Mum asked.

I nodded quickly.

'Sure?'

'Yeah,' I answered.

'Sorry.' Billy was actually chuckling. 'It took me a while to
get the hang of the camera. Saul was the cameraman, not me.'

'You have to stand back,' Saul was instructing. 'Further, further . . . Keep it steady, Bill.' A white wall, a green curtain, someone's bare feet again, the sound of Billy laughing and then, there on the screen, was a man climbing into a hospital bed, turning over, smoothing hair off his face and putting on a cap. 'Hang on a minute.' He was clearing his throat and fiddling with the tube in his nose. Then he said, 'Hi guys, it's me. Coming to you from Room 6, St Bernard's Hospital, Greenwich Village. Just three blocks down from my favourite bagels. Not that I've been eating them. As you can see, I'm skin and bones. Not very pretty . . .'

This wasn't Saul. Did Billy have the wrong video? But it was him because this man was looking straight into the camera and saying, 'How's my favourite gal?'

Mum put her arm around me and was speaking softly. 'It's just a short message for you, darling. We don't have to play it now. It can wait for another time.' But I shook my head. I had to see it.

Dotted around Saul's face were dark splotches, the colour of plums, that looked like squashed jubes. Like he'd dropped some in the bed and slept on them and now they were stuck to his face.

But what really had my attention were Saul's teeth. I couldn't stop staring at them. They looked huge, as though they'd outgrown every other feature on his face. All I could think about was that he reminded me of the grinning horse on a birthday card Justin had given me when I'd turned fourteen. *Neighly forgot to wish you a Happy Birthday.* What a crazy, stupid, demented thing to be thinking right then, but the image was stuck in my brain and I couldn't get it out.

'. . . anyway, I've been thinking about you, Gem,' Saul kept speaking. 'Tons of things keep popping into my head. Mostly the time Bill and I took you to the Boy George concert. Remember how I really didn't want to go? How I wanted to give my ticket to Andrea but your brother made me come? So I did what I was told and next thing I knew I was dancing with you on my shoulders and belting out "Karma Chameleon" at the top of my lungs. Remember?'

I was sitting there nodding, as though Saul was right there talking to me. 'That was our moment, hey, Gem? Everything was okay after that.' Saul was smiling but it was the saddest smile I'd ever seen. 'Remember how the next day you and me went to the record shop and I bought all his albums?'

'Yeah, and you drove me crazy playing them all the time,' Billy's voice piped up from behind the camera. '"Church of the Poison Mind". You played that song until I thought I was going to—'

'Well, that's my favourite—' Saul said, starting to hum the tune. But he couldn't finish because he'd started coughing.

'You want to stop?' Billy asked him.

Saul was lifting his hands as if to say *wait a minute*.

'How about a break?' But Billy's voice was being drowned out by the hacking sounds of Saul's cough. The video stopped.

A second later, Saul was back on the screen. His cap was off but his head was down. His hair flopped across his forehead and his fingers pressed at the tube sitting in his nostrils. I could tell that he was trying to settle his breath.

When he looked up, he pushed the hair off his face and smiled into the camera. 'So what I wanted to say was that

I've been tripping down memory lane with you, Gemma, and it's been mighty fine.' It felt as though he was looking right at me, as if I was the only one in the room. 'You'll always be my favourite gal . . .' For a second the smile slipped off his face. 'You know that, don't you?' He swallowed. 'My favourite gal.'

'Yes. Yes. Yes.' I kept repeating it until I realised that the screen had turned black.

It was hard to fall asleep that night. Every time I closed my eyes I pictured Saul's face, covered in squashed blackberry jubes, grinning at me like a horse with huge teeth. The other thing I hadn't seen at first, because he was wearing a cap, was how Saul's hair had thinned out and almost turned white. If it wasn't for the purple marks all over his face he would've probably just faded into the pillows.

Saul had been thirty-one when he died, but today the man I'd seen could've been a hundred.

My fingers touched the triangle on my chest because again that was where it hurt. As though under my ribs my heart was actually aching.

For me, the Boy George concert with Billy and Saul had been about more than converting Saul to our Boy Brigade. Yet for all these years, I had forgotten.

Saul and I had never discussed it. But he was right. It had been our moment. Everything was okay after that night.

The concert was during my first Christmas holidays with Saul. When Mum told me Saul was coming home with Billy I was so excited. But once they were here, my excitement began to turn sour. They were out most nights clubbing, then sleeping late into the afternoon. The door to Billy's room was always closed and the few times I plucked up the guts to knock and go in, Billy seemed uninterested in talking to me.

When I was in the kitchen or living room with just Saul I could never think of anything to say and it didn't feel like Saul was trying that hard to make conversation with me.

If I grumbled to Mum, she'd either say, 'Don't take it personally,' or the more annoying line, 'The complaints bureau is closed for the day, Gemma.'

It wasn't like I could share it with Andrea because when I'd told her Saul was coming out with Billy, the first thing that popped out of her mouth was, 'They are going to be doing it in your house. That's gross, Gemma.'

Then one afternoon, a week before Christmas, Billy surprised me.

'I have an early Chrissy present for you,' he'd said. 'And you'll never guess what it is.'

'A kitten?'

'No!' Mum called out from her workroom.

'Much better,' Saul added. 'This gift doesn't poop everywhere.'

'What? Tell me?'

From out of his pocket Billy held up some tickets. 'Boy George at the Western Showground. Tomorrow night!'

Of course I knew the concert was on but I'd given up on the idea of going because I was too young and the tickets were so expensive. So I was running around the kitchen table screaming when I realised I'd seen three tickets, which meant Saul was coming too. It was like my batteries suddenly went flat and my running faded to a feet-dragging limp.

'So, you and me and Saul are going?' I moaned, and I knew that my feelings weren't hiding in the question.

'Yeah. Who else?' Billy answered.

'Um, Andrea?' I said. 'She started the Boy Brigade.'

'Well, Andrea can buy her own ticket then.'

'Why doesn't Andrea take my ticket?' Saul offered. 'I mean, you're wasting the ticket on me, Bill. I'm no fan of the Boy.'

'No. I bought the tickets for the three of us to go together.'

'Hey, it's no big deal,' Saul said.

'It is to me, Saul. I want us all to go together.'

'But if Gem's friend is a fan and I'm not . . .'

'No. It's the three of us. End of story.'

Saul mouthed, 'Sorry,' to me before following my brother out of the kitchen and into his room where the door slammed behind them.

'Still feeling left out?' Mum asked.

I opened my mouth to answer then promptly closed it because the real answer had just dawned on me. It wasn't that I was feeling left out. It was that I didn't want to share my brother. I had to share Billy with Mum but that was different because we were blood. But now I'd been demoted further down the ladder by a non-blood and I knew it'd be impossible to scramble back up again.

Sulking wasn't my thing. I wasn't averse to putting Mum in the freezer for a few hours, but days of not talking seemed like a big waste of time and energy. However, for the next twenty-four hours, I wore a face so long it could've made *The Guinness Book of Records*.

My symptoms grew worse. I felt like I had lead in my shoes and a brick in my tummy. They were competing with each other, too, because they were both there for different reasons. The lead in my shoes was because I wanted to go to the concert with just my brother. Then Billy and I could dance as crazily as we wanted. I wanted him to lift me onto his shoulders and when everyone behind us would shout at me to get down, Billy could tell them to shut up. We would be unstoppable.

Now it was going to be me, my brother and his boyfriend. They'd be dancing together and I'd be the third wheel. The little sister hanging around like a bad smell. Everybody would probably think I was there because they had to babysit me, not because I was the real Boy George fan.

The brick was in my tummy because I hated myself for feeling like that.

Before the concert started, Saul offered to buy me the program and a T-shirt and I actually said, 'No, thank you.' Even when he suggested we should push further up the front I answered, 'It's okay.'

But when the crowd started cheering and the loud voice announced, 'Ladies and gents, I give you Boy George,' I couldn't help myself. I was screaming and jumping around like a mental case and just like that Saul scooped me up and sat me on top of his shoulders.

'Get down!' the people behind started calling.

'Shut up, would you?' Saul shouted back. 'How's she expected to see over everyone? She's his biggest fan.'

I wrapped my arms around his neck and Saul danced crazily for both of us. We were unstoppable.

Saul had been spot on. It was our moment. Simple. And it made everything okay after that.

Finally, when I fell asleep, the picture of Saul's face wasn't the main image in my head because now I had the Boy George concert to remember. But what made me feel warm inside, what allowed me to close my eyes and drift away, was knowing that just a few weeks ago Saul had been lying in his hospital bed thinking about me and him too.

※

On Sunday afternoon, Mum and Billy did that thing they always did. They chatted to each other like I wasn't even in the same room, like it didn't matter if I was there or not. But today it did matter and they still talked like I was invisible.

It began with Billy saying, 'I'd better start getting ready for Vanessa.'

That name got my attention.

'What time's she coming over?' Mum asked.

'Ten minutes ago,' Billy replied. 'Models are never on time.'

Vanessa? Model? How many models called Vanessa did Billy know?

'Are you going to cut her hair in the kitchen, Billy?' Mum even asked this while leaning over me to get to the sink. 'Or the bathroom?'

'Kitchen,' he answered. 'The light's not good enough in the bathroom. At least, not for her hair.'

Part of me wanted to interrupt with, *Isn't cutting hair in the kitchen against all the new hygiene laws?* My mother had enforced spraying and wiping down counters even after buttering a piece of bread. But there was more pressing business to attend to.

'Hold it right there!' I finally made my presence felt. 'Are you talking about *Vanessa* Vanessa? Vanessa Harding, the girl who goes to my school?' I stepped in front of my brother. 'Hello?'

Mum piped up. 'What's the drama?'

'I would just like to know if someone from my school is planning on knocking on our door in a few minutes. It is past three o'clock and I'm still in my pyjamas.'

'So – change,' Billy said.

'Isn't she in your year?' Mum asked.

'Her twin brother is,' I mumbled. 'Vanessa's repeating Year 10.'

'Ralph's the twin brother, Mum,' Billy told her. 'You know, Ralph? The one Gem thinks is Mr Spunky Monkey.'

'No, I don't!' I blurted.

'You do so!'

I was about to whack Billy over the head with Mum's bag of fabric offcuts when there was a quick little tap on the front door.

'Can you get it?' Billy and Mum sang out to me at the same time.

A second later I was opening the door and then Vanessa was standing in our kitchen hugging my brother.

I've never taken drugs but I reckon this was what it'd feel like. I was almost having one of those out-of-body experiences that I'd read about in the *Reader's Digest* at the dentist. You know you're in the room and you can hear everybody talking, but it all feels too weird to be really happening.

'I'm so sorry,' Vanessa was saying. 'I knew Saul was sick but I only heard that he'd passed away the other day. I'm so, so sorry.'

I opened my mouth but closed it straight away. I wanted

to ask Vanessa when she had heard. But there was no place for my question.

Billy and Vanessa were facing each other and holding hands like no one else was in the room.

'How are you?' Vanessa asked my brother.

'One day at a time.'

I couldn't tear my eyes away from them.

'Thanks so much for saying you'd do this, Billy. I know it's such a big ask and I feel so bad. But I don't trust anyone else to cut my hair and I couldn't believe you were actually here – just down the road!'

'Stop it! It's my pleasure. I'm super excited for you, Vanessa.' Then Billy turned to me and said, 'Vanessa's scored an audition for the new Pantene ad.'

Vanessa was grinning and I wondered if there'd ever been a Pantene girl with a big gap between her teeth. She had the hair though. Long, flowing dark locks that shone so much you needed sunnies to look at them without your eyes stinging. Ralph's hair was even darker, almost jet black, and had a way of falling over his eyes that was quite possibly the hottest thing I had ever seen apart from Johnny Depp.

'Getting a big contract at home and not having to travel for a while would be the ultimate,' she said. 'On the way here I was telling my brother that I'd trade a *Vogue* cover for this.'

'Where's your brother?' my mother asked. Of course she did. She had to open her big mouth. 'It's Ralph, isn't it?'

'Yes. He's waiting in the car. He drove me here.'

'Tell him to come in.' Now I really was having an out-of-body experience. But a bad one where it suddenly felt like everyone was staring at me. Probably since they were, because my mother was saying, 'Go and get Ralph, Gemma. He's not a chauffeur. We can't let him sit in the car all afternoon.'

'Is that okay, Gemma?' Vanessa was asking me.

'Sure,' I heard my voice reply. 'Might just get changed.'

I put on my 501s and my tight black jumper. They were lying on the floor of my room. I'd worn them last night when Billy and I went to pick up pizzas. The waiter with the permanently greasy hair had winked and called me 'cutie-pie' when he handed over the pizzas.

Yesterday that wink hadn't mattered and neither had his lame compliment. But right now it was as though Johnny Depp himself had said it – that's why I was putting the same clothes back on.

I slunk out of my room as casually as I could, picked up the front door key and asked, as though I didn't already know, 'Vanessa, what kind of car does Ralph drive?' What I really wanted to ask was, *Will he know who I am?*

'What?' She laughed. 'You mean you haven't noticed?'

'Put some shoes on!' Mum called.

But I pretended I hadn't heard her because bare feet were an essential part of the casual look I was attempting to pull off.

By the time I was walking down the path, my mouth was dry, I was experiencing intense palpitations and I had a horrible feeling that when I opened my lips, no sound was going to come out. Pathetic, considering I had been seeing this guy almost every day for the last five years. But that was in the classroom or Literature Circle or the quadrangle with hundreds of other kids hanging around. Ralph's group of friends were intense types who were into music and art and wore all black on the weekends. Come to think of it, they didn't speak much either, which could account for the lack of words Ralph and I had exchanged. 'Hi', 'Bye' and 'Did you hand in your essay?' weren't exactly earth-shattering pieces of conversation.

Up ahead I could see the lime-green station wagon that was parked outside school most days.

Andrea had wanted to snoop through the windows because she said that could tell us a lot about who Ralph really was. Every time she suggested it I'd said, 'No way,' emphasising my point with a tight, nail-piercing squeeze of her arm.

The idea of Ralph catching us was, in my books, even more embarrassing than him seeing my undies on April Fools' Day. Everyone saw my undies that day. But what excuse could I possibly give Ralph if he sprung me with my face pasted against his car window, acting like the bunny-boiling stalker lady from *Fatal Attraction*?

As I got closer to the lime mobile, I could see Ralph in the driver's seat reading a book. I'd bet it was our history textbook. It had the same dark cover with a large white title and the rumour going around class was that the end-of-term History exam answers were straight out of chapter three. There was a talking point, I told myself. That could be the conversation starter as we began the awkward walk back to our flat.

But barely a metre away, the title became clear. This was no modern history book. It was a folder called *Belle Modelling Agency 1989*, and whatever Ralph was looking at had him mesmerised. He wasn't even aware that there was a person, me, almost outside his window, arm raised and about to tap on the glass.

So I didn't stop. I kept walking. The footpath was cold and up ahead someone's garbage bin had overturned. Empty cans of cat food, dirty nappies and orange peels were scattered along the pavement. Carefully I stepped around the rubbish and kept walking as though that was what I'd intended to do all along.

My first thought was to walk all the way to Andrea's. It wasn't that far but I didn't fancy the journey in bare feet. Plus I'd been faking a sore throat as I'd supposedly been 'sick' again.

For a stupid split second I wondered if Ralph might see me walking away and call out or toot the horn. As if. There was no way I could compete with a folder of models. I had to be satisfied with a wink from the greasy-haired waiter at the Grazia Pizza Bar.

I kept walking until I reached the park right down the end of our street. It was a safe enough distance between Ralph and me, but not too long of a trudge home where I knew an interrogation from Billy and Mum would be waiting for me.

It was a sad park. Even as a kid I'd thought so. Once upon a time, before they'd filled the pond up with cement and a toilet block, there used to be ducks there. Not the cute white ones that you saw in fairytales. These ducks were mangy, skinny brown things that were always pecking holes into their feathers.

It was actually Dad who used to take me to this park on weekends. He'd bought himself a metal detector, so Dad, me and the metal detector would hang out here all afternoon while Billy and Mum were at swimming training. I'd feed the ducks or play on the swings while Dad and the device, which resembled a long pole with a steering wheel on the end of it, would cover every inch of grass. I remembered the beeping of the machine floating along on the air and Dad occasionally calling, 'I think I've got something, Gem'.

Those times with Dad weren't so bad. As we walked home he'd show me what he'd found. Sometimes we'd take a detour and Dad would buy me an ice-cream with the change he'd dug up.

The toilet block was still standing, except most of the time it was locked to stop the junkies from hitting up in there. This afternoon, the park was empty. It was late autumn and the sun was low in the sky, warning us that the day was nearly over and it was time to go home where it was warm and safe.

Still, I sat there, working on my story about why I didn't return to the flat with Ralph. I needed to know the reason as much for myself as I did for Billy and Mum.

Ralph was from the arty group; the Fink and Marty Searles were the tough guys; Sonia Darue and her clones were the pretty, oh-so-perfect, prissy girls; Andrea, Justin, now Louise Lovejoy and I belonged to none of them. Nor did we fit into the middle. We were a group of ordinary unremarkables. Not ugly, not beautiful, not arty and not tough.

The only thing that had ever brought me attention at school was last year when the *Women's Weekly* did a one-page story on Billy – and everyone had forgotten about that in twenty-four hours. There were photos of him with Cher and Demi Moore and right there in black print it was written that he had one sister called Gemma.

I could say to Mum and Billy, *Ralph was looking at a folder full of beautiful girls. And I felt unremarkable. Ordinary. Not quite enough to get his attention.*

It wasn't a great excuse but it was probably as close to the truth as I'd ever get.

It was pitch black in the park now and it wasn't the sort of place a girl wanted to be on her own. Yet I tucked my feet underneath me, sitting on them to warm up my toes. I could feel the cold night air blowing right through me because I was hollow inside.

I was beyond sad. That was the real truth and it had nothing to do with the darkness or Ralph or who was in which group at school. I was sad because Saul was dead. Because I would never see him again, and I was starting to sense that this sadness was far from over.

10

'WHERE HAVE YOU BEEN, YOUNG LADY?'
Mum huffed. Billy and Mrs C, who was wearing her black apron, were also gathered by the front door. No doubt they'd all jumped up the second they heard the click of the lock. 'It's nearly 6 p.m., Gemma!'

Mum and her support team followed me into the kitchen. 'You've been gone nearly three hours, Gemma. All you were meant to do was get Ralph and bring him back up. Two minutes! So, what the hell happened?'

I was gulping down a second glass of water because I thought that might give me a bit more time before I had to answer my mother's pretty reasonable question. Not that I had any intention of admitting that.

'I . . . I changed my mind,' I finally answered.

'You what?' Mum barked.

'I changed my mind,' I repeated. 'I don't think Ralph cared about sitting out there in the car. I think he was quite happy to. He had enough to occupy himself with.'

'That's not the point! I asked you to go and get him. Instead you disappeared for three hours.'

'Well, if you wanted Ralph to come up then why didn't you go down and get him? I'm not your slave!'

'I beg your pardon?'

'Calm down, both of you,' Billy said.

'Mamma was just worried,' Mrs C offered.

'I was more than worried, Carmella,' Mum spat. 'I was confused. I was embarrassed. I was—'

'Embarrassed?' I yelled. 'What was so embarrassing?'

'You just sneaking out like that and—'

'I didn't sneak out!'

'You just disappeared. How were we expected to know what had happened to you? You could've been abducted!'

'Get real, Mother!'

'Don't tell me to get real!' she shrieked and we all did a little jump. Maybe she noticed because she started speaking in an overly calm way like she'd just remembered she was meant to be giving a relaxation session. 'I'm not angry, Gemma. I'm upset because I was worried about what had happened to you. Billy went downstairs and spoke to Vanessa's brother and he said he hadn't even seen you. So what were we meant to think?'

I was about to surrender. I was about to wave my white flag and admit that it had been a pretty random thing to do, disappearing like that. But then my mother said, 'If you felt shy about going down and getting Ralph, then you should've told me.' She kept on with the annoying voice. 'You know you can be up-front and honest with me. We've always been so open with each other. When did we start hiding things from . . .'

Suddenly there was an opening and I hadn't even been aware that I'd been looking for one. This was my moment to say how I felt. I was never going to get it again and I was about to barge through headfirst. I had doubted all my instincts. I had been tight-lipped and well-behaved. I had sucked it all up for the sake of not causing any more upset. That very afternoon, I'd had to stand there without pulling a face or making a noise when I realised that Vanessa had known Saul had been sick way before I had. That little fact alone had run me down like a semitrailer driver on No-Doz.

So I began. 'When did we start hiding things from each other?' I repeated. 'I think you're the one who should be answering that question, Mum! You're the one who's been doing all the hiding. Not me.'

'And what on earth does that mean?'

'Have a big guess, why don't you?'

'Gemma,' Billy started. 'Leave it. She was just worried.'

'Very, very worry,' Mrs C chimed in.

I ignored the peanut gallery. Instead I stood firm, kept my eyes on my mother and said, as together as I could muster, 'You knew Saul was sick. It seems that even Vanessa knew.'

'Whether Vanessa knew or not has nothing to do with this!'

I took a deep breath because I had to say my piece. 'Mum, even when Saul was dead you let me believe he wasn't.' Mrs C blessed herself but there was no stopping me now. 'I'd hardly call that being open with each other.'

'Gem,' Billy was saying. 'Come on—'

'Don't tell me to come on! It's more than that. She didn't even tell me you were coming home,' I yelled as my fingertip jabbed towards my mother's chest. '*She* didn't tell me Saul had AIDS. And then, when she did, *she* let me go for a whole night still thinking he was alive. I lay in bed all night wondering how he was feeling. If he was scared.' My breath was rumbling at the back of my throat, my hands were shaking and my legs were too. I had never felt this angry before and it was scaring me. 'How could you do that?' I roared at my mother. 'How? Just tell me that!' Billy was trying to take my hands in his but I wouldn't have it. They were now clasped tightly behind my back, away from temptation to dole out another face-stinging slap. 'Why did Saul's death have to be such a huge secret? What's your excuse for that? Huh? Just tell me the truth! Why didn't you tell me?'

'Because I promised!' Mum hollered. 'I promised your brother I wouldn't.'

I had to get out of the kitchen before I tore it to pieces. 'What sort of a sick promise is that?' I spun around, and there face-to-face with me was Mr C, standing in the doorway.

He reached out and touched my cheek. '*Gemma mia*,' he whispered. That was all it took. I was stumbling into his arms while my sobs erupted and the heavens opened with my tears.

'She sad,' Mr C was saying, as he rubbed my back. 'She sad.'

'I know, Marcello,' Billy answered. 'We're all sad.'

Mr and Mrs C made some tea. Mr C ran upstairs and brought down a plate of freshly made cannoli, which became dinner and dessert. Mr C patted my head. Mrs C gave me one of her epic squeezes and when they thought we were all okay, they said goodbye and went back upstairs to their place.

After we heard the thud of their door closing, Mum said, 'I'm sorry, Gemma.'

'I'm sorry too,' I answered. I meant it. That explosion must've been waiting patiently somewhere in my body because I hadn't seen it coming. But when it came, it erupted like Vesuvius's big brother.

'We were just trying to protect you,' Mum offered.

'I know. But I'm not an idiot. I knew something was wrong and I would've preferred that you'd just told me.'

'Gem,' Billy said. 'I promise you it was Saul who didn't want you to know until the end. He said, "It's too much pain and worry for a kid." Those were his words. So, I made Mum swear she wouldn't tell you. And at the end, it just all happened so fast.'

'Okay.' I swallowed. 'I accept that. But why wasn't I told that you were coming home? And all these new rules in the kitchen and the bathroom?'

Billy was nodding. But he wasn't nodding at me, he was staring at our mother. She nodded too, cleared her throat, then leaned over the table, finding my hand and taking it in hers. 'Now that we're here, just the three of us, sitting quietly, it's probably time to—'

'Billy's sick too, isn't he?' I blurted out. 'That's why we have all these new rules in the house. Billy has AIDS, doesn't he?'

This time Billy looked straight at me. 'I don't have AIDS,' he replied. 'But I'm HIV-positive.'

I didn't cry. I'm not even sure I made a noise. I think I'd been waiting for this moment. I had sensed the inevitable was rolling towards us and now it had arrived in the kitchen on the second Sunday in May when I was wearing my 501s and a tight black jumper.

I thought back to all the times I had been told there was nothing to worry about because Saul and Billy were different. They were 'an old married couple', my family's favourite line. But even that hadn't protected them and now everything I'd been afraid of was right here in my home.

Billy started to explain that his T cells were good and that he hadn't had any opportunistic infections.

Mum added that not everyone would be kind and understanding. That we could lose friends and people might judge us.

But I stood up and asked if I could leave the table. I was tired. I wanted to be on my own. Mum had taken over as Polly Pessimistic and up to five seconds ago I'd never heard of T cells and opportunistic infections. I knew I'd get to know about them though. In a few weeks' time, I bet the words would be rolling off the tip of my tongue.

I asked Mum if I could make a phone call in her room, and said goodnight.

Her clock said it was 8.21 p.m. I decided that at 8.30 p.m., I would make the call to Andrea. It was pointless putting it off any longer. Andrea would most likely be pissed that I hadn't told her anything before.

You are the wind beneath my wings! I could imagine her saying. *I am your best buddy. It's my job to know everything about your life.*

But 8.30 p.m. passed and I still wasn't ready to dial Andrea's number.

I wasn't scared. In fact, I felt strangely calm. It wasn't like I didn't know what to say. There was a good chance, I estimated it at a one-hundred-and-ten-per cent possibility, that Andrea would be shocked. But she'd get over it.

For me, the real thing stopping me was the thought of having to speak those words: *Saul died of AIDS. Billy's home and he's HIV-positive.* Saying those two sentences out loud would give it life, make it real. That's what telling Andrea really meant.

In Year 8, when Andrea confessed that she had her moustache waxed, she'd laid down a rule. I wasn't allowed to ask anything about it. 'It's off limits,' Andrea told me. 'If I decide to tell you I'm having it done again, or if I want to ask you if you think it needs doing, then I can. But you can't mention it. At all.' I told her I understood and that I thought it was a fair rule.

Perhaps I could make some rules? I could talk about Billy or Saul whenever I wanted. But she couldn't. Not unless I brought it up first.

Yes, I decided. These would be my terms and conditions. I would need them to survive, because Andrea had the potential to turn the news about Billy into the biggest catastrophe of the century.

Billy was going to be okay and that was that. Tomorrow I would ask him about his cell count and whatever those infections were called. I'd seen people on talk shows who'd been HIV-positive for years and hadn't become sick. Justin had even told me about that.

Plus there was always talk about a cure being just around the corner. My biology teacher, Mr Curtain, had mentioned it the other day in class when we were learning about the eradication of polio.

The clock read 9.37 p.m. In twenty-three minutes, Andrea would be tucked up in bed starting her eight hours of beauty sleep as prescribed by Elizabeth Taylor.

I picked up the phone and dialled her number.

'Hello? Andrea beaking.'

'You sound terrible.'

'I know. I hab a cold. Probably got your germs, Mub reckons.'

'Huh?' I had momentarily forgotten about my fake sickness.

'Mub says you probably breathed on be or sneezed in by face.'

'Gee, tell Constable Germ Patrol, thanks,' I said. 'Anyway, I'm all better now.'

'Lucky you. By nose is so blocked I can't even breabe.'

'Do you want me to bring you over a magazine after school tomorrow?'

'Baybe.'

There was a click on the other end, the sound of someone picking up the phone. Then Billy's voice came through the receiver. 'Oh, Gem? Sorry.' He hung up.

Andrea suddenly squawked, 'Was bat Billy?'

My eyes were shut. This wasn't how I wanted it to go.

'Gemma! Was bat Billy?'

'Yeah, yeah,' I answered, pressing my fingertips into my forehead. 'He just got home this afternoon. That's what I was ringing to tell you.'

'How cub he's hobe? Gebba? Is Saul there too?'

'Hang on a sec.' I placed my palm against the mouthpiece, pretending someone was speaking to me. 'Yeah, okay,' I was saying to the imaginary person. 'I have to go, Andrea. I'll pop by your place tomorrow. Bye.'

I threw the phone off the bed like it was contaminated and bolted into my room.

Had my life suddenly become like Ferris Bueller's, except that I couldn't figure out how to fix mine? Because I didn't want to have one of those lives. I wanted my old one back.

'Can I come in?' Billy was at the door. 'Gem? Hey, are you okay?'

'Sort of,' I answered, trying to focus on the figure walking towards me.

'Sorry. I didn't know you were still on the phone. I hate that. When Dad started getting suss about me and Matt, he used to try and eavesdrop on us all the time.'

'That sucks.'

'Shove over,' Billy said, squeezing next to me on the bed. 'How are you, really?'

'I feel kind of weird.'

'Fair enough.'

'I knew you not being HIV-positive didn't make sense. I just really hoped you weren't.'

'I know, baby girl.'

'I was so sad about Matt. I know that's how he died. Not that Mum ever said anything to me.'

'Poor darling Matt,' Billy answered. Yet his voice sounded like it did the day he told me about his friend from the country who'd died. Sad but matter-of-fact. 'It's like all my mates, all these men I've loved, are dying at the same time. There have been days when I've almost been too scared to walk down the street in case I bump into a friend who tells me someone else has died.'

'That's horrible.'

'It's like I'm in this really bad dream,' Billy said. 'That's what it feels like.'

'I can't believe I'm never going to see Saul again.'

'Get under the rooster's wing,' Billy told me, lifting his arm so I could snuggle up under it. It always felt safe under Billy's wing.

But tonight, he felt smaller. Like he'd shrunk. My brother,

who'd been a swimmer, a fifty-metre champion whose big lungs and strong shoulders had carried him down the pool in state-record time, now felt like he'd deflated. Just a little. As though someone had pricked a pin into his chest and the air was gradually escaping until there'd be nothing left.

'I'm sad,' I whispered.

'Me too.'

'You must miss Saul so much.'

'It's like I've had my leg amputated. I still think it's there but it's not,' Billy explained and I tried to imagine what he was feeling inside, right at that very second. 'I wake up or I walk into a room and I expect Saul to be there and he's not. All our dreams are gone. Just like that.'

'What were your dreams?' I asked.

'A house in the Hamptons,' Billy laughed. 'That was the big one. We'd even picked the street in Montauk. But that wasn't going to happen until his parents dropped off the perch. Doesn't seem too big a bet, does it? They're in their late sixties, Saul was in his early thirties. Who do you reckon is meant to die first?' I wasn't sure if they were questions Billy wanted answers to. I suspected they weren't. 'This goes against all the laws of nature. That's what's so punishing about this disease, Gem. I know a guy in New York who's been to nearly thirty funerals in the last eighteen months. Every single corpse under thirty-five years old!'

I started to wiggle out of his wing. I suddenly didn't like this conversation.

'Sorry, Gem,' Billy offered. 'You don't need to hear that.'

I nestled back under. If I wanted to know stuff then I had to show Billy that I could handle it. Even if it was slightly freaking me out. 'You can talk to me about anything, Billy.'

'And you can ask me anything too,' he answered. 'All the cats are out of the bag now!'

'I do have one question,' I said. 'Is that why Saul didn't come out last Christmas? Because he was sick?'

'He wanted to spend Christmas with his family and he also had quite a lot of work on. I think he probably knew something was up, but he didn't want to say.'

'Was it . . . ?'

'Two nights before I flew out he got a temperature. We were walking home from the movies and it was maybe two degrees outside and Saul started ripping off his coat and scarf.' Billy paused. I could feel my arm across his chest rise and fall with his breath. 'I realise now that was the beginning. But you just don't want to know. So you keep the idea as far away as you can.'

'Did you know he was HIV-positive?'

'We found out we both were, about eight months ago. We kept putting the test off, like lots of couples do.' Billy pulled me in tighter. 'Sorry I didn't tell you, Gem. It's hard enough trying to digest it yourself. And then there's all the blame stuff.'

'Like who gave it to who?'

Billy nodded. 'I don't want to talk about that.'

'All right.'

I thought maybe that'd ended the conversation. But Billy kept going. 'We didn't even tell all our friends we were positive because we knew it would freak them out. Everyone's terrified they could catch it. But they don't want to say anything so they just start avoiding you.'

'I wondered if something was wrong last Christmas,' I told him. 'You were quiet. But I just thought you were missing Saul. It makes sense now.'

There was a long, slow silence. The seconds crawled on their hands and knees and I watched the clock take forever before it changed from 9.57 to 9.58. Then Billy sighed and I felt his chest go still as he held his breath. 'I was missing him,' he sighed again. So sad was the sound. 'But it was more than just missing him,' he continued. 'When I spoke to Saul on the phone his voice sounded different and I knew there was something wrong. I just knew.'

'I get that feeling all the time.'

'I know you do,' Billy answered. 'But I'm not a thinker like you, Gem. You spend hours doing it. I like to keep busy.'

'Believe me, thinking keeps you busy. It's a full-time job.'

'Not my sort of job. But you're right. I was quiet at Christmastime. I think I sensed something was wrong.'

'You just get a feeling sometimes.'

'The day before I flew back to New York, January sixteenth to be exact, Saul found that deadly purple spot on his chest. Actually, it was almost smaller than a spot, more like a dot. Then they just started spreading.'

'Poor Saul,' I whispered.

'Yeah, he looked terrible. But he was still my beautiful Saul.'

More slow, sad silence. I wondered how I would be if every day I had to look at a face that had changed like Saul's had. Could I still think a person like that was beautiful? Was that how you measured and weighed love?

'I wish I'd seen Saul properly,' I whispered. 'Just one last time.'

'Gem.' Billy squeezed me. 'I'm glad you didn't see him in real life, baby girl. You saw how he didn't look good. I promised Saul not to tell you he was sick. I had to make him many promises and that was one of them. It was hard to keep, too, because I knew you'd want to know. I knew you'd feel left out.'

'What were the other ones?'

'I promised him that he wouldn't be alone.' Billy swallowed hard. 'At the end. I promised I would be there. And I was. And it was peaceful. I promised him that too, but I wasn't sure if I could deliver on that one.'

'But you did?'

'Yeah,' he whispered. 'He was peaceful. It was like he'd slipped off to some other land.'

ON MONDAY I WAS DRESSED AND OUT THE door to school like usual. Like it was a normal day in the normal life of a normal girl called Gemma Penelope Longrigg. Not a girl who had an HIV-positive brother at home.

If you saw me walking down the street, my bag slung over my shoulder, my fluoro green scrunchie in my hair, you'd think I was a dinky-di suburban girl without a worry in the world. Smiles and cool bananas all round. I wanted people to think I was this person. So I made my strides longer and my grin bigger and when I saw Louise Lovejoy waiting at the pedestrian lights across the road from school, I called out to her in such an extra loud and bouncy tone that I wondered for a second whose voice it was.

'You're all better?' Louise asked me.

'Just peachy,' I replied. Peachy? Did I really just say that? I'd never used that word in my life. I hated that word.

'How was your weekend?'

I found out my brother's HIV-positive. Instead I said it again. 'Peachy.'

'My weekend was boring,' Louise moaned. 'My mum

117

was away and my dad and my brother hogged the TV watching sport.'

'How old's your brother?'

'Nathan's twelve, but he's almost six foot.'

'Just like my brother,' I told her. 'His foot was size thirteen when he was fifteen.'

'Did he play sport?'

'He was a swimmer. He broke a state record once.'

'And then became a hair and make-up artist? Whoa, that's a 360-degree head spin.'

'I know,' I chuckled, because that's what all our friends and family had thought when Billy announced he was going to hair and make-up school in the city.

'My mum's heard of your brother,' Louise said. 'She delivers magazines to doctors' surgeries. She said she's read about him before.'

'Probably in the *Women's Weekly*.'

'She went totally mental when I told her he was going to do my hair and make-up for the formal.'

Suddenly, an alarm started up in my head. *Whoop-whoop-whoop*, like that noise an ambulance makes before it drives away. The warning sound that tells everyone beware, watch out, get out of the way because there's a disaster up ahead.

I actually had to stop and crouch down, pretending my shoelace was untied. Eye contact and conversation would only make the alarm louder. I needed to think.

Billy was still doing our hair and make-up for the formal. Wasn't he? So much had happened that I'd completely forgotten about it. But of course he was. He'd promised.

The bell was ringing and I was starting to cause a bit of

a traffic jam, crouching smack bang in the middle of the school gates. A sea of black shoes and hairy ankles and socks in every variety of white were stepping over me and across me. Someone even squeezed in a sneaky kick.

'Oi!' I shouted, scrambling to my feet to see if I could spot the offender.

'We'd better get out of the way.' Louise took my elbow, steering us away from the crowd. 'It's a stampede!'

'I don't know why they're all in such a rush to get to class,' I grumbled, smoothing down my school skirt and dusting the gravel off my knees. 'I could've been squashed to death.'

'Imagine that,' Louise said. 'Like those soccer fans in England last year.'

'Or the students in Tiananmen Square who were run down by the army tanks.'

'I think I'd prefer dying like that. At least it'd be quicker.'

'If I had to pick a way to die I'd go for drowning or freezing to death,' I told her. 'You just fall asleep when you freeze. That wouldn't be so bad.'

'Oh my God! Why are we having this conversation, Gemma?'

Now we were both laughing. Actually Louise had stopped because it wasn't really that funny. But I was still going and it was triggering a switch inside me that I knew if pressed could turn this laughter into crazy, rib-cracking hysterics.

'Are you okay?' Louise was asking me, a trickle of a giggle still in her voice, even though it sounded awkward. 'Gemma? What's so funny?'

'Ah, nothing,' I answered. 'Nothing at all.' But Louise was looking at me and I suddenly felt caught out. Or maybe

I needed to tell someone because I heard myself saying, 'Actually everything's wrong, Louise. Everything.'

Louise and I wagged first period. We went behind the gymnasium because there was always a sewerage stink hanging around, which made it teacher-free. Yet it was the exact spot the teachers should be patrolling because it was the place to wag, smoke, get off with your boyfriend or, for some, find a moment of peace. I wondered how many times Louise had taken refuge here.

Louise lit up, blowing out a perfect chain of smoke rings that she stuck her fingers through before they curled away and disappeared.

'What's wrong?' she asked me. 'Were you really sick? Oh God, you're not . . .'

'I'm not pregnant if that's what you're thinking.'

'Phew!'

'Yuck!'

'Well, you do look pale and you've got dark rings under your eyes.'

I was edging towards the far end of the building because only a few metres away a couple were pashing and clawing at one another. They certainly looked occupied but it still didn't feel safe talking here. Louise followed me.

Our bums had barely hit the ground and I was saying those two sentences. 'Saul died of AIDS. And my brother's HIV-positive.' I heard the words come out of my mouth like I was listening to a report on the radio.

'Oh God, Gemma!' Louise said and she took my hand.

I didn't cry. I wasn't trying to be strong either. Maybe I'd cried too much yesterday because I honestly didn't even feel close to tears. Maybe I sounded the way Billy did. Sad but matter-of-fact.

Louise was super nice and understanding. Last year her uncle had been killed in a car crash, so she said she knew how I felt. But I don't think she did. You could tell everyone that your uncle had died in a car crash and they'd all feel sorry for you. But if you said that he died of AIDS, people might say something bad back. Mum had tried to warn me last night but I already knew. I wasn't an idiot.

Did she really think I'd forgotten about Aunty Penny's nursing friend Karen, who used to work in the AIDS ward at King George's? The owner of her corner store found out where she worked. Next time she went in, he told Karen that they wouldn't be needing her as a customer anymore because they were a family business.

Aunty Penny and Mum swore their heads off. They threatened to write letters to the local council and dob to the anti-discrimination people. To me, it was a story about something happening to someone else. But now that someone else could be us. Last night Mum wasn't really being Polly Pessimistic. She was just saying it how it was.

In the end, telling Louise didn't make me feel better. It made me feel guilty.

I had broken the golden rule of loyalty. Andrea was my best friend and I should've told her first. So after school I spent my current life savings buying the latest *Cleo* and *Cosmo* magazines and headed to her place.

Andrea's mother, Deidre, answered the door in a hot pink velvet tracksuit with streaks in her hair to match. Her arm, elbow deep in bangles, jingle-jangled as she pulled me towards her.

'A little bird told me Billy's home.'

'Yes,' I replied.

'Don't tell me,' she started. 'I bet he's here to do some fabulous celebrity's hair and make-up and you're not allowed to reveal their identity? Is it Olivia Newton-John?'

This is how I answered. With a question. 'Is Andrea upstairs?' And I bolted away before she could reply.

Andrea was sitting up in bed, surrounded by tissues and eating jubes.

'Want one?' she offered, pouring some into her hand. 'Don't take the green. They're by favourites.' That's probably why she was presenting me with a handful of purple and yellow ones.

'No, thank you,' I said. I hadn't realised until now but I'd never be able to stomach jubes again. Especially the purple ones. 'I bought you some magazines.'

'Thanks.'

'How're you feeling?'

'Sick. By nose is so blocked I want to chob it off. The only thing I can taste are jubes.'

'That's no good.'

'How combe you're acting weird?'

'I'm not.'

'Yes, you are. You're acting all forbal and bolite.'

'So I'm normally rude, am I?'

Andrea pulled a face and hoovered up another palm of jubes.

'How combe Billy's home?' she asked through a technicolour mouthful. 'Did you know he was cobing hobe?'

I was shaking my head because I knew that once the words were out I wouldn't be able to take them back.

'Did you?'

'There's something I've got to tell you.' I swallowed.

'What?'

'Saul died.'

'What?' Andrea punched the mattress. 'No! What habbened?'

'He – he got AIDS.'

'What?'

'Saul died of AIDS. And Billy's HIV-positive.' This time I said it much faster than when I'd told Louise.

Andrea was staring at me as though she'd just spied the Grim Reaper behind me. Still I made myself keep talking. 'That's why he's home. That's why Billy came back. I just walked in the door one afternoon and he was there.'

'Gemma!' she gasped.

'I know. It's bad.'

'It's really bad,' Andrea answered. 'What are you going to do?'

'What can I do?' I shrugged. 'I just have to try and be there for Billy. He's so . . .'

'But what are you going to do about beoble finding out?'

'I . . .'

'Have you told anyone, like at school, I bean?'

'No,' I lied. 'Just you.'

'Good.'

'Andrea, Saul died. He died. I'm so sad.' My bottom lip had started the shakes when Andrea slapped her hand over my mouth and said, 'Shoosh. Mum's coming.'

Deidre walked into the room with a plate of chocolate biscuits. 'Special treat,' she said, handing them to Andrea. 'Don't drop crumbs or you'll have rats in here before you can say Jack Robinson.'

'Jack Robinson,' Andrea said.

'Ha ha. Very funny,' Deidre replied, closing the door behind her with a wink.

'I bet I know why Bum just closed the door.'

'Why?'

'She wants me to bumb you for info because she reckons Billy's here to do some secret celebrity's hair and bake-up.'

'Oh,' I replied. 'What are you going to tell her?'

'Well, I'm not going to tell her the real reason, am I?'

'W-why?' I stammered. 'What would she do?'

Andrea's room was starved of air. I was hot and my limbs felt strange, like they'd detached themselves from my body. I suddenly couldn't feel them anymore and I couldn't hear what Andrea was saying. All I could see were her lips stretching over words and the blur of her arms waving around like she was about to topple over and off the bed.

But I sat there and nodded, pretending to take in every word. When the only ones I was actually hearing were Billy's words from last night. *It's like I'm in this really bad dream. That's what it feels like.*

Andrea wasn't at school all week. Polly Pessimistic had busted free from my head and was out in full force, playing havoc like she'd never done before. It was one bad thought after the next. And just when I didn't think they could get any worse, they did.

Is Andrea avoiding me?

Is Andrea avoiding me because Billy's HIV-positive?

Is Andrea avoiding me because she told her mother and her mother doesn't want her to come anywhere near me?

Is Andrea avoiding me because she told her mother and her mother doesn't want her to come anywhere near me because she thinks I'll get AIDS from Billy and then give it to Andrea and then Andrea will give it to the rest of her family?

Am I still the wind beneath Andrea's wings?

Just when I thought I was going to have to put a vacuum up my nose and suck Polly Pessimistic out of my brain once and for all, one good thing happened.

I spied Billy in the kitchen with his arms crossed, staring at the fridge. At first I thought I'd caught him frozen in the middle of a sad thought. I contemplated sneaking away. I wasn't sure if he'd heard me come in and I could do without hearing another sad thought, whether it was mine or my brother's.

But then he piped up and said, 'It's a really nice dress, Gemma.' And I realised he'd been staring at the photo of my dream formal dress.

'You like it?' I asked him.

'It's gorgeous. You've got the legs too.'

'Mum reckons I should—'

'—have a long train at the back?'

'Yes.'

'No way! That's Demi Moore, 1989 Oscars. So last year as we'd say in showbiz!'

'Thank you.'

'Simple but chic,' he said. 'Which fabric did you like the best? Claude knows he's on standby to send it over.'

'Um . . .'

'I'd do it exactly the same as this,' he said, pointing at the photo. 'Black velvet. Gold braid edging. Gorgeous. Slicked-back hair. Big earrings and red lips.'

'So . . . you're still going to do my hair and make-up?'

'Of course I am!' Billy answered.

'Really? Truly?'

'Try and stop me, baby girl! You, Andrea and another friend. That's what I promised.'

'Can you do Elizabeth Taylor hair?'

'I can do anything!' he answered.

※

The next day after school, another good thing happened. At least, it started out that way.

In last period, Louise had been drawing pictures of the Roxette dress. Now I had their song stuck in my head, except I only knew the one line. Maybe that was because the band were from Sweden or somewhere and they didn't really know what they were singing about so they mumbled their words. Kind of like Mr C, but he jumbled up sayings and words. 'Hit two birds with one stick' and the one that once had Saul laughing so much he had to excuse himself and run to the toilet: 'an otter he can't refuse'.

So, I was walking out the school gates, minding my own business and softly singing that one Roxette line to myself, when I heard someone call out, 'Hey, what happened to you the other day?'

How had I not noticed Ralph up ahead, maybe only five metres away, getting into the lime mobile?

Footpath, open and swallow me. I was looking so not-cool with my scrunchie falling out, giving me a loose side pony-tail that was straight out of the 1970s. The problem was that I had to walk right past Ralph. If I crossed the road it would've looked too obvious.

Ralph was half sitting in the driver's seat with the door open and one of his feet still outside on the ground. 'Apparently you were meant to come and get me,' he said, 'but you never showed.'

'I am so sorry,' I said, lingering by the car, not sure whether to stop and talk or keep walking. 'I honestly forgot. I walked out the gate and next thing I knew I was halfway up to the main road and . . .'

He made a grunting sound that I thought was probably the end of our longest conversation yet. But then he said, 'I mean, I'm hardly inconspicuous in this electric-green car.'

'Oh? Really? No. I didn't see you. Or the car.' The fibs were flowing. 'But yes, you're right. It is electric-green, isn't it? I've never noticed that before.'

'You're the only one then.'

I let out an awkward laugh that sounded more like a sheep baaing.

'Hey, do you want a lift home?' Ralph asked. 'I have to pass the end of your street anyway.'

'Oh? Sure. Okay. Why not.'

The *Belle Modelling Agency 1989* folder was on the floor in front of the passenger's seat. Nothing would've given me more pleasure than to slide my grubby school shoes across the title. For a second, I regretted dodging the dog's poo at the school gates. However, I picked it up and said, 'This looks like interesting reading.'

For a second, Ralph looked at me and I almost stopped breathing.

'It's Vanessa's,' Ralph finally said, taking it out of my hands and chucking it in the back seat, giving me a chance to quickly compose myself. 'I have a bit of a flick through it if I'm caught in a traffic jam.'

'Yeah, right,' I said. 'Thousands of traffic jams around these parts. It'll probably take us an hour to get to my place.'

'Ha ha,' Ralph replied, starting the engine and pulling out into the street that was only five blocks away from mine. 'You've always been a bit of a smartypants, haven't you, Gemma?'

'Excuse me?'

'I'm not saying it's a bad thing,' Ralph answered. 'It's good – being honest and saying what you think.'

Was I falling into a trap? Was this one of those negative-positive, upside-down compliments? I was seriously suspicious, and I was doing everything in my power not to take a sneaky look at him.

'Remember that time in Year 9, when we were studying *The Hotel New Hampshire* in Literature Circle?' Ralph began.

What I remembered was that in my copy of the book someone had crossed out 'Gemma Longrigg' and written 'Jamma Longdickupyourbum'. Andrea had wanted me to dob. But I wasn't a dibber-dobber and I didn't care about what some pathetic poofter-hater had written.

Suddenly, a thought occurred to me. Maybe Ralph was about to confess? Maybe he'd been the one to graffiti my book? Or maybe Ralph was a poof himself? He'd just told me it was good to be honest and to say what you think.

'. . . remember how you challenged Mrs Bryce?' Ralph was saying. 'You shot up your hand and started . . .' I had no memory of this. Zero. None. Zip. I wished I had, because if Ralph remembered this then maybe I wasn't so invisible? So unremarkable? '. . . you were waving your arm like crazy, Gemma, trying to get her attention but she was . . .'

No, Ralph definitely had me mixed up with someone else. And worse than that, that someone else was probably Andrea because she was always waving her arm around like a demented person trying to catch the teacher's attention.

I wasn't sure what idea tortured me more. Ralph not

noticing me or Ralph confusing me for Andrea. I couldn't prolong my pain and embarrassment any longer so I butted in and said, 'You've totally got the wrong person. It wasn't me.'

'Yes, it was! I remember everything about the Lit Circle days.'

'I think I'd know what I said. I do remember studying that book.'

Ralph was freeing up a hand from the steering wheel. 'I bet you five dollars it was you.'

'You're wasting your money,' I told him.

'No, I'm not.' His hand was still there, almost touching me. I was staring at it as though I'd never seen one before. I wanted to touch his long fingers but he snatched them away laughing, 'Too chicken to shake on it, because you know that five bucks is mine.'

I laughed back although I wasn't really sure what we were laughing at. 'I'm not really a mad hand-waver in class.'

'I know. You're more the controversial one who starts the discussions.'

'So, there you go. Not the mad hand-waver!'

'Ah, but you were on this day, Gemma. That's my point. You waved your hand and barked at Mrs Bryce, telling her she was stereotyping the characters. She was saying how awkward and weedy the brother Frank was because he was a fag and the jock footballers hassled him because he couldn't defend himself.'

I had just lost five dollars.

Ralph was right. I had totally forgotten. Blocked it out of my memory. Locked it in the box where the other ones were stored. It was the day after I'd said that to Mrs Bryce that my book was graffitied.

'You let Mrs Bryce have it, Gemma. You told her that just because the character was gay it didn't mean he couldn't be good at sport and . . .' I was nodding. Now Ralph was hitting the steering wheel and hollering, 'You do remember! You owe me five dollars!'

'We didn't shake on it.'

'Cheat! No way!'

'Anyway, how come you remembered such a stupid thing?'

This was the moment I wanted him to say, *Don't you know I'm always watching you?*

Of course, he didn't. He shrugged. Then, said, 'I knew your brother was camp so I got why you were making the point. It sucked and some of the guys were being dickheads. Didn't one of them graffiti your book?'

There was my answer. It was boringly logical and utterly unsatisfying. The lime mobile was about to turn back into a pumpkin and me into one of the ugly sisters. My Cinderella moment was over and I wanted it back so I could try again.

We were almost at the corner of our street. I wished I could say, *Turn around. Let's do that drive all over again.* Maybe Ralph felt the same way, because as we neared my place, he suddenly slowed down. Really slowed down.

The two of us were sitting there, the engine rumbling, the car hovering. We were going nowhere. It was as though we were caught in a one-car traffic jam. But now there was the world's most awkward silence between us. It was almost like that silence you get the second before you kiss someone but I was sure we weren't about to do that.

Say something, I was telling myself. *Speak. Say anything.*

Ralph kept one hand on the steering wheel but was

turning himself around to face me. *Relax!* I was shouting inside my head. *Stop looking like a freak!*

Now Ralph was staring straight at me and saying, 'Gemma?'

'Yes?'

'Vanessa told me your brother's home.'

I nodded.

'She also told me about his boyfriend dying in New York.'

'Oh?'

'I'm really sorry.'

'Thanks.'

'Don't take any shit from anyone, Gemma.'

'Sorry?'

'AIDS in the burbs. Not everyone's going to like it.'

'Excuse me?'

'Just saying.'

✳

I couldn't get out of Ralph's car quick enough. I was bounding up the stairs, two at a time. *AIDS in the burbs. AIDS in the burbs.* Those words had stuck to the lining of my brain. *Not everyone's going to like it.* Exactly what did he mean by that? Did he think my brother's germs were going to float down the drains to his house, killing him and his precious sister? Maybe Vanessa wasn't as relaxed about it as she made out. Maybe they thought my brother was going to kill the whole suburb like the Grim Reaper and his bowling ball?

I ran into the kitchen and filled a glass in the sink with water, all the time saying to myself, *I hate you, Ralph. I hate you.* How could you look me in the eyes and say that? I sculled the water, half of it running off my chin and onto my school shirt, and when I'd finished I slammed the glass into the sink like I'd just won a drinking contest.

That's when I realised I'd taken a dirty glass out of the sink and I didn't know who had drunk out of it.

We had to take our toiletries into the bathroom now whenever we wanted to use them so that we didn't accidently mix up our toothbrushes. After Billy shaved over the sink he had to clean it with some stinky bleach. Mum didn't want to use paper cups and plates. She'd thumped her fist on the kitchen table, declaring measures like that were over the top and that in reality AIDS was hard to catch.

Even Ita Buttrose had told all of Australia that you couldn't contract the virus from a mosquito. But my lips had just touched the rim of a glass that held a fifty per cent chance that my brother had too, and how did I know that his germs weren't lingering?

I stumbled to the bathroom, grabbing my toiletry bag on the way. I turned on the taps full throttle and, almost climbing into the basin, washed my face and scrubbed the inside of my mouth with a toothbrush until I could taste blood.

There was no need to sneak out of the bathroom, because if Billy and Mum were home they sure weren't making a show of it. Mum's door was closed and it was one time I could've dropped to my knees and kissed the carpet in gratitude and relief. I would die if they had seen what I'd just done.

Softly, I tapped on the door. 'You guys in there?' I said, opening it and going in.

Billy and Mum were sitting on the bed sorting through

a pile of sympathy cards. It was obvious they'd both been crying. Their red noses were a dead giveaway.

'How was school?' Mum asked. 'Do you have much homework?'

'Kind of,' I answered, swallowing a bit of blood that had gathered on the roof of my mouth.

Billy passed Mum one of the cards, saying, 'That's a nice one.'

'For the reply pile?'

Billy nodded.

'Who are those cards from?' I asked.

'From people who wrote to me when Saul was sick and when' – Billy's voice cracked – 'he died.'

I reached over and picked up a card.

'Don't get the piles mixed up,' Mum nagged.

I got comfy on the floor and opened it. It was from Rod and Carl. Not that I'd heard of them before.

Hopefully Saul is sharing a gin and tonic with Wes, Benson and Rick. If he's not doing that then maybe he's playing tennis with Frankie and Peter W or skiing with Douglas, Hank and the ever-beautiful Sam. That's how Rod and I like to think of it. As though there's a whole new world just as good or even better than this one. But wherever he is and whoever he's with, Saul knows that in NYC he was loved by so many and especially us. Thinking of you, Billy. Forever in our thoughts, Rod and Carl xx

PS Wish we could spend time with you at Martha's Vineyard but Rod too weak. Bring me home a piece of Glory's apple pie!

I handed the card back to Billy. 'I don't think I want to read any more. They'll make me too sad.' Or they'll freak the living daylights out of me – that was closer to the truth.

More importantly I needed to find out whose glass that was in the sink. 'What did you guys have for lunch today?' I began. It was good to add a yawn in these circumstances. Andrea once told me that it was important to sound bored when you really, really wanted to know something but didn't want to show it. 'There was a nice smell in the kitchen,' I fibbed.

Maybe they hadn't eaten lunch? There was no way to know these days. Mum had become even more of a clean freak Nazi. Every bit of cutlery or plate or cup had to be cleaned and put away straight after each meal. The dishwasher that Billy and Saul had given Mum was permanently running. I could vouch for that because I was the one who had to unstack it.

There had just been that one lone glass in the sink. Billy was taking so many vitamin concoctions and weird tablets that he'd most likely used it for water to swallow an afternoon dose and forgotten to put it away.

I was starting to feel sick. Could I really get HIV from drinking out of a glass? Billy and I had hugged and kissed. Just on the cheek, so it probably was safe. He'd crawled into bed with me the other night and given me a cuddle. He'd driven the car, helped Mr C fix the front gate and he still cut his nails on the couch while watching TV. He and Mum were always lying on her bed an inch away from each other. *Kissing doesn't kill.* Elizabeth Taylor had told the world that and she was an AIDS expert.

'There's some yoghurt and plenty of bread.' Mum was

listing the foods to satisfy my supposed appetite. 'I think there's some devon left.'

'Yeah, there is,' Billy said. 'It's in the vegie drawer in the fridge because I moved my Chinese herbs onto the shelf.'

'Chinese herbs?' I asked. 'What the hell?'

Billy started laughing. 'You wait,' he said. 'I haven't cooked them up yet. That's a smell you're going to have to learn to love.'

'What are they for?'

'They help boost your immunity,' he explained.

'It was very sweet of Mae to bring them over,' Mum said. 'That would've been hard.'

'Who's Mae?' I asked.

'Matt's mum,' Billy answered. 'You know, Mrs Leong.'

'Mrs Leong came over here?'

'Let's put the kettle on,' Mum said. We all got up and Billy and I followed her into the kitchen like she was our Girl Guide leader.

Before Mum touched the kettle she went straight to the sink, picked up the offending glass and put it in the dishwasher saying, 'I hope Mae got rid of that headache. It sounded like the beginning of a migraine to me.'

'Did you give her some Panadol?' I blurted out. 'Did she take it with a glass of water?'

'Yes, Nurse Gemma.' Mum was looking at me like I'd lost it, and in a way I had. In the span of half an hour I'd been humiliated by the boy I thought I loved but now hated, and imagined the sympathy cards that Billy and Mum would receive when I died of AIDS and joined Douglas, Hank and the ever-beautiful Sam.

'Tomorrow I'll buy a new saucepan for my Chinese herb

brew,' Billy was telling Mum. 'And I'll also try and make an appointment with that acupuncturist that Mae was telling us about.' Billy leaned over and gave Mum a peck on the cheek. 'You okay?' he asked her softly.

Mum did one of her quick nods back that actually meant she wasn't okay at all. 'I just really feel for Mae,' she said after a little while.

'Did she just turn up on the doorstep?' I asked.

'No, she called first.'

'But can she speak much English?'

'Her English has really improved,' Billy told me. 'Matt was always bugging her to take classes and she must've.'

The mugs were out, the teapot and milk in the middle of the table; it was our call to take our seats and begin on whatever topic was loitering in our kitchen. This afternoon it was Mae Leong's visit.

That morning Mrs Leong had called completely out of the blue. Billy answered the phone and minutes later Mum left the sewing machine and rushed to his side when she heard his sobs.

Less than two hours later, Mrs Leong was sitting at this kitchen table.

I had to ask if Mrs Leong still wore her hair in a tight bun and had pencilled-in eyebrows like upside-down 'C's. Billy started laughing and told me how when Matt and he were going out he'd fantasise about doing a makeover on her. I was glad we had that light moment because then Mum told me Mae's story about how Matt got a cough that kept getting worse, and within a week he was dead in hospital.

That night it took me a long, long while to get to sleep. Five words kept me awake. *Died after a short illness.*

12

THE NEXT WEEK, ANDREA WAS BACK AT school, standing at my locker like she would've been on any ordinary day. My brother had HIV but she was still there waiting for me. I ran into her arms and spun her around with joy.

'Have you lost the plot?' Andrea said, wrestling herself out of my hold then running her fingers through her stupid spiked-up fringe.

'I'm just happy to see you. Arrest me for my crime!'

'Which one?' Andrea mumbled.

Still that didn't burst my bubble because Polly Pessimistic had prepared herself for this. Louise and Justin seemed to be fine about my brother being HIV-positive. Andrea, on the other hand, was going to take a while to get used to the idea.

It was still too early for me to even think about how Deidre might take the news. Saul always said, 'One hurdle at a time.' Well, I had a whole field of hurdles ahead of me and some of them were going to be easier to jump than others.

'Can I just say something,' I began. 'I know that was big, big shit that I told you about Billy and Saul. And I get it if you need a bit of time to digest the—'

'Let's not talk about that!' Andrea answered, waving her hand in my face as though she was about to swat a fly. 'That's not for school.' Then she launched into the subject of her choice. Herself. And, to be honest, that was fine with me. 'Why does everything happen to me on the way to school when you're not there, Gemma?'

'Because I walk and you're lazy and catch the bus.'

'I swear I am *not* catching the bus again,' Andrea told me. 'From today on, we are meeting at Nigel every morning and walking together.'

'What happened?'

'Derr, one big guess, Gemma.'

'Martin and Sonia?'

'Plus the Fink.'

'Simon Finkler acts like their minder.'

'He has the worst breath you ever smelt.'

'How do you . . .?' I stopped mid-sentence because there was an ugly picture forming in my head. 'Andrea! You didn't?'

'Of course I didn't!' Andrea squealed.

'So what happened with the Fink, then?'

Through the locker room and amid the sound of banging metal doors and kids shouting and running up and down stairs, I strained to hear the details of what had happened to Andrea on the bus.

We walked out into the crisp May air and across the quadrangle and Andrea was only up to the part where Martin Searles and Miss Prissy Sonia Darue were going for it in the back seat of the bus. Simon Finkler hadn't even appeared yet. Probably because Andrea's description of Sonia's black lacy undies climbing up her bum went on for about five minutes.

Down the wind corridor towards the Science labs, and the Fink had finally entered the scene. Quickly, checking over her shoulder as though it was a state secret she was about to divulge, Andrea pulled me into a doorway and whispered, 'Suddenly he was almost sitting on top of me. He was panting in my face saying, "I hear you like it hard," and he was pressing himself against me and he had, you know . . .' She mouthed, 'an erection.'

'Did anyone try and stop him?'

'What do you reckon, idiot?' she squeaked. 'If they painted the Fink green he could stand in for The Incredible Hulk.'

'Are you okay?'

'I will be because I'm not catching the bus ever again.'

'I promise I will meet you every morning at Nigel.'

'And walk home with me in the afternoon?'

'Deal.'

'I don't know what was going through Louise Lovejoy's head when she got off with the Fink,' Andrea said. 'She should've just left him to Bronnie Perry. He's seriously off!'

❋

The end of May was only a few days away, which meant the start of winter. If every calendar in the world had been destroyed you'd still know it was coming because the sun had lost its power. It was like an old woman who'd once been beautiful. There was a trace of heat but mostly it was underwhelming. Still, we stretched out our limbs and, apart from Justin, hitched up our skirts to soak in the last of the rays.

Lunchtimes had returned to feeling like the old days. Not that I was sure what or when the old days actually were. But the old days hadn't been around for a while, that I did know.

Maybe the old days were before Saul died and Billy came home? Or maybe I should think of them as the simple days? Anyway, whatever it was, life felt normal again. We were sitting up on the roof of the gymnasium; Ralph and I were back to not talking; and Justin and Andrea were arguing. Today it was about whether a tunnel under the harbour was a good or a bad thing. Louise watched them like she was watching a tennis match, with me adding a comment every now and then just to stir things up.

Andrea would never back down, even though her facts were usually wrong to the point of made-up, and Justin's brain seemed to be growing by the day. Anything he didn't know about wasn't actually worth knowing at all. So their debate reached the usual stalemate and then there was a blissful silence.

I heard myself sigh, because for the first time in weeks, I really felt my body let go. Perhaps I was feeling lighter because I was accepting the situation at home? Perhaps my family and I could be okay, even though my brother had HIV? Apart from Billy going to a clinic on Fridays, you'd never think anything was wrong with him.

Suddenly Andrea disrupted the peace. She sat up and declared at the top of her voice, 'Louise, you seriously must've been off your face when you got off with Simon Finkler. How anyone would actually volunteer to touch that thing needs their head read.'

Silence. Ear-piercing silence. But Andrea was acting like she was deaf, because she didn't seem to notice it. 'What was going through your head? Because, no offence, you can't honestly have thought he was a spunk? I mean, only a—' I dug the heel of my shoe into Andrea's ankle. 'Ouch!' she squealed. 'What did you do that for, Gemma?'

'Accident,' I muttered. Andrea's skin was thicker than I'd thought. 'Sorry.'

'I mean, I'm no fan of Bronnie Perry.' Andrea kept talking. 'But that poor thing, being stuck with him for so long. If I was her I would've broken up with him the day after we'd got together. No, correction, five minutes after. Even that would be too long.'

Louise was sitting up now. 'Maybe she couldn't,' she uttered. 'Maybe it's complicated.' That's when I sat up, because I knew what that line meant. 'Things aren't always what they seem.'

Clever Justin had the sense to stay horizontal. Now Andrea was leaning towards Louise, her head cocked, her forehead folding like an accordion mid-note.

'What do you mean, Louise?' she asked.

Louise shrugged. 'I don't know.'

'But why did you say, "Things aren't always what they seem?"'

I was the unadorned meat in the sandwich. No lettuce or tomato on either side. Just me, smack bang in the middle of Andrea and Louise. I didn't know which way to look.

Louise knew something about Simon Finkler, she just wasn't going to tell us. I'd been suss for a while, but now I was convinced.

'Why are we wasting our time talking about the Fink?' I asked them. 'He's not worth it. Let's talk about something else.'

'Okay,' Andrea agreed. 'Should I get my hair cut?'

We dissected the pros and cons of Andrea getting her hair chopped less than five months before the formal. But out of the corner of my eye, I couldn't help noticing Louise's fingers, the way she was knotting and twisting them to the point that it must've hurt.

＊

That afternoon, as Andrea and I walked home from school, I started to tell her about what had happened with Ralph. She wasn't saying much back, just making lots of *hmm*s Andrea's *hmm*s usually meant that she didn't like what she was hearing, and today they were making me nervous. So, what? She didn't like the fact that Vanessa came over so Billy could cut her hair? Or that Ralph remembered that I'd had an argument with Mrs Bryce and now I owed him five dollars? Was Andrea cross that both times I hadn't called her up straight away to tell her what'd happened?

She let out the longest *hmm* when I told her that Ralph knew about Saul dying. And I stopped then. I stopped because Saul had died and all Andrea was doing was making a stupid sound. I wanted to slap her across the face again and tell her that I wasn't going to meet her at Nigel the next morning.

'So Ralph knows about Billy too?' Andrea asked. 'Did you tell him?'

'What? That Billy has H-I-V?' I stretched my lips over each letter. 'Can't you say it? H-I-V?'

'I'm just asking, Gemma. Don't bite my head off! I can't help it if I'm not good at saying the word.'

'You're not going to catch it just by saying it.'

'I know that!' Andrea opened her mouth again but quickly closed it. I wished I hadn't noticed but I had and now I needed to know what those swallowed words were.

'Tell me,' I said.

'Tell you what?'

'What you were about to say.' I paused because now I desperately wanted to slap her. Instead, I sucked the air in through my nostrils and calmly said, 'Please tell me what you were going to say, Andrea. I really need to know. If you don't tell me then I'll start imagining all the things it might have been.'

'I just . . .' Andrea hesitated. 'I just feel a bit weird. It's kind of a big deal Billy having AIDS.'

'HIV,' I corrected.

'How do you know everyone at school's not talking about it?'

'I don't. Anyway, how would they know?'

'Aren't you scared of catching it, Gemma?'

'No,' I lied. 'You catch it through bodily fluids. Like how could I get any of Billy's bodily fluids on me?'

'Yuck! Okay.'

'I get that you feel weird, Andrea. But it doesn't have to be a big deal.'

'Will Billy have to wear gloves when he does our make-up?'

'No. I don't think so.'

'I'm just a bit scared.'

'Well, don't be,' I answered and I knew my delivery was blunt.

For a while we walked in an uncomfortable silence.

'So . . .' Andrea started, 'what else happened with Ralph?'

My story about Ralph hadn't finished. But it had for Andrea. No way was I going to share Ralph's clanger. The line that made me turn from love to hate in less than a second. *AIDS in the burbs. Not everyone's going to like it.* I would keep that to myself.

So I answered, 'Nothing. That was it.'

We didn't talk anymore. We just kept walking.

I'm not a mind-reader, so I don't know what Andrea was thinking, although I'd guess her thoughts were along the same lines as mine. That AIDS was scary and that I didn't even know if I could catch HIV from doing something like drinking out of the same glass as Billy. Nothing was clear anymore. How would I know if everyone was secretly talking about me? And would Billy have to wear gloves if he was touching our face and hair?

The lightness I'd felt today, lying on the roof of the gymnasium, had disappeared. For the rest of the afternoon and evening I felt cranky. Everything and everyone annoyed me. I snapped at Billy because his Chinese herbs stank out the kitchen. I told Mum to get a life when she was dressing Neuta in a frilly blouse and talking to it like it was alive. Then, when it came to dinnertime, I had a spack-attack at both of them because they started to discuss if Dad should be told about Billy's HIV status. To me that was about the dumbest idea my mother and brother had ever had.

※

The next morning as I was walking to Nigel, I heard the hum of an engine behind me. It was Ralph in the lime mobile. I started walking faster, instructing myself not to turn around again under any circumstances.

The car kept trailing me and now I was telling myself that even if my foot got stuck under the wheel I was to keep walking. People had lived with worse injuries.

'Hey!' I heard Ralph call. 'Hey!' he called again.

I wanted to shout back that I had a name and it wasn't 'Hey'. But I didn't. Instead, I repeated his words in my head, watching my feet stride out in front of me. *AIDS in the burbs. Not everyone's going to like it. AIDS in the burbs. Not everyone's going to like it.*

'Gemma!'

Now the lime mobile was idling right next to me. The front passenger window was open and Ralph was calling out to me. 'Look, I'm sorry if I offended you. It came out wrong. I wasn't saying that's how *I* felt. Gemma?'

I had reached the park. The sad park that had been my escape from Ralph once before. Walking through the park would mean taking a longer route to get to Nigel. The chances were that Andrea would think I wasn't coming and leave and I'd end up in her bad books for the rest of the day.

One more time I whispered Ralph's words to myself, *AIDS in the burbs. Not everyone's going to like it.* Then I turned, stepped onto the grass and strode through the park. Not once looking back.

※

Mum and I came home from the grocery shopping to find Billy in the kitchen plucking Aunty Mame's eyebrows.

When we walked in, Mame jumped up out of the chair and took the armfuls of shopping bags from my mother.

'Maryanne!' Her deep voice was always a surprise at first, but you got used to it quickly. 'You shouldn't be lugging these up the stairs. You'll break your back.' Mame clicked her tongue and began to wag a finger with the longest nail I'd ever seen, painted bright purple. 'Shame on you, Billy,' she scolded. 'You're not sick yet.'

I ignored the comment because Mame wasn't the sort of person you could feel mad at.

'Miss Gemma,' she said to me. 'You are getting gorgeous. Don't touch your eyebrows. Do you hear?'

Our eyebrows couldn't be more different. Mine were thick and needed a bit of a comb each morning. Mame's were thin and mostly drawn in with a pencil, which made me wonder why they even needed plucking.

'Sit back down, darling,' instructed Billy. 'I haven't finished and we don't want you looking lopsided.'

'Billy said you're working on a new show.'

'That's right, Maryanne,' she answered, hitching up her red skirt to show long, skinny legs with knobbly knees that reminded me of Vanessa's. 'There's going to be a few Kylie numbers in this one and some other surprises.'

Billy was chuckling and I wondered what those surprises were.

I wasn't usually so enthusiastic to help unpack the shopping but I wanted to hang around because Mame was always full of stories. Imagine if Louise suddenly knocked on the door? She'd never seen a transvestite in real life but I'd told her all about Mame.

'Put this stuff in the fridge,' Mum said, handing me a bag. 'Carefully.'

Today, the shop had cost almost double the usual amount because Billy needed special food from the health-food shop that was natural and free of pesticides. Evidently before HIV entered the flat, our mother had been quite content to poison her children with pesticides and preservatives.

'Oh, these are so cute.' I held up the tiniest milk bottles I'd ever seen to show everyone. I tried to read the name on the label. '*Acidof . . . acidofool . . .*?'

'*Acidophilus*,' Billy pronounced for me.

'Good boy,' Mame said. 'He's definitely got a bit of the old candida in the mouth. I did the tongue test, Maryanne.'

'I bought some Nilstat mouthwash too. His T cell count's a bit low.' More and more Mum was breaking into this strange HIV language that I didn't understand. 'What are your thoughts on AZT, Mame? They've been talking about it at the clinic.'

'Mum!' Billy groaned. 'Leave it.'

'I can ask Mame's opinion if I want.'

'For a start Bill's count is not low enough so they won't be offering it to him yet. Personally, I hated the stuff and stopped taking it. Those AZT tablets made me feel terrible and you had to take them all the time. I couldn't exactly stop in the middle of a show and say, "Sorry ladies and gents but I just have to take my AZT!" Not a fan, Maryanne. Sorry, but that's my opinion.'

'See,' Billy said to Mum. 'I saw what it did to Saul. Endless blood transfusions. Always feeling sick, even on his good days. It stole time from us. I'm not taking that shit, *ever*.'

'But what if it helps?' Mum said.

'Please, Mum!'

'Some people are fine with AZT,' Mame offered, maybe because she could hear the desperation in my mother's voice. 'But it's not for everyone, sweetie. It has to be a personal choice.'

Mum went back to unpacking the shopping. But there was a noticeable shift in the atmosphere. Mame wouldn't be belting out in song today or telling us funny stories, like about the time a fake boob popped out of her bra and she trod on it in the middle of a dance routine. I'm not sure I could've enjoyed it anyway now I knew Aunty Mame was HIV-positive too. Some days it felt as though half the world had it.

So, it was just as well Louise didn't knock on the door. The entertainment today was how AZT had done wonders for Gavin but killed Paul; the imminent release of a new wonder drug made with egg yolk; that Chinese cucumbers were a load of bollocks; and then came the big mother of all statements of Aunty Mame's that had me wishing I'd been anywhere but in the kitchen.

'You know why your T cells are nosediving, darling,' she said to Billy. 'It's because of the trauma of losing Saul. Death of a partner is a sure way to give the virus a bit of life.' She sighed dramatically like it was just a scene in a show she was acting in. 'Opportunistic infections, here they come.'

Before I knew it, I was at the sink singing out in a voice that sounded so fake, I surprised even myself. 'How about I put the kettle on?' it said. 'Who'd like a cuppa?'

Mum didn't lift her head to answer. Her face was shielded in her hands. It was a terrible sight and it made me really, really scared.

I woke up during the night. I didn't bother to glance at my clock. I knew it was early. It was pitch black outside and the rumbling of the buses up on the highway hadn't yet started.

It was freezing out of bed. I wrapped my doona around me as I tiptoed to the bathroom.

A sliver of light flickered from under the door.

'You going to be long?' I whispered to whoever was in there.

The door opened to reveal Billy, standing by the basin in just a pair of undies. His skin glistened with sweat like he'd just returned from a run and hadn't yet showered. He was staring at himself in the mirror.

'You okay?' I asked.

'Yeah,' he answered. But still he didn't move.

'I need to go.' I pointed at the toilet.

'Oh? Oh, sorry,' Billy said and he slipped past me and down the hall.

Whatever just happened in the bathroom had given me a case of the freaks and I couldn't go back to sleep. So I took my Walkman and changed the tape from Fine Young Cannibals to one I'd made at home and labelled *Trying to Sleep Songs*.

Maybe Billy was sleepwalking? But whatever justification I tried, it didn't stop the 'bad' that I could sense creeping down the road towards us.

13

ALL THE WAY TO NIGEL, I CONCENTRATED ON
avoiding stepping on the cracks and joins in the footpath.
I had to keep my eyes on my feet and counting helped
because there seemed to be some mathematical formula to
how often a crack or join occurred.

When I finally looked up, I was totally surprised to see
Louise leaning against Nigel. She was shivering, which
wasn't surprising, because Nigel was possibly the coldest
spot in the whole suburb.

When she saw me, she waved. 'It's freezing,' she said,
breaking into a big smile that didn't match her words.
'I hope you don't mind me turning up?'

'Don't be a dag.' It was going to be interesting seeing
Andrea's face when she turned the corner. 'We can all walk
to school together.'

That same smile was still pasted on Louise's lips as
though the wind had just changed and it'd be stuck there
forever.

Her face reminded me of Tweety Bird's. She had the
same enormous eyes. But Louise looked like Tweety Bird
after he'd flown into a pole and now her beak was all
squashed and flat on her face.

'How's Billy?' Louise asked.

'He's given up coffee because he's trying to be healthy. So Mum decided she'd give up too, and it's like living with addicts going cold turkey. Not that I'd know,' I quickly corrected myself, because I didn't want Louise thinking my family was a total freak show.

'He needs to take his mind off things.'

'Exactly! Billy has to be busy all the time. You know what he's always been scared of?' I said. 'Thinking! Crazy, don't you reckon? He hates having too much time to think.'

I was wondering if all the talk about Billy was really boring, because Louise was rummaging around in her schoolbag. But then she pulled out a Rubik's Cube and handed it to me, saying, 'Give this to Billy. It stops you from thinking.'

'Really?'

'You get so lost in trying to match up the squares. It's like magic.'

'Wow.' I twisted and turned the tiles of colour. 'But this is yours.'

'I have about five of them. It can be a thank-you present in advance for my hair and make-up,' Louise said. 'Except Mum keeps bugging me to ask you what Billy drinks because she wants to buy him a bottle of something.'

'Does . . .' I almost stopped, but I pushed myself along '. . . does your mum know he's HIV-positive?'

'No. I thought it was private and that you didn't want people to know.'

'It's not a big deal anyway.'

'Exactly,' Louise agreed. 'It's not like we're going to catch it from having our hair and make-up done.'

Now I was smiling, just like Louise. It was as though

we were speaking in a secret language that had no words, yet it said everything. Everything I needed to hear from a friend these days.

'Well, heeeellloooo girls,' Andrea sang. I was trying to read her face, to understand what secret language she was speaking to me in. Surprised but not pissed off, was my verdict. 'I didn't expect to see you, Louise Lovejoy.' Andrea started laughing and pointing at Louise's legs. 'Your legs have turned blue. One thing you need to know about Nigel is that you never arrive early because you'll freeze to death.'

But Louise's smile had vanished and I wondered if Andrea's stupid joke had fallen flat. 'I need to tell you something . . .' Louise started. She'd begun to twist her fingers like she'd done the other day. 'I came here because I want to tell you guys this thing. I haven't told anyone. But I know I can trust you two.'

Andrea reminded me of a dog waiting to be given a thick, juicy bone. I wanted to tell her to shut her mouth and push her eyeballs back in.

Stretching out the time, taking every possible long cut and detour, the three of us wandered to school while Louise told us a story. A story that we and the whole school had got so wrong.

Bronnie Perry had not rearranged Louise Lovejoy's face, because Louise had never got off with Simon Finkler. He had tried to get it on with Louise but she'd pushed him away. But he wouldn't take no. So he tried again, with force this time – and that's when his girlfriend, Bronnie Perry, walked in on them.

Bronnie went to help Louise fight him off. But all it took was one push from the enormous Fink and both girls went flying. Bronnie's head smashed the once fine bridge of

Louise's nose. The only reminder of the night for Bronnie, apart from being scared of the Fink, was a tiny chip in her front left tooth.

Of course they had promised Simon Finkler that they wouldn't tell anyone and they had stuck to their word because Simon Finkler told them that if they did tell anyone he would kill Bronnie. Louise finished with, 'It took her almost six months to get away from him. She was counting the days, making excuses every time he wanted to do it. In the end he dumped her because he wasn't getting any. He's too thick to figure out what was really going on. Poor Bronnie. She was a nervous wreck.'

Andrea's first reaction was, 'Oh my God! I knew I was in danger on the bus that day!'

Mine was to ask Louise what I thought was so obvious. 'Didn't you tell your parents? I mean, he wouldn't really kill her, would he?'

'He really scared us,' Louise said. 'I told my parents that I fell over. I was already in so much trouble with them because I was drunk. Actually paralytic by the time I got home. I just wanted to disappear into my bedroom and be left alone.'

Every day of last year and probably a fair part of this one too, Louise had had to wear names such as 'slut' and 'slag'. So why had she decided to tell us now? She'd already lost all her old friends. Wasn't it a bit late for the truth?

So I asked her. It was a simple question. Just like Louise's answer. 'Because you're my friends.'

Billy and the Rubik's Cube had become inseparable.

'It's the best present ever,' he told me.

Now he was dying to meet Louise so he could thank her.

'She's so pumped about you doing her hair and make-up,' I said.

Mum had taken Aunty Penny to the airport. She was off on a girls' trip to Bali. Billy and I were watching a repeat of *Moonlighting* because we both loved Bruce Willis. At least, I was doing the watching and occasionally Billy would glance up from the cube that he had no hope of ever mastering.

'What about Andrea?' Billy asked. 'Is she still going for the Elizabeth Taylor look?'

'She's obsessed. She wants to have a meeting with you beforehand.'

'That's cute.'

'No, it's not. It's annoying. Why can't she just be normal?'

'Because she's Andrea.'

'Billy?' I began. 'Can I ask you a question? Can you promise not to get mad or think I'm stupid?'

'What?' Billy teased, screwing up his nose the way I was.

'Will you have to wear gloves when you do our hair and—'

I didn't get to finish because Billy started laughing. He was clapping his hands and thumping his fists on the couch like it was the funniest thing he'd ever heard.

'That's too much, Gem!' Now he'd run out of breath and was coughing. 'That's beautiful. The way you asked it . . .' He was starting to choke and turn red in the face.

'Billy? Billy!'

'I'm fine,' he spluttered. 'It was just funny.' He wiped his eyes and rubbed his chest. 'Ah,' he sighed. 'It's been a while since I've had a good laugh.'

'It wasn't that funny.'

'Yes it was, baby girl.'

'Are you okay?'

'Yes! I'm fine!'

'Are you sure?'

Billy reached for my hand then shook it with each word he delivered. 'Please don't freak out every time I do something like cough.'

I nodded.

'It's bad enough having to deal with Mum,' he said. 'She's turned into Polly Pessimistic. I need you to be positive with me. Polly Positive. For all of us.'

'Okay. I will.'

'Promise?'

'I promise.'

'Now about the gloves.' Billy grinned and had another chuckle before I snuggled under his wing to hear the story about the 'ever-beautiful Sam' who'd featured in the sympathy card.

'Sam didn't look so beautiful anymore,' Billy said. 'People treated him differently. But he didn't care. So it didn't matter how bad he looked, he kept going out.'

'He had AIDS?'

'What else would steal your looks at twenty-five?'

Dumb question. But surely there was someone in Billy's world who wasn't sick with AIDS?

'So one day Sam caught the bus,' continued Billy. 'He wasn't really a bus-catcher. It was always the subway. But it was the end of February, the snow had melted and the sun was out. Sam flagged down the bus, went to pay the fare and the bus driver said, "Wait a minute, sir."' I giggled at Billy's fake American accent. 'Then, right in front of Sam, the driver took a pair of latex gloves out of his pocket. You know, like the ones you do the washing-up with? He put them on, then opened his hand to take Sam's quarters for the fare.'

'Because . . .?'

'Because in New York City, if you're a young male who's lost half their body weight like Sam, then you must have AIDS. I mean, Sam actually had cancer but that didn't count. It's okay to have cancer-cancer. But it's not okay to have AIDS-related cancer. Quite a few bus drivers started wearing gloves all the time. Ambulance drivers too.'

'That sucks!'

'Some doctors won't operate on people with AIDS. Friends, gay and straight, stopped calling one another. Having AIDS is a big, bad disaster.'

'Now I feel horrible for asking about the gloves.'

'Don't,' Billy said. 'Gemma, I'm fine talking about it. It's Mum who's not. That's just the way she's dealing with it. Whatever you want to know, you just ask.'

In the ad break we decided that Louise and Andrea should both come over soon to discuss what look they wanted for our formal. It didn't matter that the formal was still months away, Billy said it would help him kill the time.

'So you're staying here?' I asked. 'You're not going back to New York?'

'I haven't decided. The lease on our apartment is up. Claude's packed it up and put our stuff in storage.'

Each utterance of 'our' felt like a little electric shock. I wondered if that's how it felt for Billy too.

'I know I can't face New York at the moment,' he almost whispered. 'It'll make me too sad and stress me out.

Everyone's dying or dead. At least, that's what it feels like,' he said. 'I'm too tired to keep hearing about it. Here I'm safe. Or at least safer.'

Billy went back to his Rubik's Cube. No wonder he didn't want to think.

I pretended to watch *Moonlighting*. I hadn't let my expression slide off my face. I'd swallowed my gasps before they left my lips. This was the way it had to be, if I wanted to be included.

But Billy's stories, in fact nearly everything that came out of his mouth, had a way of making me scared or sad or just plain pissed off with the planet.

Imagine waking up one morning and finding out that Andrea, Justin, Louise and Bronnie Perry were all dead? Sonia Darue was on her way out and Ralph and Vanessa weren't talking to me anymore because they were scared they'd catch the plague too.

Maybe people were horrible? Is that what I was starting to learn? Louise Lovejoy was hated by half the seniors for a crime she didn't even commit. But no one asked questions. All of us, including me, were happy to don our latex gloves and point our fingers at her. Louise had spent nearly a whole year alone. Demoted from the gang of Sonia Darue and the prissy girls. Had she purposely waited for the next year to roll around before she dared come and sit with us? If she'd tried six months earlier would we have told her to piss off because we didn't want to be contaminated by her and join the rank of untouchables?

It wasn't Polly Pessimistic thinking this. It was Polly Perceptive. Suddenly it was like I'd taken off my sunnies and could see the world in the harsh light it really turned in.

But I had promised Billy I'd be Polly Positive. To not freak out over everything.

So as I tried to fall asleep that night, I turned up the music on my Walkman to drown out the sounds of Billy coughing that were barking up the hallway.

*

Louise was now a fully-fledged member of Nigel. We were walking back there after school, discussing Saturday night because we were going out raging. Some guys who'd left school last year had started a band called Albatross. Louise had seen them and said they were pretty good. They were playing up at The Northern, which was renowned for being easy to get into because of the slack bouncers. Even better, Andrea's parents were away for the weekend, so we could stay at her place and get home as late as we wanted.

Our plan was sounding excellent. Louise and Andrea were coming to my place in the afternoon. First, we'd have a meeting with Billy about our hair and make-up for the formal. Then Billy said he'd do us up for going out that night.

'Oh my God, what are we going to wear?' Andrea was already squealing and there was still forty-eight hours to go. 'Like we don't want to be too dressed up, do we?'

'Jeans,' I advised.

'Gemma, can you *not* wear what you always wear?' Andrea turned to Louise and said, 'Levi's 501s, some black top and Docs. Oh and big gold hoops. That's Gemma's uniform.'

'So?' I muttered.

'So it's getting boring, Gemma.'

'I've got a really nice new jeans jacket,' Louise told us. 'So I think I'll wear that and maybe a black leather skirt.'

'You have cool clothes,' Andrea said to Louise. 'What can you bring over to Gemma's that I could wear?'

There was a good chance Ralph would be at the pub on Saturday night. The guys from Albatross were his kind of people. Black stovepipe pants, black pointy shoes and a big flop of hair over the eyes: the look that I loved.

I was avoiding Ralph now. And I think he was avoiding me too. But it was hard to know when we'd barely spoken in the past anyway.

Twice this week we'd been walking down the same corridor, seconds from colliding into one another, when one of us had miraculously disappeared into a classroom or done a step-ball-change and headed back in the direction we'd come from. That was 'avoiding' in my book.

Sure I'd been the one to jump out of his car without saying goodbye. Then I'd ignored him when he'd trailed me on the way to school. But that didn't count as me being rude. He'd been the insensitive one. I mean, how did he expect his comment would make me feel? Warm and fuzzy?

Maybe if he was at the pub, we could talk about it and I could tell him why I jumped out of the car. But the risk in doing that was Ralph telling me that he didn't even know I'd jumped out of the car; that he'd thought the conversation was over. But I could retaliate with, *Then why did you stalk me in your car the other week?* Or my latest theory, *I bet Vanessa's told you to be nice to me.* But I knew I couldn't say any of that or I'd totally come across like a freak who overthought everything, which I did. But Ralph didn't need to know that.

On Saturday night, I couldn't wear my 'uniform', as Andrea called it. Not because she thought it was boring but because that's what I was wearing the night we crashed the Fink's party and danced to Salt-N-Pepa. Ralph was there that night and what if he remembered what I was wearing? Not that he would. He probably wouldn't even remember I was there. Let alone our dance. But the problem of what I was going to wear was one I could deal with. Why not make Saturday night the night to shine? Why wait all year for the formal?

***

By Friday evening, I had a shortlist of three outfits. The one I liked the best was a black-and-white striped T-shirt paired with a tube skirt that Mum said 'hugged my curves'. To my mother that was a good thing. To me, it was not.

The second option was my 501s and a white shirt, but Billy told me, 'You can do better,' so that was out. The third was a dress, black of course, with gold buttons on the shoulders. I don't usually wear dresses so I felt weird in it, like I was playing dress-ups. But Mum and Billy both agreed it was the best.

In the end, it didn't matter, because at five-thirty on Saturday morning, when I was in my green spotty flannel-ette pyjamas, an ambulance came to take Billy to hospital.

He had a fever, he couldn't breathe and the cough that I'd heard the last few nights echoed down the stairwell as they carried him away on a stretcher.

Mum and Billy went off in the ambulance. Mr and Mrs C and me followed in their tiny car. No time to change. Mrs C had rollers in her hair and Mr C definitely didn't have any jocks on under his pyjama pants. The engine of the Fiat strained to keep up with the red flashing light in front of us. Mrs C draped her arm over the seat so I could hold on to her hand and not feel so alone in the back.

I closed my eyes and remembered my promise. I would be Polly Positive. For all of us.

14

BILLY HAD A DRIP IN HIS ARM. HE WAS
wearing an oxygen mask that whistled and had a weird
plastic bag hanging off it. He didn't speak. It seemed that
all his energy was going into taking the next breath and
then the one after that.

He wasn't in the main section of King George's casualty
ward, but in a small room tucked away off one of the
millions of corridors. By small, I mean Mum and I could
fit in there only if the door was kept open and even then
half of my body was poking out into the draughty hallway.

Rushes of cold air kept blowing under my pyjama top
as nurses and doctors hurried past, calling out things like,
'Trauma in five.' I wanted to ask for a blanket so I could
wrap it around my shoulders. But everyone was too busy to
stop. They were acting like they couldn't even see me.

I wished Mr and Mrs C were still here. Or that Aunty
Penny would miraculously reappear from her girls' tour
of Bali. Mum was present in person; she could nod and
answer. But I felt like I was probably just a blur of green to
her, a mottled shadow that existed only in her peripheral
vision.

Mum wasn't going to wrap her arm around me or ask

one of the scary nurses if there was a spare blanket. And I couldn't tell Mum how frightened I was because it was obvious she was frightened too.

'I think I'll go for a wander,' I said to Mum, because I was starting to freeze. 'Do you want me to see if I can find a coffee machine or something?'

'Sure,' Mum replied without turning her head from Billy. 'Take my purse.'

It was only then, out of the room, that I noticed our surroundings. Mrs C and I had been so frantic trying to find Billy and Mum in the labyrinth of corridors and underground tunnels that I hadn't taken in the scene around us.

Now I could sum up the situation and it wouldn't take a brain surgeon to work out that my brother had been tucked away. Tucked far away where the other patients and their families couldn't see the big sign that read *Infection Hazard*.

Outside my brother's room was a trolley filled with gloves and masks. Plus a massive bin lined in yellow plastic that also shouted *Infection Hazard* in case you'd missed it the first time.

'Can I help you, dear?' A woman at the reception desk smiled at me. She seemed pretty nice so I wondered if maybe I could ask her for a blanket. 'Are you looking for someone?'

'No, it's okay. I'm here with my brother, who's . . .' I gestured down the corridor. Her gaze followed my finger, her smile folded back inside her lips and she went back to whatever she was doing.

'Is there a coffee machine around here?' No words back. Just a finger pointing at something behind me. 'Oh?' I murmured. 'Thanks.'

The powdered milk plopped in the cups and the bitter-smelling coffee reminded me of Friday evenings at the swimming dome, watching Billy race. Some nights Dad came too. I'd sit between my parents, bugging them to let me have a sip of their coffee. Mum always said no but Dad would let me.

How simple those days had been. Maybe not for my parents or for Billy. But for me they were. AIDS, queer-haters and boys that attack girls were not the kind of surprises I'd thought might jump out from behind the couch.

At the other end of the corridor I could see a small gathering of people in white coats outside Billy's room. I walked faster, not caring about the hot coffee splashing onto my fingers.

'Excuse me,' I said. No one moved. 'Excuse me,' I said again, louder.

'That's my daughter,' I heard Mum say. The white coats parted, letting me squeeze inside and share the doorway with them.

Billy looked more with it now. He'd even taken the oxygen mask off so he could speak.

'How long will I be in here?' he was asking a doctor in a paper mask and gown, who was perched on the end of the bed. 'Can you tell me that?'

'AIDS-related pneumonia can be unpredictable. But we've got this one early . . .'

I didn't take in the rest of what he said. 'AIDS-related pneumonia', or rather just the 'AIDS' part, had jumped out from behind the couch and hit me over the head like a sledgehammer.

Billy's white cell count had nosedived. His lungs had almost collapsed with pneumonia. There was a thrush infection in his mouth that was threatening to creep down his throat. In simple terms, this meant that Billy had crossed the threshold into the dark space that was called AIDS.

Now I looked at his HIV diagnosis longingly, wishing we could go back to those simple days.

The doctor also explained that there wasn't a bed available in the AIDS ward. She didn't actually say that nowhere else would take him. What she did say was, 'With your condition there aren't any other beds available to you except on 9 South West.' This meant that Billy would have to start treatment for his pneumonia in this room, that someone had let slip was actually a storeroom.

'When will a bed in 9 South West become available?' Mum asked the doctor.

'Later today,' she'd answered. 'Or maybe even sooner.'

I looked down at my feet and ordered Polly Pessimistic not to think about what that could mean. There were two options: the first was that the patient had gone home; the second was what I told myself not to think about.

The white coats squeezed their way out of the room. Outside they ripped off their aprons and masks, stuffing them into the big plastic bin. Then they strolled off, deep in discussion on whether or not they had time to grab a coffee.

'What's the time difference in Bali?' Mum said, looking at her watch as though it would tell her the answer. 'I have the number of Penny's hotel.'

'Mum, don't call Penny,' Billy uttered through panted breaths. 'Let her enjoy her holiday. I'm in hospital now, it's going to be fine.'

Mum made the *humph* sound that usually meant she

wasn't going to take any notice of what was being said. I didn't know whose side to take, but if I had to choose, I would have gone for Penny coming home from her holiday. She was good at handling Mum.

'Gem, sorry about tonight,' Billy mouthed.

'We can do the practice make-up another day,' I told him. 'It's no big deal.'

'There's plenty of time to discuss all that formal stuff,' Mum said. But then a minute later, she added, 'I'll start cutting out a pattern for your dress. It'll keep me busy while I'm sitting here in the hospital.'

'Mum,' Billy began. There was a whine in his voice that I hadn't heard for a long time. 'I'm a big boy.'

'So what are you saying?'

'When I get a bed up on the ward you don't have to hang around,' Billy told her, pausing between words to catch his breath. 'You're busy, Mum. You've got Catrina's dress to finish, plus the bridesmaids' dresses and her mother's.'

Their bickering was interrupted by a man outside Billy's room, putting on a gown, mask and latex gloves. 'I'm here to take you for a chest X-ray,' he announced, before squeezing his way in.

As he wheeled Billy out the door, my brother wiggled his fingers and winked at me. Latex gloves. Just like the bus driver in New York.

I'd seen a pay phone by the coffee machine in the reception area, so I wandered off to make the dreaded calls to Andrea and Louise.

The mean lady behind the desk had gone and her replacement was a man with the longest permed mullet I'd ever seen. He reminded me of Elizabeth Taylor's boyfriend, Larry. Andrea had shoved so many photos of him in my face, saying things like, 'Can you believe Liz is going out with a builder?' and, 'She deserves so much better!' Andrea didn't seem to get that I really didn't care. Yet here I was, on a Saturday morning waiting with my brother for a bed in the AIDS ward, thinking about Larry, Elizabeth's Taylor's boyfriend.

Perhaps everyone waiting around in hospital could do with a Rubik's Cube? The seats in the waiting area were filled, plus there were people standing, and I wondered what random thoughts they were all having. Maybe that's what you did when you hung around hospitals. Thought of the strangest things. Anything to stop you from thinking about what was really going on.

A pregnant woman, who looked as though she could give birth at any second, was using the phone. I stood there, but not too close, because I didn't want to seem like I was hassling her. I was sure her phone call was more urgent than mine.

Finally, when the phone was free, I dropped the twenty cents into the coin slot, took a deep breath and began to dial Andrea's phone number. But suddenly I changed my mind and hit 2127 instead, the last four digits of Louise's.

Maybe I'd been having random thoughts about Elizabeth Taylor's boyfriend, but obviously my brain hadn't wandered that far. It knew what I couldn't handle today: Andrea's mother, Deidre, answering the phone.

'Hello? Louise speaking.'

'Hi.'

'Is that you, Gemma?'

'Yep.'

'What's all that noise in the background?'

'I'm at the hospital with . . . Mum and Billy.' I gulped because I nearly hadn't made it to the end of that sentence. 'Billy's sick. Pneumonia.'

'No,' Louise uttered. 'Are you okay?'

'Uh-huh.' I nodded, even though Louise couldn't see me. 'But obviously this afternoon is—'

'Don't worry about that!' Louise answered. 'Don't be silly. Is Billy all right?'

I wasn't ready to say the 'AIDS' word. 'He's going to have to stay in hospital for a few days. But he's so much better than he was this morning and the doctor said they caught it early. The pneumonia, I mean.'

'That's good.' Louise sighed. 'So you're not coming out tonight?'

'No.'

'Did Andrea say—'

'I couldn't get through,' I lied. 'Can you call her for me?'

'Sure.'

'And Louise – don't make it sound like Billy's really . . .'

'It's okay, Gemma,' Louise said. 'I think I'm getting a handle on Andrea. Leave it to me.'

'Thanks.' One word and it was stuffed full and over-flowing.

Finally at about 6 p.m. Billy was transferred up to the AIDS ward on Level 9. It sounded shallow, especially under the circumstances, but my biggest concern when we walked into 9 South West was what I was wearing.

Mr and Mrs C had come back with some clothes for me. Who knows where Mrs C found it, but she'd brought in a crocheted apricot jumper with a white lace collar that I hadn't worn since Year 8. Even then I'd hated it. I almost would've preferred to still be in my pyjamas. At least I knew there was no chance of running into Ralph here.

I was occupied with feeling self-conscious when I followed Mum into the four-bed room that was to be my brother's home for the next while, and I wasn't prepared.

The man in the bed next to Billy had shrunk so much it was hard to spot him among the pillows piled up around him.

'Hello, girl,' he whispered. 'I'm Vincent.'

He held out a hand. Pale, almost see-through, fingers long and thin. I had another one of those random thoughts: Hansel and Gretel sticking a chicken bone out of the cage instead of their fingers so that the witch would think they still weren't fat enough to eat.

I must've been staring because he said it again, 'Hello, girl,' and stretched his hand out further towards me.

'Oh, hello.' His fingers were cold to touch. 'I'm Gemma.'

'Don't worry about him.' Now the patient across the room was speaking. 'He doesn't know who he is. He's Vincent today. Yesterday he was Randolph.'

'Oh?'

Vincent, or whatever his name was, was smiling at me as though he hadn't heard a thing that the other man had just said about him. Above his bed I discovered his true identity: *Maurice Goldsworthy*.

I went up to Mum and put my arms around her because I needed to feel her close to me. She kissed me on the head. 'You okay?' she whispered. 'We'll wait till Billy's settled, then we'll go home. It's been a long day.'

I nodded. I was trying to be Polly Positive but Maurice Goldsworthy was freaking me out. His hands were out in front of him, his fingers climbing the air like he was playing 'Incy Wincy Spider'.

'Is this your first time at 9 South West?' the man across the room asked.

'Yes,' Mum answered. She had to duck her head to see him because he was hidden behind vases of flowers. 'I'm Maryanne and this is Gemma. My son Billy's behind the curtains.'

'They're good up here. Your boy's in good hands,' he told us. 'I'm Brian, by the way. I'm a haemophiliac.' He pointed to the neat bed next to him that looked as though it hadn't even been slept in. 'That's Zane's. He's probably in the TV room watching *MacGyver*.'

'Have you been here long?' Mum asked Brian.

'This admission about two weeks. My last time was about six weeks.'

'Really?'

'It's my eighth time in 9 South West,' he told us. 'I'm running out of lives.'

The curtain around Billy's bed opened and I tried to paste Polly Positive's face over the top of however I was looking now, which after hearing that, wasn't positive at all.

Two nurses were on either side of Billy's bed. One fiddled with a tap on the wall that must've delivered the oxygen, while the other was wrapping a bandage around the drip in his arm. I noticed this guy wasn't wearing gloves.

'I'll make you up some mouthwash,' said the nurse, whose nametag read *Anna*. 'You have to be vigilant about using it or you'll end up only being able to eat mush.'

'My mouth has been a bit sore.'

'The thrush will get worse if you're not on to it, Bill.'

Thrush? I'd had that before but not in my mouth. For

a second, I was scared I'd spoken that thought out loud because the nurse looked at me and said, 'Thrush, or candida, is a really common symptom of AIDS. It starts in the mouth but if you don't get on top of it it'll spread all the way down to the gut.'

I nodded like a stunned mute. I was done talking for the day.

On the way home in the taxi, Mum described what my face looked like when Mrs C took the apricot jumper with the lace collar out of the bag. 'I have never seen you pull that expression before.' Mum could barely get the words out, she was giggling so much. 'It was priceless.'

'I know.' Now I was laughing too. 'I nearly died when I saw it.'

Soon Mum and I were sliding across the back seat of the cab, squealing and shrieking like it was the funniest thing that had ever happened. But in less than a minute, the laughter had disappeared and Mum and I were clinging on to each other, crying.

The driver probably thought we'd gone mad. And in a way we had.

15

THE NEXT DAY I WAS BACK AT THE HOSPITAL
wearing my 501s, Docs and a big, baggy grey jumper that
used to be Billy's.

The atmosphere felt completely different to yesterday.
Maybe because it was a Sunday, and families were visiting.

The blinds were up and the view from the ninth floor
was incredible. You could see all the way across the suburbs,
over the red roofs and dotted swimming pools, to the sea
that looked like a band of blue at the edge of the world.

The biggest difference of all was that Billy was much,
much better. He still wore the oxygen mask but yesterday
his lips were a dusky mauve and today they were back to
normal. He could talk, too, without panting and coughing.
He gave us a little run-down of the other patients in
the room.

Brian was thirty-one and married with two kids, who
were sitting on his bed playing with Lego while he and his
wife stood by the window, their arms linked around each
other's. He was a haemophiliac and had contracted HIV
through a blood transfusion.

Maurice was forty-two and an art dealer, but today he
thought he was Greg. He had some disease in his brain

that before AIDS came along had only been seen in cats; I didn't understand what Billy meant. Whatever the disease was, it was obviously bad, because Maurice seemed to have shrunken into the pillows a little further than yesterday. I felt mean but I'd turned my chair away so I didn't have to look at him.

Zane didn't look sick! He was about the hottest guy I'd ever seen. Not that he was interested in me. Andrea would probably say he was a bit too 'Ken doll' with his chiselled jaw and perfect teeth. Maybe when he was just lying there he did look a bit plastic, but he had a killer cheeky grin that'd make any girl wish he batted for our team.

According to Billy, Zane was twenty-one and from a place called Garrandai, nine hours' drive west of here. I wondered how often his parents visited him.

Mum was off chatting to the nurses. She'd made a list of things she wanted to ask them about, like could she bring dinner in for Billy and did she need to do anything special when she washed his clothes?

Billy lifted the mask off his face and smiled. 'You still wear that old jumper of mine?'

'It's so soft. I love it.'

'Were the girls okay about having to cancel yesterday?' Billy asked.

I nodded and stretched my feet up onto the end of Billy's bed.

'What did Andrea say?'

'Nothing,' I replied.

Billy leaned in closer to me. 'You didn't tell her. Did you, Gem?'

'Tell her what?'

'That I'm sick. That I have AIDS.'

I shrugged because I didn't even know how to start talking about this.

'Don't chuck away a good friendship over it. Some people just can't handle it. They're scared.'

'I told her you're HIV-positive,' I began. 'She was . . . sort of okay about it. A bit shocked at first. But she's still excited about you doing her hair. She's always crapping on about it. It's not so much Andrea that I'm—'

'Her mother? Is that who you're worried about?' Billy asked, lying back into the pillows. 'She's an old homophobe from way back. We've always known that.'

'Still, it makes it awkward for me to talk to Andrea about it properly.' It felt as though my lips had gone to sleep and I couldn't wake them up. 'I don't know if she's told her mum. If she did, I don't think her mum would let you do her hair and make-up.'

'Probably not.'

'Doesn't that make you mad?'

'I'm used to it. My expectations are different now.'

'That sucks.'

'When the lesions started appearing on Saul's face, he was advised by his firm that it was best not to see clients anymore.' Billy almost snarled the words. 'He could still do the work, but not attend meetings. Save their clients and save Saul from suing them. The firm had a bet each way.'

I didn't understand completely what Billy was saying, but I got the gist.

'Do you think about Saul a lot?'

'All day, every day.'

Mum had made me bring homework to the hospital because we were camping out with Billy for the day and probably well into the night too. But every time I opened a book and started reading I'd get heavy eyelids. I longed to curl up on the floor and have a snooze. But the carpet looked dodgy with all types of weird stains and I wondered what disease I could catch from lying on it.

'I can't stay awake,' I told Mum and Billy, who were both engrossed in their own magazines and hadn't said one word for about half an hour. 'I think I'll go for a walk.'

I was dying to call Louise to see if she and Andrea had ended up going to see Albatross. I didn't have a life so I may as well hear about someone who did.

Louise's little brother, Nathan, answered the phone. He was a prize pain in the bum. One of those smarty-pants who pretty much interviewed you before handing the phone over to Louise.

I could still hear him in the background when Louise finally got on the phone. Then I heard a yelp and his voice disappeared.

'Sorry about that,' Louise apologised. 'He's killing me.' Then she whispered, 'I've got a thumper of a headache.'

'So you did go out last night?'

'Yeah. Wish you could've come, Gemma.'

'Who was there?'

'You mean, was Ralph there?' Before I had fully registered the comment, Louise added, 'Andrea told me. I had no idea you liked him.'

'Used to like him,' I corrected. 'Not anymore.'

'Ralph asked where you were. Like he didn't go, "Hi, Louise, how are you? Are you having a good night?" He just came straight out and asked, "Is Gemma here?"'

Something went *pop* in my chest. A little ball of hope? Or was it a little ball of fear, anticipating the answer to my next question?

'Where did you say I was?' I asked.

'Andrea did the talking,' Louise said. 'God, she's bossy!'

'What did she say?'

'She said you were dealing with family issues.'

So maybe that's why on Monday morning, on my way to Nigel, the lime mobile appeared from around a corner and stopped right next to me.

But this time Vanessa was in the car, so I couldn't just give Ralph the finger and walk off. Instead I stood there waiting, feeling like an idiot loser while Vanessa took forever to wind down the window.

The only thing on my side was that I'd washed my hair and it was still out. Not tied back like we had to have it for school. I liked my hair. It wouldn't win me the role in the Pantene ad like Vanessa, but my hair and legs were definitely my best features.

'Hi,' Vanessa said. 'Jump in. We'll give you a lift to school.'

I'd been warned about stranger danger but what about jerk danger? Still, I opened the door and climbed into the back seat, thinking the whole time, *Why am I doing this?*

In the rear-view mirror, Ralph gave me a smile that was more like a stretch of his lips. So I did the same back.

'Vanessa's had me driving around looking for you,' he grumbled.

'No, I haven't!' Vanessa answered. Then she turned around to face me and mouthed, 'He's in a bad mood.'

I smiled. A real one, this time.

'I don't want to sound like I'm interfering, but is Billy okay?' asked Vanessa. 'Andrea told Ralph that something had happened and I just wondered if it was maybe about Billy?' Vanessa looked genuinely worried. 'And I thought it was better to ask you before we got to school.'

'He had to go to hospital,' I said. Vanessa's hand slapped itself over her mouth. I didn't want to make it into a big deal so I carefully chose my next words. 'He has pneumonia. But he's fine. They caught it early.'

I had spied Ralph glancing at me in the mirror. But this time our eyes locked together. I'm not certain who looked away first. What I was certain about was that it was awkward.

'Which hospital?' she asked.

'King George's,' I answered.

'Oh, okay,' she replied. 'I know where that is. Ralph works around the corner. At Hot Spot Records. Is Billy allowed visitors?'

'No,' I said, a little bit too quickly. I actually didn't know the answer. But what I did know was that the last thing I needed was Vanessa and her twin brother rocking into the AIDS ward at King George's.

'Are you all right, Gemma?' Vanessa asked. 'If you need anything just say. Ralph and I are happy to help. Aren't we, Ralph?'

Ralph grunted and I badly wanted to tell him that I didn't need his help.

There was a traffic jam outside the school, which was usual for this time of the morning. It was all the spoilt and lazy kids being dropped off.

The three of us watched Sonia Darue spring out the

door of her father's gold Volvo like the homecoming queen she thought she was.

Ralph groaned and said, 'Hurry up, sweet sixteen, you're holding up the traffic.'

I pretended to chew my nails because I could feel a grin wanting to escape. But I wasn't prepared to give Ralph the pleasure of thinking he'd amused me. It was bad enough him thinking that I needed his help.

Sonia was bent over the boot, taking out a tennis racquet and a cello. She closed the boot, tapped the roof of the car three times and her dad drove away with a toot of the horn.

Now Ralph's face was buried over the steering wheel. 'She is the world's biggest loser.'

'Don't you reckon she'll be married with two kids by the time she's twenty-one?' added Vanessa.

'To Martin Searles. I bet you *five dollars*.' Ralph said those last words loud and clear.

I kept my head turned towards the window, telling myself not to move or speak.

The minute the car was parked, Vanessa was taking off her seatbelt and jumping out. 'I have to see my English teacher before class,' she was saying at a rate of a thousand words a minute. '*Pride and Prejudice*. But hey, I should be asking for your help, Gemma. Ralph said you got the top mark for the essay last year.' And she was off, her long, skinny legs flying behind her.

'I know Vanessa's told you to be nice to me,' I said as I got out of the car. 'But I'm fine.' Then I forced myself to add, 'Thanks for the lift,' because even though I told myself I didn't like Ralph anymore, I still didn't want him to think I was a brat.

After school, Aunty Penny drove me to the hospital. On the way we picked up honey king prawns and chicken chow mein from the Chinese restaurant across the road from King George's.

Aunty Penny and I waited in a little annexed corner for our takeaway.

'Your nails match the carpet,' I said, pointing at Penny's long purple claws. 'They fakes?'

'What do you reckon?' she answered. 'Have you ever seen a nurse with long nails?'

'Are you sad you had to cut your holiday short? I know Mum feels bad about it.'

'I'm sad. My liver's not.' Aunty Penny wrapped her arm around me. 'I'm glad your mum called me. You have to promise that if Billy is rushed off to hospital again and I'm in another exotic location, you will contact me. Promise?'

'I don't think that's likely.'

'What? Me being in an exotic location or Billy going to hospital?'

But before I had a chance to answer, Aunty Penny was squeezing my shoulder and saying, 'Billy will go to hospital again, Gem. He'll get infections and they'll need to be treated. We just have to be calm and logical about it.'

'Order for Penny,' said the man behind the counter, stuffing a bag of prawn crackers in among the plastic containers.

'So much for Billy eating healthy, pesticide-free food,' I said to Penny as we walked out. 'I've never seen him say no to a prawn cracker, so if he eats them, he's ready to come home.'

'The drugs are making him hungry,' Penny explained. 'It's good if he can eat because Bill has been on the thin side.'

The first thing I saw when we walked into Billy's room was that Maurice's bed was freshly made. Empty. There was no longer a sign above it that read *Maurice Goldsworthy*.

'Where's . . .?'

'They've moved him to a single room,' Billy explained. 'He's unconscious. All his family's here with him.'

I felt my expression crash, my smile sideswiped off my face. I'd walked in genuinely feeling like Polly Positive and not her impostor.

Billy patted the bed. I sat on the edge and Billy put his hand on top of mine. 'You okay?' he asked softly. His cherry-scented breath from the thrush medicine made me feel sick and it had left a yellow stripe along his tongue.

'Penny's just heating up your dinner,' I mumbled.

'That's not answering my question, Gem.'

'I'm okay.' Then I whispered, 'Is Maurice going to die? Is that why they've moved him to a room on his own?'

'Yes.'

'Does he have a boyfriend? Or a partner or whatever you say.'

'No. But there are lots of people with him. People who really love him. So he'll be okay.'

I'd only met Maurice two days earlier but I wanted to cry. I wanted to cry because this whole AIDS thing was unfair. It sucked. That frail, little man who had lain in the bed next to my brother was about to die. He was about to find out if there really were tunnels filled with light and people that you used to know standing there, waiting for you.

The whole thing didn't make sense. How could you be here one second and then just gone the next? Gone and never coming back. Who wrote that rule?

The smell of honey prawns wafted down the corridor. It didn't mix well with Billy's cherry breath and the bleach that must've been used to mop around Maurice's bed and the antiseptic pong that seemed to sweat from the hospital walls. Now I really did want to spew.

'Dinner's served,' Aunty Penny sang, carrying in a tray.

'I'm starving,' Billy said. 'What's wrong with me?'

'It's the Prednisone.'

'I tell you what, it's powerful stuff,' Billy replied. 'I'm buzzing. I barely slept last night.'

'That's the trade-off.'

'I'll take it, Penny. I've got this new burst of energy.'

'This is probably a dumb question seeing that you're eating Chinese. But how's the thrush?'

'Not bad,' Billy said through a mouthful. 'My throat was feeling a bit scratchy but it's settled.'

I listened to this half-adult, half-medical conversation that Billy and my aunt were locked in. There was no place for me, so I wandered out to find Mum.

At the nurses station, the ward clerk was rubbing the name 'Maurice Goldsworthy' off the patient board. She smiled and said hello to me as I passed.

There was a small crowd of people outside one of the single rooms. There, standing among them all, was my mother. She was deep in conversation with a woman in a bright red jacket. They were holding hands and nodding their heads. Whatever they were talking about, they agreed.

Mum saw me coming towards her. She broke away from

the woman in the red jacket, greeting me with open arms like a long-lost friend. The whole thing was weirding me out. Who were these people that my mother knew so well, but I didn't recognise?

'Maurice just died,' Mum told me gently. She pointed to the woman she'd been with. 'That's his mother, Eileen.'

What was this? Maurice had just died. His name had already been wiped off the patient board as though he never existed, and now it seemed like a party was starting around me. Everyone was hugging each other and saying the same thing over and over. 'I haven't seen you for so long!' But someone had actually died. Someone called Maurice Goldsworthy. Someone who'd been alive five minutes ago.

'I'm going to make myself a cup of tea,' Mum said. 'Do you want one?'

'No.'

I broke out of my mother's hold and walked away. The air around me suddenly seemed thin. I needed to find somewhere new, somewhere the air was thick and pumping. Someplace where the living breathed.

Zane and the TV room was as close as I could find to that.

He waved at me, so I went in and sat down on the couch next to him. Zane was watching the TV series *Twin Peaks*.

'Has Maurice . . .?' He didn't say the last word.

I nodded.

'Poor old bugger.' Then he said, 'Fun up here, isn't it?'

'It's okay.'

'Nah, it's not. It sucks.'

'Yeah. It sucks.'

'That's why I hang around in here and watch TV all day.'

Zane stretched his legs out onto the coffee table. His feet were sun-tanned and he had perfect toes. Not like my brother's, whose second toe was longer and wedged itself against the big one, as though it was too scared to be on its own.

'Do you miss home?' I asked him.

'Parts of it.'

'Like what?'

'The sky. I miss the big sky. That's the best thing about home.'

'What about your family?'

He shrugged and I thought I saw his Adam's apple bulge in his throat.

So quickly I changed the topic. 'What's the name of the girl in this show who's been murdered?'

'Laura Palmer.'

'That's right.' I already knew that. But it was the first thing that popped into my head to change the conversation.

'What's that smell?' Zane asked.

'Probably the Chinese we brought in for Billy. He was craving it.'

'I've been craving a cheeseburger something bad.'

'I love cheeseburgers,' I said. 'Especially the gherkins.'

'With extra gherkins,' Zane grinned. 'Don't you reckon life's better with extra gherkins?'

'Totally. I don't understand people who don't like gherkins.'

'It's not a cheeseburger if it doesn't have gherkins,' Zane agreed. 'And it has to be from Maccas. Back home I'd drive two hours just to eat one.'

'That's dedicated.'

'That's how much I love 'em.'

'Have you had a cheeseburger while you've been in here?'

'Only been feeling like one these past couple of days. Before, I couldn't have stomached one.'

'You should have one.'

'Gemma, where am I going to find a Maccas cheeseburger in King George's?'

'Why don't you get one of your friends to bring one in?'

'I don't reckon they'd drive 937 kilometres to bring me a cheeseburger,' he chuckled. 'They're good mates but not that good.'

I vowed to myself that the next time I visited I would bring Zane a cheeseburger with extra gherkins.

***

The next morning the lime mobile didn't appear from around a corner. It was parked outside my place and sitting in the driver's seat, all alone, was Ralph.

My first thought was: *Do I pretend I haven't seen him? Do I just keep walking and see what he does?* But Ralph was out of the car, the top half of him leaning over the roof and waving me down with both arms.

Don't laugh, I ordered myself, because he looked pretty funny.

'Do you want a lift?' he called.

'What are you doing here?' I answered with a question because I was terrified that a simple yes or no would be the end of the conversation.

Ralph opened the passenger door. This morning his hair was damp and when I got up closer I could smell apple shampoo. His fingers raked the wet strands off his face and close up I could see how beautiful he was.

'Please?' he murmured. 'Can you get in, Gemma? I'm starting to feel like a stalker.'

I didn't answer.

'And I'm not just being nice to you because Vanessa told me to.'

I climbed into the front seat and waited for him to close the door. If I closed the door, it'd feel like I was jumping at his offer and although I wasn't altogether devastated that he was waiting outside my place, I didn't want to seem overenthusiastic or desperate.

Ralph didn't start the ignition. We didn't drive away. Instead, we sat there like we were boyfriend and girlfriend about to break up. But the problem was we weren't. We were Ralph and Gemma who'd had one proper conversation in our lives and even that hadn't gone well.

But I would be lying through my teeth if I said that there wasn't some feeling in the car that morning. I just wasn't sure what the feeling was. I couldn't name it. However, I could say that, for me, it was suddenly like I'd known Ralph all my life. Like we were that couple who'd just had a fight and were now sitting in the broody air.

How could something feel so comfortable yet so uncomfortable at the same time? Ralph must've felt something too because why else was he here? Why did he keep turning up in his car? *Stop thinking*, I told myself, terrified that I might have a Tourette's outbreak and accidently say it all out loud.

'I'm sorry about what happened last week,' Ralph started. 'I feel like what I said came out all wrong.'

'It was pretty harsh,' I answered.

'Yeah. I get that it could've sounded like that.'

'Could've?'

'I mean, *did* sound like that,' he admitted. 'I'm sorry.'

'Thanks.'

'Are you okay?'

'Am I okay about what exactly?'

'About your brother being . . .' he hesitated, 'being sick.'

'Having AIDS, you mean?' Now I was being harsh. 'It feels like shit. It feels like everything's different. Like my whole world's changed in a month. It didn't even feel like this when my dad left. When he left everything was better at home. There's no bonus with this one. Just a whole lot of nasty surprises waiting behind the couch.' I stopped because I was aware of the sensation of hot, stinging salt at the back of my eyes. I was also aware that this was the most I'd said to anybody about how I felt.

'I'm really sorry,' Ralph said.

'It's not your fault.' I tried to smile but it came out lopsided. 'We should probably get to school. Don't you think?'

'Probably.' He started the engine. We drove away, and the awkward silence returned.

After school, Mr C drove me to the hospital. Mr C never actually came in to visit. 'No parks' is what he'd say, even though there was a huge car park. He was probably scared of walking into a ward filled with the 'pooftas'.

It took a long time and a lot more patience to explain that we needed to stop at Maccas on the way because I had to buy a cheeseburger with extra gherkins.

'Two old beef batty, special saucer, lattice, cheese on a same seed bun,' Mr C recited the TV ad, finishing with a big, proud grin. 'I know all the menu. You want to eat inside or taking away, Gemma?'

'No, it's not for me,' I told him for the hundred-thousandth time. 'It's for another patient in Billy's room.'

Mr C was nodding now. It was the next part that was going to really challenge us.

'There's a Maccas near the hospital with a drive-through.' I saw Mr C frown and close one eye the way he did when something was totally lost in translation. 'So let's just order there. Save us from going in.' I was speaking extra slow and clear. 'That means we don't need to stop and park.'

'I see,' he answered.

But he didn't. Mr C completely missed my directions at the Maccas drive-through. He had absolutely no idea what he was doing. He drove straight past the speaker, then slammed on the brakes when I yelled, '*Stop*,' giving me a slight case of whiplash. But then he couldn't reverse because there was already a car behind us. So I had to lean all the way over Mr C in the driver's seat, getting a full whiff of his BO, and shout the cheeseburger order through the window while trying to be heard over the radio from the car behind that was blasting out Men at Work.

By the time Mr C dropped me off outside the hospital with Zane's cheeseburger in my bag, I was stressed out, had a stiff neck and my throat was hoarse from shouting.

I already knew what I was going to say to Zane. I turned the corner into the room, already starting to laugh at my own joke: 'Extra, extra . . .'

But Zane's bed was empty. Stripped bare, his name wiped, bleach still lingering in the air.

I gasped, dropping the cheeseburger onto the floor and bursting into tears.

Mum jumped up from the chair beside Billy's bed and came running to me. 'Gemma! What is it? What is it?'

I couldn't get the words out. I was doubled over, my hands clutching the end of Zane's bed, the extra gherkins staring up at me from the carpet.

Now Billy was up too. Mum and he each held an arm, steering me towards the closest chair. 'Zane?' I finally spluttered. 'Where's Zane?'

Zane had been discharged. He was better. He'd left the ward at 2.30 p.m., telling Billy and Mum to say goodbye to me.

16

18 weeks to formal

THE WEEK'S CRAZINESS DIDN'T STOP THERE.
If anything it had found momentum and was ploughing
headfirst through the freak show that had become our life.

After six years of barely mentioning his name, except to
say something mean, we were suddenly talking about my
father like he was a real person who we cared about.

It was Billy's second weekend in hospital. Another one
of me doing nothing except flicking through magazines
and wandering up and down the corridor. We were seated
in the positions we had adopted from day one in 9 South
West. Mum in the big comfy chair closest to Billy, Aunty
Penny perched on the end of the bed and me in the smaller
chair down by Billy's feet.

Mum had brought up the topic of Dad. It was obvious
that she and Billy had already discussed the situation
because they were speaking in their *we're so calm and
grown-up about everything* voices. It was probably their
plan. I could imagine them conspiring. Mum saying,
*We'll bring up contacting your father and you make out like
it's a good idea because that'll stop your sister from going
berserk.*

Well, it didn't.

'He doesn't deserve to be told,' I growled. 'Why would you be so stupid as to think he'd even care? What's changed? Why would you even think about telling him, Mum? He stopped writing to Billy ages ago. He doesn't even ask about him!'

'He's still your father,' Aunty Penny said. Of course she was neck high in the conspiracy too. 'I think that's a good enough reason, Gem.'

'But he's never given a shit before, so why would he now?'

'Please don't swear, Gemma.' Mum sighed. 'Can't we discuss this like adults?'

I looked at Billy because he'd suddenly turned annoyingly quiet.

'What do you think?' I asked him. Billy gave a lame shrug and began to pick at his nails.

'Well, do you think Dad'd really care?' I pushed. 'I mean it's not like he'd drop everything and come running to see you.' Again there was no comment. No comment from anyone. So I dropped the 'A' bomb. 'Do you reckon he'd really want to know that his son has AIDS?'

'Gemma!' Mum barked.

But my eyes were locked on Billy. Billy and I had never stopped talking about Dad. Yet our conversations were never about how we longed to see him or wondered what he was doing or if he thought of us.

'It's just an idea,' Billy finally said to me. 'We weren't talking about calling him tomorrow.'

'When then?' I spat.

'When we need to,' Billy answered.

'This sucks!' I hissed and I took myself off to the TV room.

Billy was discharged the next week on Tuesday afternoon. I knew he was coming home but Andrea, Louise and I had already arranged to have a coffee after school to discuss the project we were doing on the American Civil War.

It'd been raining since lunchtime. Sheets of water poured from the sky, filling the gutters and sweeping the footpaths. Part of me wondered if I should cancel because maybe Mum and Billy would get caught in the rain and need my help. The other part of me didn't want to think about them. Mr and Mrs C were home if they got desperate and I was sick of not having any time for me. With Andrea and Louise I could at least pretend that I was a normal girl with a normal life, just like they were.

'I shouldn't be eating this croissant,' Louise said, loading up a knife with butter.

'Who cares?' I answered. We all had five dollars so each of us could afford a hot chocolate and a croissant. The flaky pastry melted on my tongue and my spoon had just found the marshmallow at the bottom of the mug. Even the cafe's red-and-white checked tablecloths weren't annoying me today.

'The dressmaker who's sewing my formal dress,' Louise replied. 'I met her on the weekend and she kept saying how you had to have a good figure to wear a dress like the one I want.'

'That's a bit rude,' I said. 'My mum would never say that to one of her brides.'

'The formal isn't for ages,' Andrea told us. 'Go on a diet the week before.'

'You can talk, Andrea,' I said. 'You've been doing sit-ups since the start of the year!'

'Oh, remember you said I could borrow your Jane Fonda aerobics videos?' Louise said to Andrea. 'The one we were doing last Saturday.'

'Mum's pinched it. I have another one though.'

'Cool.'

I listened as Louise and Andrea went back and forth with, 'I'll bring your skirt back tomorrow,' and, 'Do you have my Revlon lippie?' feeling like the third wheel, gate-crashing on a friendship that I no longer had a part in. So when Louise asked if we were still having a meeting with Billy I suddenly felt energised and excited, like I finally had a role in the play.

'I can organise it anytime,' I told the girls. 'Billy's feeling so well. He's put on weight and he's going to start swimming again. He's even lined up some jobs for the next few weeks.'

'How about this weekend?' Louise suggested.

'I don't think I can this weekend,' Andrea replied. 'Maybe another time.'

'The weekend after?' Louise asked.

'Hmm . . .' When I heard Andrea make that noise I sat up to attention. 'I don't think I can for the next few weekends.'

'This weekend or next weekend is good, Louise,' I suddenly announced. I wasn't sure what I could hear inside that *hmm*, yet it made me want to slap Andrea all over again. 'In fact they might be the only times Billy can do it for a while,' I lied. 'Like I said, he's taken on some big jobs.'

I glanced at Andrea, but her face was buried in her mug

of hot chocolate. So I made arrangements with Louise for the weekend after next.

At home things almost went back to normal, the three of us resuming where we'd left off before Billy went to hospital. Before Billy's disease was called AIDS. Fighting over the bathroom, telling stories about our day at dinner-time, then lounging around on the couch as we watched TV and ate chocolate chip ice-cream.

Even being shut out of Mum's room didn't annoy me because that was the biggest sign that life was back to normal. Hearing Mum and my brother's laughter bellowing out from under the door actually made me smile.

Billy started swimming every morning up at the local pool. Some days, he'd leave the same time as me. I'd turn left towards Nigel and he'd go straight ahead. Tuesday nights he had acupuncture and brought home takeaway. If it wasn't for clinic day each Friday, you probably wouldn't even know that my brother was sick.

The lime mobile had stopped stalking me and Ralph and I were back to avoiding each other in the corridor. Andrea, Louise and I had resumed navigating the big stuff in life. Such as, were three holes in the ear too many? Or simply way cooler than two? And was Justin ignoring us? Or had he really become a major swot who never came up for air?

Perhaps life with a brother with AIDS could be normal?

※

On Saturday morning, I put on my new black-and-white checked coat that Saul had sent me at the start of the year for no reason other than I was his 'favourite gal'. That's what the card had said. But now I knew there had been a lot more to it.

It had a silk lining the colour of mulberries and a wide collar that I could button up at the neck if it was freezing. The coat had been sitting in my cupboard waiting patiently for winter. The problem was that it hadn't actually been that cold yet, even though it was the last weekend in June.

I fastened the buttons and tied the belt around the waist, then sashayed my way down the hall and into the kitchen. Billy whistled. 'Look at you.'

I spun around, doing my best Naomi Campbell poses.

'I think it's the nicest thing I've ever owned,' I told Billy.

'It's pretty special.' Billy smiled in a sad way that I was starting to realise meant a Saul story was coming. It didn't matter how much life felt like it was getting back on track, the constant reminders would never stop. 'Saul saw the coat in the window of Saks Fifth Avenue on his way home from work. By the time he walked in the door at our place he was so excited.' Billy's smile became even sadder. 'He couldn't wait to post it off to you.'

'I love it so, so much,' I said, spinning around again. Today I didn't want to be sad. I had a whole weekend with no trips to the hospital, and Louise was coming over to meet my brother and then we were going to see *Pretty Woman*.

I picked up my purse from the kitchen table. 'Are you going out?' Billy asked.

'Just to the shops,' I answered. 'I thought I'd buy something yummy for afternoon tea.'

'Won't you be a bit hot in the coat?'

'Who cares,' I answered. 'I'm going to stroll up to the shops like I'm off to buy pastries in Paris.'

Billy was laughing now. 'Off you go then.'

'Toodles.' I waved to him from the door. 'Oh, and don't forget to wake Mum by eleven.'

The last of the autumn leaves were scattered across the footpaths. Mounds of yellow and brown that crunched under my feet as I walked through them. I loved that sound. I stamped and shuffled my way through every pile I could find.

Seasons and memories. We'd talked about this in English last week. What triggered us to remember these things – a smell, a sound. Of course one of the prissy girls shot up her hand and said, 'Summer and coconut oil,' at which all the other prissies had started giggling. One of the guys blitzed three senses in one: feeling the cold winter air, eating meat pies and hearing the whistle blow in the footy season. Lots of the other blokes nodded and grunted at this.

I didn't want to share mine even though I could squeeze in a sound, touch, sight and taste. Walking to kindy with Dad. The touch of his hand tightly holding mine. Watching my yellow gumboots as I jumped in puddles. That was another sound I loved. The splash when my boots landed. Sometimes if I jumped extra hard and the puddles were deep, the water flew so high that I could catch the droplets on my tongue.

The kids in class knew my dad had left. But that wasn't the reason I didn't want to tell them. I didn't care about their sad faces looking at me and thinking, *Poor you, you must really miss him*. It wasn't that at all. It was much simpler. I didn't want to think about my father. Let alone talk about him.

The topic of whether Dad should be told that Billy had AIDS was still coming up in our dinnertime conversation.

Often I would find myself staring at Billy, wondering if we were all actually talking about the same man. Perhaps some of Maurice's cat disease had crawled its way into my brother's brain? Telling Dad would be a disaster. It wasn't something I sensed, it was something I knew. A basic fact. Like my name and address and what day of the week it was.

I tightened the belt around my coat as I turned the corner into the street where all the shops were. There was a new bakery owned by a Vietnamese family, also called the Leongs. Andrea said their bread sticks and apple danishes were the best and the line that snaked around the corner proved that others thought so too.

I had just joined the queue when I noticed Andrea's mum's car parked across the road, outside the beauty salon. I scanned the line to see if Andrea was waiting here for a bread stick, but no luck. Deidre was probably getting her hair done. Billy always joked that she changed her hairstyle more often than her undies.

Could Andrea be at the hairdresser getting a third ear piercing? She'd been talking about it all week, telling me that three little studs up the ear were quite elegant. She'd even asked if she could borrow the sapphire studs that Saul had given me, to which I answered a flat-out, 'No way, José!' Was she punishing me? Was that why she couldn't come over this afternoon?

I ditched my place in the bakery queue and made a beeline straight for the salon. I was right. Through the window I could see Andrea sitting in a chair facing the mirror. Deidre and another woman were standing behind her, holding her hair up off her shoulders. They were talking and they kept pointing at something on Andrea's lap.

I crept up to the door, waiting for the right moment to burst in and surprise Andrea. But the woman suddenly pushed Andrea's chair so that it swivelled to face me. I ducked, just in time, then slid back up the window to get a better view.

On Andrea's lap lay a book, opened at the middle. I could see Elizabeth Taylor with her hair up in a French roll. The exact hairstyle she'd wanted to workshop with Billy.

Panic seized me, squeezing my heart into my mouth. I made a sound I had never made before. A gasp, a cry, a bleat like a newborn lamb, all rolled into one note.

I started running. Back across the street, cutting through the line outside the bakery. I ran down the middle of the road, dodging and swerving through the Saturday morning traffic, because I didn't want to run through the autumn leaves and hear the crunch under my feet.

I hadn't seen this coming. I hadn't figured out what was really behind Andrea's *hmms*. I hadn't sensed the betrayal lurking around the corner.

By the time I burst through the front door I could barely breathe. I wrestled myself out of the black-and-white checked coat, flinging it across the room so that it knocked the pepper grinder off the kitchen table.

'You back already?' Billy called, wandering into the kitchen, a towel around his waist.

I ducked around the corner and into Mum's workroom, and sat on the floor.

But Billy spotted me. 'You're as red as a beetroot,' he started, '. . . Gemma?'

Billy crouched next to me. His bare arms wrapped around me and I could smell the soap on his skin, feel the droplets from his wet hair dripping onto my face.

'Andrea . . . Andrea and her mother were in the hair-dresser.' I knew how pathetic my words sounded. 'She had that stupid Elizabeth Taylor book with her.'

I didn't have to say anymore. Billy understood. 'Oh dear,' he said, 'it's started.'

'What's started?' Suddenly Mum was standing there, in her nightie, her eye mask hanging around her neck. 'Gemma, what's happened? Billy?'

'I don't think I'll be doing Andrea's hair and make-up anymore,' Billy simply replied.

17

MUM BECAME HOMICIDAL. I HADN'T SEEN
her act like that since she'd ripped the poster off the church
billboard. She wanted to drive to Andrea's place and 'give
it to Deidre'. She told me she'd been holding back all these
years for the sake of my friendship with Andrea. Suddenly
my mother was reciting a list of grievances she had with my
best friend's mother: 'Deidre judged us from the moment
your father left. Deidre always looked at your brother as
though he was dirty, but as soon as his career kicked off she
acted as though we were all best friends. She even had the
hide to ask me one day if I was sad he would never make me
a grandmother! I am not having her in my home ever, ever
again.' If she'd harboured a desire to rip Deidre to shreds,
she'd done a good job of hiding it from me until now.

After we'd had a cup of tea, calmed down and, more
importantly, I was sure Mum wasn't going to burst into
another psycho rant, I phoned Louise. I wanted to suss out
if she knew anything. I think part of me also hoped that
she'd cancel coming over. I would have been quite happy to
lie on the couch and watch television for the rest of the day.

I told Louise what had happened. She listened to
every word, adding the occasional 'oh' and 'shit' and

'really'. She wasn't freaked out by any of it. That's what I was starting to learn about Louise: nothing really seemed to shock her.

Louise had had no idea that Andrea and her mum were going to the hairdresser today. But she did know that Andrea had been getting cold feet.

'She started talking about it when Billy went to hospital,' Louise told me. 'She wanted to ring the AIDS hotline and get some advice.'

'Did she?'

'No! Justin told her she was being ridiculous.'

'Justin was there?'

'It was one lunchtime. I can't remember where you were. But Justin really gave it to her.' Louise let a giggle escape then quickly apologised and went on. 'Justin told Andrea there was no way she could catch AIDS from Billy doing her hair and make-up unless he poured a big bucket of blood all over her.'

'Obviously she didn't listen.'

'She said her grandma was scared about her catching it from the lipstick.'

'How? Billy doesn't put it on his own lips!'

'I know how stupid it sounds,' Louise said. 'Most of it is coming from Andrea's mum.'

'Still,' I hissed, 'she's meant to be my best friend.'

For a while I lay on my bed, thinking how strange it was that at the start of the year I didn't even know Louise. Now she was someone I could ring and talk to about anything. Someone who could make me feel better.

What was wrong with Andrea? Why couldn't she be that person?

But she wasn't and she never had been and it'd never

really bothered me before. Maybe what I was really mad about was that I hadn't sensed it coming. All the signs had been there. Andrea making excuses, the long *hmms* that'd found their way into our conversations. I had known that one day there'd be some kind of outburst from her but I hadn't expected this. I was the wind beneath her wings. Wasn't I?

I'd always imagined me and Andrea getting ready for the formal together. Billy doing the final touches to our hair and make-up in the kitchen, Mum giving us a sneaky glass of champagne before we left. Outside the school hall I'd pictured us winking at each other and saying something cheesy like, *This is our moment.* A third person had never even featured. But now I couldn't imagine the night without Louise in it.

Luckily, Billy's head popped around my bedroom door just as my tragic imaginings of Andrea and me at the formal were making my jaw wobble.

'Is Louise still coming over?' he asked.

I nodded. 'Remember she's got a busted nose. She's pretty self-conscious about it.'

'Powder and shadowing can trick the eye,' he answered. 'I told you I can perform magic.'

I sniggered, thinking about the afternoon with Andrea. 'Andrea and Deidre said you were her magic bullet. They obviously don't think that anymore.'

Billy wiggled his fingers at me.

'What?'

'The gloves,' he replied. 'People are scared, Gem. Did you ever hear about that little girl who wasn't allowed to go to kindy because she was HIV-positive?'

'No. What happened?'

'All the parents became paranoid and didn't want her at the school,' he explained. 'In the end she was allowed to go only if she wore a mask all the time.'

'That's horrible.'

'The family eventually moved away. Don't ruin a friendship over this. The only thing Andrea and Deidre are guilty of is ignorance.'

'I hope the hairdresser is lousy at doing French rolls.'

Billy started laughing. 'Even a good French roll still looks like a piece of dog's poo on your head.'

'Stupid Elizabeth Taylor,' I muttered.

'Come on, Gem. You know Elizabeth Taylor is one of the biggest supporters of AIDS? Probably she and Princess Di are the ones who've helped fight the fear and ignorance the most.'

I spat back, 'Isn't that called *irony*?'

※

Louise came over with a big smile and a sponge cake covered in fresh strawberries and cream. She seemed a bit starstruck when she first met Billy, but after a while she relaxed.

Billy's make-up collection was spread out along one side of the kitchen table and his portfolio laid out on the other. Some of the pages were opened at looks he thought Louise might like: teased hair and skin dusted in bronze powder; a mop of curls with hot pink glossy lips; a sleek ponytail with smoky black eyes. The pictures of slicked hair and red lips weren't on display because that look was reserved for me.

I stood in Mum's workroom as she measured around me, watching Louise through the doorway. She sat at the kitchen table while Billy dabbed cream on her nose and dusted powder across her face.

Louise was holding the picture of my formal dress. 'I love this dress,' she called.

'The fabric should arrive this week,' Mum answered. 'It's the most beautiful, lush, rich black velvet that slips through your fingers.' Billy and I started laughing because Mum always talked about fabric like it was a man she was in love with. 'Plus I'll use some thick gold braid to edge around the bodice.'

'What about jewellery?' Louise asked me. 'Are you wearing earrings or a necklace?'

'I'm not sure. Maybe big gold earrings.'

'Start saving,' Mum the killjoy butted in.

'You're going to look stunning, Gemma,' Louise said.

'So are you,' I replied.

But my comment was met with silence. I was racking my brains, trying to think of something to say, when Billy handed Louise a mirror, saying, 'What do you think?'

Louise didn't move. There wasn't a sound. She sat there, staring at her reflection like she had turned into stone. 'Oh my God,' she finally uttered. 'I . . . Is that really me?'

Mum and I walked into the kitchen so we could see Louise in full view.

Billy had worked his magic. Again.

A tiny teardrop stained with mascara was sliding down Louise's cheek. 'I look like me again.'

On Monday morning I walked to school with Louise and Andrea pretending that I hadn't seen her on Saturday because I'd promised Billy I would. But just to rub another kilo of salt into my wounds I discovered a huge AIDS poster plastered onto the bus stop outside school. *Most parents suffer from AIDS.* What the hell did that mean?

Andrea and Louise didn't seem to notice the poster. Andrea had ended up with a third piercing in her ear and was deep in discussion with Louise about whether it had hurt more or less because the skin was thinner there. At least the school holidays were about to start because I really wanted to shout at them, *There are more important things in the world to think about.*

Most parents suffer from AIDS. All day I tried to figure out what the slogan meant.

I supposed I could say that our family was suffering from AIDS. It was like the boogieman knew where we lived but we didn't know when he was going to turn up on our doorstep. And when he arrived, how did we know if he was going to be in a really bad mood, or just a bit cross like he'd been on the morning Billy went to hospital?

We'd been lucky. I understood that now. Billy's pneumonia had been caught early, the drugs had worked and now he was back home, better than he'd been before he went to hospital. Matt Leong hadn't been so lucky. The boogieman had shown up at his place in a rage. The doctor had probably put him straight into a single room because he knew it'd all be over in a week. Brian had been to hospital eight times but he'd managed to go home eight times. Maybe the boogieman felt sorry for him because he was a haemophiliac and not a poofter or a druggie?

At dinner that night, I asked Mum and Billy what they thought the slogan was about.

Billy said he thought he knew what they were getting at because there'd been a similar campaign in the USA. '*Most parents suffer from AIDS* means that parents suffer from the fear of it and therefore they don't talk about it with their kids like they should.'

'So it's kind of like *Silence equals Death*?' I asked, sucking up the last strand of spaghetti on my plate.

Billy put his fork down. He'd barely touched his bolognaise.

'You okay?' Mum asked.

Billy nodded. I thought he was thinking about my question because he started saying, 'Same sort of message. If you walk down the . . .' but mid-sentence, he jumped out of his chair and ran into the bathroom.

'What's wrong with him?' I asked Mum.

'I think his meds have given him diarrhoea,' she explained. 'He's going to see the GP tomorrow to sort it out because clinic isn't for a few more days.'

'He's hardly touched his dinner.'

'His mouth's getting sore again with that bloody thrush.'

I rinsed and stacked the dishwasher while Mum went back to her sewing. I sang along to Crowded House on the radio and Mum joined in for the bits that she knew.

But in every microsecond of silence, that split second between one song finishing and the next one starting, the groans could be heard coming from the bathroom.

The boogieman was back. In Billy's bowel was a bug with the longest name I'd ever heard: cryptosporidium. Aunty Penny called it 'crypto' for short. Most likely Billy had caught it in the public pool where he was swimming in his quest to be healthy.

Because Billy's immune system was being so wrecked by AIDS, he would catch more and more infections from now on. Crypto was just one of them.

That made me so mad. People like Andrea and her mother and grandma were terrified that Billy was going to make them sick, when in fact it was much more likely that *they* would make *him* sick. I knew that my mother felt the same as me. As our GP explained this to us, I could hear Mum's tongue clicking and see her eyeballs changing into her mad psycho woman ones.

By the second week of holidays, I was back in the lift on my way up to 9 South West. This time, Billy was in a different room with just two beds. In the other bed was Zane.

Zane had just gotten over the crypto bug, but now he had pneumonia and his lung had collapsed. He had a thick tube sticking out of his chest. My eyes followed it all the way down to the floor where the tube was attached to a glass bottle that bubbled when he breathed.

'What's that?' I asked.

'They call it an underwater sealed drain.'

'Wow.'

'Don't knock the bottle over,' Zane told me. 'Otherwise I'm a goner.'

'Seriously?'

He nodded. 'That's what the nurses told me.'

'So you're stuck in bed the whole time?'

'Nah. I can put the bottle in a little trolley and take myself off for a walk.' He winked. 'Want to go down to the TV room? *Police Rescue*'s on soon.'

Zane swung his legs out of the bed and stood up. He had lost a lot of weight. His hospital pyjama pants were so loose he had to hold them up. He reached out to me with his other hand, which had a drip in it.

'Still a bit weak after the crypto,' he said as I took his hand. 'Lost ten kilos in three days. They reckon I was about to go into a single room.' His grip was tight around my fingers and I started wondering if he was meant to be out of bed.

He shuffled a few steps and pointed to the bottle. 'Put it in that trolley over there, Gemma,' he instructed. 'But don't lift the bottle up too high. It has to stay down below the level of my chest or I'm a goner.'

Not the kind of thing I wanted to hear again. Carefully I manoeuvred the bottle into the trolley, checking a few times that it was securely in place and not about to smash on the ground.

I could hear Zane chuckling. 'You look scared shitless, Gemma.'

But what did he expect? I was standing in a tangle of tubes with a glass bottle that if I knocked over Zane would be a goner. I wasn't scared. I was terrified. And I didn't even like *Police Rescue*.

'Now I'll take the pole with my drip and you push the trolley,' Zane was telling me. 'Okay?'

So, the accident waiting to happen – that was Zane and me – started the slow journey down the corridor to the television room.

The TV was already on but it was tuned to *21 Jump Street*, a show that I loved. Probably because the main guy, Tommy, was played by Johnny Depp.

Zane climbed into one of the big, comfy recliners.

He was breathless and I wondered if he needed oxygen, but in a second he was back to bossing me around.

'Park the trolley here,' he said, patting the side of the chair. 'Can you open the blinds too?' he asked, pointing to the windows. 'I hate the way they close everything the minute the sun goes down. It depresses me. I like looking at the lights. Wondering who's out there and what they're doing.'

The view was awesome, even at night. All those lights twinkling and sparkling as though we were looking at some exciting land that we couldn't quite get to, only watch and wonder about. I pressed my nose up against the glass, my breath leaving a circle of condensation. Before I knew what I was doing I realised I'd written the name 'Ralph' into the misty layer. Quickly, I rubbed it out, hoping that Zane hadn't seen. When I turned around he was gazing out the window. Lost in his own thoughts too. I wondered if there was someone he'd left behind at home. Someone 937 kilometres away whom he loved?

'See that light way out there?' Zane pointed. 'That tiny light way out on the horizon?'

'Yes.'

'That's a ship. Way, way out at sea. I wonder where it's going?'

'Probably to some exotic island,' I answered.

'Tahiti sounds nice.'

I laughed.

'You know, I've never been to the beach. Never swum in the sea,' Zane said. 'Swum in rivers and dams. But never the ocean.'

'But, but . . .' I started. 'How can you live here and never have been to the beach?'

'I didn't come down to the city until I was sick,' he answered. 'This is the first time I've left Garrandai. I've never been away from home before.'

I left the sparkling lights and sank into the chair next to Zane's. Why was I shocked? Zane's story was similar to the ones Billy had told me. Guys who couldn't stay in the country because they were gay. Who found that it was only here, in the city, that they could be themselves.

'I don't know if I'll ever go home again,' Zane said.

'Of course you will!'

Zane grinned at me. His teeth were straight and square and fitted his mouth like they'd been made to order. 'I'm not saying I'm going to die,' he explained. 'This bloody AIDS thing isn't going to take me. They reckon there's a new drug around the corner. Just waiting for approval or something.' Zane closed his eyes as though he'd lost his breath. I was about to suggest I get a nurse when he whispered, 'Maybe . . . I mean, I don't know if I can go home.'

This time I know I saw his Adam's apple roll in his throat. But I didn't have a how-to guide for this. I couldn't flick through the index and find the page that would tell me the reply for a line like that. I'd have to muddle my way through.

'Is that because you're queer?' I could ask about this, I told myself. It wasn't off limits. My brother was queer. I knew this story. I'd grown up with it. 'Is that what you mean when you say you can't go home?'

'It'd kill my dad, his only son being a fag. Maybe my mum too,' Zane told me. 'They think I've gone overseas. On a big world trip.'

'What? Zane! What about your friends? Do they know?'

'The only bloke who knows is our family doctor, back home.'

I hadn't even realised but I had dragged my chair closer to Zane's.

'He's pretty much told me to go. Not that I was planning on sticking around.'

'What do you mean? Did he give you a blood test and—?'

'Nah! He wouldn't even put a needle near me 'cause I told him I was a homosexual and that I was sweating at night and feeling crook all the time.' Zane's foot, those perfect toes, were tapping in triple time on the floor. He was shaking his head and bending his fingers back until I thought they were going to snap. But he kept talking and as much as I wanted to block my ears and bury my head in my lap, I knew that I had to listen to Zane's tale. 'You know how hard it was to tell the doctor I was a queer? I'd never told anyone before. Just kept it here.' Zane hit his chest. 'But I got scared because I'd read enough to know I was sick. I thought all doctors take that oath and that means they're meant to care for you and not judge you.'

He looked at me as though he was unsure whether he'd got this right or not. I nodded. Not once but about four times. It didn't matter whether you were here in the city or 937 kilometres away. I agreed. It was a fair thing to think.

'Who I was with . . . well, he was married, but he just disappeared one night. It'd been a bad harvest and everyone thought that's why he up and left. I think the doctor knew something. He said to me, "In some cases it's better to leave and not bring shame upon your family. Maybe folk think it was a bad harvest that drove you away. But maybe it wasn't.

Maybe it was your sins." So I packed up and told everyone I was going to see the world.'

'That's terrible! That doctor should be—'

'That's how we do it in the country, Gemma. We don't make a fuss.'

'Still!'

'By the time I arrived in the city I had my first dose of crypto,' he explained. 'Pretty much went straight to hospital. They put me in a single room too. But I didn't know what that meant back then. Lucky, hey?'

'Where do you live?'

'Not too far from here. Share a place with some other fellas.' Then in a completely new, sparkly voice, Zane said, 'Can you change the channel, Gemma? *Police Rescue*'s about to start.'

I couldn't contain the rage I felt inside. I thought about ringing a radio station or writing to the newspaper. Perhaps I could write a story about what had happened to a young guy from the country who had AIDS. I could even add in my own experiences. I'd call my story 'The Glove Syndrome'. It was holidays so I didn't really have an excuse not to. All I seemed to do most days was hang around at the hospital, talking to Zane or trying to study the theory of osmosis or read my school novel, *1984*, without falling asleep.

Sometimes when I opened my eyes, Zane'd be watching me, that big grin pasted onto his face. It didn't spook me because often I found myself gazing at him when he was asleep too.

I thought I had met all that sad had to offer. Seeing how Saul had changed on the video, tiny Maurice disappearing into his pillows, and catching Billy's face when he was lost in a thought and I could almost hear his heart cracking. But watching Zane sleep was perhaps the saddest.

Zane was meant to be overseas. Sunbaking on a beach in Greece. Swimming in the sea for the first time. At least, that's what his family thought. But instead here he was, asleep in a hospital bed with a tube in his chest, a drip in his arm and an oxygen mask on his face.

Somehow, I had become his visitor, his friend, his family. I didn't know anything about him. Yet I knew more than the closest people to him, the ones who had known him all his life.

When Mum had said, 'You're hanging out with Zane a lot,' I'd answered, 'That's because he has no one else.'

18

AT LAST IT WAS COLD. IT WAS AS THOUGH winter had suddenly remembered it was meant to be here and came barrelling through the sky bearing icy cold winds. People scurried through the streets, their heads down, their hands buried in pockets.

The other sign that winter had arrived was that our car had broken down. It wouldn't start and had to be towed away to the mechanic's.

Mum flew into a total panic because that evening she had a fitting with Catrina's mother and bridesmaids. She had never been so behind with her work. She still had seventy-five beads to hand-sew onto one of the bodices and she didn't know how she was going to get it all done, and also visit Billy at the hospital when she didn't have wheels. Aunty Penny was of no use because she was on night duty and needed to sleep during the day.

I told Mum to take a chill pill and that we'd make a plan. So today, we were playing tag. She would do just the morning shift at the hospital. I'd have a sleep-in (except I didn't mention that part of the plan) and then stay with Billy until evening.

I was in Mum's workroom because she had a full-length mirror in there. I couldn't stop admiring my reflection in my black-and-white coat. Was it possible to be in love with a piece of clothing? Because I was pretty sure I had fallen in love. Coats didn't talk to you, so Ralph had given me plenty of experience with this type of crush.

'*Cara* Gemma?' I heard Mrs C sing out to me. 'You ready to go to hospital?'

'Coming.' I took one last glance, then grabbed a container of Billy's pumpkin mush out of the freezer and locked up.

Mrs C was waiting downstairs at the entrance. '*Bella, bella,*' she said when she saw me. She ran her hands along the collar and down the sleeves. 'Is so smart, Gemma. Beautiful. Is one Saul buy for you?'

'Yes,' I answered. 'Isn't it the best?'

'*Cara, cara* Saul.' Quickly she blessed herself.

Outside Mr C was tooting the horn. Mrs C and I held hands as we made our dash down the path and through the mini cyclone that'd just erupted in our suburb.

The Fiat swayed in the wind and the windscreen-wipers squeaked double time as they tried to sweep the rain off the window. Poor old Mr C had to keep rubbing off the condensation with the sleeve of his jumper so he could see where he was going.

'Raining cats and pigs,' he shouted.

'Sure is!' I yelled back, instructing myself to tell Billy what Mr C had just said because he would piss his pants at that one.

'Okay.' Mrs C started on the arrangements. 'We are picking up Mamma, you are going to Billy. Later Mr C will drive you home.'

'Yes, sir,' Mr C said, saluting me in the rear-view mirror. 'I am taxi today.'

As we neared the hospital we could hear sirens howling down the streets. Police cars and fire-engines were blocking off roads and redirecting the traffic.

'I'll jump out here,' I told Mr and Mrs C.

'No! No! Gemma!'

'But we'll be stuck for ages and I know Mum's probably stressing up there because she's got hems and beads to finish by 7 p.m.,' I started. 'Wait at this corner. I'll explain to Mum where you are. Okay? Don't move.'

Mrs C was waving an umbrella in my face. 'Take, take.'

I ran across the road weaving around the traffic, my black-and-white coat billowing in the wind. *Raining cats and pigs*. I reminded myself again to tell Billy.

As I'd suspected, Mum was stressing out. 'You were meant to be here half an hour ago, Gemma!'

'Something happened. There's traffic everywhere,' I told her. 'They've blocked off the street. Mr C is waiting for you on the corner, just down from Maccas.'

'Did you remember Billy's mashed pumpkin?'

'Yes, Mum.'

'Did you write his name on the container?'

'Yes, Mum. His name and his bed number and I've already put it in the patient fridge.'

My brother and I watched Mum rush away, bags of sewing swinging from each arm. Then Billy lay back into the pillows and sighed. 'I hope they like their dresses,' he said. The thrush in his mouth was bad. He was dribbling a bit because it hurt his throat to swallow. Sometimes between words he had to stop and suck up the spit or wipe his mouth. We all pretended we didn't notice. 'Mum has put her heart and soul into them. She's been sewing beads all morning. They should be paying her a bonus.'

'Poor Maryanne.'

'Poor Maryanne,' Billy agreed. 'She needs a few days at home. I don't know why she comes in here every day. I'm twenty-five years old. Not five!'

'She likes being with you, Billy.'

'She needs a rest. And I do too.'

'Is Zane in the TV room?'

'He's having an X-ray,' Billy said. 'They took his chest drain out this morning.'

'Wow. He must be pleased.'

'Zane's mates came in last night.'

'What? From home?'

'No,' Billy answered. 'His flatmates. Kind of an odd bunch.'

'How do you mean?'

'They just don't seem to fit together. One of them was pretty old and the other one was just weird.'

'I wish Zane'd tell his family and friends back home where he really was,' I said. 'It just doesn't seem right. Does it?'

'It's Zane's choice, Gem. And it's a double whammy for a lot of families.'

'What do you mean?'

'They find out their son's gay *and* that he has AIDS.'

'Yes, but I bet his dad's not like ours.'

'You don't know that.'

I shrugged off Billy's comment. He didn't know, either. Besides, I'd imagined myself contacting Zane's family. I'd imagined the reunion they could have here in 9 South West.

I'd been thinking about asking Zane if he'd let me write to his parents. Maybe he needed someone to do that for him. Maybe that's why he'd told me in the first place?

'Do you mind if I close my eyes?' Billy said, yawning. 'Have a little nap? It hurts my tongue to talk.'

'No. You have a sleep. I think I'll go down to Maccas and get Zane that cheeseburger with extra gherkins. He'll probably be feeling like it now his drain is out.'

'He already mentioned the cheeseburger this morning,' Billy said. 'His mouth must be in better shape than mine. I couldn't think of anything worse.'

When the lift doors opened they revealed Zane in a wheelchair, that insane smile beaming from his face. 'My drain's out!' he announced. 'My lung's all good and working.'

'I'm so happy for you.'

'We have to celebrate.'

'I know,' I said, hopping into the lift and pressing the ground button. 'I'll be back with a surprise.'

The doors closed but I could still hear Zane shouting, 'Extra gherkins. Please!'

Perhaps something I had learnt these past couple of months was not to knock the simple things in life. Like a good cheeseburger with extra gherkins. Especially if you'd been trapped in a tangle of tubes or your guts had been attacked by crypto or your mouth was so sore from candida you could only look forward to eating vegetable mush.

That wasn't the case with me. I was merely a spectator. But there were days in 9 South West that I found suffocating, even after an hour. The air was fake. The sounds were muted. The lights were always on. But you could still see out to a world on the other side of the glass that teased and taunted because you were no longer a part of it. No wonder Zane liked to stare out the window and imagine how other people were living their lives.

Outside it was still raining cats and pigs and the wind was tossing up rubbish and sending it flying. But it was open space and the air was real and suddenly it felt like a type of freedom I hadn't experienced before. It was different to being allowed out past midnight or sleeping at Andrea's when her parents were away. It was so much bigger than that and yet so much simpler.

There was no point holding up my umbrella because it was only turning inside out. So instead, I held the collar of my coat tight around my neck, put my head down and made a run for it.

When I reached a barrier barely half a block from Maccas, a policeman stopped me. 'You can't go past here,' he said.

'I'm just going to Maccas,' I explained, a bit breathless and taking shelter under one of the awnings. 'It's just there.' I pointed. 'I'll come straight back. I'm not going any further.'

'Sorry, love.'

'But I have to go to Maccas and get a cheeseburger. It's for one of the patients at the hospital.'

'No thoroughfare from this point.'

'I'll only be a minute. I promise. Please?'

'I've told you, miss. You can't go past this point. There's been a gas leak in the street. You'll have to get your cheeseburger somewhere else.'

I stomped away, hissing under my breath, convinced that the policeman thought I was lying and that the cheeseburger was for me. What would he know anyway about being a boy from the country, 937 kilometres from home, sick and alone and only wanting a cheeseburger with extra gherkins? He was probably the type who'd put on gloves if he knew I'd come from the AIDS ward.

I trudged off. Too bad if I got soaked. I wasn't going back into the ward empty-handed. There had to be another Maccas close by.

Three blocks down the next street, I was stopped again and told to turn back. This policeman was even meaner and actually told me to stop being a 'drama queen'.

Now it was raining cats, pigs and elephants. My Doc Martens had water pouring out of them and my beautiful coat was starting to smell like soggy wool and stick to my skin.

'Excuse me,' I asked a woman taking shelter in a bus stop. 'Do you know where the closest Maccas is?'

'By the hospital, I think.'

'I can't get to that one! It's blocked off.'

'I know there's one on the other side of the city. But it's about a twenty-minute walk. They do good burgers over there,' she told me, pointing to a dingy-looking cafe with an unpronounceable name.

'No. It has to be a Maccas cheeseburger with extra gherkins.' My bottom lip was getting the wobbles. 'It's for my friend who's a patient at the hospital. He has AIDS and no one in his family knows.'

'Oh, sweetheart,' the lady said, gently putting her hand on my shoulder. 'That's terrible. Aren't you a good friend.'

'I can't go back without the cheeseburger.' Now I was crying. Not blubbering crying. More the sniffing and shaking-jaw variety. 'He's waiting for it because he just had the tube pulled out of his chest.'

Her head was cocked, her lips open, but I couldn't wait for her words.

'Don't worry,' I muttered, stumbling back into the downpour. I felt like I was the only one out there. Everyone else seemed to be crowded under whatever cover they could find because now it was raining sideways.

Where am I going to find a Maccas? I snivelled to myself. *Why is everything so hard? Why can't something just work out for once?* I wanted to look up to the heavens and shake my fist like they do in the movies. Yet it was too wet to even do that.

Luckily, I at least glanced up, because ahead, just visible through the thick sheets of rain, was the faintest shimmer of lime green.

I started running. I had to get there before the lights changed and it drove away. I was ankle deep in puddles, my Doc Martens feeling like they were about to float off without me. Yet I didn't stop. Not till I was at the driver's door and banging on the window of the lime mobile.

Ralph totally freaked out. He jumped away from the window like he thought I was some crazy with a knife about to carjack and kidnap him. Then he saw that it was me and wound down the window.

'Gemma?'

'Can you let me in?'

He unlocked the door, and twenty seconds later I was sitting in the front seat, bawling my eyes out. Somehow I managed to choke out a jumble of words. 'Cheeseburger,' 'Maccas,' and, 'Life's better with extra gherkins.'

Ralph drove while I told him the story of Zane. By the time we reached the drive-through on the other side of the city, I could've filled my Docs all over again with my tears.

It wasn't until we'd turned out of Maccas and I had the goods in my hands that I began to calm down. Then I started to feel really, really embarrassed. I had blubbered and dribbled snot all over myself in front of Ralph. I felt like pulling the Maccas paper bag right over my head and hiding in it.

'What were you doing in the city?' I asked, trying to speak calmly and slowly like I was a grown-up in a play.

'I work at Hot Spot Records.'

'Oh, yeah. That's right.'

'I couldn't find a park because they've blocked off the street where I usually go,' Ralph said. 'At least it gives me a good excuse for being late.'

'How late are you?'

'About an hour.' Ralph grinned.

'Oh. Sorry.'

'Don't be. This is a thousand times better than work.'

'Well, I really appreciate it,' I started. 'Especially when—'

Ralph interrupted. 'Don't go all formal on me, Gemma.'

'Huh?'

'Saying you appreciate it and stuff. And what's with your voice?'

'I don't know what you mean.'

We had pulled up at the hospital. Ralph had his hands off the wheel and was facing me. 'Gemma,' he began, 'I'm just going to say it because Vanessa says I have to. Not that I don't want to. I mean, I want to say it. But I know you've been dodging me. So I doubt it's what you want to hear . . .'

I braced myself because these days I couldn't tell what was coming at me. All I did know was that AIDS would most likely be in this sentence or at least have something to do with it.

'I think you're a really cool girl.'

I kept holding my breath but then I realised that was

it. That's what Ralph had wanted to say and I had not in a million trillion years seen those words coming.

Back in the TV room, Zane gobbled up the two cheeseburgers with extra gherkins. He didn't speak. He just ate and I watched him. I had already decided not to tell him the story about how I ran into the boy I'd had a serious crush on since Year 7 and randomly jumped in his car and he drove me to Maccas, then told me I was 'cool'.

It was a good story and Zane liked a good story. But I didn't want to tell him about Ralph. It was hard to explain. Of course Zane didn't like me like that. But I still wanted him to think that he was the only one in my heart.

19

THE SEVENTEENTH OF JULY, THE SWEET
day I wore my black-and-white checked coat, the day
Ralph Harding told me he thought I was cool, became a
night that turned sour.

The rain had dried up. There were even stars scattered
around the sky. Mr C and I were driving home from the
hospital, singing along with the radio. It was The Beatles,
'Hey Jude', which was a sad song but nothing could make
me feel sad tonight.

At least that's what I thought, until we turned the
corner into our street and saw four women coming out of
our block of flats, dresses on coathangers trailing behind
them, their hems sweeping the footpath. Mum and Mrs C
were almost jogging after them.

Something about this picture was very wrong.

By the time Mr C parked the Fiat, the ladies had driven
away.

'What happened?' I called. Mum was huddled under
Mrs C's arm.

'Bloody, bloody bastards!' Mrs C was shouting. 'They no
good, anyway.'

'They took their dresses and Catrina's too,' Mum whimpered. 'I hadn't finished the hems.'

Back upstairs I made some tea while Mum sat at the kitchen table staring into space. I tiptoed around the kitchen, making toast and heating up the teapot, as I attempted to coax just yes or no answers from her, trying to piece together what had happened.

'Was that Catrina's mum and the bridesmaids driving away?'

'Yes.'

'Catrina wasn't with them?'

'No.'

'But they took her dress?'

'Yes.'

'And they didn't want you to finish them?'

'No.'

'They told you why?'

Mum nodded. 'Catrina's mum saw Billy at the doctor's.'

The next thing Mum said I could barely believe.

'They're scared about being in the same house as Billy.'

'What?'

'They thought I should've told them,' Mum croaked. 'Because Catrina's pregnant and she uses the toilet when she comes over for a fitting.' Mum lay her head on the table. 'The world's gone insane.'

The next morning, I called Billy at the hospital and told him Mum was sick. His words, muffled in spit that he couldn't swallow because it hurt too much, were hard to understand. But we muddled through and I told him I'd see him later in the afternoon.

Of course, I didn't tell him what'd happened. When he asked how the fittings had gone, I told him the ladies had left with the dresses, so now Mum could concentrate on mine. He liked that answer.

Mum lay on the couch. *Donahue* was on the TV and the topic of the day was 'Why do some children hate their parents so much they won't even speak to them?' If that'd been the subject on *Donahue* even four months ago, I may've joined the discussion. Shouted at the audience, *Yeah, and some parents hate their children because they're queer!*

Today I didn't, because Mum looked like a zombie lying on the couch staring at the TV. She didn't need me to suck her just a bit drier.

The topic of 'Should your father be told that his son is sick?' seemed to have disappeared from the agenda. What would it achieve, anyway? It's not as though Dad would jump on his white horse and come charging down to rescue us. And if he did turn up, it'd be beyond stressful. Billy's T cells would probably nosedive and crash.

My job for the morning was making Billy's mush. I wore the blue gingham apron I'd made for Mum in Grade 6, which marked the beginning and the end of my sewing career. The hem was uneven and the pocket had unravelled after its first outing. But wearing it now added to the atmosphere. There were saucepans boiling and I was elbow deep in pumpkin and potato peels. I pretended I was working in a soup kitchen for homeless people because inside my head that made it a bit more interesting.

When Aunty Penny arrived at 4.30 p.m. I had six containers of mashed vegies lined up along the counter, the lids all reading *Billy Longrigg, 9SW, Bed 22*.

'Nice job, Gem,' she said.

'All that mashing is good for the biceps.'

'How's Mum?'

'She's asleep.'

'I could kill those women. At least they paid her.'

'I still can't believe it,' I said.

'Me neither,' answered Penny. 'It's the twentieth century. No wonder people call it a plague.'

When I arrived in Billy's room I found him sitting up in bed, a tall pile of the latest fashion magazines stacked in front of him.

'Wow,' I said. 'Where did they come from?'

'Visitors,' he mouthed, then mopped the spit off his lips before he took a spoonful of my pumpkin mash.

'Jonathon?' Aunty Penny asked. 'He called to ask if he could visit.'

'Who's Jonathon? Is he the fashion photographer? The really short guy?'

Billy nodded.

'He's not that short. He's cute. But gay.' Penny laughed. 'Anyway, hope he cheered you up. The nurses said you didn't get much sleep.'

Billy pointed to Zane's empty bed and whispered, 'He had a bad night.'

'I heard they're putting in another drain,' Penny told us.

'Is Zane going to be okay?' I hoped it didn't have anything to do with the cheeseburgers. 'Did his lung collapse again?'

'Most likely,' Penny answered.

'I might go and ask how he's doing,' I said.

One of the reasons I had to get away was because I couldn't stomach watching Billy eat. The orange mash bubbled between his lips with the effort of swallowing and

I knew that most of it would end up dribbling back out of his mouth. I was going to have to add pumpkin to the list with blackberry jubes.

The nurses station was at the other end of the corridor near the TV room. I wandered down to see if I could find Anna. She was the only nurse I'd spoken to enough to actually know something about. Anna was from Holland and here on a working holiday with her boyfriend.

Since Billy's first admission, I'd probably travelled up and down the corridor of 9 South West at least fifty times. The worst part was the middle section where the single rooms were. I seemed to have formed a new style of a walk when passing by there: head down, quick steps and most importantly, don't look in, no matter how curious you are. That was the difficult part, because often there were huddles of people crying and hugging outside the rooms. But it was the sounds from inside that freaked me out the most.

Up ahead, the door to Room 16 was wide open and a patient was being wheeled in on a bed. I glanced sideways, as quick as a flash. Yet not quick enough to miss seeing Zane disappearing and the door closing after him.

I picked up my pace, only just making it to the TV room before I collapsed into one the chairs. This was just a bump in the road, I told myself. Zane would be okay, just like Billy would. There was a cure around the corner, everyone was saying it. It was just a matter of them getting through each bump – whether it be crypto, candida, pneumonia, cat germs in your brain and whatever other strange varieties of infection AIDS had to offer the body.

The glass door of the TV room slid open. So I pasted on Polly Positive's smile.

'Hi, Gemma,' Anna said. 'I saw you coming down here.'

'Oh? Yeah.' For a second, I wondered if I was only allowed to be in here with a patient.

'You saw Zane, didn't you?' she asked. She was crouching next to my seat. Today she was wearing blue mascara. 'Your aunty said you'd be upset that Zane's not well.'

'She said they were putting another tube into his chest.'

'They did something to Zane called "pleurodedis". It's sort of like they have to stick the lung together. It's quite painful so he's had a lot of sedation.'

'Will he be all right?'

Anna shrugged, but she may as well have shot me in the stomach because that's what her silence felt like. 'We'll have to wait and see,' she finally said.

'His family situation' – I didn't want to dob, but I didn't want to do nothing either – 'is complicated.'

'We know all about it, Gemma. One of our AIDS volunteers will speak to him when he's well enough.'

'To see if they can contact the family?'

'He hasn't wanted to in the past,' she explained. 'But people change their mind.'

'So you've asked him?'

'Yes. A few times now.'

I felt better knowing that. It was another lesson I was learning. These days the smallest thing could make such an amazing difference to the way I felt.

'Can I go and see him?'

'He's asleep,' Anna said. 'But I'll take you there.'

My fingertips slid along the wall as I followed Anna back up the corridor and into the single room where Zane was.

The only sounds were the oxygen hissing and the beep of the machine that tracked his heartbeat. Zane lay as still as stone, as though he wasn't actually there at all and in his place was a mannequin. A Zane look-alike that you could practise CPR on. The hospital gown was loose around his shoulders and I could see a tattoo. Just three numbers, etched in green: *937*. The number of kilometres to home.

It was coming up to the last weekend of holidays before school went back on Tuesday. It was my turn to give Andrea excuses as to why I couldn't go out with her. *I can't deal with you at the moment. I can't deal with you. Or your mother. Or your grandmother, at the moment.* Even though it was the truth, I was too chicken to say it. So instead, I offered her the other truth because I wanted to make her feel bad: 'I can't go out on Saturday night because Billy's really sick and back in hospital.'

I hoped that wasn't going to cast a jinx on Billy because he was actually starting to feel a bit better. He'd even managed to swallow some non-mush food. Plus, he was starting to hassle the doctors and nurses about when he could get out of there.

Zane wasn't getting better. He had been in the single room for three days. Every time I went in, he was still lying there looking like the Zane mannequin. Once or twice I saw his fingers twitch, but that was it. Anna said they were keeping him sedated. She didn't explain why and I didn't ask because I never understood all the medical blah blah that came with the answers to those questions. They were the doctors and nurses, so I figured they knew what they were doing.

But I was impatient for Zane to wake up so the volunteers could talk to him about contacting his family.

So his parents could hurry up and get down to the city to
see him.

Billy had given us strict instructions that on Saturday we
were to have the whole day off and not come into the
hospital. Probably the only reason Mum agreed was
because he had a heap of old friends visiting him that
day anyway.

Mum seemed to be beating herself up for not going in to
see Billy on the day after the dress drama. She kept saying
how pathetic it was that she couldn't pull herself together
and that people like Catrina and her mother weren't worth
the heartache.

Mum and I were still in our pyjamas in the afternoon.
I had just finished my third bowl of cereal while watching
the really cheesy midday movie.

The fabric had finally arrived from New York. The
pattern was finished, the glossy black velvet spread over
the table. I stood there watching as Mum held up the
scissors about to make the first cut.

'You nervous?' I asked.

'I am, a bit,' she giggled. 'I don't know if it's because this
fabric is so beautiful.'

'Or that it's your daughter's dress and you don't want
to stuff it up?'

'Thanks for that,' Mum answered. 'I haven't stuffed up
a dress yet.'

Perhaps it'd been too early for a joke like that. Over the
past months I had watched my mother alter Catrina's bridal
gown to fit around her ever-growing belly, the whole time
telling Catrina that it wasn't too much trouble, and that

she promised her dress would be perfect and that she'd be a beautiful bride. Now Neuta stood in the corner, naked, because my brother had AIDS.

Mum took a deep breath. 'Here goes.' She lined up the scissors and cut into the velvet. I watched her steady hand work, cutting a straight line, the other holding the fabric tight. 'Phew,' she said when she reached the end. She looked at me and we both started giggling.

'Were you scared when you made your own wedding dress?' I asked.

'I can't remember.'

'I wonder why I'm no good at sewing.'

'You wouldn't know,' Mum answered. 'You've hardly tried it.'

'I've tried it enough.' I added, 'To know I hate it.'

'You'll never be good at something you hate, Gemma!'

'I have other strengths,' I announced.

'Like what?'

'Like . . .' I had to be good at something. I just couldn't think of what. 'Apparently I'm good at writing English essays. And being cool. I'm good at' – there was a knock on the door – 'I'm good at answering the door,' I said, doing exactly that.

Standing there on the other side, with a ginormous belly, was Catrina and her wedding dress.

'Is Maryanne home?' she whispered.

But Mum was already next to me, taking the dress out of Catrina's hands and saying, 'Come in, Catrina.'

Before I was even asked, I went straight to the kettle and started to fill it with water. Then I thought to myself: *Why are we making this person a cup of tea?* Catrina was a horrible person and she probably wouldn't touch one of our mugs anyway. We should be honoured she'd even walked into the flat at all.

Mum and Catrina sat down at the kitchen table. I wondered who was going to be the first to speak. It was Catrina.

'I am so sorry, Maryanne,' she began. There was a definite quiver in her voice. 'I had no idea that my mother and brides-maids had planned to take the dresses. I am ashamed. I am embarrassed. I just don't know what I can say.'

'Thanks, Catrina,' Mum said. 'I appreciate that. But this is who we are. Warts and all. You can like us or lump us.'

'I never said those things about Billy or that I was scared to come here and use the stupid toilet.'

Mum was doing the slow nod, which made me suspect that she was biding her time before she dropped an almighty clanger. 'How did you know Billy was sick?' she asked.

'We obviously have the same GP. My mother saw Billy there.'

'And thought what? Oh, he's a fag, he looks a bit thin, he must have AIDS?'

'I don't know.'

Mum was leaning on the kitchen table. She'd clipped the softness in her voice just enough for Catrina to know she meant business. I switched the kettle on because for some reason that I couldn't explain, part of me suddenly felt a bit bad for Catrina.

'Really?' Mum said. 'You don't know?'

'I have no idea,' she answered.

Mum sat back in the chair but I knew she wasn't finished.

'Please, I just really wanted to say how sorry I am,' Catrina offered. 'And . . . I also wanted to ask if you would consider finishing my dress?'

'Of course I will finish your dress, Catrina. I wouldn't trust anyone else to,' Mum said, then she dropped the clanger. 'I know your mother is friends with Sandra, the receptionist at the doctor's surgery. I would very much hope that's not how the information about my son was passed on.'

Catrina went pale. The kettle started whistling. And my mother folded her arms wearing an expression I had never seen before.

To me she was just Mum. Plus a dressmaker who worked from a little room off the kitchen sewing pretty clothes for people. But right now she was a lady not to be messed with.

Suddenly I realised that maybe it wasn't so important my armour always fit properly because my mother would fight to the death for both my brother and me.

I poured the boiling water into the teapot, hoping that when it came to my turn, I would be a mother like that too.

❊

Even before the lift doors opened I could hear it. A spine-chilling wail that made the hairs on my arm stand up.

I stepped out into the entrance of 9 South West and the sound became alive, like someone had just turned up the radio.

'No. No. No!' the voice cried. 'Please, pleeeease get me out of here.'

Straight away I knew it was Zane.

I edged down the corridor towards his room. I was terrified of what I would find.

Inside I could hear Anna saying, 'Zane? Zane! Keep still or you'll pull your drip out.'

There was another voice, maybe a doctor's. 'Zane, we need to keep you in this room until you're better.'

'Noooo!' Zane howled. My hands covered my mouth and I started crying. It was the worst sound I had ever heard. It blasted through my chest, through the bones of my ribs and stuck to my heart like the tentacles of a blue-bottle mid-sting.

'Get me out of here!' He started to sob. 'Get me out of here! Please! Please, Anna?'

'Zane!' Another voice shouted and I wondered how many people were in the room. Were they holding him down? I could hear the squeak of the mattress and the rattle of the bed. Maybe Zane was trying to fight them off?

Anna ran out. She was calling to another nurse who was gowned and gloved, running down the corridor with a syringe and a towel. Then Anna noticed me. 'Go back to your brother's room, Gemma!' She was wearing gloves too. 'Gemma!'

But my feet were glued to the ground.

Anna and the other nurse rushed past me and back into the single room. 'Gemma! You need to move.'

How could I explain that I couldn't? I literally couldn't move. I wanted to get away. I didn't want to hear the sound of Zane's terror because the situation in there was clear to me now. After four days, Zane must've woken up and found himself in the single room. The room for the dying. Zane had belted out that raging 'Nooo!' to whoever it was who told him, 'We need to keep you in this room until you're better,' because Zane knew they were lying.

Somehow I made it into the TV room. I was blubbering so hard my whole body was shaking. I wedged myself behind the door and knelt on the floor while the television played the midday movie.

I couldn't tell you if it was five minutes or half an hour later when I felt the door of the TV room push against me. I looked up and saw Anna.

'I knew I'd find you hiding in here,' she said. She reached out her hand and helped me to stand. I had pins and needles in both ankles. 'I'm sorry I growled at you before, Gemma.'

'That's okay.'

'Zane is very upset but he's also quite confused at the moment.'

'What do you mean?'

'Sometimes AIDS can affect your brain,' she told me. 'He's going to have some scans so the doctors can see what's going on.'

'Does he have that cat cancer thing in his brain like Maurice did?'

'Toxoplasmosis? Most likely. But we won't know until we get the test results.'

'I see,' I whispered so softly that even I barely heard it.

'Why don't you go back to your brother's room?' Anna said. 'I'm here till three-thirty if you want to ask me anything.'

I wandered back to Billy's room. I must've looked as bad as I felt because the minute Mum and Billy saw me they chimed, 'What's happened, Gem?'

With a wobbly jaw I told Mum and Billy what I'd heard outside Zane's room and what Anna had said. I finished with a question for Billy: 'Zane can come back into this room, can't he?'

At the same time as my brother said, 'Yes,' my mother said, 'No.'

'But Mum, he doesn't want to be in a single room and if Billy doesn't mind—'

'It's not up to Billy,' she snapped. 'It's up to the doctors and nurses.'

'So if they say he can come back in here, then he can!'

'Gem, I don't think it's that simple,' Billy said.

'Oh what, you've changed your mind now, have you?'

'If he needs to be near the nurses, they'll keep him in a single room,' he told me. Mum nodded her head in agreement.

Suddenly, I felt like slapping them both. 'If you had heard Zane yelling out, then you wouldn't feel like that, Billy,' I snarled.

'I did hear him, Gemma,' he answered. 'I heard him this morning and last night and the night before that.' It was that weary but matter-of-fact tone in Billy's voice that I could hear again. The way I'd heard myself speak when I'd told Louise that my brother had AIDS.

Right then, I could've surrendered. I could've agreed that it was up to the doctors and nurses what room Zane stayed in. I was tired and I thought about how nice and easy it would be to collapse into the recliner next to Billy's bed, snuggle up with a spare blanket, put on headphones and have a little nap. But I couldn't.

That night I started to write a letter to Zane's parents. I decided I would ask Anna for their address and if she wouldn't give it to me then I'd simply mail it to *Zane Bradbury's Parents, Garrandai Post Office*. It was a small town. It would find them.

Dear Mr and Mrs Bradbury,

My name's Gemma and I'm friends with your son, Zane.

This is a difficult letter to write. I'm not completely sure I am doing the right thing. But I hope I am.

Zane is not backpacking around Europe like he told you. Zane is actually in the city in King George's Hospital. He is very ill.

He didn't want to tell you that he's sick. He knew that it would worry and upset you both. That's why he left home saying he was going on holidays.

Zane has told me a lot about you and your family and his town of Garrandai where he misses the big sky. He is a great guy and I've had lots of laughs with him. But I know deep down he is really sad because he feels like he can't tell you the truth about himself.

I wish I could say more but it's up to Zane to tell you the rest. It's complicated, as I am realising life can be.

Please call King George's Hospital, Ward 9 South West and ask to speak to Sister Anna.

Yours sincerely,

Gemma Longrigg

20

12 weeks
to formal

THE CAR WAS FIXED AND MUM DROVE ME TO
school on Tuesday, supposedly because it was the first day
back after holidays and my bag was heavy. However, on
the morning news there'd been a story about a young gay
guy being bashed by a group of men. I wondered if this had
something to do with Mum's offer of a lift.

I got out of the car at the back gate, because I'd told
Mum my first class was in the gymnasium. I squeezed
between the loose bars of the fence and headed towards
the stink of sewerage. I needed to hang out there for a
while because I wasn't sure how I felt about being back
at school. And I wasn't sure about who to be now I was
back at school. The girl with the brother who had AIDS?
The girl who Ralph said was cool even though he avoided
her? The girl who was in the middle of a Mexican standoff
with her best friend? Or the girl who I really felt I was:
the girl who could only think about a guy she barely knew
called Zane?

The letter to Zane's parents was in my bag. After school
I was catching the train in to King George's. This morning
Mum had told me, 'There's no need to see Billy today,' and,
'Go straight home after school because you're tired.' But

I knew she meant, *Don't come to the hospital because I don't want you seeing Zane.*

Both Mum and I seemed to be caught in this funny game of not totally saying what we thought. Not fibbing or outright lying, more just skirting around the edges of the truth.

Louise was behind the gymnasium smoking. Before I had a chance to sneak away she saw me and waved.

'I haven't heard from you for a few days,' she said. 'Everything hunky-dory? I was getting worried.'

'Just hospital shit.'

'How's Billy?'

'He should be home by the end of week,' I told her.

'That's good.'

'Yeah,' I replied. 'I'm getting a bit over it.'

'I bet you are,' she answered. 'What do you do at the hospital all day?'

'Not much,' I said. 'It was pretty boring holidays. I hung out with that guy called Zane I told you about.'

'The good-looking one?'

'He looks pretty bad at the moment,' I said. 'He's really . . .' I swallowed hard '. . . really sick.'

'Is he going to die?' Louise asked.

My lips were pressed so tightly together I could feel them tingle. 'I don't want to think about it,' I answered. 'Yet it's all I can think about. I can't get him out of my head.'

'You need one of my Rubik's Cubes.'

'No offence, Louise, but I don't reckon that'll help.'

'You should try it. It worked for me.'

'What do you mean?'

'When that stuff happened with Simon Finkler and Bronnie, I was so freaked out. I couldn't eat, I couldn't sleep. I just kept thinking about what happened and what I did and what I should've done.' Louise lit up again, her lopsided jaw blowing out a spiral of grey smoke. 'It was horrible. I never ever want to feel like that again.'

'So what's the cube got to do with it?'

'One day I was at a toy shop with my brother and I just picked one up and started mucking around with it,' she explained. 'About ten minutes later I realised I hadn't thought about Simon Finkler. Not once, because I was concentrating so hard on matching up the stupid squares. It was like a holiday for my brain. So peaceful. I was addicted after that.'

Louise rummaged through her bag and took out a Rubik's Cube, a bit smaller than the one she'd given Billy. 'There,' she said. 'All yours.'

'Aren't you running out of them by now?'

'Nope.' She laughed. 'I have a stash.'

We walked around the gymnasium and I promised Louise I would give the cube a try, even though I was pretty sure I wouldn't.

Andrea saw us as we passed the locker room and came running up like nothing had happened. Like it was perfectly normal to see each other once during the holidays and not every second day like we normally would.

Even Justin appeared from a corridor and joined the walk to assembly. He'd been in Hawaii and was so sunburnt that the only part of him that wasn't red were the whites of his eyes.

'How's Billy doing?' Andrea asked me, as she twisted and twirled her new piercing.

'A bit better, thanks,' I answered. 'Hopefully he'll be out of hospital by next weekend.'

'In the States they're all saying a cure for AIDS is around the corner,' added Justin.

'I wish it'd hurry up,' I answered.

I'd figured out ages ago that Justin knew about Billy having full-blown AIDS. Sometimes, I wondered who else did too.

When I went to the hospital after school, Billy wasn't in his room. In the other bed was a new patient. He looked okay to me but I noticed the side rails of his bed were up as if to stop him from falling out.

He didn't say anything when I walked in, so I said, 'Hello.'

'Oh, hello,' he answered. 'I thought there was someone in here. Is it Bill's sister?'

'That's right.'

'I'm Patrick,' he introduced himself. 'I'm nearly blind. I always think it's a good idea to tell people that because I'm sure I look like a halfwit sitting in this bed with the cot sides up around me.'

'Not really.'

'You're just being polite, love,' he said. 'I haven't always been blind. It's the AIDS monster. I'm still trying to get used to it.'

'AIDS made you blind?'

'Cytomegalovirus. CMV for short. Must've been exposed to it before.'

'Gosh.'

'You can say that again.'

'Do you know where my brother and Mum are?'

'In the cafeteria,' Patrick replied. 'Sorry, I was meant to tell you that. Not start talking about myself.'

'No, that's okay.'

I was searching through my schoolbag for the letter to Zane's parents. I slipped it into my pocket, feeling even more deceitful for doing it in front of a blind man. I shoved my bag under the bed and told Patrick I was off to find Mum and Billy. It was a lie, but he wasn't going to know that either.

The nurses station was hectic like it always seemed to be until 6 p.m. when it became a ghost town. Phones were ringing, patient's families were leaning over the desk asking questions. There were always a few groups of white coats in deep discussion.

This afternoon one of the doctors was pointing out things on an X-ray. The rest of them were nodding and I wondered if any of them actually knew what they were looking at, because to me it looked like a smudge of black and grey clouds.

By now, I'd figured out that you just had to hang around the nurses station until someone eventually noticed you or stopped pretending that they hadn't seen you in the first place.

The ward clerk who I'd said hello to a few times waved at me and mouthed, 'Do you need some help?'

I mouthed back, 'Can I talk to Sister Anna?'

She stood up from the desk and came around to me. She must've hated having to wear that ugly brown uniform. I know I would've.

'Anna's not on duty today,' she told me. 'Do you want to speak to the nurse looking after Bill?' She scanned the patient board. Next to Billy's name was written *Darren*. The nurse's name next to *Zane Bradbury*, I didn't recognise.

Now I wasn't quite sure what to do and I didn't know how truthful I could be with this woman.

She started saying, 'I'll tell Darren—'

But I interrupted. 'Actually I wanted to ask about Zane.' I slipped in a yawn. 'If that's okay.'

'Oh?' She frowned and I was sure I'd blown it. 'Just hang on a minute.'

Within seconds a doctor was standing there and introducing himself as 'Tim'.

I remembered seeing him when Billy was first admitted because he reminded me of the singer Rick Astley. He spoke in a gentle voice and was wearing a funny tie with Sylvester the Cat on it.

He seemed trustworthy. He seemed nice. So I collected my courage, took a deep breath and started the mini speech I'd planned.

'I wanted to speak to you about Zane Bradbury and . . . his parents,' I began. 'I know they don't know he's sick in hospital and Sister Anna's told me how the AIDS volunteers have . . .' But Dr Tim had stopped listening and was looking over my shoulder. There was something going on behind me that was obviously a million times more interesting than anything I had to say. Suddenly I felt foolish and stupid and every day of my sixteen years.

'Who's the sister looking after . . . ?' Tim was waving his hand at someone.

I turned around to see Zane. He was walking up the corridor on legs that were as thin as my mother's sewing needles. His gown was untied and back-to-front so you could see every bit of him.

When he saw me he broke into a smile, cracking life into his face. But as he came closer I noticed his eyes. There was no one in there.

Dr Tim and one of the nurses were each trying to take an arm and steer him back towards his room. But Zane slapped at them like a child, freeing up his hands and waving to me.

'Hi there,' he called.

I tried not to appear terrified at the person staggering towards me who looked like he'd just escaped from a concentration camp. So I straightened my back, ordering myself to smile.

'Hi to you,' I answered.

'Where have you been, Stacey?' he said. 'Pa told me you were down in the chook pen.'

'It's Gemma,' I murmured.

'Come on, mate,' Dr Tim was saying as he linked his arm through Zane's. Now they resembled a couple walking down the aisle. 'Let's get you back to your room, buddy.'

They disappeared into his single room and somehow I managed the long journey back to my brother's room. I didn't tell Mum and Billy what'd happened. When they kept asking why I was quiet, I simply answered that I had a headache. I snuggled into the recliner. I draped a blanket over my head to block out the fluoro ceiling lights and pretended to have a nap.

But I couldn't sleep. Instead, I prayed. I didn't know what else to do. We weren't a religious family. I'd only stepped into a church three times in my life. But I needed to tell whoever it was that it was fine if Billy had to eat vegetable mush for the rest of his life, but please, please don't let my brother go blind or get the cat disease in his brain so that he wouldn't even know who I was.

The next afternoon I took the Rubik's Cube out of my locker. It was worth a try and by now I'd realised it was impossible to get any homework done at the hospital. I wasn't convinced by the power of the cube. At least, not like Louise was. She was like a Rubik's Cube addict. I was addicted to nice clothes and maybe buying earrings. In Year 7 Andrea and I had definitely developed an obsession with potato scallops. We bought one every afternoon after school but that addiction was quickly over when our jeans became too tight. But a Rubik's Cube? I certainly couldn't see myself getting addicted to one of them. Although I had to admit, these days Billy seemed to be attacking the coloured squares more often than he was reading magazines.

The cube was balancing on the palm of my hand. I was about to drop it into my schoolbag when someone behind me said, 'You have to be a genius to do them.'

It was Ralph. He was so close that if I turned around I was sure we'd bump noses.

'That settles it then,' I answered. 'I missed out on the genius genes.'

'Do you want a lift home, Gemma?'

'Thanks but I'm catching the train to the hospital.'

'I'll drive you,' Ralph said. 'The train will take forever.'

'Are you sure?'

'Come on, Gemma,' he said, touching my elbow. 'I'm parked out the back.'

Maybe the praying was paying off. Suddenly there were a couple of reasons to yell, *Hallelujah!* The obvious one, the prospect of a long car ride with Ralph. Something that was helping to get me through these days was the little private memory of Ralph and me going to get Zane's cheeseburger.

The other reason to give praise, was where his car was parked; I didn't trust what Andrea and Louise would do if they spotted Ralph and me together. A wolf-whistle would be Andrea's style, probably followed by a hundred and one questions. Louise would be fine. She was cool. That's something I was learning every day about her.

Ralph put on a cassette of the Style Council. We drove down the streets with 'Big Boss Groove' blaring. I looked out of the window, trying to hide my smile. At this moment it was easy to forget who I was and where I was headed. It was just Ralph and me. It was too crazy to believe it was happening.

'Do we need to stop off at Maccas for another cheese-burger with extra gherkins?' Ralph shouted above the music.

'No.'

'How's he doing?'

'Pretty bad.'

Ralph turned the cassette off. I told him what'd happened yesterday. I knew he was listening to every word. I could just feel it. When you know someone is really hearing you, you feel . . . lighter? When it was just the two of us, Ralph and I seemed to be able to talk easily. Over a week had passed since I'd said a word to him. But it didn't feel like that.

'Will you be going to the hospital every afternoon after school?' he asked.

'Pretty much,' I answered. 'I don't reckon Mum and Billy wanted me to come in today. They kept saying, "You're tired, have a break, go out for coffee with the girls instead."'

'So?'

'So, they're bullshitting,' I told him. 'I reckon the real

reason they don't want me coming in is because they don't want me to see Zane.'

'Really?'

'Mum said to me last night that she's worried I'm becoming too involved.'

'Zane's really lucky to have you, Gemma,' Ralph said. He took his hand off the wheel and squeezed my shoulder. I almost stopped breathing. 'Imagine being in hospital all alone,' he continued, both hands back on the steering wheel. 'I would be so scared.'

'I get a bit freaked out even looking at him. Zane's not the same person, if you know what I mean.'

'I know exactly what you mean. My pop lost his marbles. Once he thought the kitchen was filled with quacking ducks!'

'No!'

'True. It was a total spin-out. But I kept telling myself that Pop was in there somewhere. He'd just got a bit lost.'

'That's a good way of putting it.'

'I was with my pop when he died,' Ralph told me. 'I'll never forget it. It was only me and him in the room. My dad had gone out to speak to a nurse and he died. Just like that.'

'Poor you,' I said. 'Were you scared?'

'No.'

'What was it like?'

'The room just went quiet.'

Ralph had pulled up to the drop-off zone of King George's. He peered up at the building and I wondered if he was counting up to the ninth floor like I had done so many times.

'Look, if you ever need a lift here after school,' Ralph said, 'just ask.'

'Thanks,' I murmured back, but my mind had already started sorting through all the things that might go wrong this afternoon, as though I was preparing my armour, getting ready for battle inside 9 South West.

As I passed the nurses station, I checked the patient board. Zane's name was still there next to Room 11. His nurse for the shift was Anna.

I spotted her outside Zane's room. She was taking off her gown, putting it into one of the yellow infection hazard bins that were dotted all over the ward.

Let's do it, I told myself and strode over there.

'Hi, Gemma.'

'Hi,' I answered. 'How's Zane?'

'Not good. He's been unconscious since last night.'

Out of nowhere, Mum appeared, standing in between Anna and me saying, 'Hi, darling. You're earlier than I expected. It's only four o'clock.' I could feel her fingers wrapping around the top of my arm, pulling me away from the doorway of Zane's room. 'We thought we might go to the cafe across the road for afternoon tea. The doctor said it was fine and your brother is desperate for some fresh air.'

'Sure,' I answered. 'But I'm just going to see Zane.'

'Let's have—'

'No, Mum. I want to say hello to Zane first.'

Mum dropped my arm and I walked into his room.

At first glance, Zane simply looked like he was asleep. But the more I watched him, the more I saw. His face was merely a skull, the skin pulled tight with every bump of bone standing upright like a mountain. His lips were smeared with cream and his breath was almost silent.

'Come on, darling.' Mum was behind me. 'That's enough.'

'I can't leave him,' I whispered. 'He's got no one else.'

'Gemma, please. Anna's here. She'll be in and out of his room all evening.'

'I don't want him to be alone.' I was crying now and the pain throbbed in my chest, in that same place under my ribs in the little triangle with the funny name. 'Please, Mum? I can't leave him.'

I wasn't taking no for an answer. Eventually they caved in and let me stay.

I sat on a chair next to the bed and held Zane's cold hand.

His breathing had gone from inaudible to noisy. It was hard not to think of Darth Vader because that's what Zane sounded like. Often there'd be a long break between one breath and the next. Then Zane's lips would quiver and purse, blowing another breath into the world.

Anna was in and out of the room. Sometimes she rubbed cream into his heels and elbows. Other times, she dipped sticks that looked like giant earbuds into a pink drink then wiped them through Zane's mouth.

Once, Mum appeared at the doorway. It was a while before I noticed her. She didn't walk in. She didn't speak. She just stood there. She knew I wasn't going to budge.

Billy came and sat with me. We both cried. But not in a together kind of way. It was more Billy sitting in his chair and me sitting in mine, both crying. Not touching. Not speaking. He didn't stay for long.

A bit after 7 p.m., when it was just me in the room with him, Zane died.

All I wanted to do was tell Ralph that I'd done it.

I'd stayed with Zane and he wasn't alone when he died. I wanted to tell him how I wasn't scared. Ralph was right. The room had just gone really, really quiet.

So, the next morning I waited by his locker. I didn't care if Andrea saw me. We weren't living in the same world anymore.

I swear Ralph's face broke into a grin when he spotted me. He went to wave, but he didn't. He kind of dropped his hand and his pace slowed. Or maybe it was me and my sudden case of nerves that made it seem as though he was walking in slow motion, because it felt like forever until he was there, standing in front of me.

Ralph looked at me.

I nodded. 'I was with him,' I whispered.

Ralph wrapped his arms around me and we hugged.

21

WHEN BILLY CAME HOME FROM HOSPITAL
the next week, he walked in the door carrying a giant pink
stuffed bunny rabbit with long floppy ears and a plastic
carrot as a nose.

I laughed. 'What the hell?'

Billy handed it to me. 'It's all yours.'

'I don't think I'm a pink rabbit kind of girl,' I answered,
throwing it back. 'Thanks anyway.'

Billy passed it back to me. 'It's yours.'

'Huh?'

'It was Zane's,' Billy explained. 'One of his flatmates
brought it in to give to you. Apparently he'd told them that
if anything happened to him he wanted you to have it.'

'This was Zane's?' I looked underneath the ears and
inspected the carrot nose, pushing it with my finger to see
if it made a noise. 'I can't believe he wanted me to have it.
That's so nice. I take it all back, bunny,' I said, looking the
rabbit in the eyes. 'I like you, even if you are pink.'

We could hear Mum coming up the stairs. When she
appeared in the doorway she tried to snatch the bunny out
of my arms. 'It needs a good wash.'

'What?'

I was hugging it to my chest now. I wasn't giving it away.

'What's wrong with you, Mum?' I asked.

'All I said was, the toy needs a wash.' Mum pushed past me and a second later we heard her bedroom door slam shut.

'What the hell's wrong with her?' I asked Billy.

'Personally, I reckon we all need a break from each other.'

I followed Billy into the kitchen. He went straight to the fridge, loading up his arms with bread, eggs, bacon and a bottle of tomato sauce.

'Are you back on those drugs that make you hungry?' I asked him.

'Well, have you seen how much weight I've lost?' he snapped.

'Sorry!' I snapped back. 'I don't know what I've done to make you and Mum so angry.'

Billy mumbled through a slice of bread that flopped between his teeth.

'Hello? I can't understand you.'

'I said, Mum's mad that you were with Zane,' he answered, 'at the end. And she's mad that I didn't stop you. We had a big argument about it on the way home.'

'None of you could've stopped me,' I announced.

'That's exactly what I said to Mum.'

'And I've hardly burdened you all with the details of what happened in Zane's room,' I told him. 'Does she think I'm not old enough to handle it?'

Billy thumped his fist on the kitchen bench and I jumped. 'It's much more complicated than that.'

'That's the world's greatest cop-out!'

'Gemma,' Billy barked. 'You're sixteen. You don't know everything.'

Billy went away for a few days, which was a big relief because he'd ended up being in a worse mood than Mum.

So it was back to just Mum and me, like the old days. Except Mum was still giving me the silent treatment. When she wasn't in the kitchen she was in her bedroom with the door closed. She didn't even go near the sewing machine. Neuta stood there neglected, wearing only the bodice of my formal dress.

That weekend I called Louise. Andrea was away for a netball competition, but I wouldn't have called her even if she was home. A giant field of polite talk had wedged itself between us, turning us into friends we had never been before. We were suddenly acting like distant cousins who had to pretend to like each other because those were the rules. Or maybe we were more like best friends from primary school who'd bumped into each other after years apart and couldn't salvage what we used to have. What I did know for sure was that I didn't recognise us anymore.

It was a Saturday night and I badly wanted to go out. Mum even agreed it was a good idea. So Louise and I made plans. We met at Nigel because I wasn't sure exactly where she lived. I knew it was in one of the cul-de-sacs that all had names like Chancellor Drive and Magistrate Close. The houses were brand new, but to me they all looked the same. As we walked back to her place, I told her about being with Zane when he died.

It amazed me that I could talk this calmly about someone who'd died. Someone I'd been with. Someone whose skin I'd actually touched after all the life had left them. Wasn't I meant to be sobbing and wailing?

'You're so brave, Gemma!' Louise said, giving me a hug. 'I don't know if I could've done that.'

'I bet you could,' I answered. 'I don't think Andrea could.'

'When my nan died I didn't want to go to the hospital and see her. Too spooky.'

'But it wasn't. That's what I'm trying to say. It was . . . fine.'

'Maybe it's because you hadn't known Zane for that long?'

'Who knows?' I shrugged. 'As my brother said, I'm sixteen and I know nothing.'

Perhaps Louise was right though? Because for some reason since Zane had died, I was gradually starting to feel a strange detachment from him, like the whole thing had happened to someone else. Sort of like what was happening with Andrea. But I couldn't go there. It wasn't a topic I wanted to overthink. It wasn't a topic I wanted to think about, full stop. For now and for who knew until when, it was easier to make Zane into a story and Andrea into a girl I used to be best friends with.

It turned out that Andrea was right about one thing. Louise did have great clothes. I sat on the floor of her bedroom while she pulled out skirts and jackets and tops from her wardrobe for me to try on.

Albatross weren't playing at The Northern. It was another band I'd never heard of called Captain Dimples. Apparently, the lead singer was really cute and, according to Louise, the drummer had the sexiest arms she'd ever laid eyes on.

I'd never really taken much notice of drummers. They were always stuck down the back, like Nigel no friends.

Saul used to rave about the drummer from Mötley Crüe, Tommy someone-or-other. But that long black greasy hair with the bad headband didn't do it for me.

I really, like badly, hoped Ralph would be there tonight. I knew he hung out at The Northern so there was a fair chance. I had no interest in the drummer or lead singer. I was more concerned with finding something fantastic to wear from Louise's wardrobe just in case my hopes and dreams came true. I hadn't seen Ralph since our hug because he'd been on a Geography excursion for a whole week. Once I found myself standing in front of his locker, staring at the metal door. I weirded myself out so I made sure I didn't do it again.

By the time I'd picked my outfit, every piece of clothing that Louise owned was strewn across the floor and along the bed.

I stood there, looking in the mirror, trying to adjust to the sight of myself in a black dress with white spots, long sleeves and a straight skirt. What had really sold me was the open back that you tied up like a bikini top.

'I'm not usually a dress person,' I said to Louise. 'But this is cool.'

'It looks hot, Gemma. You have to wear it.' She winked at me in the mirror. 'Ralph might be there.'

I didn't want to blurt out everything that had happened between Ralph and me. I wasn't usually like that. The fact that I hadn't broken my silence and called Andrea to tell her every single detail was verging on schizophrenia. But there was something inside of me, like a little pea stuck in my heart, that wanted to keep Ralph and me away from everyone else. Especially Andrea. It was the one good thing happening to me and I was scared that if I talked about it then I was going to jinx it. But right then I knew that I had to tell one person or I was going to burst.

'Ralph drove me to the hospital last week,' I started. 'Actually, it was the day that Zane died. He was so nice, Louise. About everything.'

'No!' Louise squealed. 'You sneaky rat! When were you going to fess up?'

'Nothing's happened. Unless you count a hug?'

'I'm sure Ralph likes you,' Louise said. 'Andrea thinks I'm imagining it.'

'She would.'

Louise's parents had gone out and her brother was at a birthday party so we had the house to ourselves. When we'd finished getting dressed and shoving Louise's clothes back into her wardrobe and drawers, Louise went downstairs and nicked a bottle of champagne from the cupboard.

We drank it in her bedroom. The number one rule was not to get to the pub too early. That'd look desperate.

'To Zane,' I toasted.

'To Zane.' Louise clinked her coffee cup against mine. 'And to you and Ralph!'

'Oh my God, Louise, I'm really nervous about seeing him now.' Then I couldn't help myself. 'He told me he thought I was cool!'

'We are going to have the best time tonight, Gemma!'

We clinked glasses again and I promised myself that'd be the last thing I'd say about Ralph.

Even though Louise's mum had left out lasagne for our dinner and I was starving, we decided it'd make our tummies bloat so we didn't eat it. Instead we left for The Northern each with a honey sandwich in our hand and the rest of the champagne.

Champagne tasted a bit nicer than white wine and even though it had bubbles, it didn't make me burp as much. So it was definitely easier to drink and I think I was hogging the bottle. Louise didn't seem to mind though.

'You know, Gemma, apart from the movies this is the first time we've been out properly together.' She wrapped her arm around my shoulder and I passed her the bubbly. 'To us,' she said, taking a long swig.

'To going out raging,' I added. 'It's been a while for me.'

'I know. You poor thing,' she said, taking another sip.

'I thought this year I'd be raging every weekend. Not sitting in a hospital on a Saturday night.'

'Forget about all of that,' Louise declared. 'We are going to have the best night ever!'

As we got closer to The Northern, we could hear the lead singer doing a pretty good cover of 'Little Red Corvette'. The drums were thumping and I could feel the beat filling up my chest, making me walk even faster. I couldn't wait to get in there now. I'd been trapped in a hospital for weeks surrounded by a slow, plodding gloominess that had found its way inside me via osmosis. Maybe I would present my theory to Mr Curtin, next Biology class.

'Here we are.' Louise took my hand and we crossed the road towards the pub. 'You ready?'

'I think I'm a bit pissed,' I said.

'We'll order a Baileys and milk. That'll line our stomachs.'

'Okay. You're the boss.'

The minute the door opened the music blasted our brains. The room was swept up in a cloud of smoke, packed with dancing, sweaty bodies that bumped into us as we pushed our way through to the bar.

I scanned the crowd for Ralph. I couldn't see him, but there were people tucked away in corners and behind pillars, so that didn't mean he wasn't there.

Louise and I took our Baileys and milk with us onto the dance floor. The band were playing an INXS cover now and the lead singer was strutting around the stage doing his best Michael Hutchence impersonation. The song was a bit slow and hard to dance to and, to make things even more embarrassing, Fergus Eames had spotted us and came over. He was trying to rub up close to me, his hands running up and down my hips.

I excused myself and went for a wander but I still couldn't see Ralph, and wondering if he was going to show up was starting to get in the way of my fun. Three Baileys and milks later, my stomach wasn't feeling so good. Ralph definitely wasn't here, Fergus Eames wouldn't leave me alone and I was starting to remember how much I hated dancing.

'You okay?' Louise shouted in my ear.

'I think I'll go to the loo,' I told her. 'You can dance with Fergus.'

'Gee, thanks. Hurry back!'

On my way to the ladies, I did one more lap of the pub, just in case. But still no Ralph.

I wasn't going to tell Louise but my heart felt as though it had begun a slow slide down into her ankle boots. There was no point being here now and I wanted to go home. Not back to Louise's. Back to my place, where I could snuggle up in bed with Zane's rabbit, like I'd done last night.

There were only three toilets. I stood in the queue waiting, losing my footing every now and then and bumping into the girl behind me who had zero sympathy for my sorry state.

Finally, it was my turn. I folded onto the toilet, burying my head in my hands. Mum was probably still at the movies with Aunty Penny. I could walk home; it wasn't that far. Or maybe I had enough cash for a taxi. All I knew was that I had to get out of there.

I was counting my coins when I noticed a small Safe Sex poster stuck on the back of the toilet door. Just a small one sitting in a frame. *If it's not on, it's not on.* The words were surrounded by a cartoon of smiling, happy condoms, in a circle holding hands.

But why were they smiling? What was there to be happy about? What about the young guys who hadn't used condoms? Who hadn't said, *If it's not on, it's not on*? Who were too afraid to tell their families they had AIDS and were now in hospital dying and alone? Not just one of them. Lots of them.

I didn't have a pen but I pulled my eyeliner from my wallet. I defaced every smiling condom, turning the corners of their mouths down, drawing wrinkles to make them frown. Then I wrote a new slogan: *It's nothing to smile about.*

By the time I left the bathroom I was shaking. No one in this pub really knew about what was going on out there. They probably all thought that AIDS couldn't get them. It was a gay, fag, dirty, druggie disease that people brought upon themselves. And they didn't give a shit about those people anyway.

I'd bet no one here had ever held the cold hand of a twenty-one-year-old. Held it and not let go for almost three hours, until he wasn't in his body anymore. So only then, you knew that it was okay to take your hand out of his because you didn't want him to feel alone for one second because he was so fucking terrified.

Now it was me pushing through the crowd. I didn't even care that a metre-long piece of toilet paper had attached itself to the heel of my boot and was dragging along behind me. Catrina's mother and bridesmaids, Andrea's mother and grandmother, probably Andrea too and God knows who else all thought my family were dirty plague carriers. What difference did a bit of toilet paper make? Maybe it was the perfect accessory for someone like me.

Sonia Darue and some of the other prissies had turned up. They were dancing in a tight circle, smiling and laughing, each with one hand holding a drink and the other waving in the air. The perfect girls with perfect lives whose biggest dilemma was if their periods were late.

Suddenly I hoped that AIDS would bowl them all down, one after the other, until they all had cat cancer in their brains, the crypto bug to make them shit their pants and purple spots all over their flawless skin.

It was only when I was out the door and a few blocks away that I could stop. I crouched in the gutter and buried my head in my lap. I couldn't cry because I was too mad. Instead, I wanted to kick or hit or slap something. Tonight I wasn't scared of that feeling. I knew this person. This person was me. Gemma Longrigg, who had a brother with AIDS.

The gutter was feeling more and more comfortable. I decided to have a quick nap before I went back into the pub to find Louise and hopefully Ralph. But when I closed my eyes, the blackness started to swirl and sway in my head and suddenly I was sitting up, spewing.

My vomit was all over Louise's black-and-white spotty dress. It was dripping through the ends of my hair and out of my nose. I tried to stand up but fell straight back down. I pulled Louise's ankle boots off, noticed that they'd managed to get a bit of spew in them, rolled over onto my knees, then got up on all fours, and very slowly attempted to stand again.

One step, two steps, three. I staggered in my socks towards a tree. My hands steadied myself on the trunk while I vomited again.

I didn't hear any footsteps. I first realised someone was there because I noticed red pointy shoes on the ground next to me.

I peered up through strands of my sticky hair and saw Vanessa.

And standing next to her was Ralph.

22

THE NEXT MORNING, I WOKE UP TO FIND MY
bed covered in towels and a bucket on my bedside table.
I groaned, dragging the pillow over my head so I could find
some darkness.

The last thing I remembered was the sight of Ralph
standing next to his twin sister. Bits of the night popped
up but I honestly could not remember anything clearly after
that. Except a vague memory that maybe they'd helped me
into the lime mobile?

My mouth was dry and there was something sharp
sticking into the back of my throat that burned when I
swallowed. Carefully, I manoeuvred myself out from underneath the towels and blankets and shuffled to the bathroom
to clean my teeth. But I'd forgotten my toiletry bag. I was
about to shuffle back to get it when Mum appeared at the
doorway.

'Good afternoon, young lady,' Mum greeted me. She
was eating a piece of toast. 'Didn't you cover yourself in
glory last night.'

'Can you get mad with me later?' I moaned. 'I don't
think I could handle it now.'

'I'm not mad, Gemma.'

'You're not?'

'No. I'm relieved you're all right and that you have good friends that care about you.' I was about to smile when my mother said the most horrific thing. 'Poor Ralph, carrying you up every single stair like that. You were such a groaning dead weight. Worse than Mrs C at Christmas. He must feel like he has a broken back today.'

'Ralph carried me up the stairs?'

'Every single one. But don't feel bad.' Mum smirked. 'You thanked him enough. And told him how fantastic and gorgeous he was. Actually you kept telling him he looked like Johnny Depp.'

'Noooo!'

'Louise has called a few times. She was frantic last night, thinking you'd disappeared. But Ralph went back to The Northern to tell her you were fine. What a nice boy.'

'Mum, this is a disaster.'

'Well, sweet pea, you have no one to blame except yourself.'

'The night just turned—' I began.

'No. You did, Gemma,' Mum replied. 'It's called the drink.'

'Someone kill me.'

'Not yet, because Ralph will be here soon to drop your wallet off. Apparently he found it in the car this morning' – she stalled as another smirk appeared on her face – 'when he was cleaning up your vomit in the back seat.'

'What?'

I sat on the floor of the shower wishing I could be sucked down the drain hole and live underground with the water-rats for the rest of my life. Or at least the rest of the year.

Now I had to somehow get my act together and look

reasonable because Ralph was coming over. I begged my
mother to tell him I was out, or make up some other excuse
for me, but she flatly refused. This was why I wasn't in
trouble – Ralph's visit was my punishment.

My 501s and Billy's grey jumper were the best I could do.
At least it was casual and an outfit I liked. Sloppy chic, I'd
call it. The only problem was that I couldn't fix my bloated
face and my eyes like slits hiding somewhere in the skin.

There was nothing I could say to Ralph except sorry.
I would have to wear the 'you look like Johnny Depp' line
because I'd only look worse denying it. Maybe I'd try to
make a joke about it but I wasn't feeling very witty at the
moment.

Ralph didn't knock on the door until after 7 p.m. By
that stage I'd given up on him coming and had swung
from dreading his arrival to being disappointed he was a
no-show. So my heart jumped when I heard the tap on
the door.

Ralph was grinning his head off when he handed me
the wallet. 'Feeling better?'

'I'm so, so sorry, Ralph. I don't remember anything.'

'The bus from the Geography excursion got in late,' he
started. 'We'd only just got to The Northern when Vanessa
spotted you stumbling down the road.' Ralph's hand was
moving this way and that, mimicking the wonky trail I'd
taken. He was trying not to laugh. 'We were calling out to
you but you didn't stop.'

'Really?'

'Don't worry about it.'

'You must think I'm disgusting though.'

'Gemma, it's cool. Like I said, don't worry about it.'
Then he added, 'It was actually pretty amusing.'

'Glad I could oblige.'

'See you at school,' he said, and ran down the stairs two at a time.

Billy called to say he'd be away for the rest of the week. Jonathon had a house in the country with a twenty-five metre swimming pool. My mother said that Billy was there 'recuperating'. She kept saying how sensible it was that Billy'd decided to have more time away, because he needed the space. Plus, the fresh air would be good for his lungs. But I wondered how bad their fight on the way back from the hospital had been. I couldn't understand why Billy and Mum had argued over me staying with Zane until he died. Hadn't I done a good thing? A few times, I'd tried to suss Mum out but she wasn't taking the bait. Maybe I could squeeze the details out of Billy when he came home.

Louise, Andrea and I had agreed to have coffee after school. It was Louise's idea. I hoped she wasn't planning some sort of UN peace treaty between Andrea and me because life was about as peaceful as it ever had been between us. The three of us still met at Nigel in the mornings and some afternoons we walked home together too. Andrea had pissed her pants hearing about Ralph carrying me up the stairs. As far as she was concerned, if it wasn't for her netball competition, she would've been there too.

What neither of us had mentioned once was the formal. We'd been back at school two weeks. That's how long it'd been since we'd uttered the F word. It was as though the whole thing had been cancelled or that we'd never even had this grand plan of Billy doing our hair and make-up. I felt weird about it and I'm sure Andrea did too. But for now, not talking about it seemed to be the easiest thing to do. In ten weeks' time, it wouldn't be so simple.

Early this morning, Mum had driven off to Catrina's for the final dress fitting. Mum said that she and Catrina had agreed her place was the best option. But I had overheard Mum talking to her on the telephone and to me it sounded like it was Mum's idea and that Catrina had no option.

Mum forgot to leave money out for afternoon tea. In fact, Mum had forgotten a few things lately. My dentist appointment, her thirty-year school reunion and the Year 11 mothers' morning tea at Mrs Sylvia Darue's house that I'd just discovered after finding the invitation in her top drawer when I was raiding it for some coins.

All I had managed to scab so far was one dollar and thirty-five cents. I hit Billy's room next. Hopefully the top of his chest of drawers would be a gold mine because he always emptied his pockets of change there, stacking the coins up like towers.

Sixty-five cents. That was the disappointing grand total of his gold mine. I opened the top drawer, finding a couple of ten-cent pieces in one corner and a fifty-cent piece on top of a white envelope.

Billy's handwriting was on the envelope. Yet it was only as I was pocketing the change that I bothered to check who it was addressed to.

Mr Garth Longrigg
Maintenance and Petroleum Services
Ezzo Drilling, PO Box 188, Dampney Bay, WA

Very carefully, my fingers lifted the envelope from the drawer. It was already stamped and ready to go. Our address was on the back with 'William Longrigg' as the sender. It wasn't thick, it had to be only one page.

I turned on Billy's bedside lamp, holding the envelope as close to the globe as I dared. But I couldn't read a thing.

Billy had needed the space and fresh air. When he arrived home on Friday night he was like a brand new person. All sparkly and happy. He gave Mum the most beautiful bunch of white roses that he'd picked from Jonathon's garden that morning. He even lifted her up in the air like he used to.

'I might be a skinny old fag these days,' he joked, 'but I'm still strong.'

Mum was squealing and laughing. 'Put me down!'

Billy took his bag into his room, calling out behind him, 'I'm not home for long. I'm going out for dinner. Then I might go to a club.' He popped his head around the doorway. 'Hey, Gemma, want to come dancing? I hear you've become a party animal!'

'Can I, Mum?'

'Hell will freeze over before I let you go clubbing with your brother.'

'Next time, Gem,' Billy called from his bedroom.

So it was Mum and me again. We ate chocolate chip ice-cream and watched the video *A Room with a View*. It was an olden day story about a young woman and her aunt going to Italy. At one point, the guy picks up the girl and carries her away after she's collapsed. I thought of Ralph carrying me up the stairs. The only difference – and it was a big one too – was that the girl in the movie looked beautiful. I would have been covered in vomit plus my dress was probably over my head with my undies in full view. Again.

I'd barely spoken to Ralph all week. We'd just finished a Week B timetable, which meant only one double period of English. Ralph had arrived late and had to sit at the very front. For the full seventy minutes I'd stared into the back of his head, hoping it'd make him turn around. But it didn't. When class finished he had to see the teacher. At least I got a wave from him when I walked out.

Polly Pessimistic had been trying to bust out of her shell and tell me I'd jinxed things with Ralph. He thought I was disgusting. I'd vomited in his car. He thought I was desperate. I'd gushed that he looked like Johnny Depp. He so totally wouldn't think I was cool anymore. Yesterday, he'd winked at me from the end of the corridor but what was that meant to mean? He hadn't asked about giving me a lift to the hospital. Or home. Or anywhere.

Then Polly Pessimistic really did bust out of her shell. She shouted and hollered that Ralph didn't want me in his car because I'd held the hand of a guy who'd died of AIDS. There'd been more poofter bashings after two hold-ups in a bank. The robber threatened the tellers with a syringe full of what he claimed to be AIDS-infected blood. Plus all over the news was a story about a haemophiliac kid with AIDS who wasn't allowed to go back to school.

I was certain I'd seen Sonia Darue point at me the other day. Then whisper something behind her hand that had her gaggle of girls nodding like those dolls that hang off rear-view mirrors.

Get it together! I ordered myself. *Lock Polly Pessimistic up and chuck away the key.* She wasn't good for anyone.

Right there and then, I promised myself three things I would do. Non-negotiable.

1. Initiate a proper conversation with Ralph that didn't involve us both sitting in his car.

2. Organise a T-shirt cutting afternoon with Louise to make some midriffs.

3. Start a health kick. The formal was only ten weeks away.

23

WEEKENDS AND NO RUSHING OFF TO THE
hospital was another one of those simple pleasures I was
learning to appreciate. We had slotted right back to what
we usually did.

Mum slept in and then read the newspaper cover to
cover. Billy and I watched *Video Hits* while I ate cereal.
I stayed on the couch and Billy, Mr Exercise Health Freak,
went off to do laps at the pool.

The GP had him on antibiotics all the time now. The
doctor reckoned that if swimming made Billy feel good,
then he should keep it up. Mum wasn't happy about it.
I could tell by the way she clicked her tongue each time
she saw Billy walk towards the door carrying his goggles
and towel.

'Be back soon,' he told us. 'On the way home, I'm going
to get one of those famous bread sticks from the new baker.'

'Hurry up. I'm hungry,' Mum said. I wondered if she
hoped her words would make him ditch his laps and go
straight to the bakery.

Billy muttered something under his breath as he closed
the door and Mum did another one of her clicks of the
tongue.

Mum and Billy had stopped hanging out together in her room with the door closed. It took me a while to notice that now both their doors seemed to be closed. Each of them inside their own room, alone.

But I was starting to figure out why. Billy'd been home the longest he'd ever been since he moved to New York. Plus he was on his own. Usually Saul had been with him. I think they were starting to drive each other crazy. Or at least Mum was driving Billy crazy.

Since he'd been back from hospital this time, I'd noticed that she started to watch him. I'd even spied Mum standing outside the bathroom when Billy was in there, leaning against the door as though she was trying to hear what was going on. When Billy coughed, even just to clear his throat, she'd do this weird thing with her head that reminded me of a bird that had sensed danger.

Mum wasn't just driving Billy crazy. She was weirding me out too. She had started to light candles in her bedroom, and the other night when Billy was out, I'd caught her standing in his room, staring at the shelves. I stopped at the doorway and said 'Mum?' at least three or four times, but she didn't hear me.

I kept telling myself to ignore her weirdness because I had to be Polly Positive. Not Polly Paranoid, which is what Billy had called Mum when she'd asked him what the spot was on his hand. It was a lip liner he'd been testing out and he hadn't rubbed it off properly.

No wonder Billy wanted to get out of the house and do laps. When he was at school and training all the time, he told me he liked swimming up and down the pool because it emptied his mind. He said the best thing about swimming was that you didn't think.

'Gemma?' Mum called.

'What?' I shouted from the couch.

'Listen to this.'

'Hang on,' I said, rolling myself off the sofa and turning *Video Hits* down. 'What's happened?'

Mum was catching up on the death notices. She'd gone back to reading them and I didn't want to ask why. Maybe she was simply looking for Uncle Roddy's name? I'd given up on my quest after discovering Matt Leong in there.

'*Wayne Nathaniel Bradbury of Garrandai,*' she read. '*Beloved and cherished only son of Noreen and James, brother of Stacey and Bridget. Died aged twenty-one years. Up in the big sky.*'

'Wayne?'

'That must've been his real name.'

'Oh, Mum.' I wrapped my arms around her shoulders and nestled my head in the curve of her neck. I had chickened out of sending the letter and then it was too late. 'I wonder what his family thought?'

'We'll never know, my darling.'

'I had to stay with him. But why did it make you cross?'

'Because—' she choked. 'Because no one should have to do that twice.'

Mum's explanation only confused me. Twice? Was she talking about Zane? It didn't make sense. But right at that moment, I couldn't be bothered asking what she meant. It was only later that I'd work it out for myself.

Mum was pinning the bodice of my formal dress around me when Billy arrived home from the pool with two bread sticks that smelled as though they were just out of the oven.

'. . . oo were ick,' Mum said, through a mouthful of pins.

Billy understood Mum's language too. 'The pool was a bit crowded.'

'Don't they have allocated lanes?' I asked. 'You know, slow swimmers, fast lane, that kind of thing?'

'Must be a lot of good swimmers these days,' he answered, dropping the bread sticks onto the kitchen counter. 'We should eat these now. They're still warm.'

'Yum,' I called.

That afternoon was such a normal scene for my little family. Billy sawing through the bread. Me with my arms stretched out while Mum ducked around me, folding and pinning the black velvet to my body. The kettle on, blowing its steam, and U2 playing on the radio. The clean washing piled up on the table waiting to be folded in front of the Sunday night movie. The road outside quiet, the way it always was on weekends.

It must've been a moment worth remembering.

The next day at morning recess I was heading towards the bubbler because I'd just scoffed down a packet of salt and vinegar chips. The plan was I'd wash my face, then walk over and say hello to Ralph. I'd bumped into him on my way to first period. He told me he was sorry he hadn't been able to give me any lifts because he'd been driving Vanessa to auditions all week. So I figured it was my turn to make an effort.

I passed Simon Finkler who was sitting on one of the silver benches, his legs wide apart and his arms crossed – the way he posed in all the school footy photos. Maybe he was watching me, but I took no real notice of him because I was too busy being pissed off with myself for eating the chips. Today was meant to be day one of my pre-formal health kick and I hadn't even made it past recess.

I was bent over the bubbler, slurping up the water, when I heard, 'Oi! Longrigg!' The voice was low and deep like a foghorn. It sounded a lot like Simon Finkler.

I peered up from the bubbler, thinking to myself, *Did the Fink just call my name?* But my question was answered because Simon Finkler was walking towards me, hands in his pockets and a sneer so fierce his top lip almost disappeared into his nose.

Suddenly I noticed that everyone seemed to have already stopped and were staring at me, aware that something was about to take place in the quadrangle. But I was still straightening my back, putting my hands on my hips, looking around, and wondering what the hell was going on. It was as though I was the only person still moving. The last person to see him coming.

Simon Finkler was standing not even an arms-length from me. I wondered what would happen if he pushed me? Would I fall straight back, smashing my head on the bubbler?

But there was no more time for imagining my injuries, because this is what he said to me, in front of the whole of the quadrangle, 'I don't think you should be drinking from there, Longrigg. Spreading your dirty fag germs around for all of us to catch.'

'Excuse me?'

'Your fag brother swims in our pool, and now you're drinking from the school bubbler. You want to spread your poofter disease everywhere?'

'You're a pig!' I spat.

'What'd you call me, fag lover?'

'Leave her alone,' Ralph called. He was running over from one corner of the quadrangle, and I saw Fergus Eames coming from the other. But Simon Finkler didn't turn around. He was too busy staring at me.

'What'd you call me?' he barked.

'I said, you're a pig!' I reached out my hand and whacked him across the face.

I don't know who made the next move because I was having enough trouble just staying vertical and not passing out. I couldn't believe what I'd just done.

Suddenly, it was like an explosion. Bodies collided into one another, hairy arms and legs were rolling around by my feet, bones were crunching and skin was slapping.

Then Mr Curtin was there, yelling, 'Stop it, boys! Stop it!' And I could see his brown shoe kicking at their snorting, grunting bodies on the ground, trying to make them stop.

Someone had wrapped their arm around me. It was Louise, leading me away and saying stuff that wasn't making me feel any better, like, 'You were amazing, Gemma.'

Of course, the incident wouldn't just disappear the way I wanted it to. An hour later, an announcement came over the loudspeaker telling me to go to the principal's office. I was either in trouble or they were going to offer me some lame counselling session.

On the way, I passed Mr Curtin ushering Ralph and Fergus out of the sick bay. They both were holding icepacks to their faces. Ralph nodded as we passed each other.

The door to the principal's office was shut and I really hoped that Simon Finkler wasn't in there. Maybe the secretary was a mind-reader, because she called out from the desk that the principal was on the phone and wouldn't be too long.

I hoped he would hurry up. Lunch was only twenty-five minutes away and then the office would be crowded with students. I'd know the glances and whispers behind hands would all be for me: the girl whose brother had AIDS.

So I watched the clock. It was 12.05 p.m. and I found myself thinking about what had been happening at this time yesterday: Billy cutting up the freshly baked bread sticks; Mum pinning my formal dress around me; U2 playing on the radio. And out of everything that'd happened, that memory is what made me cry.

Simon Finkler was suspended and Ralph and Fergus had a week of lunchtime detentions. The principal had telephoned Mum, worried that I wasn't 'dealing with the situation'.

'Are you sure you don't want to talk to the school counsellor?' Mum asked when I got home.

'Mum, I was crying, that's all. I'm fine.' I turned to Billy because he was the one who really needed to know that I was fine. I was his Polly Positive. 'I'm all right,' I said again. 'Really. Honestly.'

The six o'clock news was on. Mum was stuffing lemons up a chook's bum and Billy was icing a cake because it was Aunty Penny's birthday.

Mum sighed. 'I just don't understand people. There's so much information out there about AIDS. Why is everyone so paranoid and unreasonable?'

'Can we not talk about it?' Billy snapped. 'Penny will be here soon and it's her birthday. Gemma seems fine to me. Let's at least try and have a nice night, Maryanne.'

'Who said anything about not having a nice night?' Mum began and I could sense another squabble on the horizon.

The phone rang, so I ran to answer it and to escape the kitchen.

'Hello?'

'Gemma?'

I recognised the voice straight away. 'Oh, Ralph, I'm so sorry—'

'Gemma,' he said quickly. 'I'm just around the corner from your place. At the phone box. Can you meet me here? Now?'

I was still in my uniform plus a pair of ugg boots and Billy's big grey jumper. But Ralph sounded anxious, and considering what he'd copped for me today, it'd be slack to keep him waiting for the sake of fashion.

Still, I had to brush my hair and put on some lip gloss. Then I ran.

Ralph was in the phone box, sitting up on the ledge, his long legs swinging back and forth. It was dark and it wasn't until he walked out into the street light that I saw his face. Both eyes were so swollen they'd disappeared inside his skull and there was a line of raw, shiny grazes down his cheek.

'Oh no,' I said. 'That looks painful.'

'Only if I touch it.'

'I'm so sorry.'

'Don't be. The guy's an arsehole.'

'Thank you for' – I wasn't quite sure how to word it – 'coming to help.'

'It was a bit late,' he answered. 'I wish I slammed him before he opened his mouth. Lucky Fergus Eames jumped in, hey? Wonder what that was about? I didn't think you guys were friends.'

'Not sure,' I fibbed.

'Anyway, lucky for me, or I'd be a slab of meat in the morgue.'

'Well, thank you,' I said again.

'It was a good slap you gave the Fink.'

'It's one of my specialties.'

'Hey!' Ralph was pointing at the phone box. 'Is that you and Andrea in there? That little line of messages?'

'We were in Year 7!'

'Still sounds like Andrea.'

Now I was wondering why Ralph had wanted me to come down here so urgently. I was quite happy to be here. I definitely didn't want to be anywhere else. But I had an inkling there was something else.

'Do you think someone's been hassling your brother at the pool?' he asked, moving closer to me.

I'd thought about that exact scenario today. But it didn't sit right in my head. My brother had always been tall and strong. When he was younger, that's had what saved him from gay taunts and bashings around the suburb.

Now, I supposed he was one of those skinny blokes with sunken cheeks and a hollow chest. It was hard for me to see him like that because my eyes still chose to see him as the guy he used to be. But maybe to everyone else he resembled an entrant in Mr Puniverse.

'Billy wouldn't tell Mum and me if he'd had any trouble at the pool,' I began. 'But maybe someone did see him and say stuff.'

'Simon Finkler?'

'He doesn't strike me as a swimmer. Too fat.'

'It sucks, anyway.'

'My mum had a bit of trouble with some of her clients whose dresses she was making. They came over and took them away before she'd even finished the hems.'

'No way!'

'Their problem. Not ours. That's the way we have to look at it or we'll go mad. Or kill someone.'

Ralph and I went and sat on the kerb. Beneath us, we could hear the water rushing by in the drain. I stared through the grates. The same ones I'd crouched next to all those years ago, trying to hear the cries of a missing girl.

'Do you ever feel old?' I asked Ralph. 'Or maybe what I mean is – do you ever wish you were still young?'

'Sometimes, I guess.'

'I used to listen down this drain for that little girl, Meg Docker. Actually all the drains along this road. In case I could hear her crying.'

Ralph was nodding. 'I remember Meg Docker. When she first went missing, Vanessa and I ended up sleeping in the same bed. We were terrified we were going to be kidnapped. We didn't know her but we cried when the police found her body.'

I gasped. 'So did I! It was like the worst thing that ever happened. Wasn't it?'

'Exactly. I reckon it was about the first time I realised that it could be a really bad world.'

'Me too!' I couldn't help adding, 'Wow.'

I don't know what made me do it but just like that, I took Ralph's hand. It was warm and his fingers curled themselves around mine. Strong and alive.

'Thanks for getting bashed up today,' I said.

'Gemma?'

'Yeah?'

'Will you go to the formal with me?'

I started laughing because I had not seen that coming.

Wearing my uniform, ugg boots and Billy's grey jumper, nothing like what I imagined I'd be wearing, Ralph leaned over and kissed me.

24

RALPH WAS DRIVING ME TO SCHOOL AND
driving me home. He said it was safer that way and Mum
and Billy agreed. Any feminist aspirations of being an
independent young woman who could take care of herself
were flushed down the toilet. As if I was going to argue
with that plan!

For some stupid reason, I called Louise and Andrea
that night to tell them I wouldn't be meeting them at
Nigel anymore. Even more stupidly, I told them how I'd
be getting to school. Andrea made *ooh* noises and heavy
panting sounds. Louise just sang through the phone, 'He's
in love with you. It's so obvious.'

To both of their very different reactions, I said the same
thing. That they were being ridiculous. I didn't mention
Ralph asking me to the formal. Let alone our first delicious
kiss, which I hoped there'd be plenty more of driving back
and forth from school. I still wanted to keep some of him
to myself.

The problem was the coming Friday. On Monday
morning, before everything happened with Simon Finkler,
I'd ticked the other items off my list and arranged for
Louise to come over. We had been discussing making our

T-shirts into midriffs for weeks. I'd suggested we do it at my place because my mother had the best scissors. At the time, I thought my biggest problem was Andrea finding out. It wasn't that I didn't want to invite her, but I wasn't sure what my mother would do with her sewing scissors if she found Andrea in our kitchen. I'd suggested Friday afternoon, because I knew Andrea had two hours of netball training.

But would I just ask Ralph if Louise could get a lift too? And if Ralph and I had been getting off in the car every day, then would I just tell him that we couldn't on Friday because Louise didn't know that we'd kissed? But then maybe Ralph would wonder why I didn't want to tell my friends about him and me. Maybe he'd get the wrong impression and think I was embarrassed of him?

Polly Pessimistic was slam dancing in my brain, bouncing off the sides then back again.

Yet I shouldn't have been thinking about that. I should've been thinking about what it was going to be like when I walked into school the next morning. That's what was occupying the thoughts of my mother, my brother and Ralph.

And of course, the other thing I should've realised before I went into overthinking-disaster mode was that most mornings and afternoons, Vanessa would be in the car with us anyway!

'You ready?' Ralph asked, as we drove into school.

'Fine,' I told him for about the tenth time. 'Simon Finkler's suspended. He's not going to be around.'

'But there could be other dickheads,' Vanessa said.

'Like?' I asked.

'One of the girls I modelled with in the States told me

this horrible story about these parents who started a picket line outside the school. You know, with signs and stuff? They'd found out one of the students there had a brother with AIDS.'

I hadn't been at all worried but now Vanessa was making me worried that I wasn't worried.

'I'm sure everything will be cool,' I said, trying not to picture Andrea's mother and grandmother marching outside the school with signs. 'What can I do about it anyway? It's their problem.'

The three of us walked in through the back gates, past the gymnasium and across the quadrangle: the scene of yesterday's crime.

Some kids did look up and stare – but they were looking at Ralph's face. Since last night, the purple bruising had bled across his nose and down one cheekbone. To me, he looked even more beautiful than Johnny Depp.

When I walked into the locker room, Andrea was leaning against the doorway and I had the distinct feeling she was waiting for me.

'I saw you and Ralph and Vanessa walking across the quadrangle this morning,' she said, a frozen smile on her face. 'You were all looking like a very cosy threesome.'

'Why are you saying that?' I could only pretend up to a point with Andrea. But maybe she'd forgotten that I could read her like a book. 'I told you last night that he was going to drive me to school from now on. I don't have to report in to you, Andrea.'

'No. But you couldn't wait to ring me,' she said, following me to my locker. 'Surprising, considering it was one of the rare phone calls you give me these days.'

I sighed. 'What's your problem?'

'I'm sure you rang me just so you could rub it in my face.'

'Sorry, Andrea, you've lost me,' I said.

'You and Ralph.'

'Excuse me?'

'You must be loving it.'

'Loving what?'

'Ralph paying you all this attention. You'll probably end up going to the formal together.'

'Andrea?' I started. 'You do remember the reason why Ralph's driving me to school, don't you?'

'Yes, I do,' she replied. 'And you know I think Simon Finkler is a jerk. But do you really think Billy should be swimming in our public pool?'

'Andrea, for your information, the pool actually made my brother sick. Our germs are a danger to him. Not the other way around. So I don't know where you're getting your information from.'

'You can't be that upset about Simon Finkler. Honestly? It made Ralph come to your rescue.'

'Are you serious? Do you have any idea what this has been like? Did you know I had to sit with a guy who died the other day? He was twenty-one. Twenty-one years old, Andrea!'

'Hmm.' Andrea nodded, her lips thinning into one straight line. Then out of the side of her mouth she uttered, 'I just reckon you're milking the situation a bit.'

'You're sick in the head, Andrea,' I snapped, and walked off.

Once, not so long ago, I would've ended up in a heap. Or at the very least given Andrea another one of those stinging slaps of mine. But this time I didn't succumb to either.

I'm not saying I didn't feel upset. Of course I did. Yet that 'once, not so long ago' girl was different now. I'd like to say part of me felt sorry for Andrea and her small pathetic mind but that'd be a lie. It was more that I just didn't care.

On the second morning when the lime mobile arrived at my place, Vanessa jumped out saying, 'You take the front, Gemma.'

That week, those car trips to and from school were fifteen minutes of pure bliss. It was a break from Mum and Billy squabbling; from Andrea's sulking; and from the odd kid at school gawking at me like I'd grown an extra nose. I felt like such an ordinary girl when I was in the car with Ralph and Vanessa. Ordinary in the best way possible.

I was put in charge of the music, changing the radio station or putting on a tape. If Ralph was thirsty, I passed him water. Once, when we'd stopped at a red light, he leaned over and kissed me. Vanessa groaned in the back and told us to get a room. Even though I blushed like crazy, which I don't do often, it was the sweetest heat in my cheeks.

Friday afternoon came too soon and Louise felt like an intruder on our precious car trip, which wasn't very fair to Louise, considering I'd been the one to mastermind the Friday afternoon plan.

As we walked to the lime mobile, I gave Vanessa a nudge and mouthed, 'You sit in the front.'

Vanessa frowned. So I pointed to Louise and she nodded.

Ralph didn't say anything to Vanessa when she took my seat. I wondered if they had that twin mental telepathy thing where they could read each other's minds.

'So what are you two actually doing this afternoon?' Vanessa asked, turning around to face us in the back seat.

'We're making these into midriffs,' Louise explained, pulling a plastic bag of T-shirts out of her schoolbag. 'Cutting them off. Giving them new life for next summer.'

'Cool,' Vanessa said. 'Can I join in?'

'Sure,' I answered. 'Billy would love that.'

'Will he be there?'

'Yeah. He's going to help. Billy's kind of claiming that it was his idea in the first place.'

'Ralph?' Vanessa asked. 'Can we go home to ours first so I can get some T-shirts?'

'Can I come too, Gemma?' Ralph winked at me in the rear-view mirror and I tried to eat my smile.

Now Friday afternoon with Louise had suddenly become the greatest.

Ralph and Vanessa lived in the old part of the suburb. When I was little, I'd wished that we could move there because to me it felt like a model town. The streets were narrow, the fences were all painted white and the houses joined together in neat rows. The park had a pond shaped like a peanut and white feathery ducks that nibbled politely on the bread you threw them.

We pulled up outside a gate with the number 36 painted in gold.

'I won't be long,' Vanessa said. Then she added, so casually as though it were a last-minute thought, 'Oh, Louise, can you come in and help me choose the T-shirts?'

So that left the two of us alone in the lime mobile.

'Doesn't Louise know about us?' Ralph asked. 'Is that why you're sitting in the back?'

'What's us?'

'You and me,' he shrugged. 'We're kind of a thing. Aren't we? Does she know we're going to the formal together?'

I shook my head. 'No. I haven't told anyone. Not a soul.'

'I was wondering why Andrea hadn't accosted me in the locker room.' Ralph smirked. 'Do you not want . . .'

I was shaking my head because I didn't want Ralph to get the wrong idea. Yet explaining the truth was terrifying.

'You're probably going to think I'm a freak but . . . but you're the one good thing that's happening to me, Ralph, and . . . I just want to keep it separate from all the bad stuff.'

Ralph leaned over and took my hand. I loved how mine seemed to fit perfectly inside his and the way his thumb stroked my fingers when he spoke. It was as though he didn't even know he was doing it. Like we'd been a couple for so long that it was just a habit now.

Mum actually didn't embarrass me when Ralph walked in the front door with us. In fact, they acted like long-lost friends. Perhaps it was due to the black eyes that he'd copped for me? More likely it was that they'd bonded over my floppy, vomit-covered body. But I preferred the first option.

'You're actually in luck, girls, because I have three pairs of scissors,' Mum said. 'I'm assuming you're not cutting T-shirts, Ralph?'

'No. I'm just the support team, Mrs Longrigg.'

'Is Billy here?' Vanessa asked.

'He'll be home soon,' Mum answered. 'He had to visit the clinic today. They've probably been flat out. Fridays can be manic there.'

I was surprised that Mum had just offered up that info. But this was us. Warts and all. 'Like us or lump us', as she'd said. No one uttered a sound and no one looked as though they were going to bolt out the door either.

'I'll put the kettle on,' I said.

'I've got some chocolate biscuits in my bag,' Louise offered.

Ralph, Louise and Vanessa plonked themselves around the kitchen table and started stuffing their faces with biscuits. I turned on the radio. 'Love Shack' by the B-52's was playing.

'I love this song!' Louise exclaimed.

'Me too,' Vanessa said. 'Turn it up!'

As I filled the kettle I noticed Neuta standing in my mother's sewing room wearing my formal dress. The skirt was now joined to the top and although it was still mostly pins and pieces of black velvet it did resemble the finished article.

I didn't want Ralph to see it. I didn't want to spoil the surprise. I wanted to have my big moment when Ralph picked me up that night. I wanted to see his face light up and hopefully hear him gasp and say something amazing. I hadn't quite decided what.

'I think the kettle's full enough,' Mum said, tapping me on the shoulder as the water spilled over the spout.

I gave Mum the big eyeballs and beckoned her over to the fridge.

With our heads inside the fridge door, pretending to search for something, I told my mother that Ralph had asked me to the formal and that I needed her to hide my dress. Then I put my finger to my lips and made a little *shoosh* sound.

Apart from Mum digging her fingernails into my wrist and me letting out a little squeal, it went perfectly. Mum slipped off into the sewing room and Neuta disappeared into the cupboard.

We sat on the living room floor because there was more room. We spread out our T-shirts and when Billy arrived home he gave us a how-to lecture. He held up one of Vanessa's old Wham! T-shirts in fluoro green. 'If they're big and baggy like this, then you can cut them quite short,' Billy told us. 'Just don't cut into the writing because that'll look weird.'

Louise unfolded a red long-sleeved top that looked as though it'd fit a doll. 'What about this shape, Billy?'

'Mmm . . . tight fit. I'd go just above the belly button.'

'Sexy,' I joked. Louise turned as red as her T-shirt.

'Talking about sexy,' my brother added, 'the other thing you can do is trim around the neckline. Depending on how deep you cut, you can make the "oh dear, my T-shirt's falling off my shoulder" look. That was all the rage in New York when I left.'

'This is sounding pretty technical,' Ralph said. He was flicking through our CD collection and I was hoping he wouldn't think the Rod Stewart albums were mine. 'How about I be the DJ?' he volunteered. 'Who wants to make the first request?'

'Can we choose songs or do we have to request whole albums?' Louise asked.

'Songs,' Ralph said. 'Otherwise I'm just going to be sitting here like a dork.'

'Michael Jackson, "Billie Jean"?' Vanessa called out.

'Coming up!'

We cut and ripped and measured our tops. We sang

and ate pretty much everything that was in the pantry and fridge. We turned on the lights when dusk arrived and the living room became too dark. And when I was starting to get that sinking feeling inside because our piles of T-shirts were shrinking and I didn't want it to end, Mum and Billy walked in, dumping two bags full of tops on the couch, then emptying them out onto the cushions.

'These are some old ones of Billy's,' Mum told us. 'I never got around to dropping them off in a charity bin.'

We pounced on them like hyenas.

'I remember this one,' Billy said, holding up a Rolling Stones T-shirt with a tattooed face sprawled across it.

'Yeah, me too,' I agreed.

'I bought this in 1981. It used to fit me like a glove.'

'It's cool,' Ralph said.

'Have it.' Billy handed it to him. 'Those black eyes tell me you've earnt it.'

For a second I panicked that Ralph would go all awkward over the comment. But he didn't. Instead, he and Billy high-fived. 'Take any ones you want, Ralph. I don't need them.'

Vanessa was studying one. '*Silence equals Death*,' I heard her whisper. 'That's an AIDS one, isn't it?' she asked Billy.

'There should be another one too.' Before I could say that I had it, Billy was pulling a third one out of the pile. Except this one was slightly different. It had a little pink triangle drawn above the words.

'Hey, we should all wear these to school one day,' Vanessa suggested. 'Put the Fink in his place.'

'Yeah!' Louise said, and Ralph chimed in, 'Good idea.'

'But we only have two,' I lied. Then yawned.

'Maybe we could get a whole lot printed?' Vanessa said.

'Sell them at school. They're always trying to get us to do forty-hour famines and walkathons and stuff like that. Why can't we have a cause that means something to us, for once?'

'My neighbour prints T-shirts,' Louise announced. 'I'm babysitting their kids tonight. I'll ask.'

Ralph and Vanessa were nodding. In fact, my brother was too. So I joined in even though I wasn't sure how I felt about my whole school walking around in *Silence = Death* T-shirts.

'Who can't wipe the smile off their face?' Mum teased, after they'd all left.

I was plugging in the vacuum cleaner because the carpet was covered in tiny pieces of fabric, as though someone had been married in the living room and we'd thrown it like confetti.

'He's so nice, isn't he, Mum?'

'You'll be a good-looking couple at the formal,' Mum said, taking Neuta out of the cupboard. 'I'd better make sure this dress is extra perfect.'

'Billy?' I called. 'Billy, do you like Ralph?' I dropped the vacuum cleaner and went to my brother's room.

Billy was sitting on the bed, his head in his hands.

'You okay?' I asked.

'That was a good afternoon, wasn't it?' His jolly words didn't suit the way he was sitting or the expression on his face. 'So you're going to the formal with spunky monkey? How about that!'

Billy stood up and went to the top drawer of his chest of drawers. His fingers lingered on the handle like he hadn't quite made up his mind if he was going to open it or not.

This was the drawer that held the letter to our father, stamped and ready to send. Was he going to take it out? Ask me to post it? Ask me to burn it the way I'd once suggested we do with any mail that had our father's name on it?

Billy opened the drawer. My heart started to pound. *Thud, thud, thud.*

'I was meant to wait,' he whispered, 'but I think now is the right time.'

Billy took out a small gold box. He held it and his hands were shaking. 'This is a gift from Saul,' he began. 'He bought it himself. He was pretty sick and I was out doing a job so he hailed a taxi. The shop was only about six blocks away, but the driver waited and Saul went in and bought them.' Billy was chuckling, lost in a story that must have felt like it happened so long ago. 'I was bloody mad because when I arrived home, he wasn't there. No note. No nothing. Hah, the trip could've killed him!' I watched my brother press his lips together and it was one of those times I was sure I could hear his heart crack. 'Saul knew he'd never get the chance, so he said that on the night of your formal I should give this to his favourite gal. Mr Attorney probably wouldn't approve that I'm giving it to you early. But, now,' Billy paused, 'well, it just feels right.'

I took the box from Billy and sat on the bed because my legs were starting to feel like jelly. On the lid were gold letters that read *Christian Lacroix*. How could being given something that I'd wanted for so long hurt so much now that I finally had it in my hands?

Under the lid was red tissue paper, perfectly folded without a crease, and inside the tissue paper was a pair of earrings. Giant gold crosses. Exactly the same earrings as I'd seen in the magazine.

I lay them in my palm. They reached all the way from the tip of my middle finger to the start of my wrist. Big, bold, look-at-me earrings just like I'd dreamed of.

'He remembered,' I whispered. My fingertips ran around the edge of the cross that Saul's hands had touched too. I closed my eyes and tried to imagine his neat, clipped fingernails. The smooth square nailbeds that Billy was always begging to paint because they were so perfect. On the day Saul had given me the gold hoops and seen the disappointment on my face he'd promised that one day he'd give me these. Is that why he'd gone out in a taxi when he was so sick? Because he'd promised?

But when I looked up to ask Billy, he wasn't in the room. I hadn't even heard him leave.

Billy had disappeared. No note. No nothing. Mum paced the hallway, ignoring my suggestion that maybe he'd told her he was going out and she'd forgotten. But I didn't even believe that myself.

At about 11 p.m. Billy rang us from the city, howling like a little boy, asking us to come and get him, telling us he couldn't go on anymore because it hurt too much.

Mr and Mrs C were only just back from holidays and already we were dumping our problems on them. Like always, just one tap on their door and they were there. Mr C in his new orange Hawaiian shirt, Mrs C with her black apron back on.

'Is no problem. No problem, *cara* Maryanna,' Mr C told Mum. 'You no go on your own. You and me will drive together and get Bill. Bring him home. All will be good. You will see.'

For some stupid reason Mum wanted to put on lipstick before she left. She was turning the flat upside down because she didn't know where she'd put it. I found it in her handbag along with three candles. My mother really was losing it.

Mrs C and I waved them goodbye. Then I put the kettle on.

We drank tea. I showed Mrs C my formal dress, pinned onto Neuta. Her big hands rubbed up and down the velvet as though it was a dog she was patting. 'Beautiful. Beautiful,' she kept saying. I even told her that Ralph and I were going to the formal together.

'You will be like Cinderella at the dance,' Mrs C said, pinching my cheek. Then she leaned over and gave me a kiss that prickled against my skin.

Mrs C wanted to know why she hadn't seen Andrea at our place much. She asked if it was because of 'the AIDS'.

'Probably' was the one-word answer I returned.

We went into the living room and sat on the couch. I dragged the heater closer to our feet and we watched *Tales of the Unexpected* in black and white.

Next to the stack of CDs still on the floor was a small triangle of fluoro green material. Most likely from Vanessa's Wham! T-shirt. Had that really been just this afternoon? Only six hours ago that we were laughing, playing music and cutting our T-shirts for summer.

I was asleep on Mrs C's lap when the thud of the front door closing downstairs woke me. The echo of footsteps trudging up the stairs and the sound of my brother weeping came closer and closer until it was here on our doorstep and sadness walked into our home.

Billy stood in the living room, Mum and Mr C on either side of him. His shoulders were slumped, as though it was an effort to stand. His face turned down to the floor like it was too much of an effort to look at us. I noticed a small patch of grey hair like a tiny hat on the crown of his head. He lifted then dropped his arms as if to say he was sorry. Or maybe he meant *it's too hard*? Then he shuffled out of the room and we heard his bedroom door click closed.

Before that moment, I had been certain that I'd already seen the best that sadness had to offer.

25

ALL WEEKEND, BILLY STAYED IN HIS
bedroom with the door closed. He asked us to give him
space, to respect his privacy, to leave him alone.

It was pretty hard. Especially in the quiet of the night,
when I lay in bed and listened to him cry through the thin
wall that separated our rooms.

The next Friday, exactly a week since we'd cut up the
T-shirts in our living room, I woke early to the sound of
feet padding up and down the hallway. I didn't know what
the actual time was because last night when I'd tried to
set the alarm on my clock, I'd pressed the wrong button
and couldn't be bothered fixing it. Now it said 9.21 a.m.,
which it definitely wasn't. Up the road, the highway was
still quiet.

The feet padded past my room again but I couldn't tell
who they belonged to or where they were going. When
I heard a light turn on, I knew that was in the kitchen
because it always buzzed for the first few seconds.

I hadn't decided who I wanted it to be. Mum or Billy?
There was a plus and minus to both. But I was curious and
wide awake so I went to suss out the situation.

Billy was sitting at the table, steam rising from a mug

of tea. The first thing that struck me was that he wasn't drinking from his *I Love New York* mug. It was the Ghostbusters mug that Aunty Penny had bought me at the movies. His fingers were pressing along his neck as though he was trying to find a spot that hurt.

He sighed. 'Hi, Gem,' he said as he looked up at me. 'I just made myself a cup of tea, but it's probably not a good idea. My mouth's a bit sore. You have it. I haven't touched it.'

That seemed like an invitation. Not the 'please leave me alone' request that I'd copped all week each time I popped my head around his door to say hi or see if he needed anything.

I sat down and Billy slid the mug of tea across the table. I wasn't sure whether to speak or not. Perhaps the invitation had conditions and silence was one of them?

'I had a look at your dress before,' Billy said. 'It's coming along. I love the way Maryanne's putting bone into the bodice. That's very haute couture.'

'It holds my boobs up better,' I answered.

'Were you planning on bare legs?' he asked, the tips of his fingers still poking at his neck. 'Because I was thinking those lace tights I bought you last Christmas could be nice.'

'What's up with your neck?'

He moaned. 'Nothing. So lace tights? Or have you lost them?'

'I haven't even worn them!'

'Okay. Sorry.'

Silence. Not too long. But long enough.

'Have you tried the earrings on?'

'About a hundred times.' I smiled. Billy smiled back.

Real and true, this time. 'I actually took them to school to show Louise and Vanessa.'

'You're hanging out with Vanessa now, are you?'

'I'm getting to know her,' I said. 'She's cool. Louise is cool too.'

'Andrea?' Billy asked. 'She's like the elephant in the room, Gem. I can't believe in the whole three months I've been here, I haven't seen her once. I kind of miss her annoyingness.'

I sighed. 'Well, she's still annoying.'

'Has she mentioned me doing her make-up since you sprung her at the hairdresser?'

'No.'

'And you haven't busted and told her that you saw her?'

'No.'

'I'm impressed.'

'You told me not to make a big deal so I didn't.'

'So, how's spunky Ralph?' he asked.

'Good.'

'Don't let him get too comfortable. Keep him on his toes.'

'Is that big brother advice?'

'Yes.' Billy smiled. 'Especially as I hear you're going to his place today after school. Meeting the parents!'

'Just his dad will be there. His mum will be at work.' I yawned because I was trying to convince myself that I wasn't nervous about it. 'Really . . .' I yawned again. 'It's no big deal.'

I wasn't positive but I thought I saw Billy roll his eyes.

'What?' I frowned.

'Nothing. I'm just . . .' He paused. 'Happy for you. He likes you. He copped a beating for you. I bet those black eyes have gone all yellowy green and look disgusting.'

'Well, I don't think he wants any concealer for them if that's what you're about to suggest?'

'It wouldn't work anyway. Bruises are hard to cover.' Billy sighed. 'Easier to cover those Kaposi bastards.'

'Have you ever had to do make-up on someone who's been bashed up? Like a celebrity?' Billy wasn't a gossiper, but every now and then he'd let a story slip. 'Maybe someone I've heard of?'

'Saul.'

'Saul?'

'The day I found out I'd tested HIV-positive, I punched him in the face. He ended up looking a lot like Ralph.'

Never had I dreamed that Billy would tell me how he ended up with AIDS. He'd made it clear that he didn't want to talk about it. I'd wondered often enough but I didn't want to know. That was the truth. I don't remember when I decided that. It was just that if I knew that Saul had given it to my brother, would I still miss him? Would I still get that ache in my chest when I thought of him? Would my earrings suddenly seem less beautiful?

'I can hear you thinking, Gem.' Billy's fingers were tapping the table.

'No, you can't.'

'Yes, I can, and I didn't get HIV off Saul,' he said. 'If that's what you're thinking.'

I shuffled around in the chair.

'*I* gave it to Saul.'

'What?'

'That's the truth. And I have to live with it. Or not.'

I couldn't think of anything to say and I was starting to feel sick in the stomach.

'You're the first person I've told, Gem. I haven't even told Mum.'

I stood up.

'Where are you going, Gem?'

'Back to bed.'

For the rest of the night I lay there staring at the ceiling. Now I knew the truth and there was no unknowing it.

＊

All day, I was like a zombie. My head full of fuzz and my limbs heavy. You could've punched me and kicked me and I wouldn't have felt a thing. I trudged from one class to the next. Half listening to the conversations around me. Feeling like everyone's life except mine was simple and straightforward.

Today was the one day I should've been buzzing. Leaping over clouds of happiness. Plus Vanessa had castings all day and hadn't been at school which meant I had Ralph to myself. But I wasn't. Perhaps I was reserving my energy? Perhaps I was excited but I just couldn't feel it yet?

Come on, I kept telling myself. *You're going to Ralph's place. You're going to meet his father. Isn't this everything you've ever wanted?*

But when Ralph stopped off at the bakery on the way home, I said, 'Can I be a couch potato and stay in the car?'

'You okay, Gem?' he asked. 'You've been kind of quiet.'

'Yeah,' I answered, sitting up and pasting a smile on my face. 'Peachy.'

'Sure?'

'Sure.'

'Okay.' Ralph nodded. 'Now do you like pink icing or chocolate icing?'

'Both.'

'I won't be long.'

I leaned out the window and did my best impersonation of an enthusiastic wave.

There was Ralph, the guy I had adored since Year 7, off to buy me cupcakes with pink and chocolate icing. Me. Gemma Longrigg. Not Sonia Darue or one of the other prissy girls.

I watched him walking down the road. His hands in his pockets, his sleeves rolled up. His shirt just a bit too small so that the outline of his muscles hugged the fabric.

Yet beneath my skin, snuggled under my bones, was a vast plane of flatness. Nothing moved, nothing quivered. The only thing I felt inside was nothing.

I turned up the radio and lay back in the seat. An almost spring sun glowed through the windscreen. But not even that could warm me today.

It was back in June when I'd spied Andrea at the hair-dresser, her Elizabeth Taylor book on her lap. I was wearing my black-and-white checked coat and on the way to the bakery I had stamped and shuffled my feet through every pile of autumn leaves. On the way home I'd dodged every one of them, choosing to run along the road instead.

Winter had almost passed. Now the trees were getting ready for the new season. Tips of green sat in the tops of the branches. Soon the leaves would be glossy and green. The branches so full they'd lean over the road casting a shadow that we'd huddle under come summertime.

'Time heals,' a man with a sleazy voice suddenly told me through the radio. A guitar strummed and birds twittered in the background. It was probably the beginning of some 'God Loves You' ad. I wanted to burst onto the radio and tell everyone that time didn't heal. Time changed everything.

When Ralph and I reached the gate of his house, with the gold number 36, I suddenly awoke and suffered a case of the jitters. No time to get it together, because when Ralph opened the gate there was his father, as though he'd been waiting for us.

'Hello,' he smiled. 'I'm Chris. I'm the father of Ralph.'

Ralph groaned. 'Please, Dad. Give us five minutes before you start with the dad jokes.'

'That wasn't a dad joke. Was it, Gemma?'

I shook my head, but I actually didn't know what a dad joke sounded like.

'What's in the bag?' his dad asked, opening it and having a stickybeak. 'Cakes?'

'Lots of them,' I said. It was about time I spoke. I didn't want to come across as some dumb bimbo who never opened her mouth. 'Ralph's bought so many. You're going to have to help us eat them.' It was true. For some reason there were about a dozen cupcakes in the bag, with a mix of chocolate and pink icing.

'I like chocolate icing. How about you, Gemma?'

'Both.'

'But if you had to pick one?'

I wanted his dad to stop asking me questions. I wanted to check him out. Study his face and see if I could find any of Ralph in there. So far, I'd noticed they had the same nose and dark eyes. He was like a faded version of Ralph.

I wondered if my dad was a faded version of Billy or me. Did he ever look in the mirror and catch glimpses of us? And if he did, did it make him grimace or feel a pang of regret, even for just a second?

The front door of Ralph's house was painted jade green, almost the same colour as one of the swatches Claude had sent from New York. We seemed to have lost Ralph's dad, who'd disappeared into the garden on the way up the path, and the door was closed and locked.

Ralph took a key from under the mat, unlocked the door and I followed him inside, down a hallway with walls covered in photos.

'These are way cool,' I said, stopping at a framed picture of Ralph and Vanessa dressed up as Thing 1 and Thing 2. 'So cute!'

Ralph took my hand. 'Come on,' he said. 'You can look at these later.'

I thought I knew what that meant. It wasn't the first time a boy had tugged at my hand trying to convince me that there was something better in the next room, which I could clearly tell was Ralph's bedroom.

But this time I was wrong. The next room was the kitchen, and sitting around the table were Vanessa, Louise and Justin. 'Surprise!' they yelled.

'No way!' I laughed. 'What are you guys doing here?'

'Well, I live here,' Vanessa joked. 'Hey, did you get food?'

'A dozen cupcakes,' I answered. 'From the new bakery.'

Louise started pulling something out of a bag on the table.

'Speech!' Justin called, banging a mug with a spoon. 'Speech.'

'Okay,' Louise started. 'We have done something and we think it's the right thing. But we decided, all of us, that is, that we should check with you first. Of course, if you don't like the idea then that's cool bananas. And . . .

here goes.' Louise reached into the bag and pulled out a T-shirt. It was white with thick red writing: *Silence = Death*.

'Wow!' I gasped. 'That's . . . wow. Oh my God, did you do that?'

All of a sudden everyone at the table burst into talk. Who did what and how they changed the design because someone said this and so they thought of that and everything in between.

'Mr Curtain was our biggest supporter,' Justin told me. 'Lucky you've been copying my Biology homework for all these years, because he likes you. He said, "That Gemma's a good girl."'

Louise held up the back of the T-shirt. In the same bold red letters it said, *AIDS. Talk about it.*

'That's really, really awesome,' I told them all. 'I don't know what to say.'

'We want to get a whole heap printed so we can wear them to school. If that's okay with you?' Louise asked.

'It's not a fundraiser,' Vanessa added. 'More like an awareness campaign.'

The others were all nodding in agreement.

'Every single person in Year 11 wants one,' Louise told me. 'So far, we have ninety-two orders!'

'But aren't there only eighty-six people in our year?' I asked.

'Bronnie Perry and a couple of others in Year 12 want one,' Louise said. 'Plus Mr Curtain and a few teachers. I have to put the order in as soon as possible. So they'll be ready for Monday week.'

'I like it.' I smiled. 'Simon Finkler will be back at school.

A smile burst onto Louise's face. I had to admit, it was a fitting revenge for the dickhead.

We sat around the table chatting and stuffing our faces with cupcakes. Justin even sucked the wrappers till there were five tiny wet balls of disgustingness sitting on the plate. I ate half a cupcake and even that didn't sit well in my stomach.

When I stood up to get a glass of water, Louise followed me. 'Are you okay, Gem?'

'Yes. Just thirsty.'

'If you're not comfortable about the T-shirts, just say. Really. It's fine.'

'No, I love them,' I said. It was just us two at the sink. 'And thanks. I know this would've been your idea.'

'We all did it. It was fun. I'm so relieved you're okay about it.'

'It's great.'

'Andrea wanted to come today. But she has—'

'State netball trials.'

'She must be good at it?'

'Killer instinct,' I answered.

*

Ralph drove me home. We pulled up outside the park near my place, the one I'd stomped off to that Sunday afternoon when he didn't notice me because his head was stuck in a modelling catalogue. I hadn't decided if I'd ever confess to that. Or if I'd ever confess why Fergus Eames had also risked his life to come to my rescue against the Fink.

We lowered our seats and I leaned across and kissed him. We wrapped ourselves around each other like we could've if we'd been alone in his bedroom. I wanted to feel his arms around me. I didn't want to speak. I wanted to wake my body from its zombified state and feel something.

Hours slipped by. It was as though we'd been sucked into a pocket where time didn't move. Where thoughts were muted and words weren't needed. It was so perfect and so hard to return to real life.

But then Ralph said, 'Do you ever see your dad, Gem? You've never mentioned him before.'

'I never see him and I never mention him. That's all you need to know.'

'Come on,' Ralph said. 'Don't be like that. Why can't you tell me about him?'

'Because there's not much to know,' I answered, suddenly sitting up and winding down the window. The heater was blowing into my face and making me feel sick in the stomach. 'My father's a dick and he left us because Billy's a poofter.'

'That simple?'

'I don't know. I don't think he and Mum were some great love story.'

'Does your dad know Billy's sick?'

'Nope.'

'Are you going to tell him?'

'Nope.'

'But isn't that like the Zane thing all over again?'

'Excuse me?'

'Well, isn't it?'

My brain was suddenly a mishmash of flying words and pictures. Zane; my father; sitting in the kitchen this morning with Billy; Andrea with her hands on her hips; Saul with purple spots all over his face; the mottled bruises around Ralph's eyes.

'Gemma? I'm not trying to . . .' My fingers were wrapping themselves around the doorhandle. '. . . to pry or be . . .' I heard the click of the door opening. 'Gem? Gemma?'

'Fuck off, Ralph.'

I was out of the car and on my feet, brushing down the skirt of my uniform, wrestling my bag onto my back.

'Gemma! Please get back in. I'm sorry.' Ralph was leaning over the passenger seat. 'I didn't mean it like that. I'm an idiot . . .'

I started walking. Now Ralph was driving next to me, calling through the open window. 'Gemma? Get back in. I don't want you walking through the park. It's pitch black. It's not safe.'

'I've done it before!' I yelled back. 'Not so long ago actually.'

I kept going, wondering if Ralph was watching me disappear through the trees.

26

WHEN I ARRIVED HOME OUR PLACE WAS
dark and silent. Mum was out, God knows where. The
only light was a sliver of gold at the bottom of Billy's
closed door.

Tonight, I wasn't going to accept any 'please leave me
alone' requests. I badly wanted a fight and Billy was the
perfect one to give it to me. I bet that he'd been cooped up
in his room all day. Seething away in his own self-inflicted
solitary confinement. The way he lived for days after he'd
fought with Matt. Billy would be ready and waiting.

I bashed on the door and marched in.

Billy didn't even look up. He was lying on the bed,
playing with the Rubik's Cube.

The first thing I noticed was how thin he'd suddenly
become. As though he'd lost weight since the morning.
It caught me off guard, catching my words with it. I stood
there, mouth open and ready, but nothing coming out.

'Do you hate me because of what I told you this morning?'
Billy said, his eyes still focused on the coloured squares he
was twisting this way and that. 'Do you? Hmm?' Suddenly,
he chucked the cube at the wall. 'I'm sure you do,' he spat.
'Saul's mother hates me. I hate me.'

'Stop having a pity party!' I was ready for battle now. It was like a switch had just clicked on. 'It's not always about you, Billy.'

'Swap places then?'

'No!' I barked. 'You know I think the whole thing sucks, so don't say that!'

Billy glanced at his watch. 'You've been out a long time,' he crooned in a fake *I'm so concerned about you* voice. 'Thought you'd be in a better mood after being with spunky monkey. Did something happen? Did his dad not like you?'

'If you want to know,' I growled, 'we had a fight. About you!'

'Well, come on.' Billy was almost gnashing his teeth. 'Spit it out. I'm dying to hear all about it.'

I crossed my arms. 'Ralph thinks we should tell Dad.'

'Interesting.' Billy sat up and crossed his arms back at me. 'What do *you* think? Actually' – he waved his hands at me – 'I know what you think.'

'And *I* know *you* have a letter to Dad. In your top drawer.'

'Correct, Miss Snoopy.'

'Are you going to post it?'

'I don't know. It depends.'

'Depends on what?'

'It depends on how sick I get. If you get my drift?'

'You don't seem very sick at the moment. If you get my drift?'

'I don't know about that,' he answered. 'I have a filthy big lump in my neck.'

'You said nothing was wrong with your neck!' I yelled. 'I asked you about it this morning!'

'I didn't know then, did I? But I've been at the doctor's

today, and now I'm just waiting for the results. Woo hoo! What surprise will they have for me this time?'

I watched my brother's cabaret of sarcasm as he clapped his hands and pretended to cheer. And for a second I actually hoped he had the cat cancer in his brain because I didn't want to think he could naturally be this horrible.

I didn't want a fight anymore. There was a bad feeling in this room. It danced around my brother's silhouette like a buzzing electric current. If I didn't get out it was going to zap me too.

Apparently, the doctor suspected that Billy had an AIDS-related lymphoma, which was a fancy way of saying he had cancer. And it wasn't just the lump in his neck. There were also lumps under his arms and in his groin that he hadn't bothered to mention. The doctors had booked all sorts of tests for Monday. My brain went into overload and shut down when Aunty Penny read the list: *full blood count, bone marrow biopsy, chest scan, stool sample.* On and on it went.

The boogieman was back. But he couldn't wait till Monday.

On Sunday afternoon, after Billy'd been shut up in his room coughing for most of the day, he suddenly called out to Mum.

We burst into his room. Billy was trying to stand up. His palms were pressed against his chest and his lips wide open in a perfect 'O'. 'I can't breathe,' he managed to mouth between gasps.

Even though it was much worse than ever before, Mum didn't panic. It was as though she'd rehearsed the moves.

She picked up the phone, called the ambulance and very clearly told them our address.

Mr and Mrs C and me followed Mum and Billy in the ambulance. As though the first time had been a dress rehearsal. The Fiat groaned to keep up with the red flashing light in front of us. Mrs C draped her hand over the seat and I gripped it tightly.

Over and over and over, I told myself that I had to be Polly Positive. Now, it couldn't matter what I knew or how I felt about my brother, or that things between Ralph and me had gone down the toilet. I had made a promise and I had to try and keep it.

Billy bypassed casualty and was taken straight to have an X-ray. We were told to wait up on 9 South West. Mum made a fuss, saying that she wanted to stay with her son. Hospital staff wheeling machines and wearing goggles, gloves, masks and gowns were trying to get through. Nurses were also attempting to squeeze past us.

Dr Sally Haste, according to her shiny name badge, stopped shouting orders, turned around and took Mum's hands. 'Mrs Longrigg, I understand that you're very worried. We're trying to assess what's wrong with Bill as quickly as we can. You can help by going up to the ward. As soon as I know what's going on, I'll come and let you know.'

When the lift doors opened onto 9 South West, it was like walking back into one giant hospital smell. Mum grabbed my arm as we stepped out. 'You okay, Mum?'

She nodded, which probably meant she wasn't. In the lift, I had noticed a new wrinkle on her forehead that I was positive hadn't been there yesterday. Deep, like I could run my finger through it.

Darren was at the nurses station, swinging the keys that hung around his neck on a red piece of string. He waved. Then he came over and performed some strange welcome that was probably meant to make us feel better.

'Hi, Longrigg family,' he said. 'How are we doing? It's been a while.'

I tried to smile and play along. Mostly because Mum was stuck in her stunned mullet act and I didn't want the Longrigg family to seem rude.

'We're pretty good,' I lied. 'How have you been? How's Anna?'

'Sadly, Anna has only two weeks left with us and then she's away on another adventure,' Darren told me. 'She has the weekend off.'

While he chatted, we followed him around the nurses station and down the corridor. I completely and totally missed where he was leading us. Until we were there, standing outside a single room. Room 12.

'Oh?' Mum uttered, suddenly pulling up at the doorway like she'd just slammed on the brakes. 'Is . . . is this Billy's room?'

'It's the only bed we have,' Darren answered. 'We're chock-a-block.'

'Thanks,' Polly Positive said. 'There's a nice view from this room.'

'Sea view,' he joked back. 'This'd usually cost you a fortune.'

'Do you know how long it will be before they bring Billy up to the ward?' Mum asked.

'Not sure, Maryanne. I think the doctors will put a drain in his chest while they're down there.'

'Oh?' Mum said, a sudden bounce in her voice. 'It's

pneumonia!' If Mum'd added 'only' to 'pneumonia', then I would've totally got what she meant.

'Let's wait for the doctor,' Darren said, patting my mother on the shoulder.

It was pneumonia, or PCP as Dr Haste called it. One of his lungs had collapsed and they had inserted a drain into his chest. But on top of it, they confirmed that Billy had lymphoma. She said it was B-something lymphoma and then went off on the long medical spiel that shut down my brain and put me into numb mode.

My ears perked up when I heard her asking Mum if Billy had once had glandular fever. 'Yes!' I beat her to the answer. 'He was still at school.'

'Was he?' Mum asked.

'I remember you made me that yellow top with the sunflowers and Billy was learning how to drive and you both drove me to Mandy Zoran's birthday party.' I suddenly felt embarrassed, like I'd shared a bit too much.

'Mandy Zoran?' Dr Haste said. 'Did she have a much older sister called Steph?'

Mum and I nodded like a couple of puppets.

'My sister was friends with a Steph Zoran. It's quite an unusual surname.'

Then it was back to business and stories of Mandy Zoran and my yellow top with the sunflowers were put on hold for another time.

'Tonight we'll keep Billy comfortable,' Dr Haste was saying. 'Then tomorrow we'll do more tests. We can't even think about starting chemotherapy until Bill's lung has reinflated and he's a bit stronger.'

'Chemotherapy?' Mum said, as if she had heard my

thoughts and asked the question for me. 'Billy has to have chemotherapy?'

'It's the only way to control the lymphoma, Mrs Longrigg. It's very aggressive and it's a gloomy picture without it.'

✳

I barely needed to give Mum an excuse for why I couldn't go to school. I think she was grateful to have me there next to her when we walked into Billy's room the next day.

'I'm not having chemotherapy.' They were Billy's first words to us. Our Monday morning greeting. 'Just want to get it out there now so that we're all clear on the situation.'

'Let's not make any decisions at the moment,' Mum said. The new wrinkle in her forehead looked like it might cave in and split her face in two. It made me want to put my arms around her and hug her tight. 'Dr Haste says we need to wait until your lung reinflates and then—'

'Mum, you're not hearing me,' Billy said. 'My body. My decision. No chemotherapy.'

'Billy?'

'Mum, please. Chemotherapy's not going to fix it. It's not going to change the ending. It's only going to make me really sick and steal whatever time I do still have. Please understand.'

Mum walked out, muttering under her breath. 'No chemotherapy? No AZT?'

I kept standing by the window, watching a ship way, way out on the horizon, wondering where it was going and who it was taking with it.

The foamy white horses gently rocked across the surface of the sea. My father once told me that if you saw a white

313

horse it meant they'd just dropped off a mermaid. He said they were the taxis of the ocean and that's why some days they were everywhere and other days you couldn't find one.

'Do you want me to send that letter to Dad?' I asked Billy.

'You might as well,' he groaned.

'Okay,' I said and I went off to find Mum because I couldn't stay in this room with my brother for a second longer.

When we arrived home from the hospital, the answering machine was flashing with four messages.

'I wonder who they're from?' Mum said.

'No idea.' I yawned.

Mum didn't know about my fight with Ralph. She didn't know about the T-shirt awareness campaign my friends had organised either. When she'd opened my bedroom door that Friday night and whispered, 'Gem? Gem, are you awake? Did it go well?' I'd pretended to be asleep.

Mum pressed the answering machine and the messages spat out, one by one. The first was from Aunty Penny, telling us she'd pop in to see Billy before her night shift started.

The second and third were from Ralph. 'Hi, Gemma. Call me back.'

The fourth was him again. All he said this time was, 'Hello?'

Mum was studying me. 'Is everything all right between you and Ralph?'

'Fine.'

'He sounded a bit gloomy.'

'That's just his phone voice.'

'Well, he'd better not get a job in a call centre,' Mum said, disappearing into the bathroom.

Never before had I considered myself to be particularly sneaky or dishonest. But I was amazed at how quickly I slipped into my brother's room, took the letter to Dad out of the top drawer and then called to Mum through the bathroom door, 'Going down to the phone box, Mum. To call Ralph.'

The door sprung open. 'No, you're not, young lady. It's almost eight-thirty. It's dark outside. You can use the phone here.'

'You let Billy go.' The speed of my answer surprised me too. 'When he wanted some privacy to call Matt.'

'Billy was a big, strong boy.'

'So? What's that got to do with it?'

'Gemma? Please, I'm tired.'

'Mum, I promise I won't be long.' That was a promise I knew I could keep. Five minutes later I was back. I just knew that if I didn't post the letter to our father then, I couldn't be sure that I'd do it tomorrow.

✳

The next day I was going back to school and my life would be back to normal. School all day. Hospital at night. The little extra slice of normal would be Ralph and I back to where we probably belonged. Not together.

This morning there was no lime mobile waiting outside my place. I did leave earlier than usual so I could get to Nigel in time to meet Louise and Andrea. At least, that's what I told myself.

Louise was suss about Ralph and me. When we were at Ralph's place, I'd caught her looking at us. Louise hadn't tried to drag it out of me. Nor was she acting all *I'm your friend and you have to tell me everything*, which would have been Andrea's tactic to make me confess.

I wondered if Andrea felt bad for being such a cow, telling me I was 'milking the situation' after the Fink and Ralph's fight? She deserved to. But maybe there was some truth to what she'd said.

Not the 'milking the situation' part. The bit about Ralph paying me attention. If Vanessa hadn't known Billy and Billy hadn't become sick and Simon Finkler hadn't done what he did, would Ralph and I have ever existed? And if that was the reason, or at least part of it, then should I feel bad that something good came out of something much worse? Not that any of it mattered now. And if Andrea turned up this morning and grilled me about Ralph, I could look her in the face and tell her truthfully that nothing was going on.

Up ahead, I could see Louise swinging around the pole that was Nigel. As I got closer, I could hear her singing the Roxette song.

Soon we'd be getting ready for the formal. I'd probably be sitting at the kitchen table. Billy would be doing my hair or maybe he'd be doing Louise's and I'd be standing there while Mum zipped up my dress and brushed down the velvet. Now it was impossible to see Ralph and Andrea in that picture.

But Andrea had never been a fantasy. She was the one thing I could be sure of. Yet our friendship was floating away from us like a prized balloon that we'd accidently let go. We were watching it float away and neither one of us could jump high enough to catch the string and save it.

'Hey!' Louise's lopsided face broke into a smile and she started waving. 'I didn't expect to see you here.'

'It's a bit silly me getting lifts to school,' I started. 'It's not like there's any—'

'But what about Ralph? Don't pretend there's nothing going on. It was a bit obvious the other afternoon.'

I shrugged.

'Vanessa told me he was a total sad sack all weekend.'

'Oh?'

'Are you still excited about the T-shirts? They're going to start printing them this week!'

'Billy's back in hospital.'

'Is he okay?'

I shook my head. 'Not really.'

———— ✳ ————

In second period I had English. I made sure I was the first one to class so I could take the desk at the very back that was in the Nigel no friends corner.

Without even looking up, I knew when Ralph had arrived. I could sense him. As though his presence had sucked up all the oxygen in the room.

When I dared to peer up, I saw that he was sitting three rows ahead of me. Not once did he turn around.

Lunchtime I spent up in the library. Out the window, I watched Ralph in the quadrangle, his hands in his pockets as he stood next to Martin Searles in the canteen queue.

Look up, Ralph, I whispered. *Look up.*

The next afternoon, like the one before, I purposely dawdled out of class and through the quadrangle, killing time until everyone was out and loading onto buses, or lining up for lifts. Then, the locker room would be almost empty. No Andrea to hunt me down. Or Ralph pretending he couldn't see me.

But when I walked in, Ralph was leaning against my locker. His hands were in his pockets, and he was staring at the floor. A second, that's all I needed to turn around and slip away.

Instead, I took a breath and said, 'Hi.'

Ralph looked up. 'Hey.'

I pointed at my locker. 'I need to get my bag.'

'Oh? Yeah. Sorry.'

I riffled around in there, trying to kill time. What was Ralph doing here? As far as I was concerned, the rule said that if you waited at someone's locker, you had to be the first to speak. State what you wanted and what you were doing here. Put your heart on your sleeve, then I'd put mine on too.

'Do you want a lift home?' Ralph finally said.

'No.' I nearly stopped there. But I didn't want to be that girl. 'I'm going to the hospital. Billy was admitted on the weekend.'

'I can drive you.'

'My neighbour's taking me. He's probably already waiting outside in the Fiat.'

'Gemma. I'm sorry,' Ralph began. 'I really am. You didn't ring me back. I get that you were probably still mad. But now you're avoiding me. Is it because I wasn't there on Monday morning to pick you up? I had to take Vanessa to an audition in the city and—'

'I didn't even go to school on Monday,' I answered. 'Look, I have to go.' I didn't really. Mr C was the most patient man on the planet. But I knew I was seconds away from crying.

Ralph stood there while I closed up my locker and fiddled with the padlock. He stood there while I heaved my bag onto my back and he didn't say a thing. It wasn't until I reached the door that he called out, 'Gemma?'

I stopped. 'Yes?'

'There's a new message for you in the phone box,' he told me. 'From Andrea. I saw it on Sunday when I tried to call you.'

'Oh. Okay.' I started walking. 'Thanks.'

When I stepped out of the hospital lift and into the ward, Anna was there waiting to step in. Her bag was over her shoulder and she was untying her ponytail.

'Bill's drain's gone,' she told me. 'Just oxygen therapy now. You have a much happier brother.'

'He's been a big grump.'

Anna pressed the button in the lift so that the doors wouldn't close. 'It's tough, Gemma,' she said. 'I don't think any of us know what it's like.'

'Probably not.'

'This morning, when I was helping Bill with a shower, he told me about his partner, Saul. He'd never mentioned him before. They sounded like they were really close.'

'I thought they were.'

'To lose a partner must be the worst.'

For a second I couldn't move. It was as though Anna's words had paralysed my limbs.

I did think about Saul. Not all day, every day. Not the way I thought about Ralph. But Ralph and I weren't even a thing. Yet I couldn't imagine how it would feel if one day Ralph just disappeared off the face of the earth like Saul or Meg Docker.

When I walked into Billy's room, he waved and pointed to the chair for me to sit down.

Today he was back to his old self, smiling as he listened to whatever the person on the other end of the phone was saying. He put his hand over the receiver and whispered to me, 'It's Aunty Mame. She's in the middle of a long story.' Then he started laughing at whatever Mame had just said.

Looking at him then, you would never guess what he was really feeling inside. Anna was right. Billy had been through something none of us could begin to imagine. Did it really make a difference that Billy had made Saul sick? They loved each other and I had to remember that.

Billy hadn't just held Saul's hand at the end like I had with Zane. He'd been there every day with him. Showering him, feeding him his mush, worrying when he came back to their apartment and Saul had disappeared to buy me earrings. Having to make all those promises, right to Saul's face, looking straight at him. At his thin, purple-spotted face. How could any of us know what that was like?

Billy didn't look like he was going to get off the phone anytime soon.

'I'm going for a walk,' I mouthed.

'Mum's down in the cafeteria,' he mouthed back.

Outside Zane's old room a frail man with wisps of white hair sticking out from under a black hat and wearing trousers that didn't fit properly was pacing around the doorway, a walking stick in his hand and a look on his face that I couldn't read. Was it impatience? Was he waiting for a doctor or nurse to finish in there? Or maybe he was waiting for his wife who'd been in there too long with their poofter son?

I went to the sink to wash my hands when I noticed a nurse and the ward clerk walking over to the patient board. As though she were some efficient teacher, the ward clerk picked up the eraser and wiped out the name next to Bed 15.

'That's number three this week,' I heard her say to the nurse.

'I know, and Jim won't last the night either,' the nurse replied. 'Look at darling Carlo. He hasn't left his side.'

'And he doesn't look well himself,' the ward clerk added. 'He'll be a patient here in a few weeks.'

'Weeks? I'd say more like days.'

They walked away, smiling at me as they passed.

That frail old man waiting outside the room was no father. That was the partner of whoever was in there. The partner who'd no doubt washed and fed and made promises to the man he loved who was lying inside.

Straight away, I went back to my brother's room.

He was off the phone and out of bed, staring through the window. There were yachts out on the water and their colourful spinnakers reminded me of our T-shirts laid out across the living room floor.

'They must be racing,' Billy said. 'That's my favourite one there.' He tapped at the glass. 'The one with the black-and-pink striped sail.'

'I'm sorry if I've been grumpy with you,' I offered. 'I didn't . . .'

'Don't worry about it, Gem. I've been horrible lately. I'm so ashamed of the way I've acted.'

I wrapped my arm around him. He felt small and bony, as though I could crunch him in half with just a snap of my elbow.

He nudged me. 'How's lover boy? Have you two made up?'

'No. We weren't really a thing anyway.'

'Was your fight about me? Honestly?'

'I posted the letter.'

Billy sighed. He took my hand and step by step made his way back to bed. I helped him pull up the sheets and blanket, tucking them in around him. Then he lay back into the pillows and said, 'I think I know what the fight was about.'

'Can we talk about it?'

'If you want to,' he answered. 'But usually, you don't.'

There was silence. We didn't stuff it with all our usual jokes about what a loser Dad was and how if he turned up at the front door we'd pretend we didn't recognise him and act like he was a Mormon coming to spread the word.

'Do you want to see Dad? Is that why you wrote to him?'

'It would be okay to see him. But it's totally fine if I don't.' Billy was fitting the nasal prongs back into his nostrils. 'To be honest, I care more about how you feel about it.'

'What do you mean?'

'I mean . . .' Billy closed his eyes and I could tell he was really concentrating on what he wanted to say. He looked sad and now I wished I hadn't mentioned it. 'Dad being here isn't nearly as important to me as you being okay is. You and Mum. I don't want to leave and have him hanging around and it all being horrible.'

'Leave?' I choked out.

Billy squeezed my hand.

'Please tell me. Do you want to see him?' I begged. My jaw felt like it was dragging down to my knees. Why was it that when something was hard to talk about it was also hard to speak the words? Like even your subconscious didn't want to hear them. 'I need to know.'

'Gem, all I wanted was to tell him that I love him and that I forgive him. I wrote the letter in case I don't get to say it to his face. So it's done. Whether he comes to see me or not makes little difference to me. I've done my bit.'

'Are you just saying that?' I wept. 'To make me feel better?'

'No. I promise. And it's not like I'm holding on for him, Gemma. Like you see in the movies. I made my peace with Dad a while ago in here.' Billy pointed to his heart. 'Thanks to Saul, who had to weather that storm with me. Poor bastard. I must've been so hard to live with.'

'How did you make peace?'

'I am so, so flawed. Just like him,' Billy told me. His eyes were closed as his long, fine fingers twisted a button on his pyjamas. 'It was hard. But it was also easy.'

'I don't understand,' I choked. 'Why can't I feel like that?'

'One day you might, baby girl. One day you might.'

THAT NIGHT I COULDN'T SLEEP. MUM HAD
taken a sleeping tablet and was snoring for Australia, but
that wasn't the problem. It was the conversation I'd had
with Billy.

In the whole time our father had been gone, it was the
first time we'd really spoken about him. Actually ditched
the jokes that camouflaged our pain and told some truths.
At least, my brother had.

I was the one who'd shouted Mum and Billy down,
who'd told them that contacting Dad was a bad, bad move.
Now, I didn't know what I thought. Did I just say that
because not telling Dad was the easiest solution? Because
it kept the lid on things and stopped all the mess spilling
out? Was it me who didn't want Dad to know? Who didn't
want Dad to be here?

Yet I'd wanted Zane's dad to be with him even though
Zane himself had probably wanted him as far away as
possible.

I dragged the pillow over my face and held it tightly
until I couldn't breathe. Then I threw it off and sat up in
bed. It was so obvious. There was no other solution.

I crept into Mum's room, took her handbag off the chair

and tiptoed back to mine. When I opened her green address book to the 'L' page, a business card fell out: *Ezzo Drilling, Maintenance and Petroleum Services, PO Box 188, Dampney Bay, WA*. But there was more. A phone number and next to it the words *24 hours*.

I copied all the details down and slipped the card back inside the green book.

Then I did what I'd probably never done before. I didn't let myself think.

Polly Pessimistic was tied and gagged.

I put my black-and-white checked coat on over my pyjamas, grabbed my wallet, the bit of paper and pen and shoved them all in my pockets. Then I took Mum's handbag back to her room, leaving it on the chair, exactly as I'd found it.

Outside it was dark and the chill in the air cut at my skin like a razor fresh from the packet. It was too scary to walk. If I looked at the trees hard enough, I convinced myself I could see someone hiding behind them, waiting to pounce. So I ran all the way to the phone box, hoping that my pounding feet wouldn't wake up the entire street who would think I was a robber on the getaway. But to be truthful, the thing I was running to was the scariest of all.

The last time I spoke to my father was too long ago to remember. Maybe it was on my birthday two years ago. The conversation had only lasted three minutes. Four if you counted the awkward silences.

If the silences bothered Dad, I never knew it because he'd never tried to fill them. All I remembered about our conversations was the twenty-tonne brick that had sat in my stomach for days afterwards.

The phone box was lit up, like a little safe house on the

edge of the footpath. I slipped in and straight away started to stack the coins into piles along the ledge. I hoped like crazy that I had enough. I didn't want to get to the punchline only to hear the phone go dead.

As I was counting the last pile, I noticed Andrea's message on the wall. In fresh black writing, standing out against all our faded words, she'd written:

G, I miss you. A xxx YATWBMW.

The tips of my fingers traced her words. It was Andrea who'd met me here the day my father had slammed the door and left. I'd cried and cried and cried. She'd patted my back and wiped my nose with the sleeve of her jumper. She'd sat with me just outside here, on the gutter, while I raged and shouted that I would poke out my left eye before I spoke to him again. She'd answered, 'Just your left eye?' We'd both started laughing and just for that second the pain had lifted and I'd felt like maybe life would be okay again.

'Thank you,' I said out loud, even though Andrea couldn't hear. I dropped the coins into the slot and started dialling.

'Ezzo Petroleum.' It was a lady. That was a good start. 'How can I assist you?'

'Hello.' I had to shake my head a bit to make the next words come out. 'I'm trying to find my father. His name's Garth Longrigg.'

'What department, miss?'

'Maintenance and Petroleum Services. He's tall and—'

'Miss, we have over three thousand staff. I'm just looking for his name. Bear with me.'

She put me on hold and some music started. It was a track from *Grease*: 'You're the One That I Want'. I wondered if it was meant to be some bad pun.

Suddenly, it occurred to me that the next voice I'd hear could be my father's. I started chewing my lips and puffing out the air as though the starter gun was about to go off for a race.

'Hello?' It was the lady again.

'Yes?'

'Garth Longrigg's out on one of the boats at the moment. He's scheduled to return on the twenty-first of September.'

'That's more than three weeks away. This is urgent.'

'I can try and get a message to him.'

'Yes, please! We've already sent him a letter. But we haven't heard back. It's urgent. His son's sick. Really sick.'

'Mr Longrigg's next of kin is Mrs Longrigg. Is she available to speak to?'

'No, she's not. But I'm the daughter of Mr and Mrs Longrigg.'

'Yes, I understand that,' she explained. 'But we need to speak to Mrs Longrigg. It's company policy, dear.'

'Please can you tell him?'

'I'll try and get a message out to the boat to tell him to ring home. But if you've sent a letter, it'll find him. There's a postal drop at least three times a week.'

'Oh, I see.'

'I'll do my best, dear. But we really need to speak to Mrs Longrigg.'

'Yes. Thank you. Thank you.'

That was it. I'd done it. The unthinkable. The thing I had vowed never to do.

My hands gripped the ledge and I breathed deeply, as though I'd finished a race. I hadn't won. I hadn't lost. But I'd done it.

I stumbled out of the phone box, almost tripping over my feet. I could feel my body traversing down the road. Off to the left, off to the right. If anyone in the houses near the phone box had looked out their window that night, they'd have seen a girl wearing a black-and-white checked coat over her pyjamas, cutting a zigzagged path across the streets.

Finally, I found myself outside Ralph's house. I sat on the footpath and waited until the sky turned from black to mauve and the birds began warbling their songs. Then it was light enough for me to see the golden number 36 on the gate. It'd be a disaster if this was the wrong house.

As quietly as I could, I slipped through the gate and crept around the side of the house. From memory, Ralph's bedroom was the second window along. I really hoped so because using the key under the doormat was not the option I wanted to be left with.

Gently, I tapped the glass. Once. Then twice. Ralph's face appeared at the window and as stupid as it sounds, I waved.

Ralph and I drove to a petrol station where the taxi drivers were lined up waiting for their morning coffee. While Ralph bought two hot chocolates and a stale doughnut, I called Mum from the pay phone – because thinking I'd been kidnapped from my bed was the last thing she needed.

We sat on the bonnet of the lime mobile, sipping our drinks, our hands wrestling in the paper bag as we tore hunks off the doughnut. It was a good breakfast and the best moment I'd had all week.

'Where do you want to go now?' he asked.

'Anywhere.'

Off we went. I watched the street lights flicker off. The first dog-walker of the day passed by, his labrador stopping at every tree, sniffing and peeing, as his patient owner stood by. I wondered if it was the same routine for that man every morning. Was that why he was eager to be out with first light? Because at least he knew how that part of his day went?

'Is it Thursday or Friday?' I asked.

'Thursday.'

'So it wasn't even a week ago when I went to your place and met your dad?'

Ralph nodded.

'And a week later I rang my dad,' I said. 'Well, left a message for him.'

Ralph pulled into the entrance of the Western Showground and parked the car at the edge of the stadium. It was built about seven years ago and was the most exciting thing to happen in our suburb yet.

Posters for the Crowded House tour in October were pasted along the walls. Maybe layers and layers underneath the ones for the Boy George concert were still there.

'I saw Boy George here,' I told Ralph.

'I think Vanessa did too.'

'Billy and Saul took me. It was my first big concert.'

'Good night?'

I sighed. 'Really good.'

We lowered our seats, then turned around, facing each other. I could see the many shades of green and yellow smudged like pencil sharpenings around Ralph's bruised eyes. My fingertips circled their outline, as though I was painting his face.

'Saul had purple spots everywhere,' I said. 'Kaposi's sarcoma,' I pronounced carefully. 'His back, his legs, his face and neck. Once when they were going to a fancy dress ball, Billy painted him into a zebra. He covered every single spot with white and black stripes so that no one would know.'

'That's sad.'

'Billy made Saul sick,' I whispered. 'Billy ruined everything.'

'Gem.' Ralph had taken my hand and kissed my fingers. 'I don't know what to say.'

'Remember when you said "AIDS in the burbs. Not everyone's going to like it."'

'That was dumb.'

'It was true.' I closed my eyes because I was searching for the words. Somewhere, so close, was a thought. It'd been spinning away since the moment I'd found the photo of Saul painted up as a zebra. It was catching threads, here and there, and growing bigger. 'It's not just AIDS in the burbs. It's not that simple,' I began. 'It's AIDS at home. It's the way it spreads everywhere. It's like it's infected my life. It's infected me, the way I see people, the way I see the world. I've lost my best friend and I don't know what's right anymore. And there've been days when I've been so angry, I don't even know who I am. I've been the one who didn't want Dad to know. Yet I wanted Zane's dad to know, so badly. Thank God I never posted that letter to his family, because it was none of my business.' A sob escaped. Ralph gripped my hand harder. 'Whenever I think that things can't get worse, they do. It's like this bottomless pit of sadness.'

That day while I tried to stay awake in class, studying onomatopoeia and similes, why Germany invaded Poland and the life cycle of bacteria, Mum and Billy were conspiring. Making a plan. Deciding how it was going to be.

Really, it was Billy making the decisions and Mum surrendering because he'd worn her down. He'd even managed to get the doctors and nurses on side.

No chemotherapy. Billy was coming home just with oxygen. Pain relief, if and when needed, and a few other tablets that'd keep some germs away for some of the time.

Apparently his lymphoma was everywhere and as devastated as Mum and I were about the news, Billy seemed unfazed. Casual. Almost bored. As though he'd prefer something lightning-fast and spectacular.

My mother had endured the day from hell and I hadn't slept at all the night before. So when we arrived home from the hospital that night we were both ready to collapse. I'd actually been worried about Mum falling asleep at the wheel.

Once we'd pulled in to the kerb and parked outside our place, it took us a few minutes just to collect ourselves and drag our bodies out of the car and up the stairs to our front door.

No baths. No showers. Not even a cup of tea.

We slept together in her bed. We held each other tight as though we were one another's hot water bottles, trying to soothe away a pain that was close to unbearable.

'Are you awake?' I whispered.

'Yes.'

'I'm scared, Mum.'

'I know, sweetheart.'
'Billy doesn't seem scared.'
'That's because he's not.'
'But how could he not be?'
'I don't know, Gem.'
'Do you think it's because he wants to be with Saul?'
'Probably.'
'Mum? Why aren't we enough?'

SEPTEMBER
6 weeks to formal

ON MONDAY MORNING WE MET AT THE BACK of the school. All of us, minus Andrea. I had prepared myself for her to be a no-show. Louise and Vanessa had been making excuses all weekend for why she couldn't be there. But truthfully, I had a tiny bit of hope that Andrea would miraculously appear.

'The Fink's here,' Ralph announced. 'I just saw him drive past.'

I felt Vanessa's hand on my shoulder. 'Simon Finkler is the least of my problems,' I told them. 'As long as he doesn't bash up Ralph, there's honestly nothing he can say or do to hurt me.'

'Exactly!' Louise said, linking her arm through mine. 'Let's go.'

Ralph picked up the box and off we marched.

'I promise Andrea has sprained her ankle,' Louise whispered to me. 'I spoke to her mum this morning. She couldn't even make it to the phone.'

'Really? Okay.'

'Honestly, Gem, she was totally up for this. She even asked me to reserve a medium and small for her – so she could see which one looked better.'

That made me chuckle because that was Andrea all over.

When we arrived at the locker room it felt like everyone had been waiting. In a second, a crowd had gathered around us. Some people were waving money, others shouting over each other asking what sizes we had and if we were only wearing them at recess or wearing them for the whole day.

When Louise held up a T-shirt to show everyone, there were claps and cheers and someone said that it was the coolest T-shirt ever.

Then suddenly, like a spell had been cast over us, the room went silent and everyone turned.

Simon Finkler, bag slung over shoulder and a sneer so sharp it cut the air, was standing in the doorway. His foot tapped as he sized Louise up.

'Is this a little do-gooders get-together?' he said to Louise, who'd started to roll the T-shirt up into a ball and hide it behind her back. 'What a joke, Lovejoy. As if anyone's going to wear that.'

He stepped towards her. Louise hit the ground as though she'd sensed a punch coming. She crouched on the floor, fumbling as she tried to stuff the T-shirt back into the box. I wanted to go up to her and tell her that he was a nothing.

But then he took another step towards her and the room of people sucked in their breath.

'Hope you didn't get one printed for me?' he barked.

Louise stared at the ground, Simon Finkler's fat hairy legs almost in line with her flattened nose.

'Did you hear what I said, Lovejoy?'

Slowly, Louise stood up. She straightened her back and, with grace, raised her face to look at him. Then in the calmest, sweetest voice you've ever heard, answered, 'Sorry, but they don't make an extra, extra, extra, extra large.'

Before I could stop myself, a half-choked laugh shot through my lips. A second later the entire room had erupted into hysterical, belly-aching, thigh-slapping laughter. A laugh for every horrible thing he'd ever done to anyone in that room. Suddenly we had all the power and Simon Finkler just disappeared.

※

Our place was starting to resemble a hospital. Mr C had lugged the spare bed from their flat down to ours, setting it up in the living room. Now Billy had two rooms he could rest in.

There was a small oxygen cylinder in a trolley that Billy pushed along if he was on the move. Also in the living room and his bedroom were huge tanks, almost as tall as me, that I couldn't even lift. There was tubing everywhere: one of us was going to trip and break our necks on it for sure. But that was the least of our problems.

Billy's thrush had returned. Not as bad as it had been before, but the potatoes and pumpkin were back boiling on the stove, along with broccoli, this time, so that Billy got his greens. Each time I walked in the door, the smell hit me. Broccoli had now made the list along with pumpkin and purple jubes.

Each day Billy seemed to get a little smaller and a little weaker. When he walked across a room he'd have to stop several times even with the nasal prongs delivering him the oxygen.

Billy's new thing was that he liked to sit up high, awake or asleep. If he was on the couch or in bed, whoever was closest would have to prop him up and rearrange the pillows around him. It seemed impossible to ever get it perfect. 'A bit to the right, further to the left, down a little more,' went the endless commentary. Then Billy would say, 'Oh shit. Don't worry about it.' And we'd start laughing.

What I hated most was the coughing and then the hoicking and dragging up spit and whatever else was down in his throat. Some days it'd be really loud and just keep going and going. What I found weird was that everyone'd keep talking, pretending they couldn't hear. Even I did it.

The coughing at night was the most punishing. Billy would move into the living room so that he wouldn't wake Mum and me up. But of course, we were usually already awake by then.

Some mornings I was in such a sleep-deprived fog that it was hard even getting ready for school. My homework would be piled up on my tiny desk because it was too hectic studying in the kitchen and the continual smell of boiling vegetables made me want to chuck all the time.

'Mum?' I ran into my mother's bedroom. I was late. Ralph had already been up and knocked on the door and now he was patiently waiting in the car. 'Mum! I need a ribbon. It's seniors' assembly today.'

She was still in bed with her blinkers on but she pointed to her handbag on the floor.

I emptied the contents of the bag onto the bed. Out spilled coins, a hairbrush, three white candles and Mum's favourite photo of Billy as a baby with Uncle Roddy.

'What's this picture doing in your bag? Why is it out of the frame?' I asked, still digging around for a ribbon. 'And what's this latest obsession with white candles? Have you joined some weird cult?'

'Hand me the photo,' Mum said. Her eye mask was on top of her head now. She took the photo from me, gazing at it like she was remembering that day. 'Uncle Roddy moved to New Zealand.'

'What? How do you know?'

'I asked your father,' Mum answered, slipping the photo into the drawer next to her bed. 'Apparently Roddy's a grandfather.'

'When did you talk to Dad?'

'August or July. I can't remember.'

This time Mum didn't answer me with a question. But I got her drift.

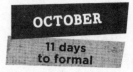

THE SCHOOL HOLIDAYS WERE ALMOST OVER
when one night, about 10 p.m., Billy started coughing. Mum
had gone to bed early with a sleeping tablet. I had a History
essay to finish so I'd told her I'd keep an ear out for him.

I heard Billy get up and make his stop-start journey
to the bed in the living room. I began to think about the
pillows and how he wouldn't be able to fix them on his
own, so I got up.

'Sorry, Gem. Did I wake you?' Billy asked. He was
sitting on the end of the bed, trying to muster some energy
before his next move.

His pyjama shirt was open and I could see his ribs rise
and fall with each breath. They seemed to stick out of his
pale skin and all I could think of were the curves and ripples
along a sand dune, because that's the pattern his ribs made
jutting out across his shrinking body.

I started to fasten the buttons, telling him that he
shouldn't get cold. Not the truth, which was that I couldn't
stand looking at him like that.

I'd developed a new system to get around the visuals
that was starting to spook me right out. If I had to talk to
Billy face to face, I'd centre my eyes at the point where his

forehead and hair met. I'd imagine that I was talking to his real face, not the one he was wearing now because that one didn't belong to the real Billy. In just a matter of weeks he had become some sucked-up, fossilised version of a man I used to know.

'Fix the pillows up, will you, Gem?'

Aunty Penny stacked them up into a pyramid so this is what I'd started doing too. 'Eleven days till the formal,' Billy said, nestling back into my work of art.

'How do you know?'

He winked. 'Can you ask Louise to come over soon? Jonathon sent me some new brushes. They're a Japanese make. I want to give them a try. I think they'll be easier to use.'

'What? For you or on Louise?'

'I've picked your lipstick too.'

'Wow, you've been busy.'

'What do you reckon I do all day when you're off with lover boy? I can't watch TV with Marcello forever. He commentates every second of every show we watch! Like I'm the one who doesn't understand what's going on.'

That made us laugh. Then that made Billy cough. For quite a while.

'I love Mr C,' I said, over the noise.

'There's only one of him, that's for sure. Now' – Billy paused as he waited for his breath to catch up with him – 'do you want to know . . . about your lippie?'

'What colour is it?'

'It's called Snow White Red. It's the colour of blood.'

'That sounds disgusting.'

'It's beautiful. Go to my top drawer and bring me the black-and-gold striped make-up bag.'

When I opened the drawer, all I could think about was the letter to Dad. He'd have to have it by now. And surely he'd have the phone message too. I was always checking the answering machine to see if he'd called. If Mum was in her room chatting on the phone and the door was closed, I'd loiter outside, trying to catch a word here and there to work out who was on the other end. The way I used to listen in when Billy would called from New York.

Before I closed Billy's drawer, I had a quick snoop and shuffle to check there were no other letters to anyone else. Perhaps Uncle Roddy in New Zealand? Or Saul's mother? But all I could see were a multitude of different-coloured make-up bags. I pulled the black-and-gold striped one he'd requested and went back to the living room.

Snow White Red *was* beautiful and it *was* the colour of blood. Billy delicately wiped a brush against the smooth tip of the lipstick. Then he drew a fine line of red across my wrist.

'Always use a brush,' he told me. 'Especially with a colour this bold. Start in the middle of your lips, then work outwards and fill in the rest. Be careful not to paint over the edge, especially your bottom lip or your mouth will turn down and you'll look like Sulky Suzy or a big, stupid clown.'

'But won't you be doing it for me?'

Billy smiled. 'I hope so.'

My pyramid of cushions was falling sideways. I built it up again and Billy lay back, closing his eyes and sighing. 'Lovely,' he whispered.

'Goodnight,' I said, kissing him on the forehead.

Before I left, I took one last look at him. My beautiful brother, the swimmer, who was now disappearing into the pillows just like Maurice Goldsworthy had.

On Saturday, it was all happening at our place.

Louise was having a tour through Billy's new Japanese brushes and Ralph had been summoned to help carry the new oxygen cylinders up to our flat. They'd been dumped at the gate. The man wouldn't bring them upstairs because he'd found out the patient had AIDS.

Poor Ralph had to carry each cylinder down the pathway, through the entrance, then up to our place. His muscles were bulging out of his T-shirt. I had to keep my hands behind my back so that I wouldn't accidently reach out and touch them. I couldn't risk him dropping a cylinder, especially when it had *DANGER* written all over it.

Once he had the last one through the front door, he collapsed onto the couch, sweating and panting. In the kitchen, Billy was giving Louise a lesson on how to use the new make-up brush.

'Sweep the powder along the bone then work up from the jaw,' Billy was telling Louise in a sing-song voice. 'Always up, up, up. Never down.'

'I'll never be able to do this,' Louise moaned.

'You will,' Billy told her. 'It's like following a recipe.'

'I should write it down,' she said.

Mum appeared. She was holding a handful of gold braid behind her back.

'Ralph, that last cylinder needs to go into Billy's room and the one in there needs to go downstairs for collection on Monday.'

I waited to hear Ralph groan. But he just said, 'Sure, Mrs Longrigg.'

'Thanks,' I mouthed.

He rolled his eyeballs, flexed his muscles like he was Popeye and jumped off the couch.

When he was gone, I snapped, 'Mum, he's not a slave! It's so embarrassing the way you're ordering him around.'

'Okay, okay,' she answered. 'But I just needed to quickly measure this gold braid on you, Gemma.'

'You don't have my dress out, do you?' I said as Mum wound the braid around me. 'Just say Ralph goes into the kitchen to get a glass of water and sees it in your workroom?'

'Neuta and the dress are back in the cupboard,' she told me. 'I'm not a complete idiot.'

Mrs C appeared in her black apron with a tray of freshly baked cannoli that actually outsmelt the boiled vegetables Aunty Penny was mashing in the kitchen.

We ended up all having afternoon tea in the living room. Our sounds of *mmm, mmmm, mmmmm* were even louder than the radio. It was the only noise I could possibly make when I took that first magical bite into the crunchy pastry, the ricotta cream squirting onto my tongue. This would be my last meal, any day.

Of course Billy couldn't eat a whole one. Instead Mrs C was digging out the filling and feeding it to him on a spoon. 'You like? You like, Bill?'

'Can I have the recipe?' Louise asked.

'Oh, Louise, you shouldn't have asked that,' Aunty Penny joked.

'There is no recipe,' Mr C said, wagging his finger at her. 'It is long, long family secret. Carmella learn when little girl. When she watch her nonna.'

Ralph's fingers were reaching over to the plate. 'Could I please have another one?'

'Take, take,' Mrs C told him.

'Yes, you need muscles for the lifting,' Mr C said. 'You eat as many as you want.'

I helped myself to a second one too (my health kick didn't count on weekends) then sat back and watched. At the start of the year, I never could have believed that this scene would take place in our living room. It was as great as it was terrible.

What made it great was the two new faces in the room. Ralph and Louise. The two most unlikely candidates to ever be having afternoon tea in our little flat.

What made it terrible was there, in the centre of it all, was a strange version of my brother. Sitting up in a bed in the living room, Mrs C feeding him the cream of the cannoli because it was all he could stomach.

But in its own way it was amazing too. We were chatting and laughing. The radio was playing happy songs because it was Saturday afternoon and most people were getting ready to party. If you were a stranger and walked in here, you'd never know that underneath it all was a really sad scene.

'Gemma? Gemma?' Billy and Aunty Penny were calling. Ralph was going to the radio and turning up the volume. It was Salt-N-Pepa.

'Come on, Gem.' Billy clapped his hands in time to the song. 'Up you get. Come on. I want to see your and Andrea's dance for old time's sake.'

'Up you get!' Aunty Penny echoed.

Now Mum and Mr and Mrs C were clapping along too. 'Gemma! Gemma!' everyone started to chant. Aunty Penny did one of her ear-piercing whistles through her fingers.

So up I got. *Can you believe it?* There I was standing in the middle of the living room, next to Billy's bed, about to break into a dance I'd never done without Andrea. 'I can't do all the moves because Andrea's not here,' I called. Really what I meant was, *Can I sit down? I don't know if I can do this on my own and I feel like an idiot – and standing over there is the boy I like!*

'No excuses!' Billy shouted. 'Come on or the song will be finished.'

Mum, Billy, Aunty Penny, Ralph, Louise and Mr and Mrs C started singing and bopping away. So off I went.

Bum to hip rotation. Spin. Bum out. Bum in. Spin. Tap hand on the ground. Arms up. Arms down. Spin. Bum to hip rotation. Down on the floor. Three push-ups. Bum to hip rotation. Arms up. Arms down. Spin.

I was laughing my head off. So was everyone else. Louise was still clapping. Aunty Penny and Mrs C were trying to copy my moves, while Mr C kept slapping his wife on the bum. Ralph was over at the radio, red in the face like he was about to keel over from laughter. And Mum and Billy were wearing the biggest smiles I'd seen in a long, long time.

30

SUNDAY WAS STILL CLEANING DAY. MUM was busy with my dress so I offered to do the vacuuming after the bathroom was finished. Billy was sitting on the couch. I'd noticed he'd stopped playing with the Rubik's Cube.

'I just have to vacuum in here,' I told him.

'I'll watch.'

'Gee, thanks.'

'There's a whole lot of cannoli flakes over there.' Billy pointed. 'I was scared the rats were going to pay me a visit last night.'

'I still can't believe you made me dance yesterday,' I said. 'And in front of Ralph!'

'He told me he'd already seen you do it.'

'Yeah, but that was with Andrea.'

'Lately, you've been doing lots of things without Andrea. Probably more things than you ever could've imagined.'

I shrugged, pushing that thought away, at least for now.

The cannoli flakes weren't disappearing. Every time I ran the vacuum back and forth over them, I looked down and they were still there. 'Something's wrong with this stupid thing. It's not picking anything up.' I turned the vacuum off.

'I bet you haven't emptied the bag,' Billy said. 'Try that and see if it works better.' I mimicked his words silently when he wasn't looking because it was all right for him sitting up on the couch giving orders. 'Open it up and see if it's full.'

'Yeah, I'm about to. I don't have ten hands, sergeant!'

The bag was stuffed. Full of little strips of multi-coloured material: the offcuts from our T-shirt afternoon, all those weeks ago.

'Look at this,' I said, showing Billy a handful. 'There's a bit of Vanessa's Wham! top. That's been turning up every-where.'

'Bring it over here.'

'What? The bag?'

'No. What you have in your hand. I've just had an idea.'

I presented Billy with my palms, loaded up with every coloured fabric imaginable, in every size and shape.

Billy began to pick pieces out of my hands. He'd give them a shake then hold them up, studying them for a second before saying either 'yes' and putting them on the couch next to him, or saying 'no' and placing them back into my hand. For a second, the thought of the cat disease made my heart skip several hundred beats.

But then Billy said, 'I want you to do something for me, Gem. Actually, it's not just for me.' Then he patted the seat next to him and told me to sit down. 'Have you heard of The Names Project?'

'No,' I replied.

'It's this giant quilt with a whole lot of names on it. People sew these huge squares in honour of one of their friends or family members who've died of AIDS. And then a whole lot of panels get sewn together and it becomes a quilt and then that quilt gets sewn onto the next piece and on and on it goes. The first one that was made was displayed in Washington a few years back and it took up the size of football field.'

'Wow!'

'Incredible, hey? It's pretty much a hundred times the size of it now. That's a lot of loved people.'

'So, so . . .' My eyes were closed as I tried to work out the meaning behind Billy's words to find the answer that I already knew. When I opened them, Billy was looking at me, copying my screwed-up nose, the way he loved to. 'What?' I smiled.

'This is what you look like when you're thinking,' he teased. 'You're lucky your nose isn't like this all the time because you do so bloody much of it!'

'Stop trying to make me laugh,' I told him. 'This is serious.'

'You're right.' And only then did he let his nose relax. 'I'd love it if you could make a panel for me and Saul. One each. And I was thinking that maybe you'd like to do one for Zane as well? I know you hate sewing. But I thought you might make an exception because I've been such a fabulous brother and you love me so much!'

Billy explained that the panel was made up of things that reminded you of that person and told other people something about who they were. He told me Aunty Mame knew all about what size they had to be and where to take them when they were finished.

'What do you want on yours?' I asked.

'You could start with these.' He held up three strips of

fabric. 'This one's from my Frankie Goes to Hollywood T-shirt and this is my old favourite Hanes one,' he said, handing me the material. Then he passed me a fluoro green piece. 'I know this one's Vanessa's but I always wanted a Wham! T-shirt.'

'Okay,' I said, staring at the beginnings of Billy's panel. 'I'll do it. I promise.'

'I knew you would.'

'Oh, Billy.' I couldn't help it. I started crying. I curled up under my brother's wing that was now like a scrawny old rooster's. But still felt as safe as it ever had.

*

On Thursday night, I woke up with a start. Almost like one of those people in the movies, who sit bolt upright in their bed. One second I was sound asleep and the next I was wide awake.

I could hear the hiss of the oxygen in the living room. Apart from that, everything was quiet. Except for the occasional creak of Billy trying to get comfortable in the bed.

It was weeks since I'd rung my father's work. I still wondered if the message had actually reached him. If he'd tried to call. Maybe they didn't have phones on these boats for him to call back? Or maybe he'd just decided not to?

Ralph and I didn't talk about it much. I think maybe Ralph was starting to understand that Dad wasn't going to just walk in the door and save the day with some dad jokes.

There was more noise coming from the living room. A moan of the mattress, something that sounded like Billy sighing, and then a hollow clunk, as though a cup'd been knocked over on his bedside table.

I wandered in there, poking my head around the doorway, saying, 'Are you okay? Do you need anything?'

'Can you get me some water?' Billy's voice was so soft I could barely hear him.

'You want some water?' I asked, walking over to the bed.

Billy nodded.

I took the jug off his bedside table and went and filled it up in the kitchen.

Mum had forgotten to turn her sewing lamp off and from the sink I could see Neuta. My formal dress was finally finished. The gold braid that had been fitted around the heart-shaped bodice sparkled against the black velvet like tiny stars in a night sky. It was the most beautiful dress I had ever seen. Much more beautiful than the picture on the fridge.

In four days' time, Ralph and I would be walking into the school hall together. I was unsure how much of my hair and make-up Billy would be able to do. He'd told me his hand was still steady, but he was weaker and smaller by the second. It was like watching someone shrink right in front of your face.

Louise knew that too. Today at school she'd said to me, 'Mum said she can do my make-up if it's too much for Billy. He's taught me a fair bit anyway.'

'I know Billy will still want to try.' Then I added, 'That's if you still want him to. I understand if you don't.' If it was hard for me, his sister, to look at him without feeling physically sick in the stomach, then I imagined it must be even harder for Louise. Let alone Andrea who hadn't seen him since he'd been back home. She wouldn't even know he was the same person.

I took the jug back to the living room and poured Billy

a cup. As I passed it to him, he shook his head and whispered, 'Can you hold it for me?'

I held the glass to his lips while he thirstily slurped at the water. It made him cough. He had to keep stopping, catching his breath before he could go back for more.

'My dress is finished,' I told him. 'Mum has really outdone herself this time.'

Billy lay back into the pillows and smiled. Then I realised he wasn't just smiling, his lips were moving – he was trying to say something.

I leaned in, close to his face, and I thought I heard him say, 'Can I see it?'

'My dress?' I asked him. 'You want to see it now?'

Billy nodded.

'Okay. I'll carry Neuta in here. Hang on.'

He shook his head. Then swept his hands down his body and pointed at me.

'You want me to put it on?'

He nodded.

'Okay. Bit weird in the middle of the night. But hey, why not?'

Then Billy pinched his earlobes and pointed to me again.

'You want me to put the earrings on too?'

He gave me the thumbs-up sign.

'You are a weirdo!'

I unzipped the dress off Neuta and took it to my room. Putting on the lace stockings was a bit of overkill at 2 a.m. But I would do the rest.

Out of my cupboard I took my black patent leather stilettos with the tiny black bow on the toes from the shoebox that I kept them in. I took off my pyjamas, stepped into the dress, slipped my feet into the shoes and, with a bit of puffing and panting, managed to do the zip up behind me. Then I carefully lifted Saul's earrings out of their Christian Lacroix box and fixed them to my earlobes.

I finished with a quick brush of my hair then tottered off to Mum's workroom to check myself out. From the waist up I was pretty happy with what I could see.

I didn't want to wake Mum up so I slipped my stilettos off and tiptoed to the living room before I put them on again. Then I leaned into the doorway, running my hands up the walls, trying to do my best movie star pose. 'What do you think?'

Billy silently applauded. Then he beckoned me over, spinning his finger, telling me to turn around. He gave another thumbs up.

'Can't you talk?' I asked, sitting by his bed where the heater was because I was beginning to freeze. 'Is the thrush making your throat hurt again?'

He shook his head. 'Too tired,' he murmured. Then he held out his hand and I felt the cool of his fingertips against my skin.

I swallowed, the spit almost catching in my throat. I remembered this feeling.

Billy smiled at me and mouthed, 'You look beautiful.'

'Thanks,' I whispered.

It was cosy next to the bed with the heater warming my legs. That plus the slow, even snore of Billy's breath, lured me away. Gradually I nodded off into one of those deep sleeps that feels like it's lasted for hours even though it's probably only been minutes.

When I opened my eyes, Billy was watching me.

'I can't stay awake,' I whispered. He smiled.

I fell asleep again. I don't know for how long, but it

must've been a while because Mum was standing over the chair, shaking my shoulders and saying my name, over and over. 'Gem? Gemma? Gemma!'

It took me a second to register where I was and then what I was wearing. And why were my stilettos on the floor next to me?

But then I became aware of the sound that must've woken Mum. The long, deep Darth Vader breathing, that Anna had told me was called the 'death rattle'.

Mum and I didn't speak. We simply nodded at one another and then she went and took her spot over on the other side of the bed.

I wrapped my fingers back around Billy's hand. It was cold. Cold like Zane's had been. Now I understood. This is what my mother had meant when she said, 'No one should have to do this twice.' Zane had been my dress rehearsal. That's why my mother had been so furious.

But part of me was glad that I had been given a chance to rehearse because now I understood how the scene would play out. I understood that there was nothing to be frightened of – except the silence.

Mum and I sat there quietly while the traffic up the highway began its hum. Then the sun rose, spilling its golden shards of light into the living room, warming us enough that we could have turned the heater off. Except that we couldn't bring ourselves to, because Billy's skin was so cold.

The tears were streaming down my face. Some of them I was swallowing. Others just kept running until they were soaked up by the black velvet of my dress.

Billy's breaths had become louder and longer. I found myself starting to breathe with him. Holding each breath so that it'd blow out at the same time as his. The break between one breath and the next kept growing. I'd keep the air in my mouth, waiting and waiting for his to let go, so I could let mine go too and at last feel my chest collapse with relief.

Finally, when my brother stopped breathing, I did too. That's when I knew. And that's when the silence came.

A sunny morning in November, when I was wearing my black velvet formal dress and my gold Christian Lacroix earrings, my brother, Billy, died.

31

BILLY'S FUNERAL WAS THE DAY OF THE
formal. It was small. Maybe only about thirty people, but
that was how Billy wanted it to be. Mum said Vanessa and
Ralph could come. They stayed quietly in the background.
But every time I looked up, Ralph was watching me.

Billy's coffin was covered with white roses from
Jonathon's garden in the country. The photo on the back
cover of the funeral booklet was the one of Uncle Roddy
and Billy.

Aunty Mame, in a wide-brimmed black hat with a
veil, sang 'Ave Maria'. I swear every tissue box was empty
after that.

Aunty Penny did a short reading. Jonathon spoke about
Billy's career. Then Mum finished Billy's farewell exactly
the way he would've wanted. My mother was like a brave
warrior woman. I watched her in total awe because there
was no way I could have got up and spoken.

Mum started with stories about Billy growing up and
then went on to his swimming career. But she left the best
story for the end. She told us all how much Billy and Saul
loved one another. Quietly she wept between words, taking
a break when she needed it.

'When Billy told me he was going to stay in New York and move into Saul's apartment, I was worried, like any mother would be,' she said. 'Your child, thousands of miles away, changing their life for someone – what if they're not the one and then your child gets their heart broken?

'So one morning I woke up and just picked up the phone and rang Billy. I couldn't even wait for the cheaper night rate because I had this burning question for him.

'I said, "Billy, can you imagine your life without Saul?" I still remember Billy's answer, word for word.

'For those of you who knew him well, you'll know why, because my son wasn't a flowery talker. I also remember his words because it was my son who taught me that morning what real love should and could be.

'This is what Billy said. "Mum, it'd feel like half my limbs had disappeared or that I was suddenly just a shadow and not a whole person. That's how much I love Saul. I can't even bear to think of my life without him because it wouldn't be worth a thing."'

Mum hadn't finished. But she needed a long pause before she could start again.

'The next words Billy said to me' – Mum started weeping – 'were, "Sorry, Mum." I couldn't work out why he said sorry to me because there was nothing more wonderful than to hear that your child had found such love.

'It's only in these past few months that I have begun to understand what that sorry meant.' Mum stopped again. Her eyes were closed and she pressed a tissue against her mouth.

I stood up and walked over to my mother. I had to be there next to her, not just so I could put my arm around her. But also because together, Mum and I were Billy's family.

Mum took a moment then kept going. 'When Saul died' – she swallowed – 'I knew that Billy wouldn't want to hang around for long. And as much as that hurts his sister and me, and as much as we'll never stop missing him, I, as his mother, understand that that's how it was always going to be.'

※

We had tea and chicken sandwiches in the hall next to the crematorium. Vanessa and Ralph had also brought a plate of cupcakes with the pink and chocolate icing.

Billy's friends came up and kissed us and told us what a good guy he was. Aunty Penny handed around a book, asking everyone to sign it. Mr and Mrs C were busy collecting the flowers that people had brought and arranging them into the back seat of the Fiat.

I had that zombie feeling back again. Watching everyone as though I was a stranger loitering on the outskirts of a person's funeral who I didn't know too well.

I couldn't feel my lips moving, yet I could hear myself saying things like, 'Yes, thank you. He was a great guy. Yes, I'll miss him so much.'

Aunty Mame snapped me out of my zombie trance, kissing me on both cheeks the way she always did, French style.

'Are you leaving?' I asked.

'I have to run, darling,' she told me. 'There's a young boy who's just arrived from the country last night. He's as sick as a dog, so I'll have to go and sort him out.'

'I'm sorry.'

'The show must go on, Gemma,' she said. 'I'm sorry that you're missing out on your formal tonight. Bill was so excited about doing his baby sister's hair and make-up. Only a few weeks ago he was driving Jonathon crazy trying to hunt down the right lipstick for you.'

'I know. Snow White Red. He showed it to me.'

'Gemma, if you do still want to go to the formal, I could do your make-up. I mean, that boyfriend of yours is pretty gorgeous! I'd like to be seen out with him!'

'Thanks. But it's okay, Mame.' I think my eyeballs may've bulged a bit at the thought of what my face could possibly end up looking like with Mame at the end of the brush. 'It's the last thing I feel like. There's always next year.'

'Goodbye, my darling. Look after your mother.'

The sandwiches were eaten. The mourners disappeared.

Mrs C was sitting in the front seat of the Fiat nursing a bouquet of red roses. Mr C was sounding like a trumpet, blowing his nose into a hanky. Every time I looked at him that hanky seemed to be covering his face. Poor Mr C, who would he spend all day watching TV with now?

I waved them goodbye because there was no room for me in the back seat of the Fiat. The bunches of flowers covered the entire back windscreen. I wondered where we would put them all.

Mum and Aunty Penny were leaning against the bonnet of Penny's car, waiting for me. Penny was telling a story in one of her semi-excitable tones that often escalated into a squeal. 'Did you see? At the very back of the chapel, Maryanne! Then just over there,' she said, pointing to the hall. 'Five minutes ago!'

For a moment I thought Penny must be talking about my father. I spun around, searching outside, wondering if it was too late to run back to the hall. But a lady was locking the door and no one else was around.

Then Penny said, 'Are you sure she's not having triplets? I have never seen such a pregnant woman!'

It was Catrina they were talking about. Not my father.

Deep down, I knew he wouldn't come. He'd probably known Billy was sick since July or August when he spoke to Mum. He would've read my brother's letter by now. He'd maybe even received it before I made the phone call. Before he'd sailed away on the ship to wherever it is that he went.

We drove down the driveway, through the gardens of the crematorium. But I wound down the window and leaned out, peering through the neatly clipped hedges, just in case.

﹡

That night, while Sonia Darue and Martin Searles were probably swanning around the school hall as the couple most likely to make everyone pea-green, Ralph and I were sitting around the kitchen table with Aunty Penny and a flat full of flowers.

Mum had gone to bed. She said she was sorry to be a spoilsport on the night of my formal, but we all told her if there was one night when it was okay to be a spoilsport, this was it.

Ralph was still in his good outfit that was reserved for weddings and funerals, and the one he said he would've worn to the formal but with a bow tie instead. Bow tie or tie was fine with me because he still looked like Johnny Depp at the Oscars. But I had stooped to the lowest form of dressing: an old pair of mustard-coloured tracksuit pants and a black Ramones T-shirt of Billy's that'd been my guinea pig on our T-shirt cutting afternoon. The neckline resembled a figure eight, dipping too low in the back and front, and the hemline was ridiculously uneven. When I'd put it on this afternoon I'd shuddered at the idea of the quilt panels I'd promised to make. What had I been thinking?

'So, ham and pineapple for Ralph.' I repeated the order to Penny. 'And you and me will share a margherita.'

'My half with anchovies,' Penny reminded me as she handed some cash over. 'Don't be too long,' she told us. 'Please?'

I knew exactly what Aunty Penny meant. Our place was quiet and sad. All the flowers did was make it creepier; their sweet scent was strange, overpowering and so unlike the smell of boiling vegetables that our little flat had become used to. It screamed, *Something is very wrong in here. Something terrible has happened.*

Ralph and I drove to the Grazia Pizza Bar. The last time I'd been here was with Billy. The waiter had winked at me and Billy had teased me all the way home.

Would everything feel like this now? Would every place and food and smell have Billy inside its story? I'd always remembered life by what I was wearing, but maybe that'd change. Maybe now, I'd remember life by Billy: Where he was when something had happened. What he was doing. If he was alive. If he wasn't.

I waited in the car while Ralph went inside to order the pizzas. On the back seat of the lime mobile was Vanessa's modelling catalogue. The first time I saw that was the day I found out my brother was HIV-positive. I had thought then that that day was the worst day of my life.

'They said it'll be fifteen minutes,' Ralph said, getting back into the car.

'I don't think I'm hungry anymore. Pizza seemed like a good idea at the time.'

'You have to eat, Gemma.'

'Are you sad you're not at the formal?'

'Do I look like I'm sad I'm not at the formal?' Ralph said. He took my hand and squeezed it. 'I'm with you. In your beautiful formal tracksuit pants the colour of shit. How could I be sad?'

We started laughing. I climbed onto Ralph's seat, squishing in next to him. He wrapped his arms around me and I nestled under his shoulder.

'I can't believe I'm never going to see my brother again.'

'It's too weird.'

'I've been with two people now when they've died. That's weird.'

'You're amazing, Gemma,' Ralph told me. 'I can't imagine how you've got through all of this.'

'I didn't have a choice.'

'But you've been so strong. I'm not sure I could be that strong if anything happened to my sister.'

'It's not like that, Ralph. It just happens.'

'I guess.'

'Thanks for hanging out with me,' I said.

'No. Thanks for hanging out with me. I was so sad after Lit Circle finished. I loved listening to you in those classes.'

'Really?'

'Yeah. Not that you would've noticed.'

'No, probably not,' I lied, because Billy had told me to keep Ralph on his toes.

When we got to the top of the stairs at home, Louise, Justin and Andrea were waiting outside the open door, dressed up to the eyeballs. Louise in her short red Roxette dress, Justin in a matching red tie – and then there was Andrea.

Andrea wore a strapless full-length hot pink taffeta 'gown', because you couldn't call it a dress. She had white gloves that reached up to her elbows and her hair was in a French roll, held together with a big golden clip.

'Is it okay that we're here?' Louise asked. 'Your aunty said it was but we can go.'

'No way!' I said. 'Come inside and have some pizza.'

'We're stuffed,' Justin said. 'School sausage sizzle.'

'Sonia Miss Priss got tomato sauce squirted all down the front of her white "I think I'm a bride" dress,' Andrea told me. 'I thought I was going to wet my pants. She was bawling her eyes out.'

Aunty Penny was calling out for the pizzas. Louise and Justin wandered into the kitchen with Ralph. I stayed behind so Andrea and I could have a private moment. Billy had been right. Whoever did Andrea's hair and make-up wasn't worth ruining a friendship over. But I just couldn't swallow the idea that Andrea and her mother and grandmother hadn't wanted my brother to touch her. I knew it wasn't Andrea's fault. But maybe I wanted her to stand up to them? Her to be the wind beneath my wings for once?

'Hi,' I said.

'Oh, Gem!'

We hugged. The hug was long and tight, not awkward like I'd imagined it would be.

'I'm so sorry, Gem,' Andrea gasped. 'So, so, so sorry.'

'It's okay.'

'I can't stay for too long,' she said. 'Mum thinks I'm at the formal. She wanted to come and pick me up early so she could have a squiz at everyone.'

'You're here. That's all that matters.'

'I know. It's just, just . . .'

'Complicated?'

'You said it.'

We had another hug. I wondered if Billy was looking down at us, giving me the thumbs up.

Andrea pointed to the closed living room door. 'Is that where . . . ?' she whispered. 'Is that where Billy passed away?'

I nodded.

Her hands touched the door, her fingertips sliding down the wood as though some of Billy was still left in there. 'Can I have a look?'

'Sure.'

I opened the door and switched on the light. The bed sat in the middle of the room. All the pillows were still stacked up in the shape of a pyramid. The Rubik's Cube sat on the table and next to it was a small tower of silver coins.

This was the scene of my brother's final weeks. The last few days I had snuck in here and stood as still as I possibly could. Trying to see if I could find a little bit of him somewhere, floating in the air, like I used to do in his bedroom when he was in New York.

Aunty Penny was sleeping in my room, so I crawled into bed next to Mum.

My formal night was over. It could not have been more opposite to what I'd imagined almost a year ago, when Billy had promised he'd come home to do my hair and make-up, plus two of my friends'. My biggest dilemma then had been choosing my dress pattern, finding Andrea a hairstyle and deciding who would be the second person. My biggest dream had been getting off with a guy called Ralph.

Time changes everything. That's what I was thinking about when I fell asleep. Sometimes it changes it for the worse. Sometimes it's for the better.

32

NOVEMBER

THE NAMES PROJECT BEGAN IN OUR HOME on the first Saturday night in November.

Andrea, Louise, Vanessa and I were sewing the three panels. According to Mum, we were involved in a 'quilting bee'. And of course, Ralph was part of it too. He was on food and beverages.

Mum said she'd help if we needed it. But I'd warned the others that she'd be a bossy pain, breathing over our shoulders the entire time. I'd already had to endure three lessons on how to use the sewing machine. I hadn't gone through all of that just for her to take over. So I told the girls it was better if we tried to do it on our own. Besides, Mum still wasn't feeling the love with Andrea. But I knew with time, she would.

Mum was going out to yet another candlelight rally, or 'vigil' as she preferred to call it because she reckoned it sounded nicer. Finally I had got to the bottom of all the candles I'd kept discovering around the place.

When I asked her why she went, she didn't give me the answer I'd expected. She said, 'Because I can cry there and no one tries to stop me.'

Poor Mum. She wore the new wrinkle on her forehead like a battle scar. She called it 'Billy's wrinkle' because it meant that he was always with her.

Aunty Mame had given me the specifications for our panels. To be honest, when she told me I felt like collapsing in a heap. We weren't talking little quilts, like the size for a baby. No, we were talking the big brother of quilts. Six foot by three foot. That was the size of each one. Non-negotiable.

Billy, Saul and Zane's panels had to be ready by the end of the month because the first of December was World AIDS Day.

Billy had thought of everything. He'd even left cash for the material for the panels. Mum had bought the fabric and cut the panels out and now they lay across the floor of our living room.

It was hard to pick the background colour for each one, but after much discussion Mum and I agreed: black for Saul, because he'd been an attorney; bright blue for Zane like the sky; red for Billy because – as Mum said – imagine the world without the colour red?

I had started three piles of bits and pieces that we could sew onto the panels. Things that told others about who these men were and also what they'd meant to us.

Ralph had already been sent off to Maccas. We'd all decided to have cheeseburgers for dinner in honour of Zane. Also Ralph's mission was to come home with something that had the face of the Hamburglar on it because that cheeky look he had reminded me of Zane. Plus Zane loved Maccas.

'This is for Zane's panel,' I told the girls. 'He told me what he missed the most about home was the big sky.

I have some leftover black velvet and gold braid from my formal dress and I thought we could make it resemble a night sky with stars.'

'Awesome,' Vanessa said, and Louise and Andrea nodded.

'This little plastic carrot is from the nose of the bunny he gave me,' I explained, holding up what looked like an orange triangle. 'It was coming loose anyway.'

We'd all voted that Andrea was the neatest with the scissors, so she had the job of cutting out all the letters of their names. She'd already done it at home, with great drama, of course, because her mother had found out what she was working on and flipped out.

The next day at school Andrea had said, 'Two words: Elizabeth Taylor. I kept telling Mum she's an AIDS Ambassador. Did you know that, Gemma?'

Andrea would never admit it, but I'd known her long enough to be sure that she was quietly impressed with herself for standing up to her mum and I was too.

Proudly, Andrea presented us with Z-A-N-E cut out in black felt. The letters were as neat as any machine could've done. 'We're not doing his dates, are we?'

'No, because I don't know when he was born. The death notice didn't say,' I told them. 'But he lived 937 kilometres away. He actually had that number tattooed on his shoulder. Maybe you could cut out those numbers?'

'Why don't you do it on this green material?' Vanessa said, handing it to Andrea. 'It's like the colour of the country.'

Andrea took the fabric with a bit of a grunt. She was, as she called it, having 'adjustment issues' hanging out with Vanessa.

'Now let's do Saul's,' I said. 'You have his name and dates cut out, Andrea?'

'Done,' she replied.

I held up a piece of mulberry satin from the lining of my black-and-white checked coat that Saul'd bought me. I had thought, overthought, then overthought some more, about whether the colour was too similar to the spots on his face. Before I could think about it any more, I'd grabbed Mum's scissors, pierced a hole in the lining and started to snip.

'Maybe this could be in the shape of a heart? It's from a present Saul gave me and . . . and I really loved Saul. He was special.'

'I found this picture of Boy George for you,' Louise said, adding it to the pile. 'But I don't know how we can sew it on.'

'Wow, thanks, Louise. Mum and I have heaps of photos we're going to sort through. Aunty Mame said it's good to have their faces on their panel. Maybe we can glue this stuff?'

'But poor Zane's going to get the face of Hamburglar!' Andrea couldn't keep a straight face and then we all burst out laughing.

Last but not least was Billy's pile.

On a white piece of fabric, Louise had painted a giant picture of the Japanese make-up brush that Billy had given her. Louise used it every day, working Billy's magic across her beaten nose.

Andrea showed us what she'd done: his full name 'William Gavin Longrigg', but she'd also cut out 'Billy'. She said that was because this is what she knew him as.

Vanessa was still working on her idea for Billy's panel. She told us that she kept changing her mind.

'You'd better get a move along,' Andrea mumbled.

I shot her a *shut up* look. She took the hint and went back to the cutting of Zane's numbers.

The three strips of fabric that Billy had picked from our T-shirt cutting afternoon were also in the pile. No one knew, but I had cut them in half. Mum had her wrinkle. I had three pieces of material that not so long ago Billy had touched with his own hands.

Some nights when playing with Billy's Rubik's Cube didn't put me to sleep, I would take those bits of fabric out of the drawer. I'd run them across my face, thinking about Billy, wondering where he was now and if he could see me. Sometimes when I woke up in the morning, they'd still be scrunched up in the palms of my hands.

33

DECEMBER

TONIGHT I WAS WEARING MY FORMAL DRESS.
For the first time since Billy died.

I stepped into it and Mum did up the zip and brushed down the velvet. I slipped my feet into the black patent leather stilettos and clipped on the Christian Lacroix earrings. Then carefully, with a brush, I painted Snow White Red onto my lips, starting in the middle like Billy had taught me.

We had finished the panels and sent them off. Today was World AIDS Day, so we were celebrating, 'formal' style.

Ralph appeared at the door. He was wearing his suit with the Rolling Stones T-shirt Billy had given him. Mum and I both lost our breath. The fit was so perfect, for a second it was as though Billy had stepped into the room.

'You look amazing,' I spluttered, while Mum just stood there nodding.

Ralph was holding a white rose corsage that he tied around my wrist. He kissed me on the cheek and whispered, 'You would've been the best one there. But I always knew that anyway.'

Andrea had organised a progressive dinner party, even

though none of the courses were taking place at her house. She was kind of still in a fight with her mum, who she kept referring to as a 'freak from the Dark Ages'. Every time she said those words her lips would narrow and she'd speak from the side of her mouth.

Entree was at Louise's. Justin was helping because they were an item now. He said he'd outgrown his crush on Vanessa along with Dungeons & Dragons. Like the night of the formal, Justin wore the same red tie to match Louise's dress. Now it was so obvious. But it had been lost on me then. Louise said not to worry, that I'd had other things on my mind.

Main course was at Vanessa and Ralph's. Vanessa was going to do all her party tricks because tomorrow she was having the gap in her front teeth filled. I liked the gap but apparently it stopped her getting modelling work.

Their father was going to dress in black and white and be the waiter. Ralph told me that his dad's shirt wouldn't be tucked in because he was wearing his tuxedo pants from his wedding and he couldn't get the zip done up anymore.

Dessert was at my place. Mum and Aunty Penny were out for the night. Mum said she might even sleep at Aunty Penny's so the flat was ours and we could go crazy.

Mr C wanted to serve dessert and wear his red-and-black checked waistcoat. But then he realised the soccer was on. Thank God!

Of course the menu wasn't fancy. I had been allowed to pick the food. Prawn crackers for entree, cannoli and chocolate chip ice-cream for dessert. But most importantly of all, cheeseburgers with extra gherkins for main course.

Because it was true. Life was better with extra gherkins.

ACKNOWLEDGEMENTS

To the early readers, thank you – Ned Pomroy, Shakti and Marg Burke, Seraphina Burke Xie, Simon Gaunt and Kelly Louise Hargreaves.

Victoria Shehadie for her early trip to the UTS Library where she found 'Discrimination – the other epidemic: report of the inquiry into HIV and AIDS related discrimination' / New South Wales Anti-Discrimination Board, 1992. Reading this report spurred me on to tell the story.

Ned Pomroy for his enthusiasm, brainwaves and encouragement.

Peter Mulley for sharing some of his stories that I know were painful to tell. Plus Shauna Flenady who shared her memories of Sydney and NYC during this period.

Library and English staff at Galen Catholic College, Wangaratta, Coonabarabran High School and MacKillop Catholic College, Warnervale, who discussed with me their 1990 fashion (mostly bad) moments; their memories of AIDS and HIV during this period, the lingo and any and all things related to 1990.

Peggy Knott and Paul Grguric, Liverpool Girls' High School.

James Scutts and his nonna for their checking of my schoolgirl Italian.

Tara Wynne, my agent at Curtis Brown Australia.

Sophie Splatt, Eva Mills, Jodie Webster and Angela Namoi from my new home at Allen & Unwin.

The ever-suffering husband and offspring – Michael, Victoria and Nick Shehadie.

To all the loved ones touched by AIDS during this era. This is my feeble attempt to not let that time be forgotten.